BRIDGE of FAITH

A NOVEL

CATHERINE WEST

Text copyright © 2015 Catherine West

ISBN-13: 9781511444675

Dedication

*In memory of my father-in-law, Colin, who read
Reid & Julia's story first, and loved it.
Wish you were here to enjoy it now.*

Chapter One

He only needed to survive one more day. Then he'd be home ... back on US soil.

A lot can happen in twenty-four hours.

He'd learned that the hard way.

"What did he say?" Reid Wallace shouted at their guide over the yells and screams as townspeople rushed by, eager to get the latest news. Sweat slipped down his back and he swatted at the flies hovering over the food he hadn't touched. He cracked a wad of gum and leaned closer as chant-ing—the call to morning prayers—began from a mosque somewhere up in the hills.

More people filled the streets, even though the air was thick with smoke. Debris littered the roads from the explosion that rocked the small town several hours ago. Children kicked at cans and tossed a dirty soccer ball to one another on their way to school. Women gathered in groups, conversing with rapid-fire words and hand gestures. Trucks rolled by. Vendors peddled their wares. The stench of rotting vegetation, stagnant water and who knew what else, sickened his already weak stomach.

Life in a war zone.

Life went on. Even here.

"Speak up, Adar. Loud. Loud!" Reid snapped his fingers and put a hand behind his ear to get the point across. Adar, a kid really, couldn't be over twenty, rolled his eyes, puffed out his chest, and yelled louder than a football coach after a missed touchdown.

"He say very bad area. Very, very bad! You stay here. No go there."

Reid glanced at Cade Connelly, his cameraman, best friend, and conscience when it came to it. Cade gave him a thumbs down. The rest of the crew sat around waiting, as they had been all night, for Reid to tell them what came next. His cell vibrated on the small scratched up plastic table, and he picked it up to take the call he'd been expecting.

"Hilary, I said I'd get back to you in a minute." His producer was quite possibly the most impatient woman he'd ever met. Another flaw that made him question his motives for dating her.

"I don't have time, Reid, are you going in or not?" He didn't have to strain to hear Hilary's clipped question. Born and raised on Staten Island, she spoke loudly whether she needed to or not. "You go live in twenty. What's happening over there?"

Reid took a swig of the lukewarm sludge passed off as coffee, forced it down, and prayed it wouldn't come back up. "There was another explosion early this morning. They say it's not safe to go any further." He pushed his fingers through his soot-covered hair and swore. "Why don't we just shoot from here?"

"You did that last night." She muttered something to somebody, probably giving the order to nix his spot. Reid clenched and unclenched the fingers on his right hand and watched dawn's first light bounce off the gold band on his third finger.

Watched Cade watch him.

If he sat here long enough, he could watch his career go down the toilet.

"Reid, are you still there?" Hilary sounded nervous and that was not normal. Not for her.

"Still here." Still nauseous. Still hung-over and wishing for something that would take the shakes away. "Do you want us to go in? I've got time to set it up."

"Wallace ..." Cade growled, his eyes darkening. Reid ignored him.

"You'd better." Hilary snapped another set of orders. "You screw this up and you're done. I'm through making excuses for you. Capiche?"

"Capiche." Reid drummed his fingers on the table and watched more smoke rise from the hills behind the town. And wondered again why he'd chosen this particular career. "What happens if I don't go?"

2

"You need me to answer that?" The line crackled in conjunction with another far away explosion. Reid closed his eyes and exhaled. If he believed God was paying attention, still listening, still looking out for him, he'd give some serious thought to prayer right about now.

"Okay, boss. You win."

"Stay safe."

Right.

He pocketed his phone and stood. "We're going in."

Adar immediately spouted off a string of words in Arabic. Reid didn't have a clue what the guy said, but could easily figure it out by his horrified expression.

Cade took Reid aside while they packed up their gear. "This is probably the craziest thing you've ever done. Don't jeopardize the safety of the team over your job, man."

"That's not what I'm doing." Reid zipped up his jacket and walked toward the truck.

"That's exactly what you're doing!" Cade jogged to catch up with him.

"They're not giving me a choice. They want the story."

"They can run something else! You're not thinking straight. I know you were up all night. If you panic while we're in there and—"

"I'm not going to panic." Reid pushed through the crowds and nodded to their driver. "Let's go."

Reid wasn't sure if he was awake, dreaming or dead.

Julia stood in front of him. Stood or floated. Hard to tell. He could just make out her face through the thick mist, but he knew the sound of her voice. Asking him to come. Asking him for help.

But he didn't know where she was or how to get to her.

And a canyon of sharp jagged rocks and oozing black tar separated them.

Something crawled across his chest and Reid opened his eyes.

What the—

He took in the scene around him and struggled to his knees. Doubled over and expelled what was left in his stomach. The ringing in his ears made it hard to think, and he could barely see through the heavy black smoke that curled around him. He wiped his mouth, blinked as something warm trickled down his cheek. He touched a stinging spot, pulled away and widened his eyes at the blood on his fingers.

His ears crackled and popped as his hearing returned.

So much noise …

Soldiers shouted in a foreign tongue, moans and groans and guttural cries punched the air and asked for mercy. Witnesses stood around on what was left of the sidewalks, shaking their fists, shaking their heads and crying out to God or Allah or anyone who could possibly make sense of this madness. Bodies littered the ground like trash after a ticker-tape parade.

So many.

He put his head in his hands, tried to breathe, tried to think, but all he could do was sit there and shake.

"Reid!" Cade emerged through the smoke, limping toward him. "You okay?"

Reid stared as his friend dragged one leg behind him. His throat closed again and he couldn't speak. So he pointed.

Cade shrugged. "Think my ankle's broken." He lowered himself to the ground and moved Reid's hair off his forehead. "That's a heckuva gash. Anything else? Can you hear me, man?" Panic flooded his friend's face.

"I don't know." Reid heard the words in his head but couldn't make them come out of his mouth. "Where's Julia?" That did come out. He could tell by the way Cade's eyes quadrupled in size.

Cade shook his head. "We need to get out of here. Where is everyone?"

The explosion had been swift, ferocious, and over before any of them had a chance to run. The last thing he remembered was a whizzing in his ears and then everything went black.

Through the suffocating smoke, Reid made out the images of the rest of his crew, crouched over two men who weren't moving. Cade saw them too and limped over there. A moment later, Cade's yell rocketed around him, confirming Reid's fears and telling him what he already knew.

He'd just made the biggest mistake of his life.

Julia Hansen picked up another dish to dry, cool Atlanta air flooding through the open window. Winters here were a far cry from months of snow and ice in Vermont. Yet she missed home now more than she could say, especially during the holidays. Christmas had been especially awful this year. Now in the first week of another new year, she had nothing to look forward to.

She jumped as the volume of the television in the living room went up. "*Yesterday's insurgence, prompted by Syrian forces in the northern town of Saraqueb, a rebel stronghold, is said to have been a bloodbath. We have received word that our news crew on assignment in the area, were caught up in the crossfire. We have no confirmation yet whether …*"

The dish she'd been drying slipped from her hands and crashed to the floor.

Julia squeezed her eyes shut and took a moment to breathe.

It could have been anyone.

Any crew. Any network.

Not theirs.

"Julia!" Frank bellowed from the living room. "What are you doing in there?"

"Nothing."

Nothing. It was nothing. She wouldn't think about it.

She stared at the broken china scattered around her feet. Watched the Christmas lights still up on the house across the street flash on and off.

What if it wasn't nothing?

What if they were there?

What if …

Photographs and fliers fluttered under the magnets that held them in place on the white refrigerator. Country music crooned from the old radio Frank wouldn't get rid of. Outside, a dog barked and children played in the yard behind hers.

Life went on while she was confined to the prison of this house. She would be thirty this year. Her life was so far removed from normal that she'd almost forgotten what normal felt like. What it felt like to come and go without interrogation. To make decisions without a second thought, without fear of condemnation or punishment.

What it felt like to love.

And be loved.

She tried not to think about the ones she'd left behind. The family she no longer saw and had limited contact with. Her parents, her sister Hannah, and her brother, Cade. She missed him most.

Cade had been her protector. Always looking out for her, watching over her and keeping her from harm. Until Frank made it impossible.

If she closed her eyes, Julia could see her brother's sparkling eyes and cheerful grin, and shock of unruly blond hair that refused to be tamed.

Cade, who might now be facedown on foreign soil, injured or ...

"This just in. It has unfortunately been confirmed that two of our news crew have died ..."

Julia froze. Closed her eyes. Prayed.

She stepped over broken pieces of white china and slowly moved into the next room.

The anchorwoman with the British accent Frank always made fun of relayed the Saturday evening news while images of burning buildings and screaming crowds flashed in the background.

"Did they say who was there?" The words stuck in her throat.

Please, God. Let him be all right.

Let them both be all right.

Julia twisted the dishcloth tight, tried to concentrate on what the woman was saying, something about an unexpected ambush in an unsafe area. She gripped the back of the wingback chair as the room began to spin.

Oh, no. Not now.

She would not pass out.

She had to know more. Had to know if they were okay.

Frank studied her from his sprawled position on the couch, his mouth curled in an ugly grin. "You don't fool me, you know. You're still thinking about him, aren't you? Even after all these years." He cracked the lid on another can of beer and took a long swig.

Revulsion rolled in her stomach. That he would do this now, when all she could think about was whether Cade was dead or alive ... typical drunk Frank behavior.

He picked up an antique Colt revolver from the side table, one of many from his collection, and rubbed a cloth over the shiny silver surface.

Something in her snapped like the dry twigs she walked over in the woods behind the house. Anger left dormant too long woke and stretched and bared its teeth.

"You're sick." She folded her arms and met her husband's accusing eyes. "My brother could be over there, Frank. *That's* who I'm thinking about!"

"Sure you are." Hostile laughter ricocheted off the walls. "Your brother and that shmuck he works with, *that's* who you're thinking about."

"Don't be ridiculous." Arguing with Frank when he was in this state was not smart. Not something she would normally do. Julia trained her gaze on the television and tried to shut him out. Maybe they'd come back to it, say who was there. Put her mind at ease.

Frank spat into an empty glass and struggled off the couch. "You talking back to me?"

She stepped backward in a hurry. "No. I didn't mean to. I meant ... I'm sorry." Lucid thought returned. Where were the kids?

Emily was in her room, playing with her dolls, no doubt. Mark was in the garage working on Frank's motorbike.

Frank started drinking early that afternoon, while the game was on. She hadn't bothered to keep track of how much he'd already consumed, just hoped he'd have enough to pass out so she could get the kids in bed and get an early night herself. But the fire in his eyes warned that wouldn't be happening tonight.

She cast a wary glance at the television and gathered courage. "Did they mention Cade at all?"

Frank swore and tossed an empty beer can her way. "I didn't hear. 'Course he's just a cameraman. They only like to talk about the big guys. Your man there got pretty beat up, s'all I know."

Julia stiffened but clamped her mouth together. She refused to be baited.

Frank sneered. "Oh, now look at that." He scratched the stubble on his chin and gave a thin smile. "Now I got your attention, don't I darlin'?" He waved the gun at her and stared in a way that made her wonder if he'd finally lost it.

"Stop it, Frank." Familiar fear threatened to take her down, but she went for the phone anyway. Picked it up and began to push the buttons.

"Oh, no you don't!" Frank stumbled across the room. He yanked the phone away with one hand, and struck her across the face with the other. "What I tell you about using the phone?"

Julia reeled backward and tasted blood on her tongue. She put a shaking hand up to her stinging cheek and stared at the man she'd married on a whim so many years ago. The man who'd promised to love, cherish and protect her, so long as they both should live. The Frank Hansen she thought she'd married slipped out the back door after those first few months, and left behind this leering, dangerous shadow that stalked her every move and pounced at the slightest provocation.

The man she'd once believed an answer to her prayers had slowly turned into the object of her nightmares.

Any other night she would have said sorry, left him alone, not given him further provocation. Tonight was different.

Tonight she'd had enough.

"Leave me alone, Frank!" She pushed against his broad frame and he staggered a bit. "I need to call home. I need to find out if Cade is all right. For once in your life, maybe you can think of someone other than yourself. The world doesn't revolve around you, Frank Hansen!"

His beefy face pinched with fury. White rage crept into his eyes and he moved toward her—a tiger eyeing its prey, about to go for the kill. "You want to apologize for that, darlin'?" He still held the gun. She never knew if he kept them loaded, wouldn't go near them to find out.

"Please, put that thing away and let me have the phone." Hot tears burned, but she would not back down. Not this time.

She was through cowering every time he spoke. Tired of jumping through his hoops, trying to meet his impossible demands. Through feeling like the poor excuse of a wife he wanted her to believe she was.

Through with him.

Frank's hand clamped down on her shoulder and he squeezed. Hard. "Apologize. Now."

Julia bit her lip as pain shot through her and shook her head. "No."

"I hope your brother is dead." His breath was warm, foul, his words filled with venom. "I hope they're both dead actually. Then maybe you'll finally get over that no good jerk."

"Let me go." Julia lurched backward, tried to extricate herself from his grasp, but he was too strong. He was always too strong.

Out of the corner of her eye, she saw Mark in the doorway as Frank's hand came down again, and she opened her mouth to scream.

Her eyes seemed stuck together, her body encased in lead, her chest too tight to take a breath. Much as she wanted to, needed to come to her senses, the effort was futile. Julia gave up the fight and let the memories she'd been visiting take her back to another place and time …

"It'll be all right, honey. You'll see." The older woman rocked back and forth, shelling peas into a silver bowl, tossing the husks into the plastic compost container beside her.

"I don't know, Esmé." Julia pulled her knees up to her chest and looked across the lake. Reid sat in his boat, his black lab beside him. He'd been out there for hours. "I hate when he gets mad at me, but I can't help arguing with him."

Esmé's laughter felt like a mug of hot chocolate on a cold winter day. Warm and filling, enough to chase the cold out of your bones and make everything okay.

"He'll come around. He always does."

"What if he doesn't?" Julia stared at the lone figure in the small tin boat, the very thought of living without him too terrifying to voice. "I just … I have these dreams where he leaves, you know? We're fighting like usual, and then suddenly he's gone. Slams the door and off he goes. And he doesn't come back." She swiped at her eyes and gave a half laugh. "I know you and my parents think we're too young to really be in love, but I do love him. I do. I'd die if anything happened to him."

"Child, you most surely would not die." Esmé pushed her long gray braid over her shoulder and smiled with the wisdom of a woman an age that, at seventeen, Julia couldn't yet imagine attaining. "You're young, yes, but you're old enough to

know what the right thing is. He'll go off to college and you'll survive it. Let him go, my love. He'll come back eventually. I promise you that. That boy out there can't live without you. I saw it the first time he brought you up here to meet me. The two of you are meant to be. You can fight each other all you want, honey, but there's no fighting God."

"Julia?" A voice pulled Julia from the safety of slumber. "Sweetheart, can you hear me?" It sounded like Dad.

But it couldn't be her father. That was impossible. She was in Atlanta with Frank. Mom and Dad were back home in Vermont.

And she hadn't seen them in years.

She flinched with the effort it took to open her eyes. Tried to move. Her head pounded like a million jackhammers were chipping away every bit of her brain.

Soft light flooded the room. Her father's face came into focus. Her mother stood at the other side of the bed, holding her hand, tears shimmering as she tried on a smile.

"Mom? What are you doing here?" Thick fog lifted as Julia looked around. "Where … am I?"

She wasn't at home. Sterile walls, a faded striped curtain pulled around the bed, the beeping of a machine and the tube attached to a needle stuck in her arm told her that. "H … hospital?" Swollen lips made it hard to get the words out. "What happened?"

Memory trickled back, a slow moving stream that picked up speed and transformed into a flash flood before she had time to prepare. "Where are the kids?"

"The kids are with us, honey. They're okay. We flew in this morning. You've been in and out since the paramedics brought you in yesterday." Her father smoothed back her hair, his gaze steady but far too serious.

Julia shivered under his touch but tears of relief pooled. "Cade … I saw the news …"

Her father pulled the covers up around her, his expression hardly reassuring. "Cade is fine, on his way home. We're going to stay here a bit, get things sorted out, but then we're taking you and the children back to Vermont with us."

"Frank? Where's Frank?"

"You don't need to worry about Frank. You're coming home."

"Home." She sank against the pillows and closed her eyes. She wasn't sure where that was anymore, but she knew what it meant.

She was free.

Chapter Two

Getting a call from the principal's office just after lunch on her son's first day at Bridgewater Middle School wasn't exactly what Julia had in mind when she'd dropped him off that Monday morning.

When she and the kids had moved to Vermont at the beginning of April, she'd kept Mark home, not wanting him to have to adjust to a new school on top of everything else. Her mother had home-schooled him so he could keep up, but by the end of summer, they all felt he was ready for a new start. Ready to start making friends.

Ready to move on.

"Fighting, Mark?" Julia shook her head as she got into the car, slid behind the wheel and counted to ten.

Twice.

The car's interior was warm, midday sun glaring through the windscreen. The remnants of yesterday's coffee run still lingered, mingling with the rose-scented air freshener that dangled from the rearview mirror.

Mark sat in sullen silence, scrawny legs stretched out, arms crossed. His dark hair was too long for her liking, but he boycotted the idea of a trim whenever she suggested it. A cut under his eye had been cleaned up, but the bluish bruise on his jaw was starting to swell.

Much to Julia's dismay, the other kid looked even worse. Since when did sixth graders pack punches like prizefighters?

"I already said sorry. You heard what he called me."

Yes, she'd heard. But that didn't make it right.

"Let's not do this again, okay?" She tried to sound angry, but sorrow quickly gained the upper hand. When would things start to improve?

"Whatever." The scowl he'd been wearing for far too long made him look a lot older than his eleven years. And a lot more miserable than any kid his age had the right to be.

Julia started the engine, and after three tries, her old Camry jolted to life. It would take at least twenty minutes to drop Mark back at her parents place, explain the situation, and then turn around and go back to work. Hopefully things wouldn't be too crazy by the time she got back.

"You know I had to skip out on Debby to come pick you up. On my first day of work, too."

"Whatever, Mom. It's just a florist shop. How busy can you be?"

"You'd be surprised."

Mark snorted. "Oh, right. I guess you must get a ton of calls for funerals in this dinky town."

Julia pulled out onto the highway, hands clenched tight around the wheel. She refused to argue with him. Bridgewater might be small, but it wasn't the worst place in the world. They'd already been there.

The gas gauge flicked and moved closer to empty. Great. The few twenties she'd been saving to do something fun with the kids on the weekend wouldn't last that long.

"Do I have to go to school tomorrow?"

"Yes, you do."

Principal Miller surprised them both by taking it easy on Mark, saying it was his first day and he deserved a chance to prove himself. He gave him a stern warning, extra homework and Saturday detention, then sent him home for the rest of the day. Julia intended to dole out a much harsher punishment. "But you're grounded. For a month."

Mark slouched in his seat, one lock of dark hair falling over his left eye. He let out a ragged sigh and sucked his teeth. "Not like there's anything to do here anyway. And I don't have any friends."

"Maybe if you tried talking to the other kids instead of beating them up, that might not be the case." She glanced his way as she idled at the intersection's stoplight. A pinch of remorse niggled her conscience. Moving hadn't made Mark any happier. But there was nothing left for them in Atlanta. Nothing but a ramshackle house she couldn't afford and didn't want, and more than a few years of bad memories.

"He deserved it."

Anger joined forces with frustration and kicked aside whatever compassion she might have had for him. Julia took a minute and prayed for wisdom. Yelling would do no good. The light changed and she pressed down on the gas again. "Mark, nobody deserves—"

"Mama, look out!"

A motorcycle crossed her line of vision from the left.

She swerved through the intersection, managed to prevent the car from fishtailing, coasted onto the shoulder of the highway and pulled up the brake. Julia clapped a hand over her mouth as she watched the bike swerve and almost spin out. The rider gained control and brought the large machine to a screeching stop a few feet in front of her car.

"He totally ran that light!" Mark voiced her first thought.

A sick feeling settled in the pit of her stomach. Thankfully there were no other cars around. She hadn't seen it coming. Hadn't really been paying attention for that matter. But the light *had* turned from red to green. Maybe. Hopefully.

The biker cut the engine, swung one long denim clad leg over the seat of the motorcycle and pushed the stand down. Then he let out a yell and kicked at a pile of gravel on the road, sending tiny rocks flying into the ditch.

"Oh, man. He's mad." Mark's eyes bugged as he looked over at her. "Let's get out of here."

"No." Julia swallowed down nerves and kyboshed the tempting suggestion. She'd thought the light was green, but maybe it hadn't been. Or maybe he'd been trying to make it through on amber. "I need to make sure he's okay."

She adjusted her sunglasses, put a trembling hand on the door handle and pushed it open. The man was already marching toward her, a black and white helmet covering his face.

Muffled words punched the air through the plastic grid in front of his mouth, whatever accusatory tone they might have held lost in translation.

Julia lifted her hair off her damp neck and gave a shrug. "Can't hear you."

He unfastened the strap around his chin, shook off the cumbersome helmet, and raked a fistful of fingers through a mess of dark hair. "I said you almost killed me, lady." Indigo eyes flashed in her direction, sudden shockwaves zigzagging through her entire body.

Oh, no. No, way.

Julia clamped her mouth shut and fought a strong urge to race back to the car.

Rage and relief sparred with one another. "Pity I missed." She let out her breath and pushed her sunglasses onto her head.

Slow recognition inched across his face.

"Julia." His helmet thudded to the ground, taking her heart right along with it.

"You remember. How shocking." She closed her eyes a minute and waited for the world to stop spinning.

His brow rippled as he narrowed his eyes. "Not gonna pass out on me are you?"

Julia sucked air and shook her head. That would just make his day.

"Good." He leaned over his knees and glanced upward. She watched him exhale, look back at the ground, and mutter a couple words she didn't quite catch, which was probably just as well, judging by how fast the blood drained from his face. Then he straightened, eased back into his six-foot-something stature and set that scintillating gaze on her once more.

"Well, well. Julia Connelly. Twelve years is a long time to hold in all that anger."

Her legs still trembled, but whether it was from the shock of their near miss or seeing him again, she couldn't tell. One thing she knew for sure though, was that this day could not possibly get any worse.

"Oh, don't patronize me, Reid Wallace. And it's not Connelly anymore. It's Hansen."

"Right. Keep forgetting that. How you ran off and married the first guy that looked your way after me."

"How dare you!" She should have run him over when she'd had the chance. "Maybe I did hit you, because you seem to be suffering a concussion. You. Left. Me. Remember?"

"Yeah." He slid his gaze from her for just a moment and there might have been a hint of remorse in his eyes. "I guess we all make mistakes."

Oh, he did not just say that.

He was right about one thing. She *was* still holding onto all that anger.

It flared and lit within seconds of seeing him again, igniting memories she'd tried so hard to extinguish. She put up a hand and shot him the fiercest glare she could muster on short notice. "I'm not doing this with you."

"So how is Mr. Hansen these days?" Sarcasm settled back into his tone.

"Dead."

His eyes widened while his mouth opened, then shut. He rubbed the back of his neck, blinked a couple of times, and shook his head. "I had no idea. I'm sorry."

"I'm not." Julia folded her arms and avoided the inquiring gaze pointed her way. "Since you don't seem to be hurt, I need to go." She pressed her shoulders back, the late August sun beating down, making her even more uncomfortable. Humidity clung to the air, but the predicted end of summer storm was nowhere in sight.

Running into Reid Wallace after twelve years had not been on today's to-do list either. Sure, she'd been relieved to hear he hadn't been hurt in that explosion in Syria, but that didn't mean she was ready to see him again. And Debby had promised her he never came back to Bridgewater.

"Cool bike."

Julia spun around to see Mark heading toward them. "Get back in the car, Mark. We're leaving." Did that shrew-like shriek come from her?

Reid's amused expression told her it most certainly had.

She cleared her throat, swallowed a hefty dose of mortification and tried again. "Please, Mark. We have to go."

Mark ignored her as usual and came closer, his eyes lit with interest. Back in Atlanta, he'd been a huge fan of all things motorbikes. She had Frank to thank for that, she supposed. Not that her late husband had shown much interest in Mark the past few years. Hadn't shown much interest in anything really, other than his favorite stool at the sports bar in town.

Julia inhaled and clenched her fists. She hadn't seen such excitement on her son's face for a long time. Certainly not since they'd come to Bridgewater.

"It's a Harley, right?" He shuffled his new black and white Vans on the gravel, his eyes covering every inch of the shiny machine while he slid his hands into the pockets of his shorts, a habit he'd recently acquired in an attempt to look cool. The annoying thing was, it worked.

"Mark. I said get back in the car."

Mark shot her a surly look, sidled past them and walked around the bike.

Reid hiked up an eyebrow, his mouth twitching with the beginnings of a smile as he looked over his shoulder at her son, and then back at her. He took another long look at Mark and his smile faded.

"Pretty old, huh?" Mark crouched beside the engine.

"Sure is." Reid cleared his throat and skewered her with a hard stare that held more meaning than any words he might have said. "Got this baby when I was in high school. Your uncle and I fixed her up and she still purrs like a pussycat. Check her out if you like. Mark, right?"

"Yeah. You know my Uncle Cade?" He ran a hand over the leather seat. "How fast does she go?"

"As fast as I want her to, buddy."

Julia rolled her eyes and put her shades back on. His voice still hummed with electricity, apparently still alarmingly capable of reaching right through her and unraveling every inch of barbed wire she'd carefully constructed around her heart over the years they'd been apart.

She kicked at a rock with the tip of her sandal. The moment she'd thought about for years was playing out in front of her. This wasn't how it was supposed to happen.

What was God trying to do? Hadn't she been punished enough?

"Okay, we're done here." She snapped out of her trance and clapped her hands together. She could still salvage this. "Mark, you're in enough trouble. Don't push it. And you ..." She steadied herself and pointed at the man standing less than two feet away. The twenty-year old that still frequented her dreams was long gone, replaced by a far more mature and way too good-looking version. "You ran that stoplight and you know it. So I suggest you pay attention and drive more carefully in future. Especially on your way out of town."

"Ouch." Reid placed a hand over his heart and staggered backward. "I'd say that was a mighty strong invitation to stay out of your life, Jules."

"Genius. Mark, get off that thing!" Julia pushed past Reid to where her son was now straddling the large bike, grinning like a five-year old on a carousel.

"Come on, Mama. I'm just looking. Chill."

The excited glow on his cheeks made her eyes sting. Julia curled her toes and forced her body to stand still while all she really wanted to do was sweep him into her arms, say she was sorry for yelling, and tell him everything was going to work out.

"Yeah, Mom. Chill." Reid's voice snuck up behind her, and she almost barged right into him as she whipped around. He stood so close she could smell the leather of his jacket and the citrus spice scent of the cologne he wore.

So close.

Too close ...

New lines curved at the corners of his eyes. A few days worth of scruff covered his hard jaw and snaked around his lips. Almost black hair curled at the nape of his neck. And his eyes captured hers just as easily as they had the moment she'd first seen him walk into their school cafeteria all those years ago.

"You're staring."

"You're standing right in front of me. What do you expect?"

He shrugged, ran a hand down his face, and backed off. "You look tired, Jules."

"Thank you." The acute observation stung. Reid never hedged. Just opened his mouth and blurted out whatever was on his mind. Usually it was the truth.

But she didn't need to hear the truth. Not today.

Not from him.

"I have to get back to work." She sidestepped him and yelled for Mark again. A glance at her watch told her she would be late picking Emily up too. "Seriously, Mark, now! Your sister will be waiting, and Deb is going to have a cow. She'll probably fire me."

"How many kids do you have?" The crunch of boots on gravel told her he was right behind her. Stalking her.

Julia yanked on the handle of the car door, and turned to face him. "Just the two. Not that it's any of your business."

"Thanks for letting me see your bike." Mark got into the front seat, still grinning.

Her belligerent son just said thank-you, without prompting? Maybe she needed to have her hearing checked.

"Anytime. I'm Reid, by the way. Your Mom forgot to introduce us."

"Cool." Mark was already playing with his iPod.

"I didn't forget."

Reid moved closer and leaned against her door, preventing her from getting into the vehicle. "How old is he?" The sun disappeared beneath encroaching gray clouds. The wind picked up and played with his hair while his eyes never left her.

Julia shook her head and prayed for the coming storm to hit.

A hurricane would be good. Even a tornado. She'd take a tornado.

"Like I said, none of your business. Now get out of my way."

Reid stepped back with a nod, his smile heading south. "Right. Well, I guess you'd better get going."

"Yes. I …" Don't look at him, don't look at him, don't … too late. Julia's breath hitched as his eyes caught hers once more. A whirlwind of feelings swirled within while common sense played tug-of-war with her memories.

"Staring again."

"What are you doing here, Reid?" She had to know. "Last I heard you were some big-shot reporter on network television. Are you just in town for a visit?" If he said yes, this unwanted and totally unexpected interruption to her life would disappear.

But she had an awful, gut-twisting feeling that her problems had just begun.

"I'm between jobs at the moment." He tucked the helmet under one arm and cleared his throat. His eyes darkened and warned that further questioning would not be welcomed. "Thought a little mountain air might be good. If I'd known you were back in Vermont, I would have opted for the ocean."

That was a nice direct hit. But not completely unexpected. Like her mother always said, don't dish it out if you can't take it. "Well. Enjoy your time off, then. I do need to go."

"Drive carefully."

Julia slammed the door on him and turned the key in the ignition. Desperation clawed, daring her to undo the locks on her emotions and let them all out right then and there. She gripped the wheel and forced back tears. No way would she give Reid Wallace the satisfaction of seeing her fall to pieces at the sight of him.

"Mama? Are you okay?"

"Fine." Julia put the car in drive, peeled onto the highway and didn't look back. For about a second. As soon as she checked her rearview mirror, she saw him standing there, hand raised in farewell. Déjà vu didn't come close.

"Well, you sure don't look fine. Are you crying?"

"No." She ran a finger under her shades and got rid of the moisture on her cheeks.

"Who was that guy?" He yanked his ear buds out and waited for her answer.

Julia fiddled with the a/c, turned it up high and let the cool air bathe her face. She needed to calm down. Needed her stomach to stop heaving, her hands to stop shaking and her brain to start functioning again. She couldn't go back to work in this state. Couldn't face what was coming either. And couldn't … stop … thinking about him.

Mark slapped his knees to a fast beat, pulling her back to the present. "He said he knew Uncle Cade. Were you guys all friends or something?"

"Something."

"So, who is he? Does he live around here? Can I go check out his bike again?"

"No, Mark. No, he doesn't live around here, and no, you may not check out his bike again. He's … nobody, all right? Nobody."

Just your father.

Chapter Three

Reid drove around for a couple hours, trying to get his head around it. He hadn't given much thought to the possibility of seeing Julia. Not really. He'd figured she was still in Atlanta. Nobody told him otherwise, and he knew for sure she wouldn't be rushing up here to see him as soon as she heard he was back.

The impact of seeing her was like a pro-boxer punching him in the gut several times over. Sent him flying. Sanity abandoned his brain. Every word that shot out of his mouth made him cringe.

He'd accused her of staring, but that was really all he'd been able to do. Stare at the attractive woman he barely recognized, but those eyes … as soon as she'd locked her gaze on him, he'd known. He was rarely at a loss for words, but Jules … she rendered him pretty speechless. Always had.

He'd wanted to ask her how she'd been, what she was doing back in Bridgewater, when she'd come home, and a million other things, but the cloak of exhaustion she wore along with the faded skirt and cotton blouse with the stain she hadn't quite managed to wash out told him more than he wanted to know. Her eyes didn't hold the same spark. And he'd been around fear enough to know when he was standing in its presence.

So he watched her drive off, waited until she was well out of sight before he doubled over again. Even sent up a frantic prayer for wisdom. And he hadn't talked to God in quite some time.

Seeing Julia again changed that in a flash.

Reid sat by the pond in the park, piecing his jumbled thoughts together—thoughts that didn't make the slightest bit of sense whichever way he spun them. Watched the ducks and swans congregate at the water's edge as little kids and their moms threw bread for them.

The weather changed, and the kids went home. Reid stayed put, staring at the rippling green water, contemplating his next move. Her face kept intruding on his thoughts. Memories launched a swift attack and pinned him down.

He sank against the doorframe and watched her. She sat at the small table by the kitchen window, head bent over a notebook, hand stilled in midair. He knew she was debating with herself, questioning the next word, wondering if it was good enough. The way she pushed her teeth into her bottom lip told him it wasn't.

Julia was her own worst critic. Never fully able to believe she was the writer he knew she could be. Never fully able to believe she was everything he wanted, always pointing out some flaw he'd never seen … always needed him to tell her what she should already know. Needed his approval, his praise, and encouragement. Needed him to be so much more, to give so much more. He was no longer convinced it would ever be enough. She needed more than he could offer, and that terrified him. After a week of sleepless nights, and shouting matches with himself as he ran in the woods, he'd made his decision.

He just wasn't sure how he'd ever be able to live with it.

Reid couldn't stop thinking about her. Couldn't stop thinking about her or that kid.

Julia's son.

Mark.

Something set Reid's mind on overdrive as soon as he'd laid eyes on him. Even though he'd only seen the boy for a few minutes, it wasn't hard to pick up on the things she so obviously didn't want him to.

Rationale said it couldn't be true. She would have told him. As angry as she had been, he couldn't imagine her keeping that kind of secret. Then again, all the arguments, all the awful words spoken between them the last few days before he left, it was possible. On the other hand, if she'd known, she could have used the fact to make him stay. She hadn't.

It couldn't be his kid.

Same eyes, hair color, nose, even the way he'd sauntered over to the bike, hands in his pockets … everything about the boy pushed the foundations out from under life as he knew it, and sent it crashing down around him.

Oh, God. It can't be. Please, don't let it be.

But every part of him said it was.

And maybe that was his punishment.

Reid tried to find some measure of comfort in the surrounding mountains as he drove along the back roads of the town he'd stayed away from so long. The leaves were changing from green to red and gold, announcing the approach of fall. Soon the hills would be blanketed in a riot of color. God's patchwork quilt, his grandmother always called it.

But nature's beauty offered him no peace today.

He pulled into the parking lot at the cemetery, shook off his helmet, and walked the gravel path for the first time in five years. Veered to the left and made his way down the rows of headstones until he reached the pink marble one with his grandmother's name on it.

The white rose bush he had planted hours after the funeral still bloomed. The area around the trunk was weeded, well cared for, one stray dandelion poking up around the back of the bush.

"I sure wish you were here, Essie." Reid scratched his head and frowned. Was it okay to talk to a piece of stone? "If you can hear me up there, I could use your advice. Because I think I'm in trouble." He crouched and yanked the stubborn weed up by the roots.

"You've gone and done it now, haven't you?" Esmé rocked back and forth in her white wicker rocker as they sat on the porch. She concentrated on her knitting, didn't look at him. She hadn't said much at all since he'd shown up two days ago. Alone.

"You don't understand." He fiddled with the strap of his watch and stared at his shiny new shoes. "This is a great opportunity for me. I may not get another chance like this."

*"Reid." His grandmother put down her needles, and fixed him with the look he'd come to understand meant she was madder than a tipped over hornet's nest. "You **had** a great opportunity, one that doesn't come around too often in this life. You had the chance to love, son. Don't be so quick to walk away from that."*

He leaned over his knees and shoved his fingers through his hair, his eyes smarting.

As usual, she was right.

Trouble was, he'd already walked away.

And there was no going back.

Reid picked at the blades of grass around his feet. He missed his grandmother with an ache he doubted would ever go away. If he could have made things right before she died, he would have. But he'd figured they'd have plenty of time for that. He'd intended to come up and spend Christmas with her that year. Instead, he'd shown up for her funeral.

He'd learned to live with the knowledge that he'd let her down, disappointed her. Somehow, over the years, he'd convinced himself it didn't matter.

It did.

And he hadn't been there for her at the end.

Reid trudged back to his bike, in more turmoil now than he had been late yesterday afternoon when he'd given in to the knee-jerk reaction to return to Bridgewater. After the hellish last few months, all he wanted was to be left alone. He planned on hibernating up here until he decided what to do with the rest of his life.

He hadn't planned on placating his past.

He parked his bike, and stomped up the wooden stairs to the loft apartment above the garage opposite the Connelly family's rambling farmhouse. He knocked once, pushed open the door, and stalked across the colorful rug, chucking his helmet on the couch, narrowly missing a glass vase on the gnarled oak coffee table.

Cade Connelly looked up from his laptop with a frown. "You want to tell me what that was about?"

Reid went into the galley kitchen and glared at the contents of the refrigerator. Cade didn't drink, which was probably a good thing given Reid's present state of mind. He grabbed two sodas, tossed one to Cade, and flopped onto the La-Z-Boy opposite the worn leather sofa. "When were you going to tell me your sister is back in town?"

"Hannah never left town."

"I'm not talking about Hannah."

Cade shut his laptop, set it beside him and took off the silver-rimmed glasses he wore for reading. Presented Reid with his classic for-a-smart-guy-you-can-be-a-real-moron expression. Lifted his hands and let them fall against his bare knees. "Reid, my friend, you had a cab drop you off here at midnight without so much as a text to say, 'Hey, I'm coming into town, okay if I crash at your place?' Then you took off this morning before the sun rose. When have I had the chance?"

"Good point." Reid leaned over and tugged at the laces of his scuffed boots.

"I take it you ran into Jules?"

Harsh laughter escaped as he kicked his boots aside and sank against the soft brown leather. "More like she ran into me."

"She what?" Cade mussed his hair as he swung his legs onto the couch.

"She tried to run me over." Okay, that was a stretch. But if she had known he was the one speeding in front of her, he bet she would have.

"Dude." Cade whistled, his eyebrows shooting skyward. "What happened? Are you all right?"

Reid waved a hand. "Okay, she didn't run me over. I ran a red light at Hogges Point Road, and she almost hit me."

"Oh, man. So nobody got hurt?"

"Nope."

"Good." Cade sighed and rubbed his eyes. "How mad was she?"

"Just about as furious as the last time we spoke."

Cade drummed his fingers over the surface of his laptop. "She had a right."

The past slipped into the room uninvited, unwanted.

Somehow he and Cade stayed friends through it all. Working together helped. He went after the stories, and Cade shot the film. There were few places in the world they hadn't been over the last decade. They could shoot the breeze, talk sports and politics, and sometimes God, but they never talked about the events that took place twelve years ago. Maybe that was their saving grace.

"I didn't know her husband died." He'd hoped she'd move on, but honestly hadn't expected her to do it so quickly. Not like he'd given her a choice. Reid's pulse jacked as he remembered that haunted look in her eyes. Dazzling honey-colored eyes flecked with gold to match her hair. Eyes he never thought he'd see again.

"Yup."

"When?"

"Just after New Year's."

"That was when we were in Syria?"

"Yes."

"You didn't tell me."

"I don't tell you everything."

Odd tension ping-ponged between them. Reid breathed in and tried to figure out how to handle it. "I thought she lived in Atlanta."

"Did."

"Cade."

"What, Reid?" Cade sat up, thunked down his soda and met Reid's eyes. The small wood-paneled apartment was hot, no air-conditioning. Cade's summer attire of shorts and a t-shirt made Reid wonder what he'd been thinking that morning, pulling on jeans and a long sleeved-shirt.

"I want answers." He shrugged out of his jacket, and waited.

"What answers? We don't talk about Jules, you and I. Ever. Suddenly you see her again and you want a play-by-play of every day of the last twelve years of her life?"

Well, yeah. That was pretty much exactly what he wanted. The very idea grabbed him by the shoulders and shook him. Hard.

"When did she come back to Bridgewater?"

Cade sighed like he was giving away the code to the vaults at Fort Knox. "She came back in the spring. I didn't tell you because you had enough going on, and you were still in New York. And what my sister does really isn't any of your business."

Reid took the blow to his pride and steeled himself for more. "She must have gotten pregnant pretty quick after they married. How old is the kid?"

"What kid?"

"Her kid. The boy. Mark. I'm thinking eleven going on twelve. Would that be about right?"

"You saw Mark?" Cade sucked at hiding his emotions. The way his jaw twitched, his eyes shifting, landing on anything other than Reid's face said his suspicions were spot on. And sent his mind spinning.

"Okay, man." Reid took a breath. "This is not the time to clam up or plead the fifth." Reid held his friend's reluctant gaze and narrowed his eyes.

"How'd you see him?" Cade asked quietly. He was supposed to start school today."

"He was in the car with her. Had quite the shiner." At least he'd had enough sense not to ask Julia about it.

"Oh, no." Cade leaned back and closed his eyes. "Oh, Lord, help us."

Reid sat forward. "Just tell me what I need to know, Cade."

"Look, Reid ..."

"Don't 'look Reid' me. I'm not an idiot, Connelly. I saw the kid! It was like looking in the mirror. Unless that guy she married was my identical twin, I'd say your sister has some explaining to do. Am I right?"

"You're the investigative reporter. What do you think?"

Reid let out a low whistle and pushed up. He fought the urge to high-tail it to the bathroom and give his churning stomach relief, and paced the room instead. Truth slammed him like a linebacker and almost sent him to his knees. "All these years, Cade? You never said a word?"

"I promised her. She didn't want you to know. You'd already left and she'd settled down south. Met Frank."

"You're my best friend."

"And she's my sister." Cade shook his head. "Don't judge me on this one."

"Some other guy raised my son, Cade! A son I didn't know I had until a few hours ago. How did this happen?"

"The usual way, I would imagine. About nine months before Mark was born, sometime during the months you and Jules—"

"You think this is funny?"

"I'm sorry." Cade rubbed his face, his cheeks splotchy all of a sudden. "It's not." His eyes shone a little too brightly. "You have no idea how sorry I am that you didn't know. But it's not my story to tell."

Reid twisted the ring on his right hand. "I'm dreaming this, right? I don't even like kids."

Cade nailed him with that you're-a-moron look again. "Sure. That's why you make a beeline for them the minute we touch down someplace. You want me to pull up the pictures to prove it?"

Cade was right. Wherever they went, Reid found the kids. Or they found him.

He'd played soccer with groups of gangly boys with toothless grins and open hearts in more countries than he could count. Sat with giggling toddlers on his lap. Doled out food and clothing to orphans, hugged them close, knowing all they really wanted was a home, and someone to love them.

He knew that feeling too well.

"Does everybody know he's my son?" Way to be played for sucker of the century.

"I doubt it. Jules didn't come home a whole lot after she married Frank." Cade coughed and let out a groan. "Don't ask me anything else."

"Are you kidding me?" Reid stifled the urge to grab his friend by the collar and shake it all out of him. "This is unbelievable."

"She did what she thought was best, Reid. I wanted her to tell you so many times, but she wouldn't. The longer she waited, the harder things got for her. You don't know what it was like … she … didn't have an easy time of it." Cade sighed and stared at the floor, his confession as over as quickly as it began.

Reid sat in silence. Cold fingers climbed up his back and sent a shiver down his spine. "What aren't you telling me?" A strange heaviness settled over him.

Outside, the dogs began to bark. Cade stood and went to the window. Tires crunched over the gravel driveway. Car doors slammed. Kids voices floated upward.

"Where is Julia staying?" Reid knew the answer before he got the question out.

"Where else? You expected her to be at a hotel?"

Footsteps pounded up the back stairs and a moment later the front door flew open. "Cade, you will not believe who—" Julia stopped mid-sentence, her long fair hair flying around her face, her cheeks pinking and getting redder by the second. Her eyes widened as they flashed under the florescent lighting. "Oh."

She was still angry. Maybe even more so now that she'd seen him again.

"Hey, Jules." Reid raised a hand and tried on a grin. "Long time no see."

Her mouth slammed shut and she pulled her hands behind her back. "I should have known you'd be here. Unbelievable."

Reid clenched his jaw. "I'll say."

"Julia." Cade went to her, tried to put an arm around her shoulders.

"Don't." She shook him off. "What is he doing here, how long has he been here, and why didn't you tell me you were keeping company with the scum of the earth?"

"That's a little harsh." Reid wanted to say more, but the lasers shooting from her eyes made him shut his mouth.

"He just showed up last night," Cade muttered. "I didn't exactly have a say in the matter."

"Oh, like I believe that!" Disbelief marred her face as she scowled at her brother. "The two of you work together."

"Not anymore." Reid worked to keep his voice level. Cade shot him a look of surprise but all Reid could do was shrug. This wasn't the time to explain. "He's right, I just showed up last night." Or this morning, but who cared. "And I think you and I need to talk. Now."

He hadn't meant to say it like that. Hadn't meant to be so abrupt. He'd intended to give her time. Give them both time, so that whatever discussion ensued might be handled maturely. But anger got the better of him and mature went out the window.

"No." Julia backed up and shook her head. She looked so afraid he almost felt sorry for her. "You and I have nothing to talk about. You made that perfectly clear twelve years ago. With divorce papers."

Reid took a step forward, risking getting close enough for her to slug him one. "I may not always act like it, but I'm a fairly intelligent guy. I saw him, Julia. *I know.* Don't stand there and try to deny it."

"You told him?" Her voice shot up somewhere near the ceiling as she turned on her brother, pushing trembling hands through her long hair. "Cade, you promised!"

Reid clamped down his anger, tried to keep calm. "He didn't have to tell me. Anybody with half a brain can see the resemblance. And I can do the math. So you want to explain why you figured it was okay to keep my son from me for the past eleven years? To not even have the decency to tell me I was going to be a father?"

Julia sank onto the couch and buried her face in her hands. Cade made a brave attempt at trying to console her but she pushed him away. Her muffled sobs pummeled Reid and made him wish it were possible to turn back the clock. Make it so that none of this was happening.

Finally she raised her head and looked his way. "You didn't deserve to know."

The cold, clipped words struck him like a slap across the face. "I didn't deserve to know? I was your husband!"

"For two months, Reid! That's all the time it took for you to decide you'd made a mistake. You didn't want to be married anymore, remember? The vows we took on our wedding day meant absolutely nothing to you. All you wanted was your freedom, and nothing could convince you otherwise. What in the world makes you think I'd consider you a good candidate to be a father?"

Her wet eyes burned holes through his chest and her words dumped a truckload of guilt at his feet. Suddenly he was twenty years old again. Too full of himself for his own good, terrified of failing, and running away from responsibility as fast as his Harley could carry him.

"You're right. Obviously I didn't deserve the chance to prove you wrong." Reid thumped into his chair, reached for his boots and yanked them back on. He grabbed his jacket and strode across the room. His duffel bag lay in the corner where he'd dropped it before crashing on the couch early that morning.

"Where are you going?" Cade blocked his path, concern etched in the lines beneath his eyes.

"No idea." He was about to lose what little sanity he had left. Staying here was not an option. Reid scratched his head and tried to avoid looking at Julia. Even as worn out as she looked, she was more beautiful than he remembered. But he wasn't going down that road.

He headed for the couch and picked up his helmet. "Thanks for letting me stay. And for storing the bike. I'll ... call you."

"You're going to leave? Just like that?" Disbelief clung to Cade's voice.

"There's a storm coming. It's starting to rain." Julia stood beside her brother and matched his anxious expression.

"Like you care?" The last few months were beginning to take their toll. Exhaustion knocked hard, and it was all he could do to stay on his feet.

"Fine. Go." Julia marched to the door and held it open. The wall was back up as quickly as it had crumbled. "With a little luck, you'll get hit by lightning."

"Jules, cut it out." Cade held up a hand, and tipped his head toward the long glass window on the other side of the room. "Look at those clouds, man. You can't go out in that."

The weather had changed for the worse, the sky now dark and threatening. The distinct sound of thunder rolled overhead. But riding through a storm would be better than enduring the hurricane in here.

"I'll go up the mountain. Stay at my grandmother's cabin."

Cade narrowed his eyes. "You haven't been up there in five years. The place is probably falling apart. You can stay here."

"No, he can't." Julia waited at the door, her lips pinched in a hard expression Reid remembered too well.

Hard drops splashed onto the dark wood deck and danced off the roof above them with a vengeance.

"I'm outta here." Reid brushed past them and pounded down the stairs. Thunder moved closer and lightning slit through the sky. Cade yelled after him but Reid kept moving.

He caught sight of the two kids standing under the porch of the main house watching the storm. Watching him. The dogs circled the driveway, barking louder as he got to his bike. He pulled on his helmet, zipped up his jacket and wished he could zip up his temper just as easily.

"Hey, Mister!" The boy called to him, giving a tentative wave.

Mark.

His son.

Reid's gut twisted. Everything in him wanted to get off the bike and run up to the porch. Hold the kid against him and promise never to let him go. The thought hit him like a wild animal crashing through the forest to escape a hunter's aim.

A little girl with blonde curls hopped up and down beside Mark, squealing with every roll of thunder.

Julia flew past in a blur as the rain pelted the ground. She ran to the kids, turned them toward the house, tried to convince them to go inside. The front door banged open and Julia's parents, and Hannah, stepped onto the porch.

Great. A Connelly family reunion.

"Reid Wallace is that you?" Julia's mother peered across the front yard. Hearing her voice after all these years almost made him quit kicking the starter pedal.

"Come on, baby. Don't do this to me." The old Harley had been giving him trouble all day. He'd had to pull over twice and give the engine a rest. The bike had been idle so long he wasn't sure how far he'd get on her. But at least she'd gotten him back to the house. And now it appeared she was taking a permanent vacation.

"It's not starting, man. Spark plug's probably shot. Give it up." Cade appeared on his other side, holding an umbrella. "Come inside."

The rain turned torrential and kept time with the beating of Reid's heart.

He'd been through a lot since he'd left home, left Julia.

Ducked sniper fire, dodged his way out of a few brawls, lived through the terror of an earthquake, even survived a bomb blast. But all that was nothing compared to the war that raged inside him right now.

"Would the two of you get on up here so we can all avoid pneumonia, please." Jonas Connelly's baritone voice rocketed through the air, brought along reason and no room for argument.

Reid hung his head, watched rain drip off his helmet and bounce off the waxed chrome gas tank. He was stuck. Either he could sit out here in the storm or find a few of the manners he'd been raised with, give in and go up to the house.

Cade grabbed his bag while Reid pushed his bike back into the garage. A few minutes later he was being embraced by the family he'd once called his own.

And Julia was nowhere in sight.

Chapter Four

"Go away." Whoever was knocking on her bedroom door clearly had no intention of going anywhere.

"Jules, it's me." Debby Jamison's voice reached her ears and Julia crossed the room to let her friend in. Debby held a tray in her hands. "Your Mom wanted me to bring this up. You need to eat something."

"I'm not hungry." Julia stood by the window, watched the rain, and ignored the rumbling of her stomach at the smell of her mother's home-made soup. "What are you doing here?"

"Cade called me."

"Figures." Julia walked around the room she'd once shared with her sister, and sat at the small desk. Hannah had long since moved to the ground floor apartment addition their father had built several years ago. "I guess you know why I never made it back to work this afternoon."

"Don't worry about it. Are you okay?"

"Define okay." Julia almost smiled. "Just when I thought I was getting my life back, he shows up and flips it upside down again. What's God trying to do to me, Deb?"

Debby shrugged, a serene look on her face. "Whatever He's up to, Jules, it's good. You know that. His plan for you is a good one. You just have to trust Him."

"That's a little hard to do right now." Julia sighed and scanned the room.

Much of what she'd left behind all those years ago remained. The awards she'd won in high school still sat in place, proud testimony to the writer she was becoming. Faded pink wallpaper, scarred in spots where the posters of their favorite bands had hung. Her old dolls and stuffed animals sat on the shelves of the bookcase her father made for them. Everything still seemed to have her name on it. Still reached deep into her soul and told her she was home.

Some things never changed.

Like Debby's friendship, solid and unwavering as ever.

Debby had been faithful to keep in touch over the years. Even when Julia tried to push her away, she showed up on her doorstep. Tried to do what she could for them, but for the last few years, Julia begged her not to make any more trips to Atlanta.

"I don't know what to do, Deb."

"You knew this would happen eventually."

"Yes." She pushed her hands into the pocket of her jeans. "But not today. Not like this."

"Come on, eat." Debby put the supper tray in front of her. "You'll feel better with some food in your stomach."

Julia picked up the spoon. Soup, crusty rolls, and a salad. It did look good. She'd missed her mother's cooking. Missed a lot of things.

The moment the hot soup slid down her throat, her stomach roiled in protest. "I can't." She put the spoon down and got up again. Better to stay on her feet, keep walking. If she sat still, the events of that afternoon came flooding back full force. "He was the last person I expected to see today. I didn't know what to say."

"I'm sure." Deb's mouth turned downward. "Between us, I don't think Cade's too happy with his sudden appearance either."

"Well. Now what? Is Reid still here?"

"Yes, but under duress. Your mother insisted he stay for dinner. Your Dad looks about ready to get out the shotgun."

"That would be too easy." Julia bit back a stupid sudden urge to burst into tears. As soon as she saw Reid get off his bike and head toward the house, she'd raced upstairs. Changed out of her wet skirt and blouse into jeans and a sweater, sorely tempted to throw on her pajamas and curl under the covers. And never come out.

She couldn't bring herself to go back down. Couldn't face him again.

"Are the kids okay? What did Cade tell them?"

"He said you weren't feeling well. The kids seemed fine when I got here. Emily was talking Reid's ear off."

Julia grinned. Her five year-old latched on to anybody who paid her the slightest bit of attention. Second thoughts slithered around her again as she stared at her friend, her eyes burning. "Was I wrong, Deb? Should I have told him about Mark?"

Debby gave a sympathetic smile. "I can't answer that. And there's no point in playing the what-if game, is there?"

"No, but maybe … maybe if I'd said something back then, things would have been different."

"Jules. You were just out of high school when you married Reid, eighteen years old. I know you guys thought you were ready, even though everyone asked you to wait. You were head-over-heels for each other, and nobody could talk you out of it. I don't think either of you knew what you were getting into."

"Reid sure didn't." Pain squeezed her heart and pushed out the tears she'd been working so hard to keep in check. She swiped her eyes and glared out the window at the dark sky. A flash of lightning made her jump. Her nerves, what was left of them, were shot. "I hated him for so long. And every time I looked at Mark, I saw Reid. Of course it wasn't Mark's fault, but … it was hard. Reid broke my heart, Deb. You know, I think I married Frank just to spite him." A cry stuck in her throat. "And look where that got me."

Debby enfolded her in a hug. "Maybe marrying Frank wasn't the smartest decision you ever made, but you thought you were doing the right thing at the time. And you've got Emily."

"Yes." Em was the light of her life and kept them laughing. "And we all survived."

Barely. And only by the grace of God.

How many nights had she spent huddled in bed, praying Frank wouldn't come home drunk and take his anger out on her?

Too many nights he had.

Julia pushed the past aside. "This wasn't quite the way I wanted today to go." The fresh start she'd hoped for when she'd left the house this morning had withered and died, like flowers left too long out of water. "I hope my boss is the forgiving kind."

"Your boss loves you to death." Debby grinned and raised an eyebrow. "But she's more than a little worried about you right now. What are you going to do about that dude sitting down there in your parents' kitchen?"

"I don't know. Pray he takes off again and never comes back?"

"Jules."

Julia shrugged off Debby's look of chastisement. "He knows Mark is his. But I don't know what he wants. And I have no idea what to tell Mark."

"How about we tell him the truth?" Reid's low voice thrummed around the room. He leaned against the doorframe, arms crossed, eyes glinting with a shade of leftover anger.

"Don't you know it's rude to eavesdrop?" Julia wiped her cheeks and hoped she didn't look as much of a mess as she felt. But what did it matter? She didn't care what Reid Wallace thought of her.

"What are you doing up here, Reid?" Debby went on the defensive, and Julia wanted to hug her.

He let out an irritated sigh and held up his hands. "Relax. I come in peace."

"Yeah, right." Julia stared at her moccasins. She hadn't actually meant to say that out loud.

Debby hesitated, looking from Reid to her. "Do the two of you need a referee or can I go?"

"Don't go." Julia grabbed her by the arm.

"Go." Reid stepped into the room and took control. Just like always.

His larger-than-life presence demanded attention. It was no wonder he'd climbed up the ranks in record time to land a spot as one of America's most popular news anchors.

Well-liked in school, he was the one they listened to, looked up to. And she had been his biggest fan.

Until he'd shown his true colors and left her, pregnant with hardly two dimes to rub together.

"Jules. Maybe you guys should talk, huh?" Debby sounded about as uncertain of the suggestion as Julia was.

"Thanks, Deb. Good idea. Shut the door on your way out." Reid pulled up a chair and straddled it, long arms hanging over the top.

Debby headed for the hallway, sent Julia a silent apology, and left the door open.

Julia had little choice but to look his way. "I really don't want to talk to you right now."

"Too bad." He stared at her for an excruciatingly long time before he spoke again. "To answer your question, yes. Yes, you were wrong. You should have told me, Julia."

He was right. He knew it, and probably knew she knew it too.

"What difference does it make now?" She sighed. "By the time I found out I was pregnant you were long gone. I wasn't about to track you down and beg you to come back to me."

"So you didn't know you were pregnant before I left?"

"No. I didn't know. That's the truth." She hated the hard look in his eyes. Like he didn't quite believe her. "Even if I had, I doubt you would have stayed."

"You really think that? That I wouldn't have wanted to be a father?"

"When would you have had the time? You were too busy getting famous."

"That's not fair."

"Isn't it?" She folded her arms against the anger his abandonment still provoked. She couldn't look at him again. If she did, she'd be a shaking mess on the floor. "If you came up here for an apology, you're not getting one."

A brief chuckle rumbled from his chest. "Oh, I didn't think I'd be that lucky."

Even with her back to him, she felt his eyes on her. Taking everything in, making mental notes through the silence. Nerves began to use Julia's stomach as a punching bag. She took slow steps around the room, trying to piece her thoughts together.

"Actually, Julia, I came up here to give you my apology."

"Really." Julia moved toward the twin bed, every muscle screaming as she sank down on the edge of the mattress. Nothing in his eyes said he wasn't telling the truth. She could spot a liar a mile away. She'd spent years living with one. "You think you owe me an apology, Reid? I'd say you're a few years too late."

"Yeah, I guess you would." He was serious, unsmiling. "I can't change the past, Jules. And neither can you."

"That's been said already." She clasped her hands in her lap. "How much of our conversation did you hear?"

"Enough." He cracked his knuckles, a habit that always drove her crazy. Tonight she welcomed the sound and found strange solace in it. "Julia, I'm sorry for—"

"If you're about to rehash it all, I don't want to talk about what happened with us. There's no point."

He clamped his mouth shut, squared shoulders that were much broader than she remembered. "All right. So let's talk about our son." He propped his elbows on the back of the chair and rested his chin on his hands. "Did your husband think Mark was his?"

"No. He knew I was pregnant when he married me." Married her anyway.

She'd been young, scared, not to mention broke. She couldn't bring herself to go home so she'd gone to stay with a cousin in Atlanta. Got a job as a waitress in a local diner. When she was about six months along, Frank Hansen walked through the doors, tipped his hat her way with a dashing smile, and she was done for.

"And I'm assuming Mark has no clue."

"No, he doesn't. And I don't want to tell him," she whispered.

"That's non-negotiable." Blue eyes pinned her and forced her to acknowledge the absurdity of her words. "You're telling him."

"I meant not right away." Julia's fingers slid to the bare spot on her left hand where her rings had once sat. Reid's had been a plain gold band he could barely afford. Frank's more elaborate, a diamond solitaire with a white-gold wedding band to match his own. "He's just lost his father, Reid."

"That wasn't his father."

"He doesn't know that."

"Well aware, Jules. Well aware." Succinct words sizzled through the air.

She couldn't do this. Couldn't step back in time to try and make it right, but couldn't move toward the future either. Both prospects were far too frightening.

"I don't want to fight with you." Julia sniffed, almost flinching under his glare. "I'm already exhausted."

"Join the club." He swiveled and played with the spoon in the soup she had barely touched. "Are you going to eat this?"

"No."

She watched him dig into her dinner. "I thought you ate downstairs."

He bit into the roll and shook his head. "The Judge was giving me the evil eye the whole time. I kind of lost my appetite." He wiped his mouth on the sleeve of his shirt. "I haven't eaten a decent meal in days. I'm starving."

"Apparently." A smile lifted her lips, unbidden. "I'm surprised my Dad allowed you through the front door."

"No kidding. The way he kept looking at me and Mark, I thought he was going to haul me into his study for cross-examination."

"He'll have to put me on the stand first."

The spoon clattered into the bowl and he jerked his head around. "Your parents don't know?"

Julia shrugged. There was so much he didn't know. So much she didn't want him to. "I'm sure they've got a pretty good idea that Mark is yours, especially after tonight. But no, I never actually told them, and they never asked. Before I moved back here, we hadn't seen each other in years."

"Why?" Consternation furrowed his brow. "You were so close."

She brushed some dog hair off her sweater and managed to meet his gaze. "I didn't leave home under the best of circumstances, if you recall. We married without their permission, Reid, without their blessing. And then the next thing they knew, you were gone, and I was marrying someone else. Hardly conversation for the church crowd."

"Surely you must have visited? They would have wanted to see their grandkids."

"They did. We tried for a while. But they didn't like Frank and he … well, Frank didn't like anybody. I wasn't allowed to come here, and eventually they stopped coming south."

"What do you mean you weren't allowed?"

Julia huffed out a sigh and gave a thin smile. "Do you think you could shut off your journalistic tendencies for the next little while?"

"Sorry." Reid got up, moved the chair around and sat on it properly.

Time appeared to have treated him well. But the dark jeans, heather-gray Henley, and that scruff on his face didn't make him look much like the well-dressed, smooth-talking news anchor who sat in front of the cameras and told viewers what they needed to know. She'd always found it ironic that the one person in the world she wanted to forget showed up in her living room night after night.

He cleared his throat. "Mark seems like a great kid. Kind of quiet, but then Emily did most of the talking. How old is she?"

"She's five. She just started Kindergarten."

"Yeah, she said. Looks like you, huh?"

"I guess." Awkward conversation wasn't helping. "You took me by surprise today. I wasn't expecting to see you."

"I figured. I wasn't expecting to see you either."

Julia decided to just get on with it. "You might as well know. I was planning on writing to you. Now that Frank's gone ... I've had time to think. It was wrong of me not to tell you about Mark. I didn't know how you'd take the news after all this time, whether you'd want to be part of Mark's life, but ..."

"Why wouldn't I want to be part of his life? He's my son." As if it were that simple. "I've missed enough already, don't you think?" He pulled at his jaw and flicked hair out of his eyes.

He and Mark were so alike it was uncanny. Julia couldn't stop staring. She didn't want to, but her eyes dragged back to his face every time she looked away. "If you really want the truth, Reid ... I think Mark will be glad to know that Frank wasn't his real father."

She might as well have sucker-punched him. His brows knit together, his mouth a thin line. She watched him process her words and prayed he would understand their meaning.

"Julia ... what are you saying?"

She held up a hand. "You don't need details and you don't need to feel sorry for me." The last thing she wanted was his pity. "Just hear me out. If you want me to tell Mark who you are, I need to know what role you intend to play in his life."

"You want me to answer that right now?"

"Yes."

Reid pushed to his feet and marched the room. The lights flickered as another round of thunder and lightning hit the sky. Eventually he lowered himself into the chair again, lines creasing his forehead the way they always had when he was deep in thought. "I need time for this to sink in. I'm stunned. I ... I never thought I'd have kids. My job takes me all over the world. And when I'm home, I'm barely there."

She nodded. He wasn't telling her anything she hadn't already assumed. "There's really no point to this conversation."

"Of course there's a point." His eyes flashed frustration. "I'm trying to figure this out, Julia, give me a break."

"Give you a break? Oh, that's rich."

He raised a brow and she stifled the rest of her rant. Part of her wished he'd just admit that this wasn't what he needed, wanted, and leave the room. Leave Bridgewater and never come back. But for Mark's sake, she would hear what he had to say.

"Fine. Go on."

"Okay." Reid looked down at his boots and she watched his chest rise and fall. "Just because this wasn't in my plan doesn't mean I'm not interested." He lifted his chin, his eyes on her again. "I'm not working right now. There was a bit of situation over in Syria a while back. Cade was there, so you probably know what happened. It hasn't been easy to get over. I put in for a leave of absence. I'm not sure what my next step is. But I've done well over the years. I have enough in savings, more than enough. I can give him whatever he needs."

"I don't want your money." Julia wrestled with her emotions. "This isn't about providing for him financially. I don't expect you to do that."

It was almost impossible to sit in the same room. She hadn't moved on as much as she'd thought or hoped. Seeing Reid, hearing his voice, reliving it all, hammered that point home. She forced herself to focus on the subject of their discussion instead. "Mark has had a hard time since Frank died. He needs somebody to be there for him. To spend time with him. Do stuff with him." She scooted back on the bed and drew her legs to her chest. "If you're planning on up and leaving town in a week or so, then I have no intention of telling him the truth right now."

Or letting you anywhere near him.

"Then I'll tell him."

"Reid." She gave a cry of exasperation. "I didn't think it was possible for you to be more stubborn than you were, but somehow I think you've managed it."

"Well, you're not as nice as you used to be." A familiar sparkle returned to his eyes.

"Oh, please. Look, I'm not about to put my son in a situation where he'll only end up getting hurt. I think it's best that we not tell him. Not right now."

"I disagree."

"It's not up to you. I have to do what's best for Mark." She saw him shut down, but went on anyway. "We moved back here to start over. The kids have left the only home they've known, all their friends. I'm trying to get them through the transition, but it's not easy. I don't need any more drama, Reid."

"And I'm not trying to make things harder on you. You think this is easy for me?" He gave a short laugh, massaging the back of his neck. "I came back to Bridgewater for some peace and quiet. I needed to get away. Needed time to think. The last thing I expected was to have my entire world turned upside down within twenty-four hours of arriving. This changes everything, Julia."

"It doesn't have to." She pushed her hair over her shoulders and watched him carefully. "You have a life in New York. A career. You'll be going back at some point. Mark doesn't need a father he's never going to see."

"You're not giving me a chance." His tone hinted at aggravation, but he remained calm. "Let me sort through this. Don't write me off as the loser you think I was when I walked out on you. I'm not that guy anymore."

"How do I know that?"

"You don't." He pinned her with his eyes, his mouth drawn. "You're just going to have to take my word for it, and let me prove it to you."

"I don't know, Reid." He was asking too much. Expecting too much.

A buzzing sound stifled whatever answer he was about to give. Reid fished an iPhone from the pocket of his jeans and shot her a look of apology. "Reid Wallace." He leaned back in his chair and closed his eyes. Pushed fingers through his hair and gave a muted sigh. "No, I can't talk right now. I'm in a meeting. What? With ... look, I'll call you later, all right? No, I'm fine. Yeah. Ciao." He clicked off and stared at the floor.

Reality crashed into the room. What had she been thinking? This would be far more complicated than she realized. The infamous Reid Wallace could not possibly have remained unattached for all these years.

"In a meeting?" She stole a furtive glance at his left hand. No ring there. But that didn't mean anything. "Are you married?" He'd asked to be a part of her son's life. Might as well know right now what she was up against.

Reid snapped his head up and stared like she'd just asked him who the President was. "What?"

Julia nodded toward the phone he tossed between his hands. "Was that your wife?"

"No." The room got a little darker and the overhead light hit his cheeks, illuminating the faint pink hue seeping into them. "Just somebody who wants to be."

Chapter Five

*R*eid rocked back and forth on the heels of his boots in front of the brand-spanking new black Range Rover he'd just parked next to Cade's dirty red Ford pick-up.

Was he completely crazy? Second thoughts slammed him and sent his mind places he was determined to stay away from. He didn't want to run anymore.

He'd gone back to New York a few days ago, not really knowing what to do. Julia's insistence on waiting to tell Mark the truth goaded him, but he saw the sense in it. And it gave him time to wrap his brain around the fact that he was a father. Whether or not he wanted to be.

Most of him wanted to be. A tiny part of him said he should ignore the entire situation and stay as far away from Mark, and Julia, as possible.

But he ignored the doubts that tiptoed around him late at night and kept him awake. He could do this. He wanted to do this.

He just wasn't convinced he'd be all that good at it.

Rather than put off the inevitable, he went back to the city to take care of a few things so he could come back to Bridgewater unfettered. After a few hours of city smog, traffic, and noise that never left him alone, he couldn't wait to leave. Couldn't wait to get back up here, inhale fresh mountain air, and try to figure out the rest of his life. The challenge was one he finally felt ready to face.

But maybe coming back was a mistake.

What if Julia never intended to tell the truth? What if he'd hurt her so badly she'd do anything to get back at him? What if she sold her story to the highest bidder? What if …

A grin slid across his mouth. He'd definitely been in New York too long.

Reid shook off paranoia and stared at the tall pines that towered above the house as the sun disappeared behind their branches. A cooling breeze picked up a handful of brown shriveled leaves and scattered them across the driveway. Scattered memories of the life he'd left behind right along with them.

The old Connelly family farmhouse, inherited from Julia's mother's side, hadn't changed. Sparkling white with green trim, the front gardens as pretty as they had been, a few stubborn summer sunflowers still holding tight to their stalks.

The surrounding farmland belonged to Julia's Uncle Walter, who ran a small dairy farm with his two sons. Reid had worked a few summers for him in his teens—long enough to convince all of them that he didn't have a future in farming, and make him very sure he didn't want to stay in Bridgewater the rest of his life either.

Time had a way of changing one's perspective.

A low whistle came from the direction of the garage. "Well, look who it is." Cade emerged from the darkness and walked toward him. "You came back."

"Did you think I wouldn't?"

"The thought crossed my mind." Cade pulled at the neck of his grimy white T-shirt, wiped his hands on a dirty rag. "Nice wheels. Rental?"

"Nope." Reid scratched his jaw and wanted to laugh at the way Cade's eyebrows almost touched his hairline. "Picked her up on my way out of the city. I flew down, drove back."

"Don't have much need for that kind of vehicle back in New York."

Reid chucked the keys from one hand to the other while his heart perfected the double flip it had been practicing the whole drive up here. "I won't be driving it in New York."

"So you're staying?"

"Looks that way." He'd made the decision less than twenty-four hours ago. Changed his mind more than a few times. But he was here now. Back in Bridgewater. Not that he would call it home.

Not yet.

"Just get in?"

"Last night. Figure I'll fix up the cabin. I went up on the roof this morning. I think I can do most of the repairs myself. The inside isn't bad. No water damage in the bedrooms."

"Reid?"

"What?" He didn't like the look on Cade's face. The one that said, 'I-know-what- you're-up-to-and-it's-not-good.'

"Don't stay for the wrong reasons."

"Meaning?" Reid backed up and leaned against the trunk, folded his arms and watched Cade measure his words.

"Meaning don't use this as an excuse to avoid dealing with what happened in Syria. Don't give up everything because you made one bad decision."

"A bad decision I have to live with for the rest of my life."

"I know. I was there."

Reid knew he wasn't the only one hit hard by the life-changing tragedy they'd somehow lived through. Cade packed up his gear and left New York as soon as he was given the go-ahead. He still worked some assignments when Reid could cajole him into it, but Reid suspected Cade's time in New York was over. Reid had continued to work and carry on as if nothing had happened. Until a few days ago when he'd finally snapped and his world crashed around him.

"You're not planning on going back to work, are you?" Cade's quiet question settled in, and forced him to acknowledge the truth.

"No." Reid squeezed his eyes shut. "Not right now. I can't."

"Have you thought this through or are you flying blind?" Cade knew him too well.

Reid scuffed the toe of his boot against a clump of weeds and ignored the hand closing around his throat. He'd had this discussion with himself about a million times. "I can't go back. I'm burnt-out. You saw it coming before I did."

"Fair enough." Cade nodded, his eyes still showing concern. "I think it's good that you take some time off. But you'll forgive me if I'm just a little wary."

"I'm sure you are. But I've made up my mind. I'll be in Bridgewater awhile."

"What's awhile?"

"I don't know, man. I need to take it day by day. It's the best I can do."

"And what did Hilary have to say about this?"

Reid appreciated Cade's look of disdain. The fact that his best friend and his girlfriend couldn't stand each other didn't make life easy. But it sure made it interesting. "I can confidently report that there are now two women in my life who'd like to see me floating face down in a swamp."

"Did you tell her about Mark?"

"Seriously?" Harsh laughter shot out of him. "No."

Cade shook his head. "Well, Miss Fairchild is not going to be happy when she finds out, I can tell you that."

"It's not her business anymore." Another snap decision, but something he'd intended to do some time ago. His current circumstances sped up the timing. Reid recalled the venom in Hilary's words after he'd laid out his plans, plans he'd made clear didn't include her, and wondered what he ever saw in the woman beyond a perfectly put together wardrobe and a stunning smile.

"You walked away from her too?"

"It's been coming. She's ready to settle down and start a family. I'm not husband material. She knows it, just wouldn't admit it. So I did it for her." He had to give Cade credit for keeping a straight face. "Go ahead and cheer if you want."

Cade didn't. The lines along his forehead burrowed deep. "Are you sure you know what you're doing? Because—"

Reid put up a hand. "You don't have to say it. I broke your sister's heart and you're not about to let me do the same to your nephew. I get it." He sucked air into his lungs and tamped his temper. "It would be nice if people around here would start trusting me again."

"Trust has to be earned."

"And how am I supposed to earn anybody's trust if I can't get within ten feet of them?" The past two weeks before he left, Julia barely looked his way. And she hardly let Mark outside. It was like the kid was in solitary confinement.

Cade looked toward the house. "Did you think it was going to be as easy as securing your favorite table at Wolfgang's?"

"No. But I didn't think it would be impossible."

"You went back to New York four days ago without a word, Reid. No explanation. Want to take a guess how well that went over?"

"You knew I was going."

Cade scratched his head and made like he was talking to a toddler. "You really need me to break this down for you?"

"I came back. I'm here, aren't I?" Exasperation merged with exhaustion. He hadn't managed a full night's sleep since finding out about Mark. Hadn't managed a full night's sleep in months anyway. "I had to take care of things, right? Had to talk to Hilary. Close up the apartment."

"I know all that. Julia didn't." Cade batted a fly. "Look, the two of you have a kid. You're going to have to start talking to each other at some point."

"Tell that to your sister." The sound of a tired car engine made him turn toward the driveway. Julia's clunker kicked up dust as she sped toward the house. She always did drive too fast. He hoped the kids were wearing seatbelts.

She parked the car next to her mother's station wagon. Mark and Emily jumped out. The little girl raced toward them and Cade picked up his niece for a hug.

"Hey, y'all." Mark sauntered past, checking out the Range Rover.

Cade put Emily down and grabbed Mark by the collar. "Excuse me?"

"Ow. Leggo." A red hue crept up Mark's neck and Cade let go with a laugh.

Mark smoothed down his Harley Davidson T-shirt and nodded at them. "Good afternoon, Uncle Cade. Good afternoon, Mr. Wallace. And how are you both today?" The kid actually grinned.

Reid stifled laughter while Cade swatted at Mark with his rag. "Punk."

"Wow! That's a big truck!" Emily skipped around them. Dressed in denim overalls, a purple turtleneck, and pink polka-dotted rain boots, Emily Hansen could have been a poster child for one of those children's stores he used to pass on his way to work every morning. Blond curls bounced around her face as big brown doe eyes held his captive. "Whooths truck is it?"

He'd understand her a lot better without that thumb stuck in her mouth, but Reid couldn't stop a smile as she stared up at him, hopping from one foot to the other.

"Mine. Not really a truck. You like it?"

"It's big!" She showed him exactly how big with her hands, stuck her thumb in her mouth again, and watched her brother complete his inspection.

"Hey, dude." Reid held up his hand for a high five. Mark didn't follow through.

"'Sup." Mark grabbed hold of Emily's backpack. "Stop swinging that. You're gonna hit someone." He jutted out his chin and settled stormy eyes on Reid. "Thought you left. My mom said you went back to New York and you weren't coming back here."

Reid tried not to flinch and managed a contrite smile. "Your mom was wrong." His pulse picked up as Julia crossed the driveway and joined them. She didn't look much happier than Mark.

"You're back?" She scrunched up her nose like he was some dead animal the dogs dug up.

"Looks like it."

She didn't need to hug him or anything, but a smile would have been nice.

"Please don't tell me this gas guzzler belongs to you." Julia stepped away from his new vehicle like he'd just driven it through a field of cow paddies.

"As a matter of fact, it does. And it gets good mileage. Need it for hauling stuff around. I'm going to fix up the cabin."

"A flatbed truck would have been cheaper."

"You're impressed. I can tell."

She crossed her arms and scowled. "You could drive up here in a Lamborghini and I wouldn't care."

Reid shoved his tongue into his cheek. Nothing he could say or do would defrost that ten-foot wide glacier she was encased in.

"You didn't sell your bike, did you?" Mark glanced his way, like he didn't think Reid was that crazy, but you never knew.

"No. She's in the garage."

"Oh." Relief crossed the kid's face, but his frown stayed put. "What cabin are you fixing up?"

Reid nodded toward the west. "Up the mountain a bit. My grand-mother's place."

"Is your grandma there?" Emily wanted to know.

Reid smiled, leaned down a little and shook his head. "No. My grandma died a long time ago."

"Oh. That's sad." She sniffed and pushed out her lower lip. "My grand-ma's inside our house. We live here now, you know. Not 'Lanta."

"All right, Em." Mark rolled his eyes. "So is it like a log cabin? We're doing a project at school about them. Is it old?"

Reid nodded. "It's a log cabin, and it's old. I think my great-grandfa-ther built it. We've owned that land forever."

"Actually, my family owned that land forever," Julia interrupted. "Your great-grandfather stole it. Get your facts straight."

"Not this again." Reid groaned and looked to Cade for support, but his friend shrugged and lifted his eyes skyward, obviously not willing to take a side. "That cabin was bought fair and square, with the land it sits on," Reid told her.

The corners of her mouth twitched. "Stolen."

Mark apparently found their altercation intriguing. A flash of a grin came and went. "Did they have a shoot out like the Hatfields and the McCoys?"

"Okay kiddo, you've been down south way too long," Cade joked. Reid noticed Mark's face redden and the boy backed up a bit.

Julia tousled Mark's hair. "Uncle Cade's only teasing, hon. Be proud of those Southern roots."

Reid caught her eye and gave her the look. The kid might have been raised down South, but he could claim as much 'southern roots' as Donald Trump.

She flushed and turned away. "Let's go, guys. I'm sure Reid's busy."

"Actually, I was just headed up the hill. If Mark wants to see the cabin … he could tag along. I can run him back down." The suggestion fell out of his mouth before he even thought about it. But suddenly he didn't want them to leave.

Didn't want to go back up there alone.

"Can I, Mama?" The kid's eyes lit like firecrackers, his stormy disposition giving way to a real grin that told Reid he'd done the right thing.

"You've got homework." Mark's usual scowl jumped over to Julia's face.

"It's Friday."

Julia stalled, staring in silence. Reid marveled at the way he could still read her mind. She was desperate for any excuse to say no.

"You're still grounded. Last time I checked, grounding means you don't get to do the things you want."

Well, that explained the not leaving the house thing.

"Aw, come on." Mark kicked at the driveway. "I haven't gone anywhere for two weeks. And I haven't gotten in any more trouble."

Reid scuffed his boots and registered the hesitation on her face. Getting involved probably wasn't the smartest thing to do, but he was running short on smart these days. "Cade could come too. I could use a hand with the lumber."

"Uh, no, Cade can't. Much as I'd love to." Cade glanced at his watch. "I need to go shower. I have a date tonight."

A smile crept across Julia's face and settled in. "Oh, do tell." For an instant she resembled the young girl he'd fallen in love with. And that smile sent his pulse soaring the same way it always had. The realization almost knocked him over.

"Not much to tell." Cade did a good job of acting nonchalant, but he couldn't get much past his sister. "Just me and Deb going out for dinner."

Julia wasn't smiling anymore. "When are you going to stop stringing my best friend along, Cade Connelly?"

"That's not very nice." Cade actually looked hurt. "Deb and I have an understanding." Reid let out a hoot. "Understanding, my foot. The only thing she understands is that you're too scared of commitment to stay in town longer than a few days at a time. She's not going to wait forever, my friend."

"Oh, I don't know." A grin propped up one side of Cade's mouth. "She's waited this long. Besides, I'm sticking around now."

"You're what?" Reid and Julia spoke at the same time.

"Well." Cade shrugged, his cheeks pinking. "Apparently I just lost the only news guy I really like working with. I'm too old to start making new friends. Maybe I'll get back to my photography roots. Start doing a little studio work. See what Vermont looks like in winter. I've been away so long, I barely remember."

"Cade, man. Come on." Reid shot him a hard look but he didn't want to get into it. Not in front of Julia.

"You can't talk me out of it."

"Watch me," he growled. "Just because I … look, you don't have to do this."

Cade laughed and punched him on the arm. "You've known me how long, Wallace? When do I ever do anything I don't want to do?"

Reid shut his mouth as Julia pulled Cade into a hug. "I think it's wonderful. Have you told Mom and Dad?"

"Not yet. I will."

"Good." She faced the kids and zipped up her beige windbreaker. "Come on guys, it's getting cold out."

"Well, you kids have fun. I gotta split." Cade took off toward his place, chuckling.

"But Mom, can't I go up the mountain with him? Please?" Mark didn't know when to quit. "I really want to see the cabin."

"Me too! I wanna go too, Mama!" Emily tugged on Julia's hand.

Reid noted the way Mark knew exactly which expression to put on to get what he wanted. Emily only had to smile and jump up and down.

Julia hesitated just long enough for him to speak up.

"You're welcome to come along." His cheeks began to tingle and he cleared his throat. "I mean, you probably haven't been up there for … a long time, right?"

She muttered something he couldn't quite decipher.

"Pleeease!" Emily danced around them while Mark looked morose. He probably figured there was no point in begging. The answer on his mother's face was a definite no.

"Oh, fine. But we can't stay long." She might as well have agreed to visit a mortuary.

"Really? We can go?" Mark's shocked expression made Reid laugh.

"Hurry up, before I change my mind. Take Em inside. Tell Grandma where we're going, and that we won't be long. Emily, use the bathroom if you need to." Julia stalked around his SUV, pulling at her hair and making weird faces. "Why am I doing this?"

"Because you don't trust me with your kids." Somebody might as well say it.

The glare that remark earned him could have frozen the lake at the bottom of their property quicker than the impending winter.

"You got that right. I don't trust anybody with my kids." Julia marched up to him, leveled her gaze and lowered her voice. "You're a real piece of work, you know that? You tell me you want to be a father to my son and then you pull a disappearing act? No explanation? For all I knew, you were never coming back."

"So now I need to check in with you whenever I leave town?" Reid pushed a hand through his hair and wanted to bite his tongue in half. *Way to be an idiot, Wallace.* "Cade told you I was going to New York, right? He said he would talk to you."

"Yes, he did. But you should have."

Yeah. He should have. "It was a spur of the moment decision. I had things to take care of and didn't see the point in putting it off."

He was that dead animal again. "Reid, one thing you better learn, and learn fast, is that when you have kids, you can't do 'spur of the moment.'"

But he didn't have kids.

He almost said it—came that close. She probably would have smacked him. It was going to take some time to change his way of thinking.

"Fine." He pulled his cell from the pocket of his jeans. "Give me your digits. I'll call next time."

"My what?" Now she was looking at him like he was a lunatic.

"Your cell number. What is it?"

"Oh." Julia shuffled scuffed brown boots she wore over faded jeans, her hair falling forward, hiding her face from view. "I don't have one."

"What?" Reid scratched his head and waited for her to look up again.

She shrugged, her eyes cool, defiant. "I don't have a cell phone. You can call the house phone if you ever need to reach me. If you don't remember the number, look it up."

"You need a cell phone, Julia. What if that piece of junk you're driving breaks down in the middle of the highway?"

Her mouth opened slightly, light eyebrows lifting. "Or what if some idiot on a Harley runs a red light and slams into that piece of junk? I suppose you're right, Reid. I should get a cell phone." She came staggeringly close to giving him a smile.

The kids raced back outside and he piled them into the Range Rover, and made sure they were buckled up, all the while enduring Julia's pained look. Sure, he probably paid too much for it, but he'd never owned his own set of wheels. Always drove his grandmother's pick-up when he was up here, hadn't needed a car in the city.

Julia refused to sit up front with him. Mark seemed happy enough to take her place. Reid gripped the wheel as he drove them up the old mountain road and tried not to sneak glances at her in the rearview mirror.

It was impossible.

Everything about her was just as he remembered.

Her hair was longer, but still fell in her eyes every now and then. She wore no make-up, never had. He'd never thought she needed it anyway. She still didn't. But there were dark shadows beneath her eyes that hadn't been there twelve years ago. Worry lines and a troubled expression on her face as she stared out the car window made him wonder what she'd been through in the time they'd been apart.

His gut told him he really didn't want to know.

Chapter Six

After maneuvering around several potholes and boulders on the winding mountain road, he pulled up outside the log cabin Reid came to call home for most of his teenage years.

He'd arrived in Bridgewater, just fourteen, and furious. Angry at the world and the way it had treated him. Esmé Wallace, the grandmother he'd only met twice, waited for him at the train station with a long hug and an old dog called Killer. The name was her idea, to give would-be ne'er do wells a warning, she confessed with a wink. Killer wouldn't kill a thing, but Reid adopted the black lab on the spot. He stared at the old cabin that still held so many memories and shook his head.

He and Mark jumped out and Reid held the back door open for the girls. Emily scrambled over the seat and hesitated, eyeing him and the ground. Reid's chest tightened. Was she waiting for him to pick her up? He took the fact that she didn't move as a yes, and reluctantly held out his arms. "Want a ride?" He didn't have to ask twice. Emily launched herself against him, little arms wrapped tight around his neck.

"Thanks, Mithter Reid." The poor kid had a definite lisp going, but that mile long grin woke forgotten feelings he'd just as soon put back to sleep.

"No problem." He set her down and shook off the strange but not altogether unpleasant sensation that having a child in his arms again produced.

Julia took her time, grimacing as she eased off the seat onto the ground.

Reid took her by the elbow to steady her. "You all right?" A smidge of concern pressed against his throat.

"Back injury." She tossed him a thin smile. "Fell down the stairs a couple of years ago. It flares up every now and then. The road was a little bumpy."

"Yeah. Needs to be re-graded, that's for sure." Something else to add to the to-do list. He kept an eye on the kids as they explored the surrounding area. The garden was overgrown, small trees sprouting up all over the place, probably a few patches of poison ivy mixed in for good measure. "Hey, Emily, I saw a couple of deer around back this morning, down by the stream."

"Ooo!" The child's eyes lit at once. "Can we go see, Mama?"

Julia nodded permission. "Mark, hold her hand and stay on the path." She shook her head at the resulting dark look that request earned her, but focused on the cabin as soon as the kids were out of sight. "Wow." She ran a hand down her face, taking it all in. "I didn't realize it was so run-down."

Reid eyed the green moss on the logs, the grime on the windows and the shutters almost falling off their hinges. "It's not in bad shape." There were sections of the cabin that actually resembled some of the houses he'd seen in Haiti after the last earthquake. He shrugged out of his leather jacket and tossed it over the railing of the porch. "There's some damage to the roof, but I can fix that. The bedrooms are livable."

Julia didn't look like she was buying it. "Are you sure it's safe? Maybe you should bunk with Cade a little longer."

"It's safe. And I'm sure you'd rather I stay up here." He scratched the bristle on his cheeks and stifled a sigh. If there was some guide he could download on how to talk to the ex-wife you haven't seen in twelve years, he needed it now.

"That's probably best." She folded her arms. "I'm sorry about Esmé. Mom called when she passed. She meant a lot to me."

"You meant a lot to her." He shoved his hands into the pockets of his jeans, the back of his throat burning. "I thought I might see you at the funeral."

Julia pushed her hair behind her ears and rolled a large stone off the pathway with the top of her boot. "I was a little busy. Em was born that day."

"Oh." Of course she was. Reid stared over her head at the mountains beyond the trees. Was there anything they could talk about that wouldn't be awkward? "Well. That's a viable excuse, I suppose."

"I didn't have a whole lot of choice in the matter." She played with the zipper of her jacket, pulling it up and down. A nervous habit he remembered. "How did she die, Reid?"

"Quite peacefully." He smiled despite the sting in his eyes. "Just fell asleep and didn't wake up. No fanfare, no warning. Typical Esmé style. Not a bad way to go, I'd say."

"Were you here?"

"No. I was on assignment in the Middle East. Your mother found her actually. They'd chatted by phone the night before and arranged to meet for lunch. When I talked to her, she said God told her something was wrong when she woke up, and she came right away."

"That sounds like Mom." Julia wandered over to his grandmother's abandoned rose garden and began to pick off the deadheads, leaving him alone with his regrets and his memories.

Reid dumped his bag in the hallway, went to the kitchen for a soda, and scanned the messages on his phone.

"You're late." Hilary looked up from where she sat at the desk off to one side of his Manhattan condo's living room.

Reid dropped his soda, cursed and reached for a cloth to clean up the mess. "My flight was delayed. Didn't you get the message?" He crossed the room and bent to kiss her but she waved a hand.

"No, I didn't." Hilary pushed her chair back, scowling. "You do realize we have dinner reservations in an hour? It's not something I can cancel." She raised a thin brow and shook her head. "Sometimes I wonder where your head is."

"You've got to be kidding me." Reid yawned and stared down the hall, bed beckoning. He looked back at her, registered the designer dress, the new haircut and carefully applied make-up. She clearly wasn't kidding. "I haven't slept in God knows when. It's not exactly an easy commute from Beirut, babe."

"I don't care." She flounced across the room and picked up her purse. *"I'll be back for you in forty-five minutes. Your suit has been dry-cleaned. There's a new tie on your bed."* She headed for the door as he stifled another yawn. *"Oh, by the way, some woman from Vermont called. Your grandmother died."*

After the funeral, he'd spent a few days at the cabin, packing things up. A chore so difficult he'd quit halfway through. Left the boxes where they still sat. Drove away and never looked back.

He blinked memories away. Time to change the subject. "Your folks are looking well."

Julia nodded. "They're good."

"Must be pleased to have you home."

She tossed a handful of rosehips into the trees. The breeze trailed through her hair and that faraway look returned. "I guess they are. Although my father hasn't said more than two words to me since your unexpected arrival. I suppose I'll have to break the bad news at some point."

Reid nodded, took the barb and did his best not to retaliate. "I always admired the way you speak your mind, Jules. There's a lot to be said for honesty these days."

She shrugged off the comment. "I'd call it blunt, but you can go with the honesty bit if you like. I'm sure the journalist in you appreciates it. No digging for facts, right?"

"Nope. No digging." A grin tickled his lips. "You just lay it all out there."

"Like you don't?"

Man, this ranked right up there with having to host a presidential debate. Definitely not an assignment he would choose, if he had a say. "So, Hannah, she's still in Bridgewater, huh? I figured she'd be married with a couple of kids by now, but she seems happy enough."

Julia laughed at that. "I'm not sure Hannah's the marrying kind. As for whether my sister is happy, I wouldn't know."

"You guys still don't talk?"

"Not really, no."

Maybe he shouldn't have asked. The two were never close. Hannah harbored a jealous streak that made her rather unpleasant to be around at the best of times. Reid had tolerated her for Julia's sake, but somehow her sister always annoyed him.

"These weeds are choking out the roots."

He watched her crouch with some effort, pulling up handfuls of the offending vines that snaked around the trunk of the old bush. There were at least a dozen rose bushes around the place. His grandmother had loved roses of all kinds, and when they bloomed, the cabin smelled like a florist shop.

If he closed his eyes he could see Esmé right there beside Julia, the two of them working away, talking about things he never attempted to guess at, tending to the roses like they'd tended to his heart.

Esmé earned his trust a little at a time, giving him the space he needed to grieve, letting him talk when he wanted to. She never pressured. Never pushed him to give more than he was capable of giving. Eventually, he dismantled the wall of self-preservation around his heart, and allowed his grandmother her rightful place in it.

Julia just moved right in the first day they met.

"Who is that?" Reid picked up his tray and turned to his new friend.

Cade carried his lunch tray and wove around chairs to find a spot for them to sit. "Who?"

"That girl over there. The one with the long hair." And the smile that reached inside of him, flicked a switch, and made him feel good again. "She just nodded our way. You know her?"

Cade Connelly seemed okay. Grandma introduced them at church yesterday, knowing they would be in the same grade when Reid started at Bridgewater High the next morning. Turned out they were in the same homeroom, and Cade lived down the mountain.

"Dude. Seriously?" Cade plunked his tray down, kicked a chair back from the table and sat.

"What? She's okay looking." More than okay, but that wouldn't be cool to say. Reid sat, swallowed hard and stared across the room into the most beautiful pair of eyes he'd ever seen. "Who is she?"

Cade bit into his sandwich and shot Reid a look that settled somewhere between annoyance and amusement. "Julia Connelly. My sister."

"You should cover the bushes for the winter." She pushed to her feet, brushed dirt off her hands and met his eyes. "I can get some burlap from my Dad, if you want."

"What's the point?" Reid shrugged. "They survived this long."

"True." Julia turned from him, her gaze sweeping over the bedraggled bushes. "But there's a world of difference between surviving and thriving, Reid." She headed for the back of the house, calling for the kids.

Reid gave himself a mental slap and forced his heart to start working again. He set his mind on the task at hand, and went to work hauling wood out of the trunk.

"My Mom said you might want some help." Mark stood off to one side of the porch a few minutes later, dark hair almost hiding one eye from view.

"She did?" He'd take the gesture without argument. "Sure. That'd be great." Reid pulled off the work gloves he wore and tossed them to Mark.

The kid was stronger than he looked, and worked hard. Reid tried to get a conversation going, but the boy sure didn't say much, so they mostly kept quiet. Soon they'd made a pile of wood on the porch. As they were lifting the last plank up the steps, he caught Mark looking at him.

"She didn't fall."

"What?" Reid almost dropped his end of the heavy two by four. They placed it down and Mark hesitated before he met Reid's eyes again.

"She told you she fell, but that's not true. He pushed her. My dad. Down the stairs. That's how she hurt her back." The mumbled words came out in a rush, but they couldn't have been clearer than if Mark had shouted them through a bullhorn.

Uncertainty hovered over his young face. "Don't tell her I told you."

"No." Reid almost gagged on the boulder-sized lump in his throat and registered the boy's fear. "Why *did* you tell me?"

Mark shuffled across the porch and leaned against the rail, picking at a scab on his hand. "I dunno. I got bored one day over the summer and looked through some of Grandma's old photo albums. You guys were pretty tight once, right? You and my mom?"

Was he fishing? Reid pushed his fingers through his hair and tried to navigate the stormy ocean he'd just unwittingly sailed into.

"I guess you could say that." He couldn't tell the truth. Not until Julia gave him the go-ahead. And the chances of that happening anytime soon were about as good as her forgiving him.

He wanted to go back to the subject of Julia's late husband, ask Mark a thousand questions, get the kid to give him every detail of their life in Atlanta, but something told him not to.

"When are you gonna start fixing up this place?" Mark kicked at a pile of leaves with his shoe.

The segue was more than welcome. "Soon. Probably start tomorrow. So, how's school going?"

"Sucks."

Reid grinned at the way the Mark's upper lip curled. "Yeah, I hear you." He opened the door to the cabin. "Got some sodas inside. You thirsty?"

"Sure."

Reid looked back over his shoulder as he led the way. "Not getting in any more trouble?"

"No." Mark coughed a bit. "Man, it stinks in here."

"Yeah, I guess." Reid hadn't quite determined where the smell was coming from. He went about finding some glasses and the package of Oreos he'd tossed in the shopping cart on a whim. "What's your favorite subject? What are you good at?"

Mark shuffled his feet and shoved his hands in his pockets. "I'm not good at anything."

"Sure you are." Reid registered the non-committal tone and the slumped shoulders. "Everybody's good at one thing, at least. Sports, writing, something."

"Well, I'm not." Mark faced him, defeat dulling his eyes. "I'm just a loser."

Reid braced his hands on the counter and felt the room get a little colder. "Who said that?"

"My dad." Mark stared at his shoes. "He always called me a loser."

Tension tightened the muscles in his neck. A very clear picture of Frank Hansen was beginning to form in his mind. Reid set his jaw and waited until he trusted speech. "Well, he was wrong. You're not a loser." What he really wanted to say would not be appropriate to voice in front of an eleven year-old.

"You don't even know me." Mark's expression darkened and dared Reid to deny it.

"I know." Somehow he found a smile. "But I've met a lot of losers in my lifetime, and I'm a pretty good judge of character. You are not a loser."

"Whatever." Mark ended the debate, checking out the room instead.

Reid poured their sodas, his mind mulling over the last twenty minutes of his life. He'd love to think the kid was wrong about what happened to Julia, but why would he lie?

"This place is a dump." Mark wandered around the small living room, running a finger along the dusty bookshelf. Books that once filled the shelves still sat in boxes in the back bedroom. "But so cool."

There was nothing cool about the neglected cabin. If his grandmother could see the state of it, she'd have Reid on his hands and knees scrubbing out the dirt. Sheets still covered the furniture, the last thing he'd done before locking the front door.

The old television probably didn't work. There was about a foot of dust on the floor and gray dirt streaked the windows. A huge cobweb hung from the thick wood mantle and reached all the way down to the stone hearth. Thankfully he still had power. He'd called before leaving the city to have it turned on again.

A lot of changes would have to be made if he intended to live here.

The door banged open as Julia and Emily came inside. "The wind is picking up." Julia's eyes widened as she took in the condition of the once pristine cabin. "This is your definition of 'not in bad shape'?"

Emily skipped around them, her face flushed with cold. "We saw deer! Two of 'em."

"That's awesome." Reid smiled at her excitement and wondered if he could bottle it. Maybe give some to her mother.

"Are you certain you can stay here?" Julia inspected the room like an army general. Her eyebrows rose as she caught a whiff of the offensive stench. "I think there's something dead back there."

"Probably. I'll find it." The window above the kitchen sink had a cracked pane, allowing a bit of fresh air in at least. He wouldn't tell her about the bird's nest in the bedroom or the hole in the side of the wall in the bathroom. Coons or worse. He'd find out sooner or later. "I haven't had a chance to clean yet."

"No kidding."

Reid popped the top of another coke can and Julia jumped. The lump in his throat came back. "You want something to drink? I've got soda. Or … I could make tea, I guess." Did he buy tea? Did she drink tea? Reid rummaged through the kitchen cupboards and coughed at the dust he churned up.

"I don't want anything. Mark, be careful with that."

Reid turned in time to see Mark fiddling with an old china vase he'd forgotten to pack away. The kid fumbled and it slipped out of his hands, crashed to the floor and splintered across the rug.

"Oh, Mark. Look what you did!" Julia's voice rose an octave.

"It's not a problem. It was just an accident." Reid found a broom and dustpan in the pantry. As he walked toward Mark, the kid backed up against the wall, practically cowering.

"I'm sorry. I didn't mean to. Please don't be mad."

Reid stopped in his tracks. "I know you didn't mean to, Mark." The kid was whiter than a first snowfall. "I'm not mad."

Emily hid behind her mother's legs, and Julia just stood there, hand over her mouth, her eyes wide and wet.

His heart thudded hard as harsh reality almost knocked him over.

Mark was scared out of his mind.

They all were.

Mark hadn't made it up.

Julia moved first, went to Mark and pulled him into a hug, kissed the top of his forehead and whispered something. Then she walked to where Reid stood. Her fingers closed around the handle of the broom. "I'll clean up the mess."

Reid couldn't move. He'd reported on unimaginable tragedies over the last ten years. Stood among the dead, recorded the cries of the tortured. Seen starving children sitting at his feet. But nothing he'd experienced thus far in his career created anything close to the suffocating emotion that blanketed him the moment he met Julia's eyes and saw the truth in them.

Reid moved his hand downward to cover hers. "Jules."

"Don't go there, Reid," she whispered, two tears trailing down her pale cheeks.

His other hand moved almost by instinct, his thumb brushing the moisture away. A faint scar he hadn't noticed before ran across her cheek. Another small white line was visible just above her top lip.

"Julia, I …" There was so much he wanted to say. Wanted to ask. So much he had to apologize for. So many regrets he needed to voice. Most of all, he just wanted to take her in his arms and make everything okay.

But that probably wouldn't go over well with any of them.

She pulled back too quickly, almost recoiling from his touch. "It's not your problem." She pried the broom from him and began to sweep the splintered bits of painted pottery.

The trembling began before he could control it. In another minute he'd have to hit the bathroom in a hurry.

Julia was right.

It wasn't his problem.

But it was his fault.

Chapter Seven

"Who let you in here?" Cade entered his apartment, arms laden with grocery bags.

Reid looked up from his laptop. "Let myself in. With the key you hide so surreptitiously under the mat at the front door." He'd waited three days since that afternoon at the cabin, but couldn't stand it any longer. He needed to get online.

"Oh." Cade hauled the bags into the kitchen. "Any joy on an internet connection up there?"

"Nope. Waiting list. I'm like a hundred down." Part of him didn't really care. Didn't want to check his inbox and sort through the multitude of messages he didn't feel like reading, let alone answering.

There were several messages from Hilary, still trying to convince him to change his mind. Still negotiating deals, sweetening the offer with every email she sent. As a producer, she was thorough, got straight to the point and went after what she wanted. He liked that. In their business, she couldn't afford to be anything less than ruthless.

As a woman, she was a pain in the rear.

Reid scrawled a few things down in his notebook. Heard Cade coming back but was too slow to click off the website before his friend looked over his shoulder.

"What are you working on … dude … spousal abuse … what?"

Reid waited for him to round the couch and sit.

"What did Julia tell you?" Cade sat forward, worried.

"More like what she didn't tell me." Reid rubbed his eyes and wished his chest would quit threatening a heart attack every five minutes. "All the signs are there, Cade. Did you know?" Silence suffocated him in the already warm room. "Cade?"

"Sort of."

"Sort of? You either knew or you didn't, and if you did then for the love of—"

"What, Reid?" Cade shot to his feet, his cheeks darkening. "Tell me what, exactly, you would have had me do? We tried to get her to leave him, she wouldn't. He was a smart man. Ran a two-bit insurance company in a small town outside of the city, where everybody knew everybody and you didn't talk to outsiders. He twisted everything around. Other than the bruises she claimed were accidents, I had no proof." He sat down again and put his head in his hands.

"You should have told me."

Cade pinned him with a hard stare. "Yeah. I should have told you a lot of things, huh? What would you have done? Gone riding in there on a white charger and whisked them all away?"

"How bad do you think it got?" Reid's stomach lurched like a ship on the Indian ocean, heaving so hard he thought he might throw-up. Cade's bland expression was all the answer he needed. So he gave himself permission to ask the next question. "What happened to her husband? All I can find on the Internet is that his death was an accident, unexpected, a shock to the family, yada, yada … what's the real story?"

Cade kicked off his shoes and shoved fingers through his hair. Uttered a low curse, something he hardly ever did, and shook his head. "This isn't some piece you can put together for the nightly news, Reid. This is my family."

Reid closed down his laptop and locked his gaze on his friend. "Julia was my wife. Mark is my son. I think I have a right to know."

"I think you gave up your rights a long time ago."

"Wow. Thanks." He knew Cade would say it.

Knew he was right. Knew he deserved it.

But that didn't make it any easier to hear.

"Well. You had it coming." Cade's gaze remained steady as he lifted his hands and let them fall against his knees. "This is why we never talk about the past. It reminds me just how much of a jerk you can be."

"You're not going to tell me."

"No, I'm not. But this is what you're dealing with, Reid. They've been hurt. They're still hurting. All of them. Just—"

"You really don't trust me, do you?"

"It's not that I don't trust you. I'm worried about you too, man. This might be too much."

Reid pressed his palms to his forehead and sucked air through his nose. "I can handle it." Not that he had a choice. If he packed up and left now, there would be little chance of ever seeing his son. Julia would make sure of that. And he didn't relish the thought of a custody battle. "But I want to know—"

"No." Cade's eyes flashed anger. "If Julia wants you to know, she'll tell you. But right now she's still trying to get her head around having you back in her life. So please, give her some space. Okay?"

"Give her some space?" Reid almost laughed. If Julia had anything to say about it, that wouldn't be a problem.

Wouldn't be a problem at all.

Reid drove back from town the following Friday after stocking up on hardware supplies and hitting the grocery store again. Back in New York, he rarely ate at home. After finding a few dead mice, fumigating the cabin and using almost lethal doses of Clorox in the bathroom and kitchen, plugging in the fridge and making sure the stove worked, he made a shopping list. He hadn't cooked for himself in a long time, wasn't altogether sure he remembered how, but unless he intended to starve, he was going to have to learn, and quick.

He rounded the corner of the mountain road, turned up the volume of the stereo, and thought about Julia. The kicker was, he hadn't been able to get his mind off her all week. He was desperate to know the story she didn't want to tell. A story he couldn't bear thinking about, yet knew he needed to uncover.

A story that no matter what she claimed, he knew he was responsible for.

"How can you do this to me!" She hurled a china plate against the wall, just shy of his forehead. She was a lousy shot, but Reid ducked anyway.

"Stop throwing stuff. I'm doing this for you, Jules. You'll see." He hoisted the strap of his duffel bag over his shoulder, propping open the door of their tiny apartment with one foot.

"It's like you think leaving me is performing some act of God! Like you're doing me a favor! Reid ... stop ... wait ..." She ran to him and yanked his bag off his shoulder. "Don't do this. Please." Tears streaked her flushed face and rolled to the corners of her mouth.

Reid shook his head and tightened the locks around his heart. "We were too young to get married, Jules. Stupid. I should never have ... Jules ... just let me go."

"I can't."

"You have to."

They'd been at it for three days. Her screaming. Him yelling. Both of them crying. But his mind was made up.

"Reid! What am I supposed to do?" The whispered question felt like somebody pulling a roll of barbed wire right through him.

Reid inhaled and picked up his bag again. "Go home. Start over. Forget about me."

"Forget about you?" She moved toward him, unbelieving. "That's like asking me not to breathe."

"I'm sorry, Jules." He dared to place his hand against her wet cheek, but she didn't slap it away. Just stood there, crying.

"I don't think you are." Her puffy eyes narrowed into thin slits. "I don't think you're sorry right now. But one day you will be. And by then it will be too late."

He was sorry all right. Sorrier than he'd ever imagined. He needed her to know that. Needed her to listen, to hear him, and understand.

And maybe, if he was lucky, forgive.

If only he could figure out how to get beyond the electric fence preventing him from getting anywhere near her.

Reid made the turn that would take him off the highway toward home, and spied a figure up ahead, pushing a bicycle.

Even from a distance he already knew his son's lanky frame.

The clock on the dash read three-thirty. Mark must be on his way back from school. That was a heck of a long way. No wonder the kid was pushing. Reid flicked his indicator, slowed, pulled onto the shoulder and honked.

Mark stopped, turned and headed back toward him.

Reid stepped out onto the road and met him halfway. "Hey, dude. Need a ride?"

"I got a flat." Mark's flushed face said he'd been walking awhile. His hair stuck to his forehead under a ratty Braves ball cap, but he grinned and took a deep gulp of air. "Man, I'm about to die."

Reid crouched beside the bike and found a rip in the rubber. "Flat as the Kalahari."

"Tell me about it." Anger flickered over Mark's face as he kicked the tire and spat out a word Reid was pretty sure his mother wouldn't want him using. "Stupid bike must be older than me. Mama found it at a yard sale a couple years ago. I fixed it up, but it's all rusty now. Probably just needs to go to the junk yard."

"Well." Reid picked up the bike with one hand and clapped Mark on the shoulder with the other. "Let's get her in and I'll drop you home. I just went to the store. Bet you could use a coke huh?"

"Yessir." Mark wiggled his backpack off his shoulders and swung it in the air. "Thanks, Mr. Wallace."

Reid opened the trunk, made room for the bike, and lifted it in. Maybe he should think about getting a bike rack. "You can call me Reid."

Or Dad.

He lifted his eyes skyward and wondered for the hundredth time how his life got so crazy.

"Cool."

He handed a soda to Mark and they stood in silence. It was the weirdest feeling in the world, standing beside this miniature version of him. Did Mark pick up on the resemblance? If he had, he was keeping it close to his chest.

The warm soda fizzed in his throat and he wasn't sure he could drink it. Reid wracked his brain for conversation. He'd interviewed diplomats, royalty, faced down a hundred or more reporters at a time during press conferences, yet he couldn't come up with a thing to say to a kid.

His kid.

Reid took a few more gulps, blew out a breath and tipped the rest of his drink out. "You ride your bike to school all the time? That's a long way to go."

"Nah. My mom usually drives me but she had an appointment this afternoon. I don't like taking the bus. Just a bunch of little sissy kids on it who don't never shut up. So I rode."

"Oh. Well. If you get stuck again you could …" What? Call him? Julia would love that. "Um. You could call your uncle. He's not doing too much these days."

Mark ground his foot on the gravel, making a large circle in the dirt. "I don't have a cell phone. Mama says they're too expensive. I'm going to look for a job though, so I can get the cash for one."

"Yeah?" Reid pushed back a pinch of pride. "I can give you a few jobs up at the cabin to get you started, if you want."

"Sweet." Mark's eyes brightened. "If Mama lets me. She kind of thought that place might fall down any second."

"She did, huh?" Reid tapped his foot and watched a flock of geese fly west. He didn't have any friends with kids. Didn't have any idea how this whole parenting thing was supposed to go. And hadn't intended to find out. But here he was.

"Hey, how old are you?" Mark asked, a grin inching around his scowl.

"Old." Reid choked on laughter and adjusted his shades. "How old are you?"

"Me? Gonna be twelve on the twenty-sixth of November."

Reid smiled. And clearly pretty proud of it.

Right around Thanksgiving. His smile faded as he allowed his mind to venture back into the past. What had he been doing the year of Mark's birth? Probably at some big party with his new city friends, not thinking about Julia at all.

Mark kicked at the gravel again and finished his soda in three big gulps. He belched and tossed his empty can over the road into the ditch. Reid figured it wouldn't be wise to make him go get it, much as he wanted to.

"So, you're how old?"

"Ancient. Like a hundred."

"Nah, man, Serious. My English teacher said she taught you and my mom. And Uncle Cade too, but she said she wished she hadn't taught him. But she don't look that old. I mean you guys are what, forty something?"

"Watch it." Reid flicked the top of Mark's baseball cap and tried to look offended. "Your uncle and I are 32. Your mom is turning 30. None of us are old. Miss Carter on the other hand, is old. She just likes going under the knife."

"Going under the knife?" Mark's mouth hung open.

"Plastic surgery. But don't spread that around."

"Oh. That figures." Mark made a gesture in front of his chest with one hand, giving a rather wicked cackle Reid unfortunately recognized.

"Yeah, okay. Get in, kid."

Mark was still laughing as he buckled up and fiddled with the radio. "Hey, y'all got XM? Sweet. Can I change the channel?"

Not country. Not country. Not …

Reid nodded and tried not to clench his jaw. "You like country."

"Well, I don't know who doesn't." Mark sat back with a happy grin. He turned up the a/c and laughed again as the cool air hit his face. "Man, that feels good."

Reid sat back a moment and watched him.

Watched the way his eyes—blue with just a hint of gray, exactly like his own—sparkled in the afternoon sun. Watched the way his upper lip lifted with a rare smile that brought out the dimple in his left cheek. Watched him just being a kid.

Watched his son find joy.

"Reid, you gonna drive or we getting out to push?"

"You want to push?" Reid let go a chuckle as he pulled out onto the highway. "That can be arranged."

The drive home went too fast even though Reid made a point of driving slow. Mark told him about school. He'd made a couple of friends and was going to try out for the swim team. Reid shared how he used to play water polo in high school, and they talked baseball. He told Mark about Esmé and Killer.

Mark didn't ask why Reid had lived with his grandmother and Reid didn't offer the information.

The kid agreed that moving to Bridgewater wasn't the funnest thing he'd ever done, but he was sorta starting to like it.

They didn't talk about Atlanta.

"Uh oh. Mama's back already." Mark slapped his thighs as they pulled up next to Julia's car and glanced at Reid. "Dude, you're dead meat."

"Why? What was I supposed to do, let you walk?"

"No, but she hates your guts." Mark picked up his backpack.

"Hate might be a bit of a strong word."

"Nah. I heard her and Uncle Cade talking one night. She hates you. What'd you do to her anyway?"

Reid cut the engine and felt his son's eyes on him. He blinked a couple of times, lifted his shades and faced him. "I broke a promise, Mark."

"That figures." Mark's lips twitched, like he wanted to say something else, then he shook his head and grinned. "Girls. Thanks for the ride, Reid." He jumped out, ducked past his mother as she came down the front steps, then raced into the house.

Smart kid.

Reid eased out of his seat and prepared for battle.

She waited for him, arms folded, eyes flashing danger signals he recognized too well. If he had any sense left he would have let Mark out and backed up in a hurry.

"What were you doing with my son?"

"Whose son?" He whipped off his shades and pinched the bridge of his nose. An oncoming migraine tightened the back of his neck.

"Just answer the question."

"He was walking home. His bike got a flat." Reid marched to the back of the Range Rover, popped the trunk and pulled out Mark's old bike. "Care to inspect it yourself before you press kidnapping charges?"

She did.

"Well, he could have called. I got home and was worried."

"He doesn't have a cell phone."

"No. But you do."

"Touché." Reid put his shades back on and hauled Mark's bike to the garage. Julia trailed him at a distance.

"What did you talk about?"

"Hum?" He wiped his hands on his jeans and walked back to where she stood, still staring at him like he'd stolen her life savings.

"I asked what you talked about. What did you say to him?"

Reid huffed, shoved his hands in his pockets and slammed a lid on his temper. "We talked about stuff, Jules. School. Sports. You want me to recount every word or what?"

"No. I just want to make sure you didn't say anything stupid."

"Like, 'hey how's it going, by the way I'm your father'?" He rubbed at a grease mark on his hand, anger simmering. "I don't know what you want from me, Julia. You run hot and cold like the taps at the cabin. Do you want me in Mark's life or not?"

Her eyes gave away the depth of her emotion, but she did a remarkable job at riding its waves. "Don't yell at me."

"I'm not yelling." Reid exhaled and moved away from her. Trying to reason with Julia proved pointless. He'd already been charged and convicted.

Maybe one day they'd be able to carry on a normal conversation without bitterness blistering off her tongue. Maybe one day her eyes wouldn't be so sad when she looked his way. So filled with betrayal.

But today they were, and he didn't know what to do with that.

So he messed with the grocery bags in the trunk and tried to ignore the hurt in his heart.

Her steps crunched leaves on the driveway and stopped just behind him. "I'm sorry. I overreacted. I just worry about him."

Reid turned, and his anger and confusion slid away as he noticed the change in her appearance. A change that started a slow stirring inside him and set free feelings he'd locked up a long time ago.

New dark jeans fit well over her long legs, and the deep brown turtleneck matched her eyes. Her hair sat just above her shoulders, cut and maybe colored just a bit, if he wasn't mistaken. Soft golden threads shimmered in the sun, her cheeks lit in the cooling breeze that lifted around them or perhaps with the fact that his gaze lingered a little too long.

"Why are you staring at me?"

"You cut your hair." Yeah. That didn't sound stupid. He studied the patch of mud on the top of his boot. Something that sounded a little like laughter pulled his head upward.

"This afternoon, actually." She lifted a hand to push a thick strand back behind her ear. Manicured nails flashed light polish at him, pink to match her cheeks. "Deb's idea. She insisted on taking me to the salon."

"Good for Deb. I mean, not that you didn't look all right before." Reid struggled for something else to say that wouldn't make him sound like the dolt he was. "You look … um … good."

Good? Pot-roast was good. A hoagie looked good. Weather could look good. But a woman…man, you never, ever, tell a woman she looks 'good'.

"Good, huh? Like a meatloaf sandwich?"

"Uh, no, not … I meant …"What exactly did they pay him to do? He couldn't come up with a coherent sentence to save his life. He should probably move back to the city before he forgot how to communicate entirely.

But that wasn't going to happen.

He was staying right here. Whether she liked it or not.

Her giggle chased off tension and reminded him again of the girl he'd fallen for so many years ago. "Well. Thanks for bringing Mark home."

"I'll let him walk next time if you'd prefer." His mouth wasn't big enough to fit his whole boot in, but it needed to be. And he needed to get out of here pronto. But he didn't want to leave things like this. He shoved his fingers through his hair. "Mark said he wants to earn some money so he can buy a cell. I could use a hand up at the cabin, if you'd let him work a few hours on weekends."

"With you?"

Reid rubbed a hand over his face and wondered when he'd turned into an axe-murderer. "No. All by himself. I'd go into town and wait until he was done."

She pressed her lips together. What he wouldn't give to crack the code of sudden silence she seemed so prone to when she was around him.

Enough.

"Okay. You know what, Julia? If you want this thing to work, you're going to have to cut me some slack. As much as I'm sure you enjoy ripping me to shreds whenever you get the chance, it's gonna get old pretty fast." He lifted his hands and let them fall. "I'm here. I'm willing to do whatever it takes to get you to trust me again, but you need to put some effort in as well. I'm not going to go behind your back and tell Mark the truth. I'm not going to whisk him away and sue you for custody or whatever other horrible scenario you've conjured up where I'm concerned. But I'm also not willing to live under your constant scrutiny." He took a breath and she opened her mouth, clearly about to blast him but he put up a hand. "I'm not done."

Calm crested over his anger and he waited a moment before he spoke again. "I know I hurt you, and I've also picked up on the fact that your life hasn't been easy since Mark was born." She started to speak again and he shook his head. "I know you have things you don't want to tell me. You don't want to trust me, you probably don't even like me all that much, and I don't blame you. But I'm not leaving, and I'm not waiting much longer for you to come clean. I want Mark to know that I'm his father. So figure out what you want, Julia, but do it soon."

"Are you threatening me?" Hands on hips, flecks of gold in her eyes accentuated her aggravation—she was a wildcat waiting to pounce, and a pretty gorgeous one at that.

Reid bit back a smile and shook his head. "Not at all. Just laying out the facts." He sauntered past her, not bothering to hide his grin this time when he glanced over his shoulder and saw her shooting blazing arrows in his direction.

He slammed the door, gunned the engine and backed up. Drove a little too close to where she stood and slid down his window. "By the way, you're still super cute when you're sizzling mad."

Chapter Eight

*J*ulia stood outside the red brick building that housed her father's law offices, squinting up at the structure she knew so well. The clock in the small tower at the top still ticked out time. The windows still shone and the two potted palms still stood sentry outside the black wooden door with the brass lion knockers that she, Cade and Hannah had loved to play with.

Glancing down the main street of town, most of the other buildings in the vicinity looked pretty much the same too. It was hard to believe so much in her life had changed while everything in Bridgewater seemed to stay the same.

Dad wasn't in court today. She'd checked the calendar that hung on the wall in his study at home. October 1st. The date told her time passed too quickly. Frank was ten months gone. She and the kids had been home for almost eight. Reid had been back in Bridgewater about five weeks.

And she still hadn't told anyone the truth.

Dad was easing into retirement, only a few years left on the bench, or so he said. His two younger partners had been running the firm the last couple of years, but he still kept an office here. Julia mounted the stairs and pushed open the glass door.

Her father's secretary looked up from behind her desk, blinked once and before Julia could say a word, the heavy-set older woman rounded the desk and pulled her into a hug that just about pushed her over.

"Well, it's about time!" Joyce Fitzgerald looked her up and down and her smile faded. "Hmm. Now I know why you waited so long to come see me. You're as thin as a rail, child." She spanned wide hands around Julia's waist and clucked her tongue. "You okay, baby?"

The tears burning the backs of her eyes were precisely the reason Julia had stayed away. One hug from Joyce was all she needed to turn into a blubbering mess.

"We're doing fine." She ducked out from under the scrutinizing gaze she remembered too well. "I'll bring the kids in to meet you soon."

"You could come to church Sunday. I could meet them then."

Julia flushed under the pointed look. They'd attended church in Atlanta for a while, but then Frank decided he didn't want them going and that was that. And she hadn't felt up to facing the stares and whispers that she knew her reappearance in Bridgewater, two children in tow, had created within her parents' congregation.

"I'll think about it." She forced her eyes toward the closed door on the other side of the room. "Is he in?"

"He is." Joyce sat at her desk again. "Probably taking a nap, but go ahead and disturb him."

"All right." Julia tried to make her smile convincing. "I'll call you soon."

"You better."

Trepidation almost made her back up and exit the building. But she determined to get this done, clenched one hand by her side and rapped on the door with the other.

"Come." Her father's gruff bark did nothing to settle her nerves.

Julia went in, closed the door behind her, waited a moment, then found her voice. "Permission to approach the bench?"

"Well, this is a surprise." Jonas Connelly leaned back in a beat-up leather chair that was years older than him. He pulled at his tie and undid the top button of his shirt. His sleeves were already rolled, his jacket discarded on another chair. "Have a seat."

Julia scanned her father's office, looking for any signs of change. She'd loved coming here as a girl. Loved the smell of the books, the excitement in the air when he was working on a particularly difficult case, but most of all she loved this room because it was his.

She picked up his jacket and hung it properly over the back of the chair. "I was just walking by, thought you might be here." She sat and fidgeted, all the words she'd prepared beating a hasty retreat the minute his graying brows knit together.

"And here I am." He didn't look anywhere near sixty, but he would be next year. Dark hair now flecked with gray framed his face. Deeper creases around his eyes bore the passage of time and his bland expression hid his thoughts. "How do you plead?" A shadow of a smile crossed his face but his eyes hadn't quite warmed yet.

"You're angry."

He ran a hand down his face and lifted his shoulders. "No. Disappointed perhaps. Reid Wallace is Mark's father, yes?"

"Yes."

He gave a slow nod. "I've had my suspicions, but seeing them together leaves little room for doubt. Is that why you ran off and got married against our wishes?"

"No." Julia crossed and uncrossed her legs. Her palms began to sweat. "I got pregnant afterward. We got married because we loved each other. At least I thought we did."

"Afterward?" His brow furrowed. "Reid knew you were pregnant and left you anyway?"

Julia stared at the ground. "No. He didn't know. I never told him." She looked up at his sharp intake of breath and met his angry eyes.

"What on earth were you thinking, keeping that kind of secret all these years?"

"He walked out on me." She was eight years old again, tattling on her brother when he'd left her alone in the park after yelling for her to come home at least ten times. "I found out I was pregnant a month after he left. He'd already filed for divorce. He had no idea until he came back to Bridgewater a few weeks ago."

"Mark doesn't know." It wasn't a question and Julia simply shook her head. Dad's expression softened, his eyes sad. He didn't have to voice his opinion. She knew what he thought. But he didn't know the truth. He might have pieced together some variation of it over the years, but he didn't know the whole story.

None of them knew the real reason she'd been so compelled to keep Mark's paternity to herself.

"All right." Her father lit the pipe he only enjoyed here in his office, probably the only reason he still paid rent here. "Well, now that he knows, what does he plan to do about it?"

"Do about it?" Julia pressed her back against the chair and fiddled with a loose button on her cardigan. Debby had some appointments this afternoon and insisted on Julia taking a long lunch. She hadn't wanted to put this off any longer. Now she wished she had. "I don't know, exactly. I think he's still trying to figure it out. We both are."

"Not much to figure out is there?" He tapped a pen against his desk. "Don't try to go after him for child support. I'll wager his New York lawyers would serve you up as breakfast for their Rottweilers."

"I don't want Reid's money."

"Then what do you want, Julia? Absolution? I doubt he'll be offering that up any time soon."

"I know. He's angry." She stared at her hands, examining her nails. "He says he wants to be involved, wants to be a father to Mark. I just ... I'm not sure I can trust him."

"You don't think he deserves a second chance?"

Julia wondered why he looked so surprised. "You're the judge. You tell me."

"Julia." Her father sat forward, studying her intently. "A man deserves the right to know his son. And Mark needs a father. A real one."

"But ..."

He held up a hand. "Don't make Mark pay the price for wrongs that were done before he was born."

She pushed her hair out of her eyes and groaned. "They don't make a handbook for these kinds of situations, Dad. It's not that easy."

"Maybe it is, Julia. Maybe it is simply as easy as asking God for the wisdom to know when to tell Mark the truth, and the strength to follow through."

She caught herself before she rolled her eyes. "God doesn't answer prayers, Dad." Not hers anyway.

"You don't think so?" A pained expression crossed his face, and his cheeks darkened. "You're back home. That's an answer to my prayers."

Julia lowered her head, tried to fight the stifling emotion she wore like an extra coat these days, but it was a lost cause. Time to deal with the rest of it.

"I know we haven't talked much since I came back, but I want you to know how sorry I am, about everything that happened. I should have come home after Reid left. I shouldn't have gone down to Georgia. Should never have married Frank without you even meeting him. But ..."

"But you did. You were scared, stubborn, and maybe a little too wounded to believe we might actually forgive you." He placed his pipe in a blue and white striped ashtray, a piece of pottery she'd made for him in fourth grade. "Julia, if I could have saved you from all the heartache you and those kids have endured, I would have. But I knew the last time we visited you down there that I was too late. I asked you to leave with us, and you wouldn't, remember? You were in too deep and too terrified to get out. And I'm sorry I didn't have the guts to force you to come home."

"I don't think you could have, Dad." She wiped her eyes and looked at the framed photographs on the wall. All the family portraits over the years, from the time they were toddlers to the last one taken before she left home. All their graduations, hers included. A lifetime of memories of the family she'd abandoned.

"You broke your mother's heart when you ran off with Reid in the middle of the night. You deferred college a year and that was fine. I was happy to have you working here with me. But the last thing I expected was for you to take off like that. Calling to tell us you were married after the fact ... it wasn't what we'd planned for you, Julia."

He didn't have to say more. She knew how distraught they had been.

Reid had come for her on a snowy night in February, his sophomore year. He'd gone back to college after Christmas break, but they'd both been miserable. So they made their plans. Plans she knew her parents would not approve of. But she'd gone anyway. And lived with the guilt of that, combined with the pain of survival, a lethal mixture that kept her up nights and dogged her during waking hours.

"You're not making this easy, you know." Fresh tears pricked her eyes and she swiped at them with the back of her hand. "I don't expect your forgiveness, but I just want you to know that I've lived with that regret all this time. Marrying Reid was a mistake. Marrying Frank was an even bigger one. But I think I've been punished enough."

"Yes, you have. We all have." He pressed his thumb and forefinger between his eyes, the old ship's clock on the wall ticking out the minutes.

Julia studied the Norman Rockwell painting on the wall—the happy family around the Thanksgiving table. For the first time in years, she looked forward to the upcoming holidays.

Her father pushed his chair back and rounded the desk. "Come here."

Julia stood on shaky legs, placed her hands in his and smiled.

"You are my daughter, Julia Rose Connelly, and don't you forget it. All was forgiven a long time ago. We just never had the chance to tell you." He pulled her into his embrace and she rested against his chest. Unbidden emotion tumbled out of her in a sob. "That's right. You need to cry, honey, do it here. Get it all out." He patted her on the back and Julia gave up fighting the feelings she'd tried so hard to keep at bay.

She was finally safe, protected and loved.

Back in her father's arms, the place she'd once run so many times for comfort.

Back home.

Chapter Nine

Reid parked by the shed behind the Connelly house and hoped he could pick up the chainsaw without having to interact with anyone. He'd summoned the nerve to ask Jonas if he could borrow a few tools now and then as he went about repairing the cabin. Jonas agreed, but beyond the grunt of affirmation, their conversation remained sparse. Like he was the one in the wrong.

Well, maybe he had been back then ... but now? If Jonas was angry about not knowing who Mark's real father was, he needed to take that up with his daughter.

Weeks had passed since that day up at the cabin, the day he'd realized just what Julia had gone through over the years they'd been apart. It was the middle of October now, hard as that was to accept. Cade still questioned his being here, Julia and Jonas hated him, Mark didn't seem to know what to make of him, and everyone else appeared blissfully unaware of the tension running rampant around the place whenever he showed up.

As he loaded the machine into the trunk, he heard the sound of somebody chopping wood. Reid glanced at his watch. It was pretty early on a Saturday. Couldn't be Jonas. Cade had mentioned his father having shoulder surgery earlier that year. It definitely wouldn't be Cade. He never got out of bed before ten.

The methodical chopping rang around him and kept time with the second hand on his Rolex. Whoever was out back with that axe was not a happy camper.

Reid walked around the house, shoved his hands in the pockets of his jacket and watched Mark split a log in half like he'd been doing it his whole short life. He picked up the two pieces of white pine, chucked them on the impressive pile he was making and went to work on another one.

His face got a little darker each time metal connected with wood.

Reid pushed down the lump in his throat and realized what he was seeing.

Fury.

Mark wore that same look he'd seen on too many of the subjects he'd interviewed over the past few years. Kids who'd seen and heard too much—boys and girls with childhood stolen from them—children of war, of tragedy. Terrorized by circumstances they could not control. Alone and afraid and convinced that nobody cared.

Reid shifted from one foot to the other as familiar fear cloaked him. He watched the axe come down again. Watched Mark wipe sweat from his brow, blink moisture from his eyes.

He saw himself, not much older than Mark was now, out back of the cabin, hacking away at a pile of wood until there was nothing left to chop. The memory justified his reasons to simply ignore the scene in front of him, let the kid be, and head on home.

But something, some crazy notion—God, guilt or a combination of both—made him clear his throat and raise a hand as Mark looked his way.

"Did your dad teach you to do that?" He hated referring to Frank Hansen as the boy's father, but didn't know what else to call him. The devil's brother probably wouldn't be appropriate.

Mark shook his head and brought the axe down with a crack. The wood split into two perfect halves. "My dad never taught me nothin'."

"Feels good, huh?"

"What?" Mark glared and threw another log on the old tree stump. Brought the axe down hard, his jaw set in a stubborn grimace.

Reid stepped a little closer. "You see his face when you do that?"

Mark swung, split the wood, kicked it aside and swung again. And again.

And again, with a gut-wrenching yell that pierced the morning air and sent Reid's pulse shooting skyward. He moved in quickly, came up behind him and wrapped his arms around his son's thin chest.

"Okay, bud. That's it. That's enough."

Mark bucked against him and yelled again. "Leave me alone! What do you know? You don't know nothin'!"

"I know enough." Reid held tight. "I know what it's like to lose a family. I know how bad it hurts. How angry it makes you. And I know that taking out your anger on a piece of wood doesn't make it go away."

Mark quit struggling and Reid let him go.

"You don't know jack." The kid picked up his ball cap and pulled it down low, spat across the lawn and shoved his hands in the pockets of his jeans.

Reid sucked in air and wondered what he'd been thinking, trying to take on this kind of pain. Trying to reason with a kid he barely knew.

But that kid belonged to him.

Whether Mark knew it or not. Whether Reid wanted it or not.

He had to try.

Reid exhaled and shook his head. "I was a couple years older than you when my parents died. I had a sister Emily's age. She died too. Nobody asked if it was okay. Nobody asked if I minded being the only one left, if I could handle being alone. It just happened. And it sucked. But that's the way life works sometimes, Mark. Sometimes it just sucks and there isn't anything we can do about it."

Mark stared through wide eyes, the flame in his cheeks lessening. "How'd they die?"

Reid looked over the kid's head toward the house, the place he'd found refuge and comfort during those early days in Bridgewater, when he'd thought his whole world was ending. "Car crash. They went out for the day, a family picnic. I thought I was too cool to go, so I stayed home. And they didn't come back."

"Man. That does suck."

"Yup. It did." Birds sang around them, the dogs barked out front, but all Reid heard was the sound of a police car's siren and the three sharp raps on his front door that changed his life forever.

"But you didn't want them to die." Mark crossed his arms and stepped back. His blue eyes held a million questions that Reid was pretty sure he didn't have answers for. "You were sad when they died, right?"

"Yeah." *Don't say it, kid. Please don't say it.*

"Well, I wasn't sad when my dad died. I hated him." Mark bent to pick up a stone, tossed it far into the trees behind them. "So you don't know how I feel, do you?"

Reid shrugged and walked to where a few stray pieces of wood sat. He stacked them on the pile and pitched around for words that wouldn't ring hollow.

"Maybe not. But I know what it's like to have to start over."

"Is that when you moved here? After your folks died?"

"Yes. Came to live with my grandmother. I wasn't happy about it."

"I'd rather be here than Atlanta." Mark threw another stone. "But I don't like it much.

The kids at school think I'm weird 'cause I sit off by myself sometimes instead of hanging out with them. And I like to read."

"You do?" Reid managed a grin. "That's not weird. Reading is cool. Sticking to yourself is a little anti-social maybe."

"Yeah, well."

"Have you tried making friends, Mark? Talking to kids?"

"Not exactly." Mark ran the sleeve of his sweatshirt across his mouth and revealed a grin that tugged Reid's heart a little too tight. "Uncle Cade keeps trying to get me to go to some youth group thing at church. He and Aunt Deb help out there every Saturday night. Sounds kinda lame though, right?"

"Well." Reid laced his hands behind his neck and stretched. "It could be fun. I mean if Cade's running it then yeah, it's gonna be a little lame, but maybe you could check it out anyway. Give him a few pointers."

"Yeah, right." Mark's dark mood floated away on a laugh. "So long as they don't talk about God the whole time. I got nothing to say to that dude."

Reid could relate.

He sank his teeth into his bottom lip and watched a flock of birds take flight. "I guess you don't know what it'll be like unless you go. Why not try it out tonight?"

Mark raised a brow, contemplative. "There's some Harvest Fair thing tonight, they're going. I guess that'd be sorta fun."

"Sounds all right." Reid smiled.

The Harvest Fair. He'd forgotten that. He and Cade and their buddies would hang out down there all day, and well into the night. Playing the games, checking out the girls and then in later years, dancing with them. By that time though, there was only one girl Reid wanted to dance with.

The back door slammed and Julia came down the back stairs, pulling on a purple hoodie over skinny jeans that made her look ... Reid grinned and stifled the thought.

"What's going on out here?" Julia narrowed her eyes and stared at him.

"Nothing." Mark and Reid spoke in sync.

"Can I go to the fair tonight, Mama?" Mark shuffled his feet and gave her a half smile. "Uncle Cade's taking those church kids. Thought I might go along."

"Uh ..." Julia didn't hide surprise well. "Sure."

"Thanks. See ya, Reid." Mark raced toward the house, took the stairs two at a time and disappeared inside.

Reid was left to face Julia alone.

"How did you do that?"

"Do what?"

She sighed and sent him a look that pretty much took his breath away. "I've been trying to get him to go to youth group since school started. You show up, talk to him for ten minutes and he's all gung ho about it."

Reid scratched his head and tried not to smile at her annoyance. "It just came up."

"We've been talking about the fair all week, trying to get him to go with the group. I suppose I should thank you."

"You don't have to. Just get your mom to send up an apple pie or something once a week. That'd be good." Reid chuckled, tempted to duck incase she felt the need to slug him one.

"She would too. She still thinks the sun rises and sets for you." Her grin came and went. "What are you doing here anyway?"

"Borrowing the chainsaw." He tipped his head toward the garage. His throat tightened at the memory of Mark taking out his vengeance on all those pieces of wood. "Heard the chopping and came round to check it out. He's a pretty angry kid, Jules."

It wasn't meant to be an accusation, but the way her lips pinched together told him she took it that way.

Julia marched across the grass, picked up a log, grabbed the axe and swung. "He's got a lot to be angry about." A thick piece of pine split in two and fell off the block onto the grass.

Apparently Mark wasn't the only one with pent up anger. And he'd learned his chopping skills from his mother.

Reid watched her work on a few logs and doubted he could do as well. He should probably make a quick exit while he had the chance.

"I've been thinking about what you said a while back." She swung the axe again, then returned to where he stood, barely out of breath. Her face flushed with exertion but her eyes remained guarded. "About how I need to cut you some slack."

Reid glanced at the axe in her hand and took a step backward. "You want to put that thing down?"

She grinned, but placed the axe against the stump. "I'll let Mark come work with you up at the cabin. You're not to pay him over minimum wage though. And I'm not telling him anything right now. He's doing much better here, but we've got a ways to go. Take it or leave it."

"I'll take it."

"All right." A hint of a smile slipped across her lips and his heart jumped a bit.

"Does this mean you forgive me?"

"Not in the least." The dogs rounded the corner and she bent over to pat them. They soon raced off and she set her gaze on him once more. "I'm tolerating your presence for Mark's sake."

Okay, then. Reid contemplated counting to a hundred before speaking again. "Oh, I almost forgot." He slapped a palm to his forehead and fished in the pocket of his jeans. "I have something for you."

"For me?" Curiosity crept into her eyes.

Reid held out the new cell phone he'd purchased yesterday. "In case some moron on a motorbike tries to sideswipe you again."

"Reid." A blush colored her cheeks, but the smile he hoped for didn't show. "I really don't need that. And I don't have the extra cash right now."

He tipped his head, ready for the fight. "It's already bought and paid for and the monthly charges are coming to me, so you can just say thank you."

"Reid." And there it was.

"Oh, wait … was that …" He staggered back, hand over his heart. "Was that an actual smile?"

"Shush." She took the cell phone from his hand like it would blow up any second. "It looks complicated."

"It's pretty simple, actually." He stood beside her and flicked a finger over the screen. "I've already programmed a few numbers. Cade's, Deb's, and there I am."

"There you are."

He'd used an old stock photo from the network, the one all the ladies apparently went nuts over. Looked pretty darn good too, if he did say so himself.

"This was taken a few years ago, huh?"

Ouch. Reid ran his tongue across his bottom lip and decided not to answer that.

"So how do I call you? If I need to. Which I probably won't."

"Just punch the button." Reid demonstrated, and the other cell in his pocket began to ring. "See? Easy."

"Okay." Julia studied the phone, glanced upward, one eyebrow raised in question. "So whenever I want to call you, I just punch you in the face."

"Punch away. But try not to look so ecstatic about it."

A sly grin flashed his way as she pocketed the phone. "I can work with that."

"I thought you might."

That odd silence ran between them again.

The years had turned them into strangers.

"Well, thanks." Another brief smile lit her face. "I'll tell Mark he can go with you."

"Great. You want him back at a certain time?"

"Maybe. I'll punch you in the face and let you know." She patted her pocket, her eyes finally free of the ice chips he'd grown used to. "You have food for lunch?"

"Yeah. Some worms and centipedes. Maybe a leftover hot dog or two."

"I'll fix you some sandwiches." Julia turned toward the house.

"Don't spit in mine."

She stopped on the bottom step, swiveled, and tossed him a smile that sent his heart racing. "You'll never know."

Chapter Ten

*J*ulia walked the fairgrounds while Emily raced on ahead with some friends. Couples moved past her, hand in hand. Kids zipped through the crowd. The air seemed charged with excitement. Music played from the overhead speakers and mouth-watering aromas from the barbeque pit hung tantalized her taste buds. There would be chicken and ribs, corn with plenty of butter, baked potatoes and huge bowls of coleslaw. Watermelon for dessert, and probably a few pies and ice cream too. The folks of Bridgewater took their food as seriously as their faith.

The sinking sun set the sky on fire and cast a pink hue across the scene. Happy shouts and delighted screams floated around her, reminding her of years gone by and how life used to be.

"How did you do it?" Cade cornered her behind the bouncy castle, grinning like a kid high on cotton candy.

"Do what?" Julia was in no mood for a heart-to-heart with her brother.

"Do what? How'd you get Mark to agree to come to youth group?"

"I didn't." Might as well get it over with. "You've got your best friend to thank for that little miracle."

"Serious?" Cade's eyebrows shot skyward. "Reid talked Mark into this? So you've told Mark that Reid's his—"

"No." She pushed up against her brother's shoulder. "No, Mark does not know. Go away, Cade. Your motley crew is escaping."

Sure enough, a group of kids of various heights and ages, her son included, shot past them, hooting and hollering, Debby bringing up the rear. She glanced over her shoulder as she ran by.

"A little help here, hon?"

"Coming!" Cade pecked Julia on the cheek. "We'll catch up later."

"Okay." Julia smiled as she watched her brother run off, and then continued her explorations of the fairground.

She'd asked Reid to drop Mark down at the church so he could come on the bus with the youth group. Her son looked happy as he ran by, even giving her a wave and that cocky grin of his. The one he'd inherited from his father.

Memories skirted her heels as she passed the game stalls, neighbors and old friends calling out greetings. Some days being home was a balm on her gaping wounds. Other days it made her question everything about herself and every bad decision she'd ever made. And since Reid Wallace barged back into her life, her regrets were multiplying by the second.

His very presence confused her. It was too easy to get caught up in the past, in the good memories. Those blue eyes of his still captured hers too quickly and she found it near impossible to stop studying him, making note of the changes the years had brought. Worst of all, she hated the way her heart still did that little flutter when she caught sight of him.

And he certainly didn't appear to be going anywhere.

Mark needed to be told. Especially now that they were spending time together, getting to know each other.

But not before she did a little digging into Reid's real reasons for coming back to Bridgewater.

Trust was not an attribute she handed out at whim.

Not anymore.

"Mama, play this one!" Emily skipped back to her and pulled her in the direction of the stall with the hoops you had to land over coke bottles. Julia groaned in dismay.

"Oh, no, Em, I'm really bad at this game."

"Please, Mama, try! I want the pink bunny."

"That pink bunny?" The most gargantuan stuffed animal Julia had ever seen.

Of course she did.

"All right. No promises." She paid the kid behind the booth and tossed four hoops. Each one missed by a mile.

Wicked laughter snuck up from behind and Julia turned to find Reid watching her, arms crossed, a grin playing around his mouth. "You're right. You are really bad at this game."

"Thanks, I know." She sent Emily a look of apology and ignored her daughter's pout.

"I didn't think I'd see you here."

He'd cleaned up. Shaved the scruff and combed his dark hair back. Julia stifled a sigh and wished he wasn't quite so good looking. He might be easier to tolerate if he'd gained fifty pounds and gone bald.

Reid cracked his knuckles and gave that grin that still sucked her under. "I wouldn't miss this for anything. Haven't been to a good county fair in years."

"No, I don't suppose you find many over there in the Middle East."

"Mister Reid!" Emily quickly abdicated sides and tugged on his arm. "Can you take a turn?"

Julia put her hands on her daughter's shoulders. "Emily, no. Reid's not going to play. We'll find something else to do."

"Actually, I'm really good at this. Remember?" Reid nudged her out of the way and smiled at Emily. "Which one do you want?"

"I want the pink bunny, please."

"No problem, princess. Hold my jacket, Jules." He tossed his jacket her way, gave the kid behind the counter a couple of bucks, pushed up the sleeves of a hunter-green cashmere sweater, sent Emily a wink and tossed the first hoop.

A few minutes later, Emily clutched the pink bunny to her chest and swung a bright blue teddy bear from her other hand. Reid would have continued, but Julia quashed any further macho displays for the small crowd that had gathered to watch their hometown star at play.

Her friend Marla hovered nearby. Marla's little girl Jessica was the same age as Emily, and they played well together. Marla was one of the few people Julia had bothered to reconnect with.

"Hey, Julia, why don't I take the kids over to the rides? You guys can hang out a while."

Julia raised her eyebrows. "No, really. We're not … no." Hanging out with Mr. Celebrity Man was not how she planned to spend the evening. She glowered at her friend's grin. "No. You are not leaving me here with him."

"Bye, sweetie. Come find us later." Marla herded the little kids up and disappeared before Julia could argue. She watched Emily skip off and tracked the area with some reluctance. Reid stood surrounded by several adults and a few kids. Signing autographs.

"You've got to be kidding me." Julia shook her head as he glanced up and caught her staring. She didn't return his smile.

She moved off to look at the homemade jewelry Carrie Mason had on display. Checked out a few bracelets and earrings and hoped nine o'clock would come soon. Then she could stick to the curfew she'd given Mark, pack up the kids and hightail it out of here.

"What is he doing?"

Julia turned at the sound of her sister's whine. Hannah stood beside her, arms crossed, mouth set in its classic pout.

"Hi, Hannah." She picked up a silver bracelet. "This is nice, don't you think?"

"Sure." Hannah pushed her light brown hair over her eyes and squinted through her spectacles. Her nose was squished tight, practically disappearing between her pink cheeks. "Is he actually giving out autographs?"

"So it would seem." Julia studied a pair of dangly earrings.

Hannah squeaked in protest. "That's ridiculous! He reads the news. You'd think he was some movie star for crying out loud. What's all the fuss about?"

"I don't know. I guess he's done pretty well. People like him." Julia moved along, taking her sister with her.

"You're defending him?"

"There's nothing to defend." Julia groaned inwardly and wished Hannah would go away too. "He's a small town boy who made it big. You can't expect people to just ignore that. Stop staring at him. I don't want him coming over here."

"Too late."

Sure enough, Reid had abandoned his adoring public, and headed their way.

"Hello, Hannah." Reid sidled up beside them, his leather jacket shoved under one arm. Julia shifted, his nearness setting her nerves on edge.

"Reid." Hannah's mouth formed a thin line. "Or do I need to call you Sir?"

"Your Highness will be fine."

Julia watched Reid's smile fade into the familiar scowl that always appeared in the presence of her sister.

Hannah adjusted a yellow top that was a tad too tight, made a face like she was sucking on a lemon and narrowed her pale eyes. "I can think of a few other things to call you."

Reid stuck his hands in his pockets and planted his feet in a defensive stance. "Oh, I'm sure you can. How's that broom of yours holding up? Taken it in for a tune-up lately?"

"Okay, that's enough." Bloodshed would totally ruin the night. Julia squeezed Hannah's arm and pointed across the crowded fairground. "Mom was looking for you. She needs help getting more pies over to Mr. Crossway's booth. And I think I heard Bryan Crossway asking whether you were here."

"Seriously, Julia." Hannah lifted her eyes skyward, her cheeks pinking. "You're still a jerk, Reid Wallace." She stalked off, yelling something Julia wished she hadn't heard.

Reid shook his head and growled a few choice words of his own.

Julia stifled a giggle and walked along the row of craft booths.

"What are you laughing at?" He shadowed her, not letting her escape.

She stopped and looked his way, noting the annoyance in his eyes. "You still let her get to you."

"She's so good at it." Reid grimaced. "Just has to look at me and I want to strangle her."

"That's Hannah. Ignore her. It works for me." She shifted the strap of her purse to her other shoulder. "Enjoy the fair."

"Are you trying to ditch me?" A grin tickled the corner of his mouth, mischief playing in his eyes.

Julia waved at Emily as her daughter looked back over her shoulder from the group a few yards ahead. "Do you really want me to answer that?"

His low laughter set her nerves jumping again. "Are you here with someone?"

"Am I what?" Julia stood still and stared him down. "Yes, Reid. I am. I'm here with my five-year old."

"I was just asking." He trailed her as she checked out another booth. "So ... you're not seeing anyone?" He fingered a couple of silk scarves, acting like he'd only asked for the time.

"*Seeing anyone?*" Julia swung around to face him. Was he serious? "Other than my psychiatrist on a weekly basis, you mean?"

"Oh." That shut him up.

Julia ducked through a few teenagers and picked up her pace. He was doing a remarkable job keeping up with her.

"Well, if you're wandering around alone, do you mind if I keep you company?"

The man was clearly trying to drive her crazy.

Julia put her hands on her hips and studied him. If she didn't know better, she'd have said he almost looked a little shy, perhaps a tad afraid of her answer. "Why?"

"Why what?" Now he just looked confused.

"Why me?" She tipped her head toward the group of girls trailing them at a respectable distance. "If you haven't noticed, you've got quite a following. I'm sure they'd be happy to keep you company."

His dramatic eye roll didn't convince her she would succeed in getting him to leave her alone. Or that she really wanted to.

"They're barely out of high school. I'd rather stick with you, if you don't mind. You're safer."

The cocky grin returned and Julia raised an eyebrow. "You sure about that?"

"Quite."

"Suit yourself." Julia gave up. There was no point in arguing and causing a scene. Emily and her friends were nearby. And she had come here to try to have a good time.

"Come on, Mama!" Emily headed toward the Ferris wheel.

"Em, wait!" Julia glanced back at Reid. If he planned to stalk her, he might as well be useful. "Remember how I'm afraid of heights?"

"Gotcha covered." He smiled as he jogged past to catch up with Emily and her friends. "Hey, Emily, wait up. I'll go on with you."

After the ride, Emily and the other kids disappeared with Marla. Julia made her way down a row, stopping here and there to check out the wares. Talk about the proverbial walk down memory lane. Nothing had changed, really. Just the faces of the people she knew so well with the passage of time.

Mrs. Menkle with her apple butter and homemade jellies. Jessup Brady peddling his painted birdhouses. The church ladies, selling their baked goods and hot apple cider. A few familiar stalwarts no longer with them, some newcomers stood out, but if she closed her eyes, Julia could have been a teenager all over again.

"Oh, man." Reid pulled her back into the space between two booths. "Check her out."

"Who?" Julia squinted in the direction he looked.

"Miss Carter." Reid let out a long whistle. "Mark was right."

"That is not Miss Carter." Julia stared at the woman in the tight jeans and a colorful blousy top, platinum blonde hair and other … attributes. Their old high-school English teacher looked nothing like that. "Miss Carter's like a hundred. You need to get your eyesight checked."

"Nah, look at her …" Reid rested an arm over her shoulder and pointed. "That's definitely her." He was laughing so hard he had to lean on her for support.

"Would you stop," she hissed, elbowing him in the ribs. "Oh, wow, I think you're right. Has she had surgery?"

"More than one, I'd say." He doubled over, trying to catch his breath between the hoots he was letting out.

"Shh!" Julia yanked his arm as the subject of his mirth walked their way.

"Why, Mr. Wallace." The not-so-beautiful Miss Carter spied them and came to a standstill. "And Miss Connelly. You're both looking well. Are you still together?"

Julia cringed under the piercing gaze she remembered and prayed Reid would come to his senses.

"Yes, Ma'am." Reid straightened, cleared his throat and pushed hair out of his eyes.

Julia elbowed him again. Hard.

"I mean, no, Ma'am. We're not. Um ... together. But it's nice to see you. Looking so ... uh ... healthy."

"Indeed." Her smile was a brilliant white glare as she clasped Reid's hand between florescent pink claws. "We're all so proud of you, dear. Such a tragedy that happened over there, but I was so glad to hear you weren't hurt. I trust you'll be thrilling us with your presence on the evening news again very soon?"

"We'll see." Reid's smile seemed set in place but the light faded from his eyes.

"Well, I must be off. You kids behave now." She batted thick eyelashes in their direction and sauntered away.

Reid practically collapsed the minute she was out of sight, leaning over his knees.

"Healthy?" Julia gave him a push and he almost fell over. "That's the best you could come up with?"

"What?" He wiped his eyes and let out a long breath. "Artificial applies, but probably wouldn't have gone over so well."

Julia laughed and wagged a finger at him. "You're bad. I'm not so sure you're the best influence for my son."

"Oh, come on." He swaggered along beside her as she walked. "You're kidding, right?"

"Maybe." She smiled as they passed a few more booths where people recognized them, waved and called out their names. Somehow they'd stumbled into a time warp.

A few minutes later she felt his hand slip into hers. Her fingers tightened around his automatically. Didn't even think about it.

The whole fairground came to a screeching halt.

Julia stopped walking.

"Whoa." She yanked her hand from his. The sheer surprise on Reid's face no doubt mirrored her own.

"Yeah. I have no idea why I did that. Sorry." He widened his eyes, color rushing to his cheeks. "Old habits die hard, I guess."

"I guess." Julia buried her hands in the pockets of her down jacket.

"Jules, I didn't mean to upset you." Embarrassment, regret and probably a whole bunch of other things she didn't want to know about stormed his face. His eyes held hers, seeking forgiveness. "That was really dumb. I'm sorry."

"It's okay, Reid. Forget it."

Mr. Fitzgerald had his woodcarvings on display like always, and she went that way.

Holding her hand? What was he thinking? What was *she* thinking? She wanted to kick herself several times over. Worse that he'd taken her hand was how she'd responded to his touch.

The feel of his fingers entwined with hers was like warm spring rain, waking her from deep sleep. Refreshing, new, yet providing familiar comfort at the same time.

And she did not want it.

Not in the slightest.

Well, maybe she did a bit. But that was just her memory having its way.

Reason over-ruled emotion and made her put some space between them. "Oh, look at this. Nice." She picked up a beautiful wooden bowl and admired the weave of the grain in the wood. Flipped it over, checked out the price tag, almost dropped it. "Wow. Never mind."

Reid lifted the bowl she'd just put down and whistled. "What is this made of, Trevor, solid gold?"

The older man behind the booth chuckled as his pair of snowy eyebrows knit together. "My time is worth what I'm asking."

"Right." Reid shot Julia a look that said he knew better. "If Essie saw you ripping people off like this she'd have your hide strung up to the highest beam in Faith Bridge. Seventy-five."

Trevor Fitzgerald crossed himself with a look of chagrin. "Eighty, and may she rest in peace."

"Done." Reid's face cracked in a winning smile as he handed over the cash. He presented Julia with the bowl.

"Oh, no. Really." She held up her hands. "I ... no."

"What?" Confusion played over his face. "You liked it."

"Sure, but I ..." She clenched her fists at her sides and tried to think. "I don't have a place to put it."

He stepped around her, grabbed a plastic bag from Trevor, and put the bowl into it. "Don't do that."

"Don't do what?"

Why did he have to be here? She couldn't even enjoy one evening without worrying about Reid Wallace and how to behave in his presence.

He sent her a sidelong look and moved to the next stall. "Don't make up excuses when you don't know what to say. That always drove me nuts." He shrugged and held onto the bag. "You don't want it because I bought it. Call it what it is."

Was he trying to pick a fight? What else had she done that drove him nuts, drove him away? She glared at a bunch of dried flower wreaths at the next stall. The poor woman in the booth gave her a startled look and moved back.

"I didn't ask you to buy it, Reid."

"No, you didn't." He stood so close their shoulders were touching. "I bought it for you because I wanted to. The polite thing to do would be to say thank you and accept the gift."

"But I don't want you to buy me stuff. The phone, the bowl ... you can't barge in and buy your way back into my life. It doesn't work that way."

"*Buy* my way ..." His mouth fell open but he shut it in a hurry. "Is that what you think I'm doing?"

Julia didn't answer, stalked down another row of stalls and prayed he wouldn't follow her. His laughter did.

"Are we seriously arguing about a stupid wooden bowl I just paid way too much money for?"

"No, we're arguing because ..." She turned to face him, the angry retort on her tongue retreating as her eyes met his. His dark hair lifted in the autumn breeze, his eyes glinting under the glow of the overhead bulbs that cast a shadow around his jaw line.

"Because?" He lifted one eyebrow and closed the gap between them.

"I don't know."

He took her hand and curled her fingers around the plastic bag. "Just take the bowl, Jules. You can still hate me in the morning."

"Promise?"

"If it makes you happy, Julia, you can hate me for eternity." Reid's expression landed somewhere between teasing and totally serious. She never could get past that one.

"I don't hate you," she whispered, watching the light dance in his eyes.

"You what?" He leaned in close, the corners of his lips lifting ever so slightly.

Julia cleared her throat and moved backward. "I don't hate you. I'm just ... I don't know how to act around you. You're so different."

"Different how?"

Great. Now she'd just opened the door for a conversation she so did not want to have. "I don't know exactly. You're pretty much a celebrity around here for one thing. And you ... well ... you're a little full of yourself, to be honest. We used to be on the same playing field. But now you're miles ahead. You live in a city, travel the world, you know things I could never begin to understand. You've become somebody else, Reid. Somebody I don't know."

He stared at her for longer than she was comfortable with. Rubbed his jaw and cleared his throat. "Let's go find Em. I'm hungry."

She'd offended him.

As they walked on, people stopped to say hello, ask Reid how he was, ask when he was going back to work. The attention didn't seem to bother him a bit. He was every inch the celebrity they all thought he was. The young man she'd fallen in love with was nowhere in sight.

And she missed him.

She'd been missing him since the day he left.

They came to the dining area. Reid found her a place near the table where the kids sat and went to get their food. She saw him nod at Mark, saw them exchange a grin, and saw Cade and Debby share a knowing smile when they thought she wasn't looking. If her parents were anywhere in sight, well, she didn't want to know what they were thinking.

All of a sudden she and Reid were like goldfish in a bowl.

It wasn't difficult to catch the way everyone around them tracked Reid's every move. A group of younger women giggled and talked behind their hands as he walked by. A few older folks, friends of her parents, gave her curious glances. Julia sighed and massaged her throbbing temples. Being in a crowd was bad enough. Being watched by the entire town was more than she'd bargained for.

Reid returned with two plates of steaming hot fried chicken legs, baked beans and potato salad and the coleslaw she loved. He disappeared again for drinks, came back and dug into his food.

"Eat that up." He pointed to her plate with a stern look.

Julia stared at the feast he'd set before her. She was hungry, but there was so much, and her stomach was still protesting the fact that the man she'd once given her heart and soul to sat across the table from her.

"Julia, eat." Reid wagged his fork at her. "You're too thin."

"You think I'm too thin?" She blew out a breath and stuck her fork in the potato salad. What other compliments would he throw her way before the evening ended?

"Just eat. Pretend I'm not here."

"That's a little hard to do." She tried not to look at him and picked at her food. "Everybody's staring at you."

"Staring at you too, wondering what we're doing together." He flashed an amused smile that said he couldn't care less.

"I don't like it." Actually, she hated it. Hated being watched. She'd been under Frank's scrutinizing gaze far too long.

"Just keep your head down. They'll find something else to gawk at soon enough."

"I hope so." She tried some macaroni and cheese. It was just as good this year as she remembered.

"It's crazy, huh?" After a few minutes, Reid broke the silence. He tipped his head toward a group a few tables down. Julia recognized their former classmates. Many of their friends who'd been couples in high school had stayed together, now had families of their own.

"What's crazy?"

He shrugged and popped the lid on his can of coke. "Just how they're all still together, still happy. Living out the great American dream."

Julia stiffened at his acrid tone. "There's nothing wrong with the American dream, Reid. Nothing wrong with wanting to settle down and have a family."

"No, of course there isn't." His smile didn't quite reach his eyes. "It's just not for everyone."

"It was what I wanted," she reminded him, twirling her fork in a mound of coleslaw. "Once upon a time you wanted it too."

"Once upon a time was eons ago." His eyes clouded over and he looked away. "But I'm sorry you didn't get your happily ever after."

"Yeah. So am I." Tears too close to the surface, she concentrated on her food again.

"What you said to me back there ..." Reid pushed his plate away, captured her eyes with his. "I know you think you shouldn't have. But I'm glad you did. I needed to hear it. And if you want the truth, I feel the same way." He propped his elbows on the table and rested his chin on his hands. "I don't know who I am anymore either."

His words pulled her back in time. Instantly. Without warning.

"What do you want from me, Jules?" He'd given up. She could tell.

She ripped another sheet of paper from her notepad and balled it up. "I want you to tell me what to do. Tell me who I'm supposed to be, Reid. Do you really think I can do this? Go to college? Become a writer?"

He rounded the desk in two seconds flat. Crouched beside her and slid his hands around her face. "You can be anything you want to be, Julia Connelly. All you have to do is believe in yourself."

"I want to. I just ... I don't know who I am anymore."

"You do know." His stare pierced through her, stripped her soul bare. "You're a talented writer, a wonderful person, and you're going to be my wife. And we can figure out the rest after that."

"What would I do without you?" She leaned in to kiss him.

"Well, you won't have to find out." He laughed, stood and began to gather their things. The library would close in ten minutes. "But you'd be just fine."

He'd been wrong.

Chapter Eleven

"So you don't know who you are. Care to explain?" Julia tapped her foot on the ground in nervous habit and hoped he wouldn't notice her leg shaking.

"I can try." He shoved fingers through his hair and shrugged. "I guess I'm feeling kind of stuck between the kid I was when I left, and the man everyone around here thinks I am. And now I'm a father. That scares me to death. I don't have much experience with kids. I don't know the first thing about being a parent. Maybe you're right not to tell him."

She leveled her gaze and saw the fear in his eyes. "You think you're going to screw up again."

Hesitation and doubt crossed his face. "I hope I don't, but I can't sit here and promise you I won't. I'd just like to know for sure that I'm where I'm supposed to be. Who God wants me to be."

She gave a short laugh. "Don't ask me about God. We're not exactly talking these days." Julia swallowed a mouthful and set her fork down. The words she'd just spoken hit hard.

Reid leaned forward, his eyes intent on holding hers. "Do you feel like that too? Like God gave up on you a long time ago?"

"Sometimes." Laughter and happy conversation floated around them and she envied it. Envied people who were free to enjoy their time without worrying how to get through tomorrow or even make it through tonight. "I've felt like He abandoned me. But maybe I abandoned Him. I don't know. Some days I found it hard to believe God loved me. I sure didn't feel loved during my marriage to Frank. Or protected."

"Jules …"

She shrugged and tried to smile. "Don't look at me like that. Don't pity me. I'm getting by. I've been thinking about going back to church actually. Just haven't found the nerve."

Reid drank his soda and got that faraway look again. "I haven't been to church in years." He rubbed his thumb over a couple of carved initials on the wooden table. "I have a dozen excuses why, but the truth is, I didn't care enough. Didn't believe God cared about me."

Julia nodded. "I tried taking the kids when Mark was small, but ... it didn't work out so well. I haven't been since we moved back here. Scared of what folks will think, I guess. But I want to change that. I can't very well ask Mark to go to church if I don't." She clenched her fists under the table. "And there's nobody to tell me I can't go anymore." The admission popped out, too late to take it back. "I just need to find the courage to walk through those doors. Maybe tomorrow." She managed a small smile. "Except I say that every Saturday night."

His smile warmed her in a way she wasn't prepared for. "I might give it a try too.

Although I'm not so sure I won't get hit by lightning the minute I darken the door."

She didn't like the insecure look he wore. So far removed from the suave and self-assured man she'd watched on television for years. The man she'd just accused him of being. And that made it even harder to voice her next thought.

"Well. Given my intentions to get things right with God, I ... I'm going to work on forgiving you, Reid." There. She'd said it. Didn't feel a whole lot better for it, but at least it was out there. "It may take awhile."

He lifted his shoulders, a smile flickering. "Don't strain yourself. I don't deserve exoneration."

"I thought everybody did."

"Not everybody."

One thing hadn't changed. He was still way too hard on himself. "I'm not so sure about that." Julia saw a little relief come into his eyes. "While we're at it, I should probably ask you to forgive me too." She looked down at her hands, her pulse picking up. "For not telling you about Mark."

"I understand why you didn't." A trace of the past stamped out his smile. "I was a jerk. You had no way of knowing what my reaction would be. Truth is, Jules, I don't even know what I would have done back then. So there really isn't much to forgive on my part. Let's just move on."

"You make it sound easy."

If only she could sort out her feelings. Could stop her heart beating a little too hard whenever he was around. Stop all the memories cascading over her, reminding her how much she had loved him. How much she'd lost.

And how long she'd hated him for ruining her life.

"How do we do that, Reid? How do we move on?"

"We just do, Julia." He folded his arms. "We can't afford not to. It'll drive us both crazy."

"More than we already are, you mean?" Julia smiled at his laughter, a lightness floating through her, unearthing some of the good memories she'd buried. "For what it's worth, I think Mark likes you a lot. And I think you're going to be a great dad."

"You do?" He leaned back so far he almost slipped off the bench.

She gave a nod. "Shoot. I guess this means I'm going to have to stop using your picture as a dartboard, huh?"

Reid tipped his head, a slow grin starting. "Nice visual. But not entirely impossible to imagine."

Awkward silence snuck up and sat beside them again. Julia watched other people in easy conversation and wondered how it was done. "We don't really have to talk, you know."

"What?" He got that confused look and she scrambled to make sense of her words.

"I mean, I don't want you to feel like you need to explain yourself to me. I don't need to know about your personal life."

"You mean you don't want to know." Reid pressed his lips together with a look of chagrin.

Did she want to know? "I know you're not married. Is there anything else for me to know? A girlfriend you haven't told me about?"

Like the one who called you that first night we talked?

She could sit here and pretend she didn't care, but somehow she knew he'd see right through that. The smile he wore told her he already did.

"You do want to know."

"All right, yes. If you're in a relationship that's going to matter when it comes time to tell Mark, then, yes, I want to know."

"Well, I'm not." The dimple in his cheek deepened. "There was someone for awhile, but it's over. You've got me all to yourself."

"I'm overjoyed."

"I can tell."

Julia caught her brother staring at them, and made a face at him. "Cade and Deb are right over there. You want to go sit with them?"

Reid swiveled, then turned back to her. "Do you want to go sit with them?"

"And all those kids?" She laughed and took another bite of potato salad. "No, thanks."

"Well, if it's all the same to you, neither do I. So if you don't mind, I'll just stay put." He picked up his fork again and she noticed the tremor in his hand.

She managed a smile when he looked up. "How was Mark today?"

His eyes lit and her heart twisted a little.

"He was great. Seemed to like helping out. He works hard, doesn't complain. He's a good kid, Jules."

"Yeah. He is." Julia fiddled with her watch, but couldn't look away. Reid's smile reached right into the depths of her soul, shoved off the debris and let it breathe. "I have a bunch of photo albums in boxes at the house. I could get them out for you sometime, if you want."

"Thanks. That'd be great."

"He's really smart, but he hasn't done that well in school the last couple of years. Things were … well … I hope now that he's here, things will get better."

"I'm sure they will." Reid's smile was reassuring. "You think we could do something about that Southern twang though?"

Laughter bubbled from somewhere deep inside. "Are you kidding? If you think Mark's accent is bad, you should hear the good ole boys down there. Mark's got nothing on them."

"Oh, wow." He laughed and pushed his empty plate away. "Guess he'll lose it after a while. Like you said, he's a smart boy."

"Obviously. He takes after his mother."

"Of course." Reid gave her a half salute and a grin that did nothing to quell the hammering of her heart. "And maybe a little after his father."

"You can take credit for his temper and stubborn streak."

"And his good looks."

"Those too." Julia took another sip of soda, sudden tears springing to her eyes.

"What's wrong?"

Julia laughed and shook her head. "This is hard for me. I mean it's okay, but it's a little weird. I thought he would never know you."

Reid reached across the table and took her hand. "If you start blubbering, I'm going to have to throw caution to the wind and hug you. And that's a scene I'm betting you do not want to create right here."

"If you hug me I'll probably hit you." She sniffed, pulled her hand from his and wiped her eyes. "And then we'd be all over People magazine. Miss Carter would be first in line for the local interview."

"Okay. No hugging or slugging allowed." He leaned back on the bench and folded his arms, a smile settling on his lips. "This is good."

"What is?" She couldn't finish what was left on her plate. The way his eyes danced in the early evening light chased her appetite away.

"This. You and I, having a real conversation." Reid nodded toward the small group on the dance floor. "Being here. Being home."

Julia watched her daughter dancing with a group of younger kids. The band had started up some time ago and the dance area was starting to fill. Couples of every age came together on that dance floor. Old Mr. Howard and his wife, both outlived all bets on their longevity. Young couples dancing together or with their kids. Her dad, swooping Emily up in his arms and twirling her around to the country music she loved so much, Mom standing off to the side, clapping, a happy smile on her face.

"Yes. It is. It's good."

When she looked his way again, Reid was on his feet, holding out a hand toward her. "Come on, Miss Connelly. We can't let them have all the fun."

Her heart thudded against her rib cage and she shook her head. "Oh. No. That's not a good idea."

"Why not?"

"Because it's …" All argument died as he took her hand in his and pinned her with that intense gaze that always took her breath away.

"When is the last time you kicked back and really enjoyed yourself, Julia? I'm betting it's been a while."

"I'm not much into kicking back." But she stood anyway, moved around the bench and let him lead her to the dance floor. "And what happened to keeping a low profile?"

"Who cares about a low profile?" He pulled her close, one hand around her waist, the other clasping hers to his chest. "I'd much rather do this."

She would too, but didn't dare admit it.

But being back in Reid's arms was making her more than nervous.

He felt different, yet the same. Taut muscles still rippled under his sweater. His hands still held her in that tender way while just a hint of mischief hid behind his smile. And unless she was totally losing it, she recognized the odd sensation that started somewhere deep inside, sparked and lit and turned her veins to livewires the moment he drew her close.

It was almost terrifying enough to make her push him away and run home. But the way he held her eyes, reassured her without saying a word, made her relax. She could enjoy this.

Just this once.

Julia hadn't danced in years, but he moved her expertly from one position to the next, keeping time with the country music the band played. She figured they could have fooled anyone.

Anyone who didn't know better might think they'd never been apart.

Mistakes of the past skipped off into the night and she was just the young girl who actually believed Reid Wallace hung the moon.

As darkness approached, the music slowed. People around them came and went, but he didn't let her go. And she didn't want him to.

Nothing mattered but the beating of his heart in time with hers, the way his thumb traced circles over the top of her hand, the feel of his breath near her cheek, his low humming to the tune they danced to, and the memory of how things used to be.

She lost track of how long they stayed on the dance floor. The air grew colder, the crowd got bigger, the music louder.

And then the fireworks began.

The first explosion split the night, hushed the music and threw down bright sparks of colored light from the sky.

Reid stopped moving and tightened his grip around her.

"Julia."

The way he said her name caused her to look at him in a hurry. "What?" The fear in his eyes sent a chill down her spine. "What's wrong?"

"Mama, fireworks are starting!" Emily raced to them, her eyes wide and filled with excitement. "Mister Reid, can you pick me up?"

"Hey, Reid." Cade appeared out of nowhere and put a hand on Reid's shoulder. "You okay, man?"

Julia didn't know what was happening, but the expression on Reid's face was morphing into one of sheer terror.

"No." Reid held her eyes, squeezed her hands and shook his head. "I ... no. I have to go." He disappeared through the crowd before she could stop him.

"Where's he going?" Emily cried. "I wanna see the fireworks!"

"I'll pick you up, Em." Cade hoisted her onto his shoulders and they walked off the dance floor to where the crowd was gathering to watch the display.

Julia stared at her brother. "What just happened? I thought we were having fun. I was actually being nice."

Cade smiled, but his eyes were worried. "It wasn't you, Jules. I didn't even think about the fireworks tonight. I should have warned him. He's been struggling for a while now. Longer than anyone knew."

"Struggling? With what?" She didn't like the tremor in her brother's tone. "What are you talking about?"

"I guess when you cover one war zone too many, it's bound to happen." Cade held tight to Emily's little legs and stared up at the fireworks painting the dark sky. "Reid's got PTSD, Julia. Post Traumatic Stress Disorder. That's why he's not working right now."

Chapter Twelve

*J*ulia shuffled her feet on the gravel path outside the old white church. Stared at the sunlight bouncing off the stained glass, inhaled sweet mountain air and waited for courage that wasn't coming. Red leaves swirled on the wind and fluttered around her. Grey clouds loomed above the mountains, inched closer to the sun and put a chill in the air that threatened an early snow.

Music and voices raised in praise floated out through the open door. The service started five minutes ago. She'd even arrived early. Drove with her parents, but then asked the kids to go on ahead inside with them. She needed a moment. That moment had turned into several, and somehow she couldn't make her feet move.

"You'll probably be able to hear better from inside."

Julia turned to see Reid walking across the grass toward her. Strange relief surged through her. But admitting she was glad to see him was not going to happen. So she shrugged and found a smile. "Fancy seeing you here."

"Everything okay?"

After last night, she could ask him the same. "I'm just having a little freak-out."

"Thought you might be."

He'd traded his casual, faded jeans and rugged hiking shoes for smart, indigo denims topped with a chunky gray wool sweater layered over a plaid button down. His vintage brown leather bomber jacket gave him a bad boy look, yet he still managed to look sophisticated.

She recognized the man in front of her as the one she'd watched on television for years. The one the whole town cheered on and celebrated. The award-winning news anchor that no doubt deserved every accolade he got.

When he took off his sunglasses, smiled and held out his hand, he was simply Reid.

"How long are you planning to stand out here, Miss Connelly?"

"Um, not sure, really. You?"

He gave a low chuckle. "Just waiting for you, Jules."

Against her better judgment, she placed her hand in his.

"You waited for me?" Fear fled the minute his fingers closed over hers. A new sensation uncurled within. The possibility of a fresh start was suddenly not so out of reach. They had been friends once. Perhaps they could be again.

"Saw you guys pull in, the rest of them go inside, and watched you try to talk yourself out of it." He pushed back a strand of her hair with his finger. "So what if we do this together?"

"What if we don't and say we did?"

He raised a brow. "Come on. How bad can it be?"

She laughed at the question. "Bad enough me going in there alone." Julia widened her eyes. "You think people won't notice the two of us walking in together? We'll probably shut down the service."

His eyes got a little darker with the downturn of his mouth. "I'm sick of worrying about what people think, Julia. You should be too. Let them talk if they want. Who cares?"

Hesitation hovered nearby, but she kicked it aside and resolved to follow through. Today she was going back to church. "Okay. Let's go."

She wanted to sneak in and sit in the back row, but, true to form, Reid led her right up front to where the family sat. Emily launched herself at him with a gleeful squeal, squashing any chance of slipping in unnoticed. Her daughter promptly plopped down on his knees as soon as he sat. And he didn't seem to mind a bit.

It might have been her imagination, but Julia heard whispers from all sides of the church. Cade practically sliding off the pew as they came in was definitely not her imagination. Mark's sidelong glances and Emily on

Reid's lap didn't do much to help her nerves. But somehow she made it through the service, wedged between Reid and Mark, avoiding her mother's smile and Hannah's glare.

Once they were outside, Debby grabbed her arm and pulled her off to the side of the church. "What in the world is going on?"

Julia foraged in her purse for her sunglasses, even though the sky was now gray. "Um. I came to church?"

"With Reid."

"Yes. Well, not exactly. He was standing outside, so we came in together." Something like that. Julia gave her friend a little push. "Do not give me that look. If you must know, I've decided to bury the hatchet. And not into his skull. We were friends once. I'm sure we can manage it again."

Debby gaped. "Honey, you and Mr. Fine Looking over there were a lot more than friends."

"Don't need the reminder, thanks." Mark was proof enough.

Her son stood near Reid, listening to whatever he was telling the group surrounding him. He glanced at Mark every now and then and smiled, and the look of admiration Mark wore almost made her march over there and blurt out the truth. "Do you think everyone sees it, Deb, or just me?"

"That they're the spitting image of each other? Probably everyone sees it."

Julia let out a sigh. "We're going to have to tell him before somebody else does."

"I was going to suggest that, yes." Debby squeezed her hands. "It'll be fine, Jules. God's brought you this far. He's not going to let you down now."

"Maybe not." Her eyes began to sting and she closed them against apprehension. The sermon she'd just heard had intimated the same. "But I'm more than a little afraid Mr. Fine Looking over there will."

"Mama, time to go!" Emily bounced toward them, Reid following. "Mister Reid's comin' for lunch!"

"Is he?" Julia inched down her shades and gave Reid the once over.

"Your mother invited me." He shrugged, looking a little sheepish. "I said I'd check with you. Is it okay?"

"Come on, Em." Debby held out a hand and led Emily in the direction of the parking lot. Julia zipped up her coat and looked up as the first few flakes of snow began to fall. It wasn't cold enough to stick, but the sight of it made her smile just the same.

"Jules?" Reid still waited for her answer.

He looked pressed and put together, professional enough to fool a casual observer. But the dark shadows under his eyes and the unease lurking in them told her something different. Something she wasn't all that sure she understood. Or wanted to.

"Of course. Come for lunch." She pulled on her gloves and sent him a sidelong glance. "Thanks for the moral support in there."

"No problem." A grin slid over his mouth. "I think the prayer chain will be buzzing all afternoon."

"That's for sure." Julia laughed. "So, what happened last night?"

"Ah." His smile of acknowledgement only lasted a moment. "I was wondering when we'd get to that."

"We don't have to." It was obvious he didn't want to talk about it, and she didn't want to pry. "I was worried about you, that's all." Julia began to walk toward the cars.

Reid caught her up. "You were?"

"I was. Shocking, isn't it?"

"A little." He snorted. "Who am I kidding? I may actually pass out."

She stopped walking, took a deep breath and let it out. "Reid. Whether we like it or not, fate or God or whatever you want to call it, has brought us together again. So I'm going to accept it, and suggest we be friends. If you think you can manage it."

"If I can manage it?" His eyebrows shot skyward as he gave a hoot. "Baby, that's the pot calling the kettle black all over town." His teasing tone made her cheeks a little too warm but she laughed anyway.

"Good. Friends then." She stuck out a hand and he shook it ceremoniously. "Oh, just one more thing."

"What's that?" His eyes sparkled with familiar mischief, his mouth curled in a grin.

Julia raised an eyebrow and picked up her pace. "Call me baby again, and I'll bring you to your knees."

Julia made her way through the stacks of bookshelves in the Bridgewater Library. She let her fingers trail over the old bindings of the books. Her mother said there weren't enough writers in the world to churn out stories faster than Julia sped through them. They'd spent their childhood here, literally. Mom loved to read, and the three of them were dragged to the library almost every day when they weren't in school.

Cade hated every minute of it, wouldn't read a thing and howled in protest whenever Mom turned the car toward the large white building. Julia and Hannah were drawn to the place. Eventually Julia discovered that not only did she love to read, she loved writing more. She would be the one to write the next great bestseller they would all talk about. Hannah on the other hand, would become the keeper of the books.

The keeper of their memories. The good, the bad, and the ugly.

Julia stood at the end of a long row, hid in the shadows and watched Hannah at work. Her younger sister chatted with an elderly gentleman while she checked out his books.

As usual, her brown hair was tied back, her face void of any make-up, her wardrobe plain as ever. Sensible brown cords, a white blouse, beige wool cardigan and penny loafers.

The smile she gave the older man tugged at Julia's heart. Hannah rarely smiled at her that way. But they'd never been close. Two years younger, Hannah constantly engaged in the game of catch up. Always wanted to be better than Julia. Get better grades. Have better hair. Have more friends. Except Hannah could never meet the grand expectations she placed upon herself. In her estimation, Julia would always be prettier, smarter and more popular. And Hannah loathed her for it.

The man moved off and Hannah caught sight of her. "Julia? What are you doing here?"

"Looking for a book." It was the obvious answer. Julia shifted the strap of her purse to her other shoulder and hoped her cheeks weren't burning. "You don't have it though."

"What's it called? I can order it." Hannah went to her computer, studied her through black-framed glasses while she waited.

Julia waved a hand. "That's okay." She shifted from one foot to the other. "Um. How's it going?"

"It's quiet." Hannah grinned at her joke, and moved her swivel chair back to the other end of the desk. "Aren't you working today?"

"Lunch break. Actually, I thought maybe we could go get something to eat? There's that new café in town I'd like to try."

"I can't." Hannah shut down almost at once. "I don't usually take lunch."

"Oh." Julia stifled a sigh. "You could make an exception, couldn't you? We haven't spent that much time together since I came home."

"No, we haven't." Hannah typed something into her computer, whatever she was reading on the screen obviously far more interesting. Hint taken.

Off to one side of the room sat a few cubicles, each with a computer on them. They were all vacant.

"Can anybody use those?" Julia tipped her head toward them.

"The computers? Sure." Hannah shot her a strange look. "But you can just use the one at home. In Dad's study."

"Oh. Yeah." This wasn't going as planned. "Hannah … could you show me how to use the computer? Get on the Internet?" Julia pushed the words off her tongue before she swallowed them back, and endured Hannah's astonished reaction.

"Did you just ask me to show you how to use a computer?" Thankfully she didn't break into hysterical laughter.

"Yes." Julia picked a loose thread on her wool sweater and wished she'd never come in here. "I mean, I know how, I just …" The ones they'd worked on in high school didn't look anything like the sleek machines sitting on the far side of the room. "You can find out information on there, right? About events, people?"

Hannah's hazel eyes doubled in size. "You do realize what century we're living in?"

Julia's temper stirred and asked to be let out. "Hannah, are you going to help me or not?"

"Come on." Hannah led her over to one of the cubicles. "I'm sure there's a perfectly valid explanation for this, because you're so good at coming up with them, but why in the world don't you know how to use a computer?"

"Forget it." She wasn't about to stand here and play twenty questions with the sister she'd barely spoken to since she was eighteen. "I shouldn't have bothered you."

"Jules, wait." Hannah grabbed her arm, her eyes softening. "I'm sorry. Sit down."

"Are you sure?" Julia surveyed the empty room. "Wouldn't want to keep you from doing your job."

Hannah pushed Julia into a chair, pulled up another chair and flicked a button. The screen came to life almost at once. In only a few minutes, her sister gave her the briefest of tutorials. Julia listened and tried to make sense of it all, wishing she were brave enough to pull out her pad and pencil and take notes.

"And that's all there is to it, really." Hannah sat back with a smug smile. "So now you can tell me why you don't know this. Surely you must have had a computer in Atlanta? I know it's the South and all, but you're not that backward."

Julia chewed on what was left of her fingernails. "We didn't have one."

"But everyone has one."

Not kept under lock and key in a room she wasn't allowed to enter. "Not us."

"What about the kids? Didn't they need one for school?"

"Mark used the school computer when he needed to. Em's only five."

"So weird. Well, whatever." Hannah stood and waved toward a couple walking up to her desk. "Be right with you."

Julia sighed with relief as Hannah moved off. Left in peace, she tried to remember her sister's lesson, and began to explore a bit.

She'd barely seen Reid the past week. When he did show up they didn't talk much, and she was too afraid to ask him about that night at the fair again. But she wanted answers. She stared at the empty box in the Google Search engine, pointed the mouse toward it, then clicked and typed in two words.

REID WALLACE.

Chapter Thirteen

*J*ulia pulled in after dark that evening. Debby was doing the flower arrangements for a wedding on Saturday so Julia offered to help her with some last minute details. Mom agreed to watch the kids so she could stay later. The blushing bride had been more like a glowering Bridezilla, with a petulant mother in tow. Julia needed to bite her tongue on more than one occasion but Debby kept calm, somehow smoothed out every wrinkle, and the young woman left the shop with a smile.

By the time Julia pushed open the back door, she was imagining the wonderful aroma of pot roast. She slipped into the mudroom, hung up her coat and took off her boots. Her nose wasn't disappointed.

They were all in the kitchen. Julia took a moment to watch her family going about their business undetected, a habit she'd picked up since returning home. She hadn't realized how much she'd missed them until she was back here. It wasn't spying exactly.

It was healing.

Hannah set the table and Cade leaned up against the counter with a bottle of Perrier, fiddling with his phone, while her mother bustled around the stove, peering into pots and whistling whatever the hymn of the day was. *The Old Rugged Cross*, if her memory was any good.

"Dang it, Sox lost again." Cade stamped his foot on the tiled floor and sent the dogs racing around the table.

"Cade, you're not listening. I'm telling you, it was the weirdest thing." Hannah put down a knife a little too firmly. "I mean, come on, who doesn't know how to use a computer?"

"Give it a rest, Hannah." Cade sounded un-amused, like always whenever Hannah got on a tangent about something. Unfortunately, this time it sounded like she was the subject of her sister's angst.

"Well, it makes you wonder. The guy was super strange. I wouldn't be at all surprised if he had them locked up in some abandoned farmhouse the whole time she was down there. And we all know he was violent."

"Hannah, seriously!" Cade's voice rose at the same time as Julia decided to step into the room. Hannah clapped a hand over her mouth and Cade blanched. "Jules. Didn't hear you come in."

"Honey, you're home." Mom came to her and placed warm hands around her cold cheeks. She tried to hide her worried expression with a smile. "Did you have a good day?"

Julia could only nod, Hannah's horrid words reverberating in her head. And then father stood at the door to the kitchen and stared them down like he would an undecided jury.

"What's going on in here?" he demanded. "Cade, why were you yelling?"

"Because Hannah was being a moron, as usual."

"I was not!"

"Everything's fine, dear." Her mother shot Cade a look of warning and went back to dishing up. "Dinner is almost ready. Hannah, are you finished?"

Her sister mumbled something under her breath and hurried past Cade to the cupboard where the plates were kept.

As much as Julia wanted to sit down and eat and pretend nothing had happened, she couldn't. It was like somebody just turned on the lights after the power being knocked out awhile. Things needed to be said. And the smirk on her sister's face as she walked past her was all the incentive she needed.

"No, I don't think Hannah is finished, Mom. I think she's only getting started."

"Julia, I didn't mean anything by it." Hannah tried to laugh off the last few minutes like they meant nothing.

"Really, Hannah?" Julia clenched her fists, calm slipping away. "You never say anything you don't mean. Isn't that right, Cade?"

"Jules, forget it. She was being ridiculous."

"Hannah, ridiculous? Can't see it." Julia spat out a laugh. "Is that what you think, Hannah?" She faced her sister, faced her fears and knew she was at the moment of truth. "You think my life was like one of those morbid family saga novels you're always reading?"

"I don't know, Julia." Hannah mumbled. "All I know is that Frank wasn't a very nice person. And I know you landed in the hospital the night he died."

"Yes, I did. And you're right. He wasn't a nice person." Julia accepted the awkward tension that took over as they all stared at her. "He wasn't a nice person at all. But I think you all knew that. And I guess you figured there was just nothing you could do about it. So did I. So, I suppose it will please you, Hannah, to know that you're not too far off the mark."

"Julia, come on, I didn't mean …"

"No." Julia held up a hand, tears blinding. "You want the truth? Here it is. Frank Hansen was a no-good, poor excuse for a man who enjoyed his liquor and lifted his hand to me if I so much as sneezed wrong. I lived every day of the past twelve years in fear, afraid of what he would do next, afraid for my kids." She took a deep breath and tried to ignore the horror on their faces. Her mother let out a cry and clutched the cross at her neck. Her expression said this might be too much, but Julia went on.

"I wasn't allowed to do anything without his permission. I could leave the house for an hour in the morning. Long enough to drop Mark at school and get groceries if I needed to. If I didn't get back to answer the phone by the time he called, I'd pay for it that night. I was afraid to sleep when he was awake." She swiped her eyes, tightened her arms around her chest.

"He scrutinized all my friendships—anyone that might ask questions or show concern was out—so I stopped making friends. And he hated my being in contact with you. The last few years, he wouldn't let me see any of you. All those excuses I gave you every holiday about having other plans were bogus. But you probably knew that. The day Frank Hansen died was, sadly enough, the happiest day of my life." Julia took a deep breath and let it out as slowly as she could.

"So now you know. You don't have to tiptoe around the issue anymore, wondering what you can and can't say. Wondering what the truth really is. That's it. Happy now, Hannah?"

Mom was crying. Cade gave a low exhale, his eyes wet, and Hannah may as well have been facing a firing squad. Julia didn't dare look at her father.

That familiar sinking feeling slammed her and she struggled for air. Blood began to drain from her cheeks and her head started to spin.

It was something that always happened when she got over-stressed. Growing up, her classmates thought she did it on purpose. But fainting at the slightest provocation wasn't something she'd wish on anyone. Her body just shut down and there wasn't a thing she could do about it. In retrospect, it was probably the one thing that had prevented Frank from actually killing her.

"Julia, sit." Reid's low command shattered the silence.

What was he doing here?

He stood behind her father, Mark at his side. His voice pulled her back for a second, but then her vision blurred at the same moment her knees buckled.

Somehow Reid managed to get to her in time.

He and Cade got her into a chair despite her protests. How had she not noticed his car when she'd pulled in? He must have parked on the other side of the garage. If she'd known Reid was here, listening to her every word, she would never have spoken.

"Julia, I'm really sorry." Hannah hovered, wringing her hands.

"Shut up, Hannah." Cade and Reid spoke in sync and Hannah stalked out of the room.

"She's okay. Just get her some water." Mark's voice sounded far away but very much in control. "Mama, did you take your pills today?"

"What pills?" Reid asked.

Julia emerged from the fog enveloping her, met his worried eyes and decided he didn't need to know. "In my purse, Mark." Breathing was becoming impossible. The fact that Reid now knew the truth made it even more so. "Why are you here? Why are you always here?"

"Sweetheart, calm down." Her father moved Reid aside and bent a little to look at her. His face was more solemn than she'd ever seen it and made her want to cry all over again. He put a hand around her wrist and one under her chin. "You're going to pass out for sure if you don't breathe, baby."

"Daddy, you're a lawyer, not a doctor." Julia sniffed and pulled her hand from his. Reid crouched on her other side while Mark stood in front of her with a glass of water. She took it with the two pills he held, swallowed them down and tried not to notice the way Reid was watching her.

Almost as if he cared.

She concentrated on Mark instead. "Where's your sister?"

"Watching that stupid Dora show. It'd have to be an earthquake to get her off the couch when that's on." He took the glass out of her shaking hands. "You need to go lie down?"

"No, sweetheart." She stood on wobbly legs and gave a shaky sigh. "I'm just ... going to get some air. Go ahead and start dinner without me. I'm not very hungry."

"Julia, wait." Reid's hand came around her wrist, his touch warm on her cold skin.

She sucked in a breath and managed to look at him. "What?"

He didn't seem to care that Mark stood by, watching them. As she stared into those deep pools of blue, that familiar longing worked all the way through her, and they could have been the only ones in the room.

But common sense prevailed and she pulled away from his grasp. "Go home, Reid.

There's nothing you can do here."

Chapter Fourteen

Reid's flight instinct kicked in the minute Julia finished telling her story. He'd managed the feeling before. Knowing he was in an impossible situation he needed to get out of PDQ but couldn't because he had a job to do. He simply ignored fear and moved on automatic pilot.

He doubted he'd be able to do that this time.

Mark gave him a curious glance and followed his mother out of the room. Julia's dad comforted her mom. Cade sank into a chair at the kitchen table and put his head in his hands.

Reid didn't know what to do, didn't know where his place was. There wasn't anything to say. They were all processing the past few minutes in their own way. As each second passed, his desire to go check on Julia increased.

But he was the last person she wanted to see right now.

"Did all of you know what was going on down there?" He could barely speak, but he needed answers.

"We knew." Jonas filled a glass with water and drank deeply. "But I didn't need the visual." He uttered a few choice words under his breath and walked to the window, staring at the darkness, his back to them.

"I already told you, there was nothing we could do." Cade sat back with a shaky sigh. "When I asked questions she'd just brush it off. The last time I showed up to see them, the snake threatened me with a rifle if I didn't get off his property."

"My poor, poor baby." Madge moved around the kitchen with slow steps. "Those poor children." She'd aged ten years in the last ten minutes. "If only we'd known for sure, had some proof, we could have done something. Couldn't we, Jonas?" She looked to her husband for affirmation, but he shrugged.

"I tried, honey. You know that. Tried to get her to press charges. Tried to get her to leave him. She wouldn't."

Reid had done several shows about spousal abuse over the years. Done the research, the interviews, viewed the stats. More often than not, the victims stayed. As well meaning as her parents were, he doubted they could have intervened.

He grasped what little composure he had left, and accepted their answers with a curt nod. "We can't change what happened. What can we do for them now?"

Jonas swiveled, his eyes kinder. "Love them through it. Pray for them."

"What about counseling?" Reid asked. God was all well and good, but from what he'd just seen, Julia needed some professional help. Maybe her crack about seeing her psychiatrist once a week hadn't been a joke.

Jonas glanced at his wife. "She is already seeing someone, Reid. This isn't the first outburst we've experienced, although it was the most detailed. Mark is also seeing Dr. Spencer."

"Mark?" Reid's stomach heaved as he realized what Jonas was getting at. His son had not escaped life under Frank Hansen's roof unscathed.

He hadn't wanted to think about it.

Hadn't wanted to face the fact that his own son might have suffered under the hands of the man he believed to be his father. But fact stood right in front of him, fists up, daring him to challenge it.

Now he definitely needed to throw-up.

A hand slipped into his, and Reid almost hit the ceiling.

"I'm hungry." Emily stared up at him through wide innocent eyes. "Dora's done. We gonna eat now, Mister Reid?"

He raked his other hand through his hair and felt the sweat on his brow. Breathe. Think. "Uh, yeah, sweetie. Looks like it's all ready."

"Well, Emily. I was just about to call you." Julia's mother sprang into action, sent her granddaughter a smile and instructed Jonas to bring the plates to the stove where she began to dish up.

"I ... um." Reid wasn't sure whether he was wanted, didn't want to stay if he wasn't. "I think I should probably go."

"I think you should probably stay." Jonas leveled his gaze and anchored him to the spot where he stood.

"Where's Mama?" Emily tugged on his hand again.

Reid ignored the two-by-four that kept slamming into his head and swept the child up in his arms. For no good reason other than he needed to give somebody a hug. And the one she gave him back felt like a warm bath of sunshine over what had turned into a very dark day.

"Mama's got a bit of a headache," he whispered with a smile he hoped would allay her fears. "You can eat dinner with the rest of us, though. Would that be okay?"

"Uh huh. Can I sit beside you?"

"Sure can." Reid set her down on the chair with the cushion on it and lowered himself down beside her, his heart still juggling fireballs of unwanted emotion.

"Uncle Cade, sit here." Emily patted the table on her other side.

"What, hon?" Cade lifted his head, his eyes a little brighter than they should have been. Reid tried to use telepathy to tell him that this would not be a good time to lose it. Thankfully Cade clued in and moved to sit beside his niece.

Mark returned to the kitchen, sank into his seat and glanced at his grandmother. "Mama said she'd be down in a minute." The kid looked remarkably put together. "Hey, Em." He flashed a half-smile. "How was Dora?"

"Good. She went to Brazil." Emily's eyes lit up, oblivious to the sadness that smothered the room. Reid wondered how many times Mark had dealt with things a boy his age should never witness, how many times he had to be strong for his mother and sister. The thought was enough to make him want to slam his fist into the nearest wall.

Mark took a drink of water and glanced at Cade. "Should I go get Aunt Hannah?"

"No. Let her wallow." Cade's eyes still simmered with anger.

Jonas said the blessing. Slowly they began to eat. Or pick. The only one showing any real interest in food was Emily. The two dogs prowled the table waiting for leftovers. Reid forced a mouthful of pot-roast down his throat with a huge gulp of water.

"Hey." He nodded when Mark looked his way. "I'm going to take my bike out this weekend. Don't know how many more chances I'll get before snow comes. Maybe I'll talk to your Mom and see if she'll let you ride with me. What do you think?"

"I think you're nuts." Mark's grin came and went but he began to eat. "She'll never let me ride with you. Not in a million years."

"Want to bet?" Jonas entered the conversation, his eyes twinkling with unexpected humor.

"Oh, boy." Cade snorted, making a valiant effort to eat as well. "Here we go."

Jonas pointed his fork at Mark. "I'll bet you a carwash that I can get your mother to let you ride with Reid. You in?"

"Grandpa, you're crazy." Mark eyes bugged out of his head. "You'll really talk to Mama?"

"I will. But of course, if she lets you on that bike, Reid won't be able to go one lick over the speed limit."

"Well, that won't be no fun." Mark complained, still grinning.

"I drive pretty carefully, sir." Julia definitely wouldn't agree, but Reid figured he had a right to stick up for himself. Jonas' lips twitched with the hint of a smile. Reid looked across the table at Mark again. "And you'll wear a helmet."

"Of course he will," Jonas concurred. "Right, son?"

"Yessir!" Mark widened his eyes and did a little fist pump.

Reid gave a muted groan. The Judge seemed to think it was a done deal. Julia was going to have a cow. And he was going to be dead.

"Well, a bet's a bet, boy. You in or out?"

"In."

Reid tried not to laugh out loud at the way Mark's whole demeanor changed. Jonas Connelly was a smart man. Always had been. Reid's respect for him doubled right then.

"Sounds like I'm missing out on important conversation." Julia came into the kitchen and sat at the empty spot beside Mark. "Did I hear something about a bike?" The direct look she gave him made Reid suck in air.

She'd tied her hair up, accentuating her finely sculpted face and slender neck. Her cheeks were still red, her eyes a little bloodshot. Dressed in an old red and white striped rugby shirt and jeans, she could have passed for the young girl he'd married so long ago, but the face staring him down was decidedly all woman.

"Still here and still causing trouble, Mr. Wallace? Really?"

Reid's stomach flipped and his fork clattered against his plate. "Um. We were just ..."

"Talking about the weather," Mark piped up. "How it's gonna snow soon."

"Is that right?" Amusement tickled her lips and brought light back into her eyes.

"Can I ride on your bike too, Mister Reid?" Emily pulled on his arm. Mark shushed her and Reid shot a furtive glance at Julia. She was no longer amused.

Reid turned back to Emily, put a finger to his lips and leaned in close. "No, you can't ride on my bike, sweetheart," he whispered. "But we could go for ice cream. In the car."

"Excuse me?" Julia cleared her throat but Reid figured at this point it was best to pretend she wasn't listening.

"Okay. Buts I only like strawberries." Emily took a drink of milk, a white moustache covering her upper lip when she smiled back at him.

Reid winked and gently wiped her face with the tip of his napkin. "Strawberry it is, princess. Chocolate's my favorite."

Mark let out a groan of appreciation. "Mine too."

"You don't say." Cade leaned forward and sent Reid a look of mock astonishment. Reid ignored him too.

Fortunately, Julia didn't press the matter and they passed the rest of the meal without having to talk to each other.

"So how come you're not on TV anymore?" Mark was done eating. He pushed his plate away and focused on Reid.

His son definitely had a knack for asking hard questions.

"Mark. That's not polite." Julia stabbed at her mashed potatoes and moved them around her plate, but he saw a glimmer of curiosity in her eyes.

"Why can't I ask?" Mark lifted his chin, defiance dancing around him. "Everyone at school thinks he got blowed up or somethin'. But you don't look hurt to me. Did you get blowed up?" The intense expression on Mark's face, so much like his own, was enough to put him under the table.

"No. Not exactly." Reid scratched his jaw and registered the rapid rate at which his pulse rose. He couldn't talk about it. Could barely talk about it with Cade, and he'd been there. Somehow he put a lid on his emotions and managed a smile. "It's kind of a long story. Let's just say it was time for me to move on."

Mark folded his arms, clearly not buying it. "You got fired?"

Reid sputtered into his water glass. "No, I did not get fired."

"So you don't want to be on TV no more?"

"I don't know, Mark. I don't know if I want to be on TV *anymore.*" Somebody needed to give the kid a lesson in grammar. Reid adjusted the collar of his shirt, heat prickling his neck. "Maybe I'll go back one day. Just not right now."

"Okay, Mark, if you're done, you can help clear." Julia gave him a pointed look that went ignored.

Mark shrugged. "My dad thought you sucked. Whenever you were on, he'd holler at us all to come watch. Even if my mom was busy doing something, he made her come watch you. He'd throw empty beer cans at the television and call you bad names."

"Mark!" Julia stared at her son through wide eyes, her expression a toss up between horror and mortification.

Silence ruled the room for a few uncomfortable moments. Reid's unrequited anger turned into a dragon, shooting flames and clawing its way to the surface. He sank his teeth into his bottom lip and clenched his hands under the table.

Cade reached around Emily and placed a hand on Reid's shoulder, sending a silent message. *Don't blow.*

But he'd never come so close.

He wanted to yell or cry or hit something, and he wasn't sure which reaction would win.

"Maybe I shouldn't have told you that." Mark's face got red. "I always thought you were good. I thought it was cool the way you went all those places where people were fighting."

"Thanks, bud." Reid's anger deflated like a popped balloon. It wasn't the kid's fault. None of this was Mark's fault. Or Julia's.

"I'm sorry. I can't ..." Julia was on her feet and out of the room before he could say a word.

Cade let out a groan and Julia's parents exchanged a worried look.

"Great. Shoulda kept my big mouth shut." Mark pushed his fingers through his hair and said a word nobody scolded him for.

"Hey." Reid got Mark's attention and forced himself to meet the boy's startled gaze. "You didn't do anything wrong. Okay?"

Mark only blinked, tears shining in his eyes.

That automatic pilot kicked in again and Reid pushed his chair back. "Would you all excuse me?"

He heard the back door slam and went that way.

Chapter Fifteen

He found Julia at the far end of the porch, staring out at the darkened fields. A few stars dotted the night sky and a horse whinnied somewhere off in the distance. It was so quiet he could hear her labored breathing and the sob she was doing her best to stuff down.

Reid grabbed an afghan from the two-seater swing and gently placed it around her trembling shoulders. She turned to face him, her cheeks shimmering under the soft glow of the porch light.

"Why can't you just leave me alone?"

"Because you shouldn't be alone right now." He gripped the soft wool, tightened the blanket around her, drew her closer and waited for her to resist. As expected, she pulled back a bit, and Reid arched an eyebrow. "Would you stop fighting me for one minute? Please? Just let me hold you."

Julia lowered her eyes, wet lashes touching her cheeks. Finally she sank against him and began to cry. Reid granted his own emotions freedom as he put his arms around her, blinked moisture and held tight.

He couldn't tell her it would all work out. Couldn't tell her everything would be okay. He could barely get his own trembling under control. But there was one thing he needed to know.

"Why did you marry him?" The question, whittling away in the confines of his brain for weeks, finally escaped. He'd wanted to ask it since that day at the cabin, just never found the nerve.

She stared in surprise, wiped her eyes and shrugged. "Frank was everything you weren't. He was older, had a steady job, he made a good living. When we first met he was charming and kind. Made me feel special. I don't know. I was vulnerable, young and scared and all out of options. He offered me security. Offered me a new start, offered to be a father to my child. He promised me the world, and I was stupid enough to believe him."

Her breath hitched and cracked on another sob. "I made so many mistakes. Put the kids through so much. The minute I think we've finally moved on, finally started to heal, something like tonight happens, and the pain starts all over again."

Reid pulled her against him, listened to her anguish and wondered if God heard it too.

Wondered where God had been the last twelve years.

And where He was now.

"Don't blame yourself, Jules. If you want to blame anyone, blame me."

She lifted her gaze, confusion streaking through her eyes. "This has nothing to do with you."

He shrugged, tried to find a way to voice the thoughts that had been dogging him for days. "If you hadn't run off and married me, if I hadn't left you ... don't you see?"

"No." She gave her head a firm shake. "Don't make my problems yours, Reid."

She didn't see. Didn't understand at all.

"Do you remember the night I came for you? The night we left?" Reid's throat hurt with the effort it took to get the words out. Julia nodded, her reply muffled against his sweater. "What did I say, Jules? What did I tell you?" He moved a few strands of hair off her wet cheeks with his fingers and watched shadows of the past drift by.

Julia stepped away from him and leaned against the porch railing. "You said, no guarantees. You said, as much as you loved me, you couldn't plan the future. Couldn't say where we'd be a year from now. And if that wasn't enough for me, then I shouldn't go with you."

"Yes." The weight of it sent his heart crashing to his feet. "I had no right to do that to you, Julia. I put you in an impossible position. I knew you would come with me. I wanted to be at college, wanted to start the next phase of my life, but I didn't know how to live without you." A ragged sigh caught in his throat. "And then I didn't know how to live with you. I wasn't anywhere near ready to be a husband, ready for that kind of lifelong commitment. I wanted to make it work, I just didn't know how."

"Neither did I," she admitted. "I didn't know how to be a wife. How to cook or clean … we were both so young."

"And maybe a little stupid." He exhaled with a muted laugh. "Did you ever learn to cook?"

"I did." Her eyes were still wet, but a smile lifted her lips. "Did you ever learn to do your own laundry?"

Reid laughed and closed the gap between them. "Not well," he confessed. He fought the urge to pull her to him again and folded his arms across his chest instead. "Jules, I'm trying to say I'm sorry. And I'm trying to figure out how we go on from here too."

"Like you said, we just do." She shrugged, then smiled. "You seem to be a hit with the kids."

Changing the subject was a good idea. But he wasn't sure what the right response was. "I admit to being a little smitten with your daughter."

Julia's eyes brightened. "You've got the touch with Em. She's attached herself to you like Velcro."

He grinned. "She reminds me of Rachel."

"Your sister."

The shriek of a night owl pierced the air. Reid nodded, battled emotion and watched the moon disappear behind some clouds. "Rach was Emily's age when she died." The old wound, never fully healed, opened again. He hadn't talked about it for years. And the last person he'd shared the story with was Julia. "She was all curls and freckles, just like Em. All I really remember is her goofy grin, how she would never leave me alone, and how she drove me nuts with stupid knock-knock jokes."

"I remember the pictures you had." A sad smile crossed her lips.

"I wish I'd been a better brother." He put his back to her. "Wish I'd been a better husband to you. Maybe if I had been …"

"No. None of this is your fault, Reid. Not really. Yes, you left me, yes, I was angry and maybe I still am a little. But when I said I wanted us to be friends, I meant it."

"I know what you said." He found a smile. "I'm still waiting for you to change your mind."

"I won't change my mind. Well, unless you bail on me again. And trust me, if you do, this time I will come hunt you down."

"I don't doubt it."

A bit of the past disappeared into the dark night. Reid studied her face, drawn to her the way he'd always been. Tried to fight off feelings that wouldn't back down, no matter how much he told himself they weren't real.

Right then it didn't matter whether they were or not.

He stepped a little closer, cupped her cheeks. Ran his fingers through her hair and gave in to the overwhelming pull he'd been ignoring since seeing her again. He brushed the base of his thumbs over her cheeks. Wanted to kiss her so bad it was killing him.

"Reid." Her voice was husky, trembling just a bit.

"Yeah." He rested his forehead against hers and inhaled the perfume she always wore. The fragrance he'd spent hours searching for, finally found and given to her on her sixteenth birthday. The scent that turned his head and jacked his pulse whenever another woman walked by wearing it.

Julia placed her hands on his chest and pushed him, gently but quite firmly, away. "Back off."

Reid retreated in a hurry and ran a hand over his face. "I'm sorry. I didn't … I wasn't thinking straight." No duh, Sherlock.

He knew better. Knew she wasn't ready for any physical attachment. With him or anyone. He counted himself lucky she hadn't slapped him. But she was so vulnerable, so sad, and so beautiful. He'd spent years trying to forget that face. Or conjure it up in somebody else's.

It was too easy to remember those first few nights after he'd slipped that ring on her finger and they'd moved into the small apartment he could barely breathe in. As the sun went down and he took her in his arms, nothing else mattered. She completed him. He'd never felt so happy, so alive.

And so scared out of his mind.

"I guess it wasn't all bad, was it?" Julia asked. "What we had." She read his thoughts the way she always could.

Reid smiled a little too. "No. Most of it was good, Jules. Really good."

Her eyes held more questions than he had answers for. And maybe still told him just how much he meant to her, how much she depended on him.

No. That was an illusion, a mirage in the middle of the desert. He was only seeing what he wanted to see. And the fact that he wanted to see it scared him more than he was willing to admit.

"I know what you're thinking." She lowered herself onto the swing and pushed off.

"I hope you don't." He leaned back against the railing and put his game face on.

Julia rolled her eyes, then grew serious. "You want to know why I stayed. With Frank, why I put up with it." She stopped the swing with her feet and looked up at him. Her hair framed her face like a halo in the golden light above them, her brown eyes still shimmering.

"Why did you?" He shoved his hands in his back pockets, not sure he really wanted to know. Her answer would only pile another block onto his wall of guilt. But he resigned himself to it and waited for her to speak again.

"I stayed because I didn't think I had a choice. I tried to leave once. That little adventure landed me in hospital and Frank took the kids to his mother's. She drank more than he did."

"Why didn't you press charges?" He could figure out why just by looking at her. "Julia, did he ever ..." Reid balled his hands, unable to say more.

He had to know. Had to ask the question. But the words wouldn't come.

That she'd been hurt, physically and emotionally, was enough of a nightmare. But if he'd hurt those kids ...

Julia put her head in her hands. After a few moments she breathed deep, and shook her head. "He never touched Emily. Crazy as he was, he loved her and spoiled her rotten."

"And Mark?"

"Not so much. As he got older, Frank really resented the fact that Mark wasn't his. They were total opposites. Mark could never do anything right. Frank was always too hard on him. Always coming down on him, telling him he'd never amount to anything. He went after Mark once a few years ago, when he started getting mouthy and sticking up for me. I threatened Frank with a knife that night, and he didn't do it again. But there was always that unspoken threat between us. I knew—if I tried to leave him or tell anyone—Mark was collateral."

Reid uttered a low curse, put his back to her and curled his hands tight over the railing. Every sinew stiffened as he processed that picture.

A mother defending her son.

To the death, if it came to it.

His son.

Life as he knew it disintegrated and scattered at his feet like the pages of an ancient book handled improperly. Everything he'd worked so hard for, clawed his way to the top for, it all meant absolutely nothing.

All the fame and money in the world suddenly turned to dust.

He'd betrayed those who needed him most. Turned away from God's plan for him.

It took one finite moment to realize it.

It would take years to get over it.

Years to make up for the damage he had done.

"Reid." Julia's light touch on his back sent him reeling again. "Do you see now why I couldn't contact you? Why I begged Cade not to tell you? Frank threatened Mark's life more than once. I knew if I got hold of you, if you knew ..." A sad sigh slid out of her. "I believed that either Frank would kill him or you'd do everything in your power to take Mark away. And even though I knew that would be best, for Mark to be safe, selfishly I couldn't take that chance. I didn't want to lose him. I needed him. I wasn't willing to give up the one good thing that came of our time together."

Reid nodded, not bothering to wipe away the tears that wet his cheeks. If he'd known they were in danger, he would have stepped in. Would have rescued them. At least he hoped he would have. "I don't suppose it occurred to you that I would have been concerned for you as well?"

"Honestly?" She raised a brow with a bland expression. "The way things ended between us, I didn't think you would be."

His stomach churned with a familiar dread.

The same feeling he'd had at fourteen, that day he'd stayed home while the rest of his family went out to enjoy the warm summer day. As the hours wore on, he wondered just how long they were going to stay away. As it got closer to dinnertime, he got a little jumpy. His heart pounded harder than ever when the sun went down. And then he heard the sirens in the distance.

Somehow he had known.

When the two men in uniform began to walk toward him, he knew what was coming. Knew what they were going to say before they said it, and knew that his whole life was about to change.

"How did your husband die?" He swiveled to face her, put his hands on her arms and braced himself. "Julia, did you …"

Fresh tears formed in her frightened eyes. "I thought he was going to kill Mark." She wore that same anguished expression he'd seen on the faces of his friends and neighbors the days after his parents and sister's funeral.

"Julia, what happened?"

She stared at him for a long silent moment. "I can't talk about it. Not right now."

He hesitated, then sighed. "Okay." He wouldn't push it.

"Believe it or not, Reid, I'm actually really glad you're here." She stood close again, another smile trembling on her lips. And then she slipped her arms around his waist.

As he felt her lean against his chest again and tighten her arms in an embrace he wasn't expecting or prepared for, he knew one thing for certain.

This whole *'let's just be friends'* thing was not going to work for him.

Chapter Sixteen

"You can't work at a florist shop the rest of your life." Cade slurped the remainder of his Coke and studied Julia from across the table, completely serious. His blond hair curled around his face, his dimple disappearing when she didn't give him the *'Omigosh, Cade, you're so right!'* response he was looking for.

"You need a haircut."

Her brother narrowed his eyes. "My hair is fine, thank you. Let's talk about your future."

"I'd rather talk about that scruff on your chin. You know Deb hates it, right?" Julia poured dressing over her salad and glanced around the new restaurant. The freshly painted brick red walls combined with the yellow trim around the windows and colorful artwork made the café a fun place to sit for a few hours. She didn't work Saturdays, and Cade insisted he had nothing better to do than take her out for lunch. Her parents were home with the kids, and Julia had been enjoying herself. Until two minutes ago. "Thanksgiving is three weeks away. You should shave before then."

"Deb's fine with my scruff. What she's not fine with is you wasting your time working for her. And neither am I."

"I knew you didn't just want to have lunch with me." She could see right through him. Always had. A knack she'd mastered at six years old, when he'd stolen a cookie from her plate, eaten it and told her the dog had grabbed it when she wasn't looking. "We're not kids anymore, Cade. You can't sit there and lecture me about my life. I'm perfectly capable of making my own decisions."

"And you've made some doozies." He raised a brow and dared her to deny it.

"Not nice." She stuck her tongue out and pushed her shoulders back. "At least I have a job. And I'm working for your girlfriend. Are you telling her she shouldn't work in a florist shop the rest of her life?"

"No. 'In Bloom' is Debby's dream. And she's good at what she does. You're not."

"I resent that." Julia tried to look annoyed, but laughter crept up her throat. "I just don't have the same touch as Deb." The few arrangements she'd attempted on her own were pretty hideous. Emily could do a better job. And she kept forgetting to refill the tubs with water. Debby delegated her to the front desk, taking orders and answering the phone. "I can't help it if I keep killing off the inventory."

"Well, we know you didn't inherit Mom's green thumb, that's for sure. What about your writing?" Cade bit into his turkey panini, mustard dripping down his chin.

"What about it?" She wished he'd quit yammering so she could just eat. The arugula salad with goat cheese, cranberries, beets, and candied walnuts was the best she'd had in a long time. "I haven't written anything in years."

"I thought you wanted to be a writer."

"I wanted to be a lot of things." Working for Deb was better than not working at all. The money wasn't much, but it was enough to feel she could at least contribute to groceries and buy the kids things they needed. The sale of Frank's house was still tied up in litigation.

She broke a crusty roll in half and dipped the bread in a plate of spicy olive oil. "What are you getting at anyway?"

Their waitress wiggled over to give Cade a refill and he waited until she was done before he answered. "I'm going to be doing a bit of freelancing. A friend in Burlington runs a magazine, one of those town and country type things. *Vermont - Yesterday and Today*, I think it's called. Anyway, she wants to do a piece on covered bridges. I suggested you could write it."

"I could what?" Julia choked on water and sat back, staring at him in horror. "Have you lost your mind?"

"Jules. Give it a shot. What have you got to lose?"

"Cade." She wanted to hammer him on the head and hug him at the same time.

Writing had been her passion. And she'd been pretty good. Editor of the school newspaper. Then yearbook editor. She'd even written a play in high school that the drama department put on and received rave reviews. But that was years ago.

"No." She shook her head, fear squashing hope. She hadn't unpacked all the journals and notebooks she'd secretly stashed away over the years, out of sight and harm's way. "I haven't written anything in forever. I don't know if I can."

Her brother eyed her with a long look that said he knew better. "I have to let her know in a few days. Write up a few pages, anything will do. I'll send it to her and she'll let you know if you can have the job."

"I don't think so." She looked down at her plate.

"Hey." Cade put his hand over hers.

Julia raised her eyes. Cade leaned forward a little, a smile lifting the corner of his mouth. "Do it, Jules. Don't listen to that voice inside your head trying to talk you out of it. Do it because you want to. Do it because you can."

Julia squeezed her brother's hand. "Thanks, Cade."

He shot her a wink and dug into his food again. "Talked to Reid lately?"

"No, not really." It had been two weeks since that awful night. Reid had shown up a few times, wanting to borrow this or that from her father's tool shed. Some nights he'd stay for dinner, but most times he'd head on back up the hill. Since their last conversation, she sensed he was keeping his distance. Probably trying to process it all, just as she still was almost a year later.

"He asked about the night Frank died, but I couldn't tell him. I suppose it's driving him crazy not knowing the whole story."

Understanding settled in and Cade gave a slow nod. "That explains why he's looked ready to slug someone the last couple of weeks."

"We used to talk about everything. But this ..."

"He's Mark's father. He needs to know. Are you going to tell him the truth?"

The lump in her throat crowded out conversation for a moment. "It's so hard, Cade. Like we need to tiptoe around each other, always afraid of saying the wrong thing. And part of me can't help feeling I'm going to wake up one day and he'll be gone."

"I don't think that's going to happen, Jules. Reid's pretty convinced he's got nothing to go back to." Cade ordered a coffee for himself and a tea for her.

Julia waited until the waitress was done, making up her mind as she spoke. "I'm going to tell Mark soon."

"Good. Reid will be happy." Cade fiddled with his watch. "He hasn't told you much either, has he?"

Julia stiffened, shook her head. "About why he's back here? No."

Cade averted his gaze, his fingers taking up a more insistent beat. "It's not something he likes talking about."

"I goggled him." The admission brought heat to her cheeks but she enjoyed his astonishment.

"You what?" Cade hollered, making people stare at them.

"Oh, whatever it's called. I got on the Internet and looked him up. The three biggest rumors seem to be that he got fired, he's got cancer or that he's dead. The news articles said that the deaths of his two crewmen in Syria were his fault. That he acted on his own accord and the network had no choice but to fire him."

"Don't believe everything you read, Jules."

"So he really didn't get fired?"

"No. He took a leave of absence, but I think in his head, he's already quit."

Julia knew by Cade's expression that the subject was closed. "You won't tell me what really happened, will you?"

"I've said enough already. If you want to know that badly, ask him."

"Maybe I will." Julia sat in silence, letting her tea cool. "How is he getting on with the repairs up there?"

Cade lifted his eyes to the ceiling. "At least the roof doesn't leak any-more. Between you and me, I'm about to tell him to give it up and hire a few professionals. Not like he can't afford it. He's going to fall off a ladder and break his neck one of these days."

"I hope not." Panic popped into her words and Julia studied her salad. "Interesting."

When she looked up again, Cade was grinning. "Oh, don't even." She held up a hand and gave him her best glare.

He tipped his head. "I didn't say a word."

"No, and you're not going to."

"Julia."

"Cade." She wanted to stare him down but a smile slid across her face before she could stop it.

The memory of that night on the porch stayed close at hand. When she'd allowed Reid to hold her, it was almost easy to forget the horrors she'd endured with Frank. Even easy to forget the pain Reid put her through by leaving.

She knew he hadn't intended to kiss her, not really. But part of her desperately wanted him to. The other part was terrified he would. And she'd been somewhat disappointed when he hadn't.

Her brother let out a victory whoop and smacked the table. People looked over at them. "I knew it. You still have feelings for him, don't you?"

"I do not." She moved her plate aside, her appetite waning fast. "I mean, not those kinds of feelings." Definitely not those kinds of feelings.

It sounded good in theory.

Light jazz filtered through overhead speakers and Cade tapped along while he waited for her to speak.

"We were married. He's the father of my son. We can be friends. But that's it. I don't intend to enter into another relationship for a long time. Maybe not ever. Do not get any ideas and stop talking to Debby about this."

"You think he's pretty hot, huh?" Cade didn't know when to let go.

Julia sat on her hands to keep herself from swatting him over the head. "I think you're extremely childish and you need to finish your lunch."

"He thinks you're pretty hot." Cade smirked and took a huge bite, choking on his laughter.

"Would you hush? You're making a spectacle of yourself." She twisted her napkin and tried to ignore the fact that her heart rate had just tripled. "Did he say that?"

"Wouldn't you like to know?"

"Cade, you're a beast." Julia shook her fist, laughing.

"Oh, come on, Jules. Don't you believe in second chances?"

"Are you kidding?" Second chances were good in romance novels and movies. She wasn't all that sure they worked in real life. "Not where Reid Wallace is concerned. He burned all his bridges with me a long time ago."

Cade tapped his spoon against the rim of his cup. "Bridges can be built again, Jules. Rebuilt stronger, made to last this time."

Julia smiled at their server as she began to clear the plates. "That's very poetic, Cade. You should write that down." He was impossible, but she'd missed him. Missed him more than she could say.

"So, when are you going to tell Mark the truth?"

"Cade, stop. I'll figure it out on my own, okay?"

"How's he doing?"

"As well as can be expected, I suppose. He still has nightmares. So does Em." So did she, but he didn't need to know that. "Dr. Spencer thinks we made the right decision to wait. Thinks he'll be able to handle it better now, since he's spent more time with Reid. I know it's not what Reid wanted, but like I told him, I have to do what's best for Mark."

"Okay." Cade put his hands behind his head and nodded. "But Jules?"

"What?"

"Just make sure you do what's best for you too."

They managed to enjoy the rest of the meal without further mention of Reid Wallace. While they walked to Cade's car afterward, Julia took note of things she never had, despite growing up here. The town square, a mini-park really, boasted a new children's play area, bordered by maples, a few red leaves still clinging to their branches. Most had fallen and children raced through the golden piles with glee. Some new shops caught her eye, and she promised to make some time to check them out. Familiar faces waved as they walked by.

The sun chased away the November chill, hit her cheeks and coaxed a smile.

Cade jangled his keys. "What are you grinning at, Jules?"

Julia stopped walking, made a half turn and hugged herself. "I never realized how beautiful it is. We took so much for granted growing up here." She pushed her hands into the pockets of her jeans and watched children take turns down the slide. "I used to dream of getting out of here. Then all I dreamt about was coming back."

He smiled and drew a deep breath. "I'm glad you're back, Jules. Glad we're both back." Her brother pulled her against him in an impulsive hug. Right there on the street for everyone to see. Cade Connelly, the man who kept his feelings to himself for the most part. Times had changed indeed.

The hum of a motorcycle engine behind them widened Cade's grin. "Guess who?"

"Do I have to?"

Reid pulled up beside them, flipped up his visor and revealed a broad smile that made Julia want to hightail it in the opposite direction. "Hey guys, what's up?"

"Just had lunch." Cade glanced at his watch and pulled on his shades. "I was going to drop Jules home, but I have some errands to run. Are you heading back that way?"

"Cade. No." Panic pressed against her throat as Julia caught the glint in Reid's eyes. "I don't mind waiting. Go run your errands. I'll just poke around the shops."

Low laughter came from the direction of the motorcycle. "What's the matter, Jules? Afraid of a little bike ride? You used to love riding on this thing. Where's your sense of adventure?"

"I used it up the night I left town with you."

"Is that so?" Reid pulled off his helmet, dismounted and retrieved a spare helmet. He walked around the bike and stood in front of her, his eyes filled with challenge. "I don't believe you."

Cade gave her a nudge. "You know I could just make this real easy and scram."

"And I would kill you." Julia glared at both of them. She stared at the bike and shoved down that odd tingling feeling—the one she knew so well—the one that pulled her into every lick of trouble she'd ever landed in. The tug was still strong. Still as tempting as ever.

"Oh, she's caving." Cade and Reid smacked palms.

"Come on, Jules. What've you got to lose?" Reid still knew how to be persistent.

She lifted an eyebrow. "The way you drive?"

"I'll let you drive if you want."

"Uh, no." But she stepped a little closer to the bike.

Whether it was the heat of the sun, the depth of her brother's smile or the daring look on Reid's face, the look that said some chances are worth taking, something made her give in. Maybe she was just tired of trying to push him away.

Julia wasn't sure what possessed her in the end, but she took the helmet from him, put it on and found herself astride his Harley a few moments later, arms wrapped tight around his waist.

Chapter Seventeen

The familiar music of the old bike's engine soothed her, but the scent of leather, spicy cologne and fresh mountain air assaulted her and common sense threatened to abandon ship altogether.

If it hadn't already.

Because the last place Julia ever intended to be again was on the back of Reid Wallace's Harley.

Enjoying herself.

She took in the views as they coasted around the mountain roads, zipped past lush green pine forests, raced the river and slowed down through old covered bridges. Reid was going the long way. She realized it after they missed the turn to the road that would take them home.

He wasn't taking her home at all.

The further up the mountain they rode, the more beautiful their surroundings became. When he shifted gears and hooked to the left, she knew exactly where they were.

The Lookout.

Reid pulled to a stop, cut the engine and Julia hopped off. She removed the heavy helmet, put it on the bike and fairly skipped across the gravel parking lot to the round walled-in area that provided an expansive view of the whole of Bridgewater and beyond.

"Oh, look at it!" Julia pulled cool air into her lungs and let her breath out on a smile.

A perfect pale blue sky dotted with puffy clouds presided over the picturesque scene. Beyond the crest of the mountain range she could see the entire town—the large white water tower, small clapboard houses, sprawling farms and fields of varying size spread out for miles, the land divided by a rushing river—and the church spire presided over all.

Reid planted himself a few feet away, leaned over the ledge and looked down. "Best view in the world."

He would know.

"It is. Thanks for bringing me up here, Reid. I needed this." She folded her arms and basked in the pleasure of simply being free. Free enough to enjoy the moment and not worry about what came next.

"Been a long time since I saw anything this beautiful." He sounded so serious that she turned around.

And found him staring straight at her.

Her traitorous cheeks heated to a color she was sure could compete with the red leaves on the ground by her feet. "For a journalist, you sure have a lot of lame lines."

"Best I can do without the teleprompter."

She tossed his smile back to him. "It was always so peaceful up here. I'd almost forgotten."

"Yeah." He threw a small pebble over the wall and released a sigh rich with regret. "Being back here reminds me of a lot of things I'd forgotten."

Julia tipped her face to the sky and closed her eyes. The sun warmed her. A cooling breeze trailed through her hair and her heart finally felt at peace. Almost. Because he'd stepped a little closer, making her afraid to open her eyes.

"Julia." His light touch on her arm forced her to move. Forced her to settle her gaze on him and try not to see things she didn't want to. How his eyes sparkled in the afternoon sun, how his dark hair had grown longer. How his dimple came and went as he flashed a smile that didn't last long enough. "Are you cold?"

"No." She shook her head, saw the questions in his eyes and knew why she was here. "We can stay." She moved across the area and sat on the wooden bench. "You want to know the whole story. What happened the day Frank died."

Reid perched on the far end of the bench. "Yes." He let out his breath and leaned over his knees. Then he looked her way. "Tell me." He pushed fingers through his hair and cleared his throat. "Tell me what happened that day. All of it."

Julia drew her knees to her chest and locked her trembling hands around them. And then she began to talk.

Somehow she could relive that night now without horror. Without terror.

But not without pain.

Or regret.

She was laid bare under his penetrating gaze as she relayed the story. "The next thing I knew, Frank had a gun to my head. He collected pistols. They were all over the house and I hated them. Mark came in, saw what was going on and jumped him. I tried to get Mark to stop, but he was so angry. It was like he'd snapped too. Frank wasn't steady on his feet, but he was strong. He sent Mark flying. I'm not sure what he would have done next, but I didn't get to find out because the gun went off."

"So it was an accident." Reid's voice shook and he pressed his thumb and forefinger to the corners of his eyes.

"I'd probably be in jail if it were anything other than that. Mark was horrified. Screamed louder than anything and ran straight for the phone. But Frank was dead. I don't remember much after that. Just waking up in hospital."

At first she'd been numb. Not able to think about it at all. She relived that moment where her life hung in the balance every night in her dreams. But as each month passed, the dreams became less intense, and she was slowly beginning to believe they were safe.

"Were the police involved?"

"Of course. My parents flew down right away. Police, social services, we weren't left alone for weeks. They ruled Frank's death as accidental, things wrapped up in March, and we were allowed to leave Atlanta."

Reid slid down the bench beside her, put an arm around her and held tight. "Thank you," he whispered. "I know that wasn't easy. And as hard as it was to hear, I needed to know."

She nodded, sat up and fiddled with the button on the sleeve of her jacket. "The kids are doing much better since we came here. I don't think Em saw any of it. She hardly talks about Frank now. Mark is still moody, still has trouble sleeping, but he … I think he'll be okay, you know? At least I hope he will." Her throat clogged. The truth was, she was terrified he wouldn't be. Terrified that none of them would walk away unscathed, terrified that her children would carry those scars for the rest of their lives.

A tidal wave of fear crashed over her and took away all confidence. Just when she thought she was in control, her emotions contradicted her. She swiped at her eyes and gave a feeble laugh. "I'd really like to get through one day without falling apart."

He didn't say anything. Just inched closer and put both arms around her this time. Somehow she forced her body to relax. To remember that this was Reid. No matter what he'd put her through in the past, he was still incapable of hurting her like Frank had.

But being in his arms was asking for trouble. They'd already proven that.

Julia pushed off the bench and walked the area again, taking in the view she would never tire of. After a while, he walked to where she stood.

"Hey." Reid put his hands on her shoulders and moved her around to face him. Put a finger under her chin and tipped her face upward to meet his eyes. "When are you going to stop running from me?"

"Is that what I'm doing?"

The sun's rays danced with the blue flecks in his eyes as he ran a finger down her nose. "Pretty much sprinting in the opposite direction when you see me coming."

"I'm sorry." She didn't know how to tell him what she needed to. "You scare me, Reid."

Concern and confusion marred his face. "How do I scare you?"

Julia shrugged. "You remind me of too many things. What it was like to be happy. What it was like to love. I don't know what to do with that. Because part of me thinks I'll never feel that way again."

"You will, Jules." He sounded like he meant it. Believed it. "You're too young, too beautiful to spend the rest of your life alone. You'll heal, in time, and then some lucky cowboy will come along and sweep you off your feet again."

"If you say so." Julia studied his face and wondered at the regret she saw there. Maybe he believed she would find love again, but it was clear he didn't count himself as a candidate. Which was just as well.

Reid cleared his throat. "Can I ask you something?" A cloud crossed the sun's path and cast them into shadow.

"You probably will anyway." She watched his smile come and go.

"Did you love him?" Questions hovered in his eyes. "I suppose you must have at the beginning. And you had Em, right? So ..."

"No." Julia tasted her tears and blinked them back. "No."

"No? Not at all?"

Julia shrugged. As she stared at Reid, it was impossible not to feel ... something. She'd loved him so long. Then hated him. Then just missed him.

She let her finger trail across his cheek, wiping away the wetness she found there. The stubble beneath her fingers stirred up sensations she wasn't ready for. She pulled her hand away.

"I was infatuated with him, maybe. When Frank and I first met, he certainly seemed to be the perfect gentleman. Emily was a gift, no doubt, but she wasn't conceived with my consent."

"What?" Anger inched into his eyes. "Julia."

She shrugged, not caring now. "Frank forced himself on me more times than I can count. At the end I hated him too much to love him. Maybe I thought I loved him, at the beginning. But ..." To go on required too much effort. Too much risk.

"But?"

He would pull the truth from her eventually.

If not today, somewhere down the road in another moment like this, when all the years and pain and loss were stripped away.

"Loving anyone after you just didn't make sense. How could I?"

His frown convinced her he didn't quite believe it. "Even after everything I did?"

"Old habits die hard."

She smiled as he pulled her closer and placed his lips on her forehead. "That they do."

The cry of an eagle startled them, and before Julia could take her next breath the majestic bird flew by in a flurry of wings on the wind.

"Whoa." Reid's laughter floated through her, filling her with unexpected joy. "We could have touched him."

"Almost." The eagle circled the scene below, let out another cry and then flew off, up into the clouds and out of sight. A reminder that sometimes even the most beautiful things remain out of reach.

Like what she and Reid had.

They could never get that back. It was stupid to think they could, to think that he would want to. But her heart was reacting to him in ways she didn't understand, tugging her back to when things were simple and safe. Making her want things that lay in the land of the impossible.

Julia moved out of the shelter of his arms and stared up at the sky. "I wonder what she's trying to tell us."

"Who?"

His confusion coerced a laugh. "Esmé." She held up her hands to the wind. "Don't you remember? She always joked that if there wasn't enough room in Heaven, she'd like to come back to earth as an eagle. To soar through the clouds and above the mountains, keep an eye on everyone without any of us knowing she was watching."

Reid's eyes misted over again. He didn't veer his gaze, but let her witness the grief he still grappled with. "Yeah. Something else I'd forgotten." He sniffed and lowered his head. "Now look who's falling apart." His lopsided grin created a lump in her throat she couldn't push down.

"You miss her, don't you?"

He released a low sigh and shrugged. "More now that I'm back here. She was all the family I had."

Julia nodded. "I'd like to think if that was Esmé checking up on us, she'd be glad to see we're finally trying to make sense of the mess we made of our lives."

If he tried not to look startled, he failed.

Reid took her hands and moved her away from the edge of the wall. Then he pulled one hand free and ran his fingers down the side of her face. "Are we?"

"I don't know. I hope so." She could barely breathe with him so close. Julia stepped backward and broke the spell his eyes held her under. "Esmé must have been very proud of you."

His smile faded too soon. "In a way, she was. But I disappointed her. You weren't the only one I let down the day I left." He walked to the wall, rested his hands on the rounded stones, his back to her.

As much as she'd tried to avoid this moment, there was no way to go on without getting through it. If they hoped to move out of the past and begin again, she needed closure.

"Why did you leave me?" The question left to rattle around her brain for years, finally spoken, incited a surge of relief that took her breath away.

His too.

Reid jerked his head around, his face ashen. "What?"

Surely he'd been expecting it at some point. But his pained look told her he hadn't. Not today at least.

She made her feet move until she stood before him, crossed her arms and lifted her chin. "I want to know why you left. What did I do? Why didn't you want me anymore?" The young girl, abandoned at eighteen, stepped out from behind the shadows, kicked aside logic and demanded answers.

Reid's reply was slow in coming. "It wasn't like that." There was such intensity in those words, in his voice, that he commandeered her full attention. "It wasn't anything you did or didn't do. It was all me. I woke up one day scared out of my mind." He rocked back on his heels, a defeated shrug lifting his shoulders. "I lost my parents when I was fourteen. My grandfather had already passed away when I moved here. I didn't really know what marriage looked like. I think I was just afraid of being alone. I wanted to be with you, but I never thought it through. Being responsible for another person. That terrified me. I didn't want to be responsible for you. For making sure you had all you needed. For giving you the life you deserved. I didn't think I had it in me. I knew I would screw it up somehow, and I didn't want to watch what we had come crashing down around us."

"But it did, Reid." The memories roared back, sucked all life from her. "The moment you walked out that door, my world ended."

"I know." He brought his lips to her forehead, his fingers threading through her hair, drifting down her back. "Mine did too."

"No." Julia shook her head. "You moved on. You created a world I wasn't a part of. You became somebody."

"Maybe it looked that way." He traced the curve of her cheek and gave a thin smile. "But I thought about you every day. Thought about what a mistake I'd made. Wondered if I could ever go back and fix it."

"You didn't try."

"I thought you were better off without me. I thought you were happy."

"I wasn't." Her whisper hung in the air between them. "Nowhere near it."

Reid pulled her a little closer and wiped her tears with the base of his thumb. "If I'd known, Jules, I would have come for you. I swear it."

Boldness allowed her to rest her hand against his cheek once more, her thumb tracing the hard jaw line. "I used to lie awake at night and wish you would."

"Julia ..." Reid's voice caught in his throat. "If I could change things ..."

"You can't."

There was nothing left to say. Nothing left to do except mold herself to him as he brought his lips to hers the way she remembered, in tentative query. Grazed hers and asked permission for more. And she conceded.

Reid tightened his arms around her as she received his kiss and returned it with another. She slid her arms upward, around his neck, curled her fingers through his hair as his lips crushed hers in a kiss that exploded, shook the dust off every negative emotion ever connected to him, woke her soul from slumber and pulled her into that intimate connection she'd been missing all these years ... and lasted much, much longer than it should have.

Julia pulled back first, reeling. Waited to see whether her body would betray her and send her to the ground, but it didn't. She let out her breath and took a quick walk around the area. "Okay. What was that?"

"That was ... me being completely impulsive and out of control." He looked just about as stunned as she was, but nowhere near remorseful.

"No kidding. You still react first, think later, huh? I can't imagine that's a helpful attribute when you're out in the field."

Reid cleared his throat and put some distance between them. "It's definitely not."

The intimate moment left her shaken and unsure. Where had it come from and what did it mean? Julia shivered in the wind. Her cheeks burned, her heart still hadn't calmed. She hadn't been kissed like that in ... she didn't even know.

That kiss was unlike any of the kisses she remembered Reid Wallace giving her. He'd always taken her breath away, but that ... that was new. And what shocked her even more, was that she had allowed it. Wanted it. Maybe even needed it.

Needed him?

Impossible.

"It won't happen again." She put her back to him.

"Are you sure about that?" He was beside her before she could think, turning her to face him. "You weren't exactly shoving me off." A sly smile ripped across his face. "In fact, I might go as far as to say you enjoyed it."

Julia looked at the ground. If her cheeks got any hotter they'd burst into flames. But she forced her eyes upward and held fast to the facts they faced. "We're just kidding ourselves, Reid. We can't go back in time."

He pressed two fingers against her lips. "Who says we have to go back?"

Reid brought her hand against his chest and held it there, letting her feel the beating of his heart. His eyes roamed her face, studying her so intently that she wondered what he saw. Whether he saw any trace of the girl she'd been, the girl he'd loved, the girl he left behind. Or did he only see the sad, tired, washed-out woman she'd become?

"I never imagined you'd be more beautiful than you were, Jules, but you are."

His words took her breath away. "Don't say things like that."

"Why not? It's true." His smile bordered on scandalous. "I think you want me to kiss you again."

"No. I absolutely do not." She'd never been a good liar. She could stage her own Occupy Wall Street right here in Bridgewater to prove it, but if he brought his lips to hers again, she'd give herself away.

He didn't. Instead, he let her go, sauntering toward the set of binoculars cemented in place near the edge of the wall. "Seen enough?"

"What?" Julia stared.

He straightened, tipped his head toward the valley. "The view. Seen enough or do you want to stay longer?"

"No. I ..." The sensation of standing so close, waiting for the next moment that didn't come still sang through her and made any clear thought impossible. "I ... thought you ..."

Okay, this was too ridiculous. Julia shook her head and headed back to the bike.

He was faster.

Reid blocked her path, a smoldering smile reaching right through her, actually making her believe life might be good again. He lifted her chin and captured her eyes with his. "Was I going to kiss you again? Yeah. But I changed my mind."

"Oh." Should she kick him? "Well, thanks for letting me know. Next time you want to go all Rhett Butler on me, give me a heads up." She spun away, but he reached for her, preventing her from going anywhere.

"Did I want to kiss you again? You bet. Do I still want to? Like you wouldn't believe. But you're right, Jules, we can't go back in time. But we can't go forward either. Not until we both know what we want. And I'm not sure we do. So, kissing you again wouldn't be playing fair."

Her heart sagged with the reality of his words.

He was right. She knew it. And his conciliatory smile said he knew it too.

"Since when do you play fair?"

"Since two minutes ago." He walked away, grabbed her helmet and tossed it to her. "Let's get out of here. You better start praying that kid of ours isn't waiting for you when you get home or you're gonna owe him a bike ride."

Julia did pray.

All the way down the mountain and along the road that led them home. But her prayers had nothing to do with Mark. Which was unfortunate, because, as Reid predicted, he came barreling out the front door as soon as they pulled up and parked.

"Mama, that's so not—"

Julia hopped off the bike, whipped off her helmet and pressed it against her son's chest before he could get another word out. "Have fun." She pitched Reid a glare over her shoulder. "Harm one hair on his head and that's the last ride either of us will take with you."

Chapter Eighteen

Reid heard the car pull up around front of the cabin and took another swing at the punching bag. Boots crunched on the leaves and came closer.

He swung, hit, swung again and launched into a round of one-two punches that gave his heart more than a healthy workout, but did little to relieve the hundred pound weight bearing down on his soul.

"You can beat the stuffing out of that thing all you want, but Frank Hansen will still be dead." Cade stood near the knotty pine that held the chain they'd secured on a high branch many years ago. Taken turns at punches for hours until Esmé called them in for supper or told Cade it was time to go home.

Reid grabbed his towel from a tree branch and wiped sweat off his face, slowed his breathing and jogged in place. "I wish to hell he wasn't, Cade. I wish I could have had the pleasure." It wasn't something he was proud of, but something he spent too much time thinking about. Ever since he'd learned the truth about the life Julia and the kids had lived, it was all he could focus on.

"Get in line behind me." Cade zipped up his jacket and shivered in the cold. "It's thirty degrees out here. Probably going to snow soon. Can we go in?"

They went in through the back door and Cade uttered a sigh of relief as the warm air of the cabin hit them. Reid went to work building the fire. Cade settled on the couch.

"So, how are you?" His friend got right to it.

Reid occupied an old armchair and flung one arm across his face. "Other than the fact I can't sleep, can't eat and can't stop thinking about what I'd like to do to Frank Hansen, things are peachy."

"You're not drinking, are you?"

"Nope." Reid pulled a throw-cushion to his chest. He knew enough to stay away from the stuff now. It wouldn't help. Wouldn't erase the pain. Only trick him into believing it was gone for a few hours. "I haven't touched a drop since I left New York."

"Still having nightmares?"

"Some. But lately they've got nothing to do with the things I normally dream about."

"Reid."

"What?" He stared at Cade through bleary eyes. If he didn't get some real sleep soon he was going to be in worse shape than he already was.

"Why don't you leave it up to God, dude? What's done is done. Let Him handle the rest."

Reid registered the slow thumping of his heart and put his head in his hands. "How do you do that?" He glanced up at Cade and wondered at the compassion on his friend's face. "How do you keep your faith when everything around you decomposes and starts to stink like dung? How do you see God in the face of evil?"

Cade pushed his fingers through his hair, his eyes suddenly wet. "It's the only thing I have to hang on to. It makes me sick to think about what happened, what they went through. I don't know why God lets stuff like that happen. Why to my family? Or anyone. But at the end of the day, we still have hope. If we can't hope, we may as well give up now."

Hope.

When was the last time Reid felt even so much as a glimmer of it?

He sat back again and studied his hands. Calluses had formed from all the work he'd been doing around the place. He fiddled with the band of gold he wore on his right hand. When he'd taken off the wedding ring Julia had given him all those years ago, as relieved as he'd been, he somehow hadn't been able to part with it.

Time had turned it into a reminder of his failures and he refused to remove it.

"God feels very far away to me." He forced himself to meet Cade's eyes.

"You didn't always think that."

True enough. His faith had been as strong as Cade's. He'd done his best to live life in a way he thought would honor God. Even in the weeks after marrying Julia, when he knew he wanted out, he'd wrestled with himself. Wrestled with the knowledge that breaking his vows went against all he'd been taught to believe in. He'd prayed for wisdom, a clear yes or no. Prayed for answers. God hadn't given him any.

Or maybe Reid just hadn't been listening.

"You think I deserve a second chance, Cade?"

Cade got up, moved around the room with slow steps. Stood in front of the mantle in silence for a while. "I believe everything happens for a reason. Even the mistakes we make."

"What if those mistakes are too costly?"

Cade's chest lifted and he exhaled. "What happened to Julia wasn't your fault. I don't think she blames you, so you've got no business blaming yourself. You made mistakes, but they're done. Same with what happened in Syria. You can't change it. The real question, Reid, is when are you going to forgive yourself?"

Reid couldn't answer that.

The mountain of guilt was too high and too wide for him to get around or climb over. So he sat at the bottom of it and watched life, real life—the kind of life where love and faith and family came first—pass him by.

"I wouldn't know where to begin."

"Begin with God. Start talking to him again. I mean, really talking. You think He wants to see you like this? That it brings Him pleasure?"

"People died, Cade. I didn't have to follow orders that day. I was thinking of myself.

Just like when I left your sister. I never once considered how my leaving would impact her life. I ..."

"You can't go back. Make peace with this thing. Make peace with Jules and move on." Cade ended the conversation, making a wide sweep of the room with his arm. "This is starting to look more like home." He nodded approval. "I see you've begun unpacking."

Reid's stuff had arrived from the city, and he'd hauled some of Esmé's things out again. The living room was dust free, the windows repaired and clean, the floors buffed and brought back to their original shine, the rugs washed and vacuumed.

"It's a start."

"TV work?"

"I don't know. I haven't tried it." Didn't want to either. He'd heard Bryan Andrews had taken his place. If he had to watch that chump stumbling over his words he'd probably barf on the clean rug.

"You know your Facebook page has about a bazillion comments on it."

"Don't care." Reid shut his eyes, wishing for sleep. Wishing for Cade to hurry up and leave so he could attempt to crash for a few hours.

"The latest rumor is that you were abducted by aliens."

"Amish aliens?" A grin lifted the corners of his mouth.

Cade chuckled. "Might have been some mention of zombies too." A sigh of frustration rang around him. "You really think this dropping off the face of the earth idea is a good one, don't you?"

"Cade." Reid didn't bother to open his eyes. "Go. Away. Far, far, away. Now."

"Well, I would but I actually came up here to give you a message. You haven't had your landline connected and your cell phone doesn't always get service up here. How is anybody supposed to reach you in case of an emergency, Wallace?"

"What emergency? What's going on?" Reid's pulse picked up and pulled him to a sitting position.

Cade lifted a hand and flashed a grin. "Relax. There's no emergency. Jules just tried calling you, that's all."

"Julia called me?" Slow heat crept up the back of his neck, followed by regret that he hadn't been able to receive the call. When he was outside, service was sporadic. Inside the cabin it was nonexistent. And he'd forgotten to take his cell out with him that afternoon.

"Yup. Punched you in the face a few times." Cade's laughter filled the room, filled a bit of the hole in his heart. "Then she got ticked when you didn't answer."

"What did she want?"

"To talk to you about Mark's birthday. It's coming up after Thanksgiving."

"Oh, right." Reid closed his eyes again. "Why didn't she just come up here herself?"

"And risk being alone with you? Maybe you really are living with those aliens."

Reid tossed the colorful cushion across the room and hit Cade square in the face.

"Ow."

"Don't you have anything better to do on a Friday afternoon than come up here and harass me, Connelly?"

"Matter of fact I do." Cade stood before the fire, warming his hands. He glanced over his shoulder with a grin. "But I wanted to talk about something else too. A favor."

"Uh oh." Cade's favors usually consisted of lending considerable amounts of cash or attending boring social soirees. "Cade, I'm broke, man."

Cade snorted. "You are as far away from broke as Bill Gates. But I don't need any money. This is about Julia."

Reid pushed to his feet, moved around Cade and adjusted a few pictures on the mantle. The picture of the three of them at the lake when they were kids, sitting on the dock, cheeky grins and sun bleached hair, held pride of place. There was an old picture of him and Killer. One of him and Esmé at his college graduation.

And then there was the one in the silver frame that he had taken out of the box that morning on odd impulse, placed on the mantle and stared at for a very long time. And promptly forgotten to put away.

He put it facedown, turned around and knew it was too late.

"I already saw." Cade's thin smile said what he didn't. Said he knew Reid was still holding onto the past, still holding tight to feelings he didn't have any right to. "You probably want to tuck that in a drawer before Mark comes back up here. Seeing a picture of you and his mother on your wedding day might raise a few questions."

"Yeah." Reid grabbed the picture and retreated to the couch. Stared at the two stupid kids smiling up at him and wondered what they'd been thinking. What he'd been thinking. And why he still carried around a cruise ship-sized load of regret that sucked him under whenever he thought about his short-lived life with Julia, and what might have been.

Cade rocked on his heels and let out a whistle. "Please tell me I'm not seeing what I think I'm seeing."

"What do you think you're seeing?"

"You're still in love with her, aren't you?"

Reid rested his head against the back of the couch and scratched his jaw. It was a good question. A valid one.

Was he still in love with Julia?

Did he even know what love was? Real unconditional love—the kind that weathers all storms of life and lasts forever—what did that look like?

Questions settled heavy on his heart. He'd been turning them over in his brain for hours on end, especially on nights when sleep wouldn't come. Pretty much since the moment he'd seen Julia again. But he was nowhere close to getting answers.

"Well?" Cade was really pushing it.

"You can leave anytime, you know."

Cade clapped his hands, his grin too gleeful. "Not now, man. Things just got interesting."

"I kissed her."

"You what?" His friend's jaw practically hit the floor.

"Yeah. That day you conjured up some excuse and had me take her home. I drove her up the mountain first. So we could talk about Mark. It's your fault, really."

"Dude. I don't see any bruises."

"No. She …" Reid smiled even though his face felt like it was on fire. "I know I shouldn't have. But she didn't exactly complain."

"Oh, boy."

"Yeah."

"I don't suppose I have to tell you to take it slow."

"You don't." He circled the face on the frame in front of him.

He was no longer sure how to make sense of things that made no sense.

He'd done it for years. All those interviews, reports and broadcasts from the darkest, saddest corners of the world. He'd said what he thought people wanted to hear. Said what he thought were the right words. Words he hoped would bring clarity and hope and maybe some healing. He'd done his best to be objective.

He'd only pretended to be good at it.

"It won't happen again. It was a mistake."

"You don't sound too sure of that, my friend."

Reid let out a groan. "I don't want to put her through any more, Cade. If I could get her out of my head, I would. But I wasn't exactly expecting to be blindsided the minute I saw her again."

"Well." Cade's sigh said more than he probably meant it to. "If you're still carrying around feelings for my sister, may I suggest you figure them out soon? It's not as though you're going to be able to avoid her."

"I know that." Unless he packed up and headed back to the city. Which would only prove he was an even bigger jerk now than he'd been when he left her. "It'll work out. We can be friends."

"Uh huh." Cade's low chuckle set Reid's nerves on edge. "You and Jules being just friends is so not possible."

"Why?"

"Because she never got over you, that's why. And from the sounds of it, I'd say you never got over her."

Reid paced the living room, his head throbbing and his heart aching.

If second chances were possible, he didn't deserve one.

He wasn't what Julia needed. He'd do his best to be a good father to Mark, and he wanted that, but that's as far as it would go. "Where do I go from here, Cade?"

"Try being honest with yourself for starters. But if you do want a second chance, it's going to take more than one kiss to convince her you're not about to pull the rug out from under her again. And you're going to have to be honest with her too."

"I hear you. Point taken." Time to change topic before he totally lost it. "So what's this favor?"

"Oh, right." Cade's smile returned. "Well, I've asked Jules to work on an article for me, for a friend of mine. It's not a big deal, just a feature in a local magazine, but I figured it might set her back on track. I'm not sure how much she's done on it though. I think she's scared to start. Scared to fail."

Reid knew that feeling too. "So what do you want me to do?"

"I don't know." Cade sent him a wicked grin. "Maybe you can help her out. Give her some advice. You're writing stuff all the time. Or you used to be. Just encourage her."

Laughter shot out of him and Reid bent over his knees. "Cade, what are you smoking? Yeah, okay, Jules and I are getting along, sort of, but I hardly think she's going to take advice from me."

"Well, you could be right." Cade jangled his keys and headed for the front door. "But give it a shot anyway. It's her birthday tomorrow. Use that as an excuse to go see her. I don't know. Get her flowers or something. Be nice. If the subject comes up, cool. If not, no sweat. I'll talk to you later, man."

Reid watched him drive off, walked down the hall to his bedroom and searched for his cell. Sure enough, no service.

Julia's birthday.

If Cade hadn't mentioned it, he might have forgotten.

Who was he kidding? He had that date emblazoned on his brain. He couldn't forget it, even during the years he wanted to. He just hadn't figured out how to handle it this year.

Reid glanced at his watch and calculated how much time he had before the stores closed. He had some planning to do.

Chapter Nineteen

Reid shaded his eyes with his hand and peered in the window of the florist shop.

Debby stood behind the counter serving a white-haired gentleman bundled up in a black coat. Julia was nowhere in sight. Reid watched the man leave carrying a dozen red roses and wearing a smile that made him wonder who those flowers were for. A wife perhaps, to celebrate more than a few decades of true love. Or perhaps his first wife had passed on and they were for a new wife—a second chance at love. That was worth celebrating. Reid grinned and almost waved as the guy got into an old Buick and drove away.

A bell above the door jangled as he poked his head around it.

Debby looked up and her eyes widened. "Well, well. Look who it is."

"Is Jules here?" Reid whispered.

"No. She already left for the day. Are you coming inside? You're letting all the cold air in."

Reid stepped into the warm shop and inhaled. A million sweet scents bombarded him, widened his grin and questioned his sanity. "Um." He walked to the long glass cabinets and took stock of the inventory.

"Can I help? You don't have to keep glancing over your shoulder. It's not like you're in Victoria's Secret or anything."

"Uh huh." He pushed his hands deep into the pockets of his jacket and rocked on the heels of his boots. "Deb, does uh … does Jules still like those purple things with the long thin stems?" He tipped his head toward a bucket way in back.

Debby rounded the counter and came to where he stood. She made no attempt to hide her amusement. "They're called orchids. And, yes. She does."

The bell on the door jangled in sync with Cade's deep chuckle. "Do my eyes deceive me? The infamous Reid Wallace in a florist shop? What is the world coming to? What are you doing here, man?"

"What does it look like?" Reid glowered. He pointed to the purple things. "I'll take a dozen of them. No, two-dozen. Is that better?"

"Two dozen would be pretty amazing." Debby stepped into Cade's arms for a kiss. "Okay, good. And put them with something … green."

"Something green. Duly noted." Debby nodded, still smiling.

Reid frowned. "No. Wait. A dozen. Make it twelve, Deb."

"Twelve it is. You want to take them with you?"

"Can I pick them up tomorrow?"

"Sure. What time?"

"Um. Well, see that's the thing. I was wondering if, well, could you give Jules the afternoon off?"

"Dude." Cade began to laugh. Debby shushed him and led Reid over to the counter. "Absolutely. I already tried getting her to take the day off but she wouldn't. So, what time?"

"Around noon. I'll come by. But she might need some convincing."

"I'll say." Cade's laughter got louder.

Reid pointed a finger at his friend. "I'm about this close to wiping the floor with you, Connelly, so shut it."

"All right, you two. Cade, go in back and make sure everything's locked." Debby rolled her eyes as Cade took off, singing a really bad rendition of *Chapel of Love*. "Just ignore him," Debby said as she put the arrangement together. "How about you pick these up at eight-thirty? Jules comes in for nine."

"Sounds like a plan." A plan he prayed wouldn't backfire on him. He handed over his credit card and left the shop a few minutes later. Sleep definitely wouldn't be coming tonight.

Julia entered the week's inventory into the computer, looked up as the bell on the door rang.

Reid strolled into the shop like he was a frequent customer. "Hello, Jules."

"Hi." If he was about to order flowers for his girlfriend or ex-girlfriend or whatever she was, Julia would kick him out. Her cheeks started to tingle at the mortifying thought. "Do you need something?"

"Yup." Reid placed his hands on the counter, a smile curling the corners of his lips. "You."

"Excuse me?"

"You heard me."

"Have you been drinking?" She tipped her head and tried to get a whiff, but all she smelled was his cologne and the faint scent of peppermint.

"Oh, hey, Reid." Debby came in from the back. Holding Julia's coat. And purse.

Julia stared at her. "What's going on?"

"You're leaving." Debby held out her coat and nodded toward the handsome guy with the goofy grin. "With him."

"Oh, no I'm not." Were they both nuts? Julia folded her arms and glared at Reid. "Go away. I have work to do."

"No, you don't." Debby shook her coat and scowled. "It's your birthday and you're taking the afternoon off. And if you don't leave right now, you can consider yourself fired."

Reid whistled and raised a brow. "Well, that's a little extreme. You really think she needs that much convincing, Deb?"

"Yes, actually, I do." Debby grinned.

"Well, you heard the woman, Jules. If you want to keep your job, I guess you're going to have to come with me." Arms akimbo, his deep chuckle wrapped around Julia and pulled her reluctant eyes his way.

Dang the man for being even better looking than he had been twelve years ago.

"Okay. Fine." Julia shoved her arms into her coat and grabbed her purse. "But I refuse to have fun."

"That's a relief," Reid growled, taking her by the elbow and escorting her to the door. "There's no fun allowed on this road trip. Besides, we wouldn't want your brain to explode or anything. See ya, Deb."

"Road trip? I think this counts as kidnapping." Julia slid into the front seat of the Range Rover and clicked her seatbelt in place. Reid was rummaging around in the trunk. When he came around front, he hopped in and handed her the most beautiful arrangement of deep purple orchids she had ever seen.

"Happy Birthday, Jules."

"Oh. Wow." She could only whisper. "Thanks." What was he trying to do, give her heart failure?

"There's twelve."

"I see that."

"Yeah. One for every birthday I missed."

She sighed and stared out the window. "I got that too, Reid."

"I'm starting the engine now. Don't jump out."

"I'll force myself not to." Her smile escaped without permission and she caught his grin out of the corner of her eye. "Where are we going?"

"Some place we've never been. There's a new resort over the mountain, The Briar. Supposed to have a great restaurant. You haven't been there, have you?"

"Can't say that I have."

"Good. Neither have I."

She stared at the flowers, glad she'd chosen to put on the new silk blouse and gray wool slacks that Cade had presented her with that morning over breakfast. Wait a minute ...

It was a conspiracy.

But a few hours later, she'd resigned herself to being perfectly happy in this dream world Reid Wallace had dragged her into.

Julia couldn't remember when she'd spent a more relaxing afternoon. They started with drinks in front of a roaring fire, then moved to a sequestered table set with beautiful china, crystal and silverware. Wine accompanied a four-course gourmet meal that made her wonder if he'd secretly transported her to New York.

Last year, Frank had taken her to Chick-fil-A. Then he'd gone out, come back a few hours later completely trashed and ...

Julia dabbed at her lips and pushed back bitter memories.

"You okay?" Reid's brow furrowed as he stared at her across the table.

She nodded and managed a smile.

"You look really pretty today, Jules. I wouldn't put you a day over twenty."

"Liar."

"Twenty-five then." He pulled at the back of his neck and grinned. He looked pretty good himself in a navy V-neck sweater over a light blue oxford and black jeans. Julia had noticed more than a few heads turn in their direction when they'd walked in. He was recognizable, but even if people didn't know him as the guy on TV, they'd look his way.

The maître d' was excellent, and made sure nobody bothered them throughout the meal. Conversation finally flowed freely.

They talked about Mark, and Em. About Cade and Debby, laid bets on when Cade would propose. They even managed to talk about their time together, laughed over the two by four space they'd lived in. Recalled the meals Julia had managed to burn and the white laundry Reid had turned blue. Remembered Esmé coming to the rescue on more than one visit, unannounced of course.

They didn't talked about the future.

"Did you want more coffee?" Reid asked, finishing his second espresso.

"No. Thanks." Julia sat back and luxuriated in the feeling of being full after a good meal. "I don't think I've ever been anywhere this nice, Mr. Wallace. A girl could get used to this."

"Oh, yeah?" He lifted a dark eyebrow. "You mean I won't have to force you into my vehicle next time?"

"Will there be a next time?"

"You never know." He shot her a wink and reached under the table, coming up with two colorfully wrapped presents. He handed both her way. "Happy Birthday. Again."

"Okay, this is too much." Julia laughed and put up her hands. "What do you want?"

"I want you to take these boxes." He held the wrapped square boxes until she took them.

She placed them on the table in front of her and sighed. "I hope you didn't get me anything expensive. Honestly, Reid."

"Now give one back to me."

"What?" Julia smiled at the mischief in his eyes. "You want my present back?"

He nodded. "Hand one over."

"You are a very strange man."

"So I've been told. Ready? Open." He waited for her to start ripping the paper before he touched his.

Julia fumbled with the wrapping and slid off the top of the box. Laughter crept up her throat. She lifted out a small shiny black chalkboard. Looked up and laughed louder as he held up an identical one. "What is this?"

"What does it look like?"

"A chalk board, dummy."

"Try again."

"Reid." She shook her head and stifled her laughter. "It's a chalk board."

"Which is made of what?"

"I don't know. They used to be made of … slate?"

A clean slate.

The answer pealed around her, louder than the church bells on Sunday morning.

A lump jammed her throat and she let out her breath. "It's a clean slate."

"And the winner is …" Reid smiled. "One for me and one for you."

Julia hugged the board to her chest and tried to come up with something to say that wouldn't send her running to the bathroom. Because all she really wanted to do was sob. "What is this all about?"

Reid's eyes blazed into her, his gentle smile warming her in a new way. "This is about you and me. Starting over. I'll try not to be a jerk, and you can work on that whole not hating me thing. We might make a few more mistakes, because last time I checked, we weren't exactly perfect. But I think it's worth a shot." He reached a hand across the table. "Okay?"

Julia smiled, embraced the future, and slipped her hand into his. "Okay."

Chapter Twenty

*J*ulia heard the rapping on the back door but knew Hannah was sitting in the kitchen. She pressed her fingers to her temples, counted to ten and faced Mark again.

"Do it over. You're not leaving this table until you get these fractions done."

"Well, you're not exactly helping me." Her son glowered and made a few deep scratches on his scrap paper.

Julia sighed, got up and went to the sideboard for a placemat. If he ruined her mother's dining room table they'd both be in trouble. She glanced down the long hallway. Couldn't see as far as the kitchen, but she heard Hannah letting somebody in.

"What are you doing here?" Hannah's monotone sounded about as welcoming as the surly kid at the drive-through window at Wendy's.

"Nice to see you too, Hannah." Reid's deep tenor bounced off the walls toward her. Julia jumped back, then leaned a little closer outside the door. She hadn't seen him for a few days, but was still dreaming about the wonderful day they'd spent together.

"What's in the box?"

"Something for Julia."

"You already took her out for her birthday. I heard all about it. The Briar. Pretty fancy, huh? I've never been there."

"Too bad. Maybe one day your Prince Charming will take you. If he ever shows up."

"So, what's with the box? Looks like a laptop. What's she want with that? She doesn't know how to use a computer."

"Hannah, I came to see Julia, not to argue with you, as appealing as the prospect may be."

"Well, she's busy. You can just leave it there."

Julia squeaked in disbelief. Hannah was too much.

"Busy doing what? I saw her car, so I know she's here, Hannah. Can you get her for me?"

"No. But I'll tell her you stopped by. If I remember." Hannah let out a little sigh. "I'm sure you have better things to do on a Friday night, Reid. Did you know there's a new nightclub in town?"

"Uh, nope. That's not my scene."

"No? From everything I've read about you, I could have sworn it was. You've garnered quite a reputation over the years. Not one I'd be all that proud of, but to each his own."

"I wouldn't be all that proud of it either, Hannah, if it were true. You do realize that rag-mags like *The Enquirer* make their money by printing slander?"

"I don't read *The Enquirer*." Her sister sounded quite contrite. Julia grinned and wished she could see her face.

"No. Or trashy romances either."

Something slapped the table, most likely Hannah's book. Reid had a short fuse where her sister was concerned and Hannah knew just how to light it.

"It's a best seller."

"It's a load of crap." Julia heard Reid sigh, probably counting to a thousand. "So, Hannah, what are *you* doing home on a Friday night? Oh … wait … never mind."

Julia shoved her fist against her mouth to stifle her laughter and went back to the table. Put the placemat under Mark's books and leveled her gaze. "You can sit here all night if you want, but you're going to finish your homework."

"Homework sucks and so do you." Mark snapped a pencil in half and glared.

"Julia!" Hannah's voice floated down the hall. "Your boyfriend, I mean your ex … oh, bother. What is the status of your relationship these days, Reid? I never can keep up."

"Reid's here." Mark pushed his chair back but Julia clamped a hand on his shoulder. "Sit." She left the room and met Reid in the hall. His face was as furious as Mark's. He started to spew when he saw her coming.

"Where did she come from? Are you sure she's not adopted?"

Julia put a finger to her lips. "You've been in New York too long. That was not nice."

"She deserved it." He glanced over his shoulder and shook his head. "Can we not do something about her? Give her some of your happy pills or something?"

"I don't share my happy pills." She folded her arms and glanced downward at the big white cardboard box he carried. "What's that?"

"Something for you. Where is everyone?"

"My parents took Emily to a kids' night at church. Mark is in the dining room trying to get out of doing his latest math assignment."

"You're not helping him are you?" A half smile lifted his lips. "Because as I recall, you and maths were not the best of friends."

"If you think you can do a better job, go right ahead. I don't understand a bit of it. We never learned any of that stuff in sixth grade. It's like college math, for crying out loud."

"Multiplication tables are like college math for you, Jules." The wink he sent her way dried up her throat in a hurry.

"Mama! I need help!" Mark hollered.

"Want me to give it a shot?" Reid asked.

"Be my guest." She tipped her head toward the doorway at the end of the hall. "But I'm warning you, he is not in a good mood."

Forty-five minutes later, they were still at it.

Julia made tea, ignored her sister's questioning gaze, and went back to the dining room with a mug for Reid and juice for Mark. She stopped in the doorway and caught her breath as she took in the scene.

Mark slouched in his chair, elbow propped on the table, his head resting on his hand. He looked about as bored as she would have been, but she could tell he wasn't making the slightest effort to think about whatever Reid was patiently trying to teach him.

Was this how things were supposed to look? A father taking the time to help his son ... the kind of father Mark should have had. One she'd denied him. Regret pressed against her throat and brought more unwanted thoughts of what might have been.

"So, if you try it this way ... see?" Reid stood over Mark, his dark head bent over the papers in front of him as he wrote something down. He'd discarded his jacket, and sweater, and now had the sleeves of his white button-down shirt rolled up.

A beam of light bounced off the ring on his right hand.

Julia blinked and craned her neck to get a closer look. It couldn't be.

She'd noticed it before, but figured it was just a ring.

But the longer she looked at the band of gold with the tiny diamond in the center of it, the more convinced she became.

He still wore the ring she'd given him.

His wedding ring.

What she didn't know, wanted to know, was why.

"I'm never going to get this. It sucks." Mark let out a loud exaggerated sigh.

Reid echoed it, looked up and saw her standing there. "*Get me out of here*," he mouthed, the soft glow from her mother's chandelier coloring his eyes a brighter shade of blue.

"*You offered*," she mouthed back. "I have tea and juice. Ready to take a break?"

Mark drank his juice, wolfed down an oatmeal cookie and tipped his chair back a bit. "Can I go now?"

"No, you're not done." Julia sipped her tea and walked around the room. Her mother's violets sat along the windowsill and she stopped to pick off a few dead leaves.

"But I want to watch Lord of the Rings. It's a marathon."

"You've seen them a hundred times, Mark." Julia went back to the table and put down her mug. She waited until he looked up. "I told you, if you want to go up to the cabin tomorrow, and to the movies with the youth group tomorrow night, this needs to be finished."

"Well, I don't want to finish it!" Mark got to his feet, rounded his chair and thumped it up and down. "I hate math, it sucks! And you suck for making me do it! You're a—"

"Whoa." Reid shot Mark a look of surprise. "Don't talk to your mother like that." He didn't raise his voice, but his tone held clear warning that Julia hoped Mark would heed.

"I'll talk to her any way I like!" Mark's face was beet red, his nose squished, lips pinched, and Julia knew he'd already lost it. "You can't tell me what to do! You're not my father!"

Reid placed a hand on Mark's shoulder, holding him firmly in place. "Mark. Sit down."

"No."

"Mark." Julia put her trembling hands on the table, met Reid's anxious eyes and nodded. Unspoken agreement passed between them.

It was time.

"Mark, do what he says."

"Why should I?" Resentment dripped from his words, his eyes bright with emotion. "He can't come in here and tell me what to do!" He tried to wriggle out of Reid's grip. "He's *not* my father. My Dad's dead."

The grandfather clock in the hall ticked out the time it took for her to make up her mind. There was no point in putting it off any longer.

"Mark." Tears slipped down her cheeks as Julia watched her son stare at Reid, watched the wheels turn in his head as he processed what he probably already knew. "Your dad is dead, yes. But Frank Hansen wasn't your father. Reid is."

"He is not." Mark's voice wavered, but she knew he believed her.

"Honey, listen to me ..."

"No. I don't want to listen to you!" Mark's cheeks flushed a deeper shade of scarlet, anger sparking in his eyes. "You're lying."

Reid still didn't let him go. "No, she's not, Mark. She's telling the truth."

Mark jerked out of Reid's grasp and pushed him away. "If it's true then why didn't I know about you?"

Julia wiped her eyes and resisted the urge to crumple against the man who stood just a few steps away, sending her silent messages of support. "Reid and I were married a long time ago. We ..." How to explain what she still hadn't come to grips with?

"No!" Mark's tone edged toward panic. "You're lying! If he was my real dad he would have come for me!"

Pain slashed across Reid's face but he braved the storm of furious words Mark unleashed and stepped a little closer. "Mark, enough. Calm down and listen to what we're saying. We wanted to tell you—"

"Then why didn't you? If you were my dad, you would have known where I was! You would have come for me and helped us. So why didn't you? Why did you let him do all that stuff to us? Why did you let him … hurt us?" Mark yelled another hate-filled word and pummeled his fist against Reid's chest. "I hate you! And I hate you, Mama! This is all your fault!" He ran from the room, slamming the door behind him. A few minutes later the front door slammed and the walls shook with Mark's anger.

Julia watched one of her mother's violets fall to the floor, almost in slow motion, unwilling, unable to move in time to stop it. The terracotta pot splintered and spread brown dirt, green leaves and purple flowers across the floor. Mirroring her life, splintering into tiny pieces she couldn't begin to try to put together again.

Invisible hands slid around her throat and squeezed. Frank's face appeared in front of her, his mouth oozing venom. *I told you this would happen, Julia. You're so stupid, aren't you? You think you know best? Think you have all the answers? You don't know squat.*

"Easy, easy." Reid sprinted around the table before she gave in to the powerful emotions that sparred with common sense. "Breathe. Nice and slow. Breathe, Jules. Just breathe."

Julia sank against him and stifled her sob. Much as she still hated to be held, hated to feel so vulnerable in his arms, she knew if she didn't let him support her, she would hit the ground.

She waited for her breathing to slow, listened to the beating of his heart and the sound of his own ragged breaths. And eventually found her voice.

"That didn't go as well as planned."

Reid hiked up an eyebrow, staring at her with a stunned expression. "Did you have a plan?"

"Oh, sure." She shrugged and moved off. Distance between them at this point was a necessity. "I thought we'd take him to his favorite pizza place. We'd break the news over dinner, he'd be thrilled, throw his arms around us both, and the two of you would ride off on your Harley and live happily ever after."

"Sarcasm doesn't suit you." Reid bent to pick up a few pieces of the broken pot. "Where do you think he went?"

"The tree house." A place of refuge when she'd been Mark's age and older, her son had found the structure almost at once after arriving. It was the one place he could go without his baby sister tagging along.

"It's freezing out tonight." Reid pulled on his sweater and grabbed his coat. "He probably didn't bother to get a jacket. Can you grab it?"

"Reid, I don't think ..."

He whirled to face her, eyes flashing. "My son is out there in the dark. Don't think. Just get me his jacket."

She scooted past him into the kitchen.

Hannah looked up from her book and feigned surprise. "What in the world is going on? Did I hear a door slam?"

Julia fumbled with the windbreakers and jackets hanging on the coat rack in the entryway, found Mark's and handed it to Reid.

"Reid, you're still here? Then who ..." Hannah stood, clapped a hand to her mouth, her eyes glinting with caustic humor. "Oh, oh my, what a tangled web we weave. So you two finally decided to fess up, huh?"

"Shut up, Hannah." Julia pulled on her coat and gloves and followed Reid out the back door.

Reid raced over the hill, Julia following behind with a flashlight. It had rained the day before and the ground was slick and sticky in patches. The dogs ran ahead, barking as though caught up in some imaginary game.

He wished they were.

A light snow began to fall. By the time they reached the bottom of the garden and stood a few feet away from the gigantic oak where he and Cade had built their tree house his first summer in Bridgewater, Reid was gasping for breath.

He really needed to work out more.

"Do you think he's up there?" Julia stood beside him, teeth chattering, but clearly not as wiped out as he was.

"He better be. How are you not even out of breath?"

"I'm used to running."

Reid caught her pained expression before she shone the light on him. He pushed the flashlight away. "Are you trying to blind me? Go back inside. You can't stand out here shivering."

"I just ran all the way down here and you want me to go back? You really want to go up there by yourself?"

"I do. I don't think he can handle both of us. I think I should be the one."

"Well, you're probably right." Julia stared up at the haphazard wooden structure settled in the highest, thickest branches of the tree. "I didn't really want to climb that ladder anyway." She sucked in her bottom lip and shook her head. "You don't have a flashlight."

Reid grabbed his phone and pressed a button. Bright light shone across the grass. "I have an app for that."

"You're hilarious." She shivered in the night air, tears standing in her eyes. Whether they were from emotion or cold, he couldn't tell. Probably both. "All right. You go." Julia shuffled her feet and lowered her head. "God, please let him be up there. Please let him listen to Reid and not be angry. And please let him understand."

Reid sniffed moisture, took a step forward and reached for her hand. "And give me the right words. I need him to know he's not alone. I need him to know ..." He couldn't finish.

Julia squeezed his hand, kept her gaze on him and waited.

Reid knew he should say more, but was totally unable to.

He couldn't remember the last time they'd prayed together, if they ever had.

Couldn't remember the last time he'd prayed with any fervent faith at all.

"Just let him be okay." It was all he could think to say.

"Amen."

"I know we never made a habit of doing that," she whispered, voicing his thoughts. "Figured now was a good time to start."

"Couldn't agree more."

Silent snow ascended from the heavens, as if to cover their transgressions. The moon disappeared beneath a cover of gray and a night owl's call sliced through the frigid air. Fast moving clouds continued east as flakes of snow fell on her hair, her nose and lips. She'd never looked more beautiful. Or sad.

"I'm so sorry, Jules." He held her gloved hand up to his mouth, unwanted tears warming his eyes.

"Don't. Just go." Julia stepped back and tipped her head toward the tree. "Go talk to your son."

Chapter Twenty-One

Reid stuffed Mark's jacket under one arm and climbed up the wooden boards, praying they would hold his weight. When he reached the top and looked in, relief seeped through him.

Mark huddled in the corner of the tree house, lost inside a thick purple duvet, only the upper half of his face visible.

"Go away."

Okay, that was a start. Reid caught his breath and hung onto the top rung. "Mark. It's freezing out here. I am not climbing back down this ladder without you. Your mother will kill me."

"Good." Mark's eyes followed Reid as he pushed through the opening and fell onto the cold boards. A splinter nicked the palm of his hand, but he bit his lip and moved forward.

"Haven't been up here in years." He settled a couple feet away from Mark. "Your Uncle Cade and I built this place when we were just a bit older than you."

"Couldn't care." Mark pulled the comforter tight around him and glared at the wall.

Reid waved the checkered fleece coat toward him like a flag of surrender. "Looks like you're all set under there, but just in case." Mark made no move to take it, so Reid chucked it his way. "Where'd you get the comforter?"

"Stole it off Aunt Hannah's bed. Her room was closest." He pulled out a battery operated Coleman lamp and turned it on, shedding soft light around them.

Reid grinned and switched off his iPhone. Resourceful kid. "You got food under there as well?"

Mark held up a crumpled bag of Doritos. "Aunt Hannah's too. I already ate them all."

Reid waited a minute, shot up another prayer, then went for it. "I need to tell you what happened, Mark. Why you didn't know about me." He sat cross-legged and pulled the end of the comforter over his knees.

"I don't care." Mark's face was streaked with dirt and tears, mud caked hair stuck to his forehead. There was a small cut above his lip, still bleeding.

"You fell?"

"Face-planted coming down the hill. Think I broke my ankle. Hurts like heck."

"Can I take a look?" Reid scooched closer and pulled back the comforter. Mark stayed quiet while Reid took off his dirty shoe and wet sock, rolled up his pant-leg and examined his ankle. Sure enough, it was red and ballooning in size rather impressively. Mark yelped when Reid tried to move his foot a bit. "I think we're going to need an X-ray for that."

"Shoot." Mark hung his head. "Mama's gonna be mad."

"She'll be fine."

"I shouldn't have yelled at her. Shouldn't have said all that stuff. Is she okay?" He looked up, an angry storm still churning in his eyes.

"She's okay. She's just worried about you."

"Always is. She should worry about herself for once."

Reid squeezed his eyes shut and wished he could take on Mark's pain.

"Sorry I yelled at you, too." Mark gave a shaky intake of breath and rubbed his cheek.

"I had it coming." Reid hiked himself up and sank down next to his son. "We should have told you sooner." He sighed deep and found the nerve to speak again. "Your mom and I ran off and got married when I was in college. She'd just graduated high school, was taking time to figure out what she wanted to do. We thought we were doing the right thing, but we were just kids. It didn't last long. Couple months, that was all. I … I walked out, Mark. I was the one who ended things, and I didn't do it well. She …"

"She was pretty mad, right?" Mark almost grinned.

"She was. And she had every right to be. But ... she didn't know she was pregnant when we split up, and I guess by the time she found out ..." Reid clenched his fists and made his decision. Telling Mark the whole truth wouldn't be fair to Julia. "By the time she told me, I didn't want to know."

"You didn't want me?"

"I'm sorry." Tears burned his eyes but Reid put an arm around Mark's scrawny shoulder and pulled him in tight. "I was a stupid kid, Mark. I didn't know what I wanted. But I know now that leaving your mother was the biggest mistake I ever made."

"Is that why you're back? To make things right?" Mark lifted his chin, hope standing in his eyes, daring Reid to deny it. Daring him to choose.

He could walk away again. Or he could stay. Do the right thing. For once.

"If I can. I want to try, Mark. What do you say? Will you give me a chance?"

Mark's fight bowed out and left the ring. He didn't say a word. Just let out a gut-wrenching wail and began to sob.

Reid held tight and sat in silence. He remembered that kind of pain. Remembered what it felt like to cry so hard you thought your chest would explode. Remembered how it felt to question everything you ever believed in and wonder if things would ever be the same.

They wouldn't.

After a while Mark sat up.

"I kind of figured it out already," he choked out in a half-whisper. "One time when my dad got real mad at me, he told me I wasn't his real son. Told me he was glad too. Told me who you were, but I didn't believe him. He said a lot of crap when he was drunk. Said you didn't want me, neither. That you'd never want me."

Reid sucked air and bit back what he really wanted to say. "Mark. That's not true." He placed his hands around his Mark's dirty, tear-streaked face and looked into his own eyes. "I wish I could have been there for you. The minute I saw you that first day on the road, I knew who you were. And I wanted you to know who I was. You're my son, Mark. I couldn't be prouder or happier about that."

"For real?" New light crept into the boy's eyes and brought a wavering smile.

"For real." Reid held him close again and buried his face in Mark's thick hair. When he felt Mark stiffen, he inched back, watched a different kind of fear move in.

"Are you going away again? Go back to work in New York?"

"I don't know." It was the only answer he could give, the honest one. "But I won't leave you, Mark. No matter what happens, I'll always be there for you."

"You really want to be my Dad? You won't hurt me or my mom or Em? You won't be like him?"

"I won't, Mark, I swear it. Men like ... Frank ... they're sick. Understand? He had something wrong with him. He didn't know how to treat people, didn't understand what love was. I'm not like that. I will be there for you, no matter what."

"You mean it?"

"I mean it." Reid folded the boy against him, his heart jumping as he tried to contain his own anger and desperate sorrow. No matter how much he wanted to, he didn't have the means to fix this kind of pain.

How long would it take for them to get through this? To heal?

He didn't know. Didn't know how to help or make it hurt any less.

And so he prayed in silence for his son.

Reid drove them back from the emergency room, shattered and having trouble focusing on anything other than the figure stretched out on the backseat.

After a few hours of waiting to be seen, Reid snapped. Marched up to the desk and demanded to speak to the doctor on call. That hadn't gone over so well with the triage nurse. It had been a while since he'd used his name or the clout that came with it to get what he wanted, but he had tonight. The Chief of Orthopedics ended up setting Mark's ankle.

· They pulled up to the house a little after eleven, and he shut off the car engine. Breathed deep and gave his head a shake.

"You haven't said a word since we got in the car. Are you all right?" Julia's quiet voice split the silence.

Reid gripped the wheel and tried to make sense of the overwhelming mess of feeling surging inside him. He turned to face the questions in her eyes. Wished he could tell her what he needed to, what he knew he had to do, but the words wouldn't come.

"Let's get Mark inside." He got out and went to open the door where his son lay, half asleep.

Mark was too exhausted to worry with his crutches so Reid carried him.

Julia's parents waited at the front door. Cade and Debby were in the kitchen. Julia stayed upstairs with Mark to clean him up and get him into bed and Reid filled the rest of them in on the events of the evening. Jonas sat at one end of the table, his hands cradled around a mug of steaming coffee.

Madge put a plate of cold chicken salad in front of him and produced a root beer from the depths of her well-ordered fridge. "I remembered you liked this kind."

"Still do, thanks." Reid lifted his fork and noticed his hand shaking. As much as he wanted to eat, nausea was biting.

"What's wrong, honey?" Madge stepped back and folded her arms, her brown eyes worried. "You want something else?"

Reid shook his head. His emotions perched so close to the edge, he knew it wouldn't take much for them to jump, for him to lose it.

And he couldn't go back there.

Julia's mom had been like a second mother. She'd taken him in like a lost pup, cared for him, disciplined and nurtured him right along with the others, like he was one of them. Nobody had been happier when he and Julia started dating. He knew she and Esmé had dreams of throwing them a big summer wedding out in the garden. He knew she'd been secretly saving and purchasing bolts of the best satin she could buy, poring over patterns of wedding dresses and waiting for the right time. Waiting for them to make the announcement that never came.

Madge Connelly's name sat right under Esmé's on the long list of people he'd let down all those years ago. He met her eyes now, searched for any hint of judgment or condemnation and came up wanting.

"I'm sorry." Reid ran a hand over his face and cleared his throat. "I should have said this when I first got back. I should have come to talk to you, to you both." He glanced at Julia's father and swallowed a fistful of nerves. Jonas watched him carefully, but with no hint of antagonism. Reid steadied his breathing and looked around the room.

These people were his family.

Cade, Debby, Madge and Jonas. Even Hannah, on a good day.

They loved him, cared for him and knew him best. When he walked away from Julia, he'd walked away from them too.

"I never meant to hurt her like that. Or you. You have my apology and I hope that one day, I'll be able to earn your forgiveness, and your trust."

Reid put his head in his hands.

It was done.

Years of regret and resistance to acknowledge his failures finally crushed him. He breathed deep and tasted tears.

"Honey." Madge leaned over, put her arms around him. Cade and Debby talked in low whispers, Jonas slurped, and the dogs prowled the table, but all he cared about right now was getting rid of the weight on his chest that made it so hard to breathe.

"You're a good man, Reid." Jonas's voice jerked him to his senses. He wiped his face and looked across the table at the judge. "Maybe you weren't following the right road map for awhile there, but you're home now."

"And we couldn't be happier that you and Mark will be able to know each other." Madge hugged him again. Cade nodded agreement and Debby wiped away tears, left her chair and hugged him too. Reid sat back and basked in their acceptance, and knew he was being given far more than he deserved.

"Excuse me for interrupting this little love fest," Hannah's whine winged its way into the kitchen as she walked across the tiled floor and demanded their attention. "But has anybody seen my duvet?"

Her bewildered expression set a smile twitching his lips. Laughter was close at hand and there wasn't a thing he could do to control it. Deep, soul-filled, sidesplitting laughter that shook his entire body, shattered all the stress, and made the tears run down his cheeks.

Chapter twenty-two

Julia stopped at the bottom of the stairs and listened.

Reid was laughing. Really laughing, like the way he did when she shot him those one-liners she used to come up with so easily. Laughing like maybe the world was about to end but who cared, life was good.

She couldn't imagine what he found so funny, but somehow it didn't matter.

The sound was a soothing salve on her stinging soul.

And she wished it wasn't.

She marched into the kitchen. "Reid, Mark wants you." She filled a glass with water and glanced at her mother. "Tylenol?"

"Third cupboard down, honey. How is he?"

"He's tired. Sore. But I think he'll live." She found the bottle of pills and turned to Reid. "You coming?"

He nodded and pushed his chair back.

Julia trudged upstairs, hating the feeling of his eyes on her, hating the confusion she wrestled with. This was what she wanted, wasn't it, for Mark to know his father? But she hadn't considered how hard it would be to have Reid back in her life.

She entered the room and put on a smile for her son. He didn't smile back, but at least he wasn't glaring.

Reid settled on the edge of Mark's bed. "Hey, bud. How's the ankle?"

"It's all right." Mark shifted and let out a yawn. "I guess I'm not going to get a ride on your bike again before snow comes after all."

"One ride was enough, if you ask me." Julia handed him two pills and the glass of water, ignoring Reid's grin.

"We'll have to wait for spring," he told Mark.

If you're still here.

Julia moved around the room, picking up discarded clothes and putting shoes in the closet. Mark had taken over the guest room, and she shared her bedroom with Emily. One day she hoped they'd have their own place, but the way the economy was going, she doubted she'd be able to afford much.

She listened to the two of them talking, making plans. Plans she wasn't a part of. Plans that she was terrified, for Mark's sake, might not come to pass.

"Well, you better get some shut eye." Reid glanced her way, then turned back to Mark. "I'll come back in the morning."

Julia watched Mark grab hold of Reid's arm.

"Stay." His eyes were almost closed, but a smile rested on his lips. "'Till I fall asleep."

Reid met her eyes, questioning her through the silence. She couldn't exactly say no and send him up the mountain. So she shrugged and crossed the room to put away the clean clothes she'd placed on a chair earlier in the day.

"You got it." Reid swung his legs onto the bed, put an arm around his son and closed his eyes. "'Night, bud. 'Night, Jules."

She stuffed down a reply, turned out the light, and left him there.

Julia sat up in bed and listened for the sound that had startled her a few minutes ago. The digital clock read 3 a.m. She didn't hear anything for a while. Emily curled in slumber in the bed next to hers, one arm around the huge pink bunny she'd named Hoppy. The dogs slept in the kitchen with the door shut so it couldn't be them. Perhaps it was Mom or Dad, up for some water or the bathroom.

Floorboards creaked as somebody walked over them. Somebody with a rather heavy step. She threw on her robe and went into the hall. Even though she knew she was perfectly safe here, knew she was overreacting, fear had her heart pounding to a frantic beat she could barely keep up with.

She checked in on Mark but he slept soundly. There was no sign of Reid.

The door to her parents' room was closed.

A thump came from downstairs, followed by a low curse.

Burglars didn't make that much noise.

Julia smothered a grin and entered the darkened living room, switched on a small table lamp and scanned the area. Reid sat on the couch holding one foot over his knee.

"I thought we'd been invaded by elephants, but then I figured it was you." She stepped a little closer and raised a brow at the swollen red toe he was nursing. "You could have turned on the light."

Reid glowered. "Didn't want to wake anyone. When did your mother move all the furniture around? That chair was not supposed to be there."

Julia crossed the room and stood at the glass doors. The moon shed a silvery glow over the fields. Snow fell in a thin curtain across the expanse of land around the house. The peaceful scene outside mocked the storm raging inside of her. "It's really snowing out there. Were you heading home?"

"Not exactly."

She turned, saw his face and shivered.

He hadn't slept long, that much she knew.

He'd been chasing ghosts.

And by the looks of it, they'd turned the tables on him.

"Reid, are you okay?"

He sat forward and put his head in his hands. "I will be once the sun comes up."

His ragged breathing pulled her feet forward until she reached the couch. She sat next to him, waited a moment, debating whether or not it was the right thing to do, then put a hand on his back. "Cade told me. About the PTSD. Can I get you anything?"

"No." He stiffened like she'd given him an electric shock, swiveled to face her and breathed out a shaky sigh. "You should go back to bed, Julia."

Yes, she probably should. But her conscience wouldn't let her.

"I have nightmares too." She gave a thin smile, pushed hair out of her face and pressed her back into the thick cushions of the couch. "Mine usually hit around 2 in the morning, and then I can't go back to sleep. I always dream about him. Frank. Part of me still believes he's going to come back. That he's not really dead."

She exhaled, strange relief sizzling through her. Admitting she still struggled with fear brought a bit of healing, something she hadn't expected. She didn't share her sleepless nights with her parents. They worried enough. But as she looked at the man who sat next to her, Julia somehow felt that he would understand. "What do you dream about?"

Reid sat back and wiped his eyes, raked his fingers through his hair. "Death."

She shouldn't have been surprised. Shouldn't have flinched a little, but she did. Yet her eyes wouldn't leave his.

"I see them all the time." His hoarse whisper scared her. "The faces of the dead. Paul was fifty-five, expecting his first grandchild. Scott was only twenty, interning for us, headed back to college in the fall. Sometimes I dream I can save them, stop it from happening. Most nights I see it exactly how it happened. That day in Saraqueb. How they died. And I know I'm responsible."

"Reid." She put out a hand but he stood, paced the room in an agitated state.

"It was bad enough before. But now I can't sleep at all. You don't know, Jules. If you knew … you wouldn't want me here. You wouldn't have told Mark I was his father."

Julia took in his wild eyes, drew her legs up and hugged them to her chest. "It's a little late for that." Nerves rumbled through her, but she forced calm. "I read that you went against orders and walked your team into an ambush. What's the real story?"

"How do you know that isn't the real story?" He leveled his gaze, crossed his arms.

She wondered at the hard look that came into his eyes. "Because I know you."

"You think?" Reid pinched the bridge of his nose, inhaled and turned from her. "See, that's where you're wrong, Julia. You don't know me anymore. You don't know me at all."

The wall went back up. Higher than the mountains, wider than the rushing river her dad fished each summer, impossible to get around or cross.

Even if she wanted to.

Julia sat in silence. The clock in the hall ticked in tenor. Crickets chirped under cover of the jasmine bush outside the window, and a night owl pitched its cry across the fields.

He had a point.

She didn't know him.

She'd believed the young man she'd married would never turn his back on her. Would never walk out with little to no explanation, and never, not once, try to get in touch with her again. Had the prospect of a life with her really scared him that much? Or had he been running from himself?

The years between then and now held secrets she wasn't privy to.

"I guess I don't," she whispered. "Maybe I never did."

Chapter Twenty-three

"Is that coffee?" Reid's sleepy voice slipped through the silence of the kitchen.

Julia looked up from where she sat at the table as he came in. "Help yourself. Is Mark still asleep?"

"Yeah. He woke up once and I gave him some more Tylenol. Hope that was okay."

"Sure." She sat at the table, bleary-eyed and wishing for a few more hours of sleep. Disconcerting images and their disturbing conversation pervaded her thoughts, prevented her from getting any real rest. Just before dawn, she remembered the box Reid had shown up with last night, still sitting in the dining room, and retrieved it.

She stared at it while Reid went about finding a mug and getting his coffee.

"It works better if you take it out of the box and plug it in." He pulled out a chair opposite her. His dark hair was sticking every which way, his T-shirt rumpled over wrinkled jeans. But his voice held familiar warmth she didn't quite know what to do with.

"I thought I told you to stop buying me stuff." Julia sniffed and pushed the offending object away. "I can't take this."

"Sure you can." He studied her over the rim of his mug. "I get a ton of free things all the time. So I didn't buy it. You can think of it as re-gifting, if you like."

"But you haven't even used it."

He smothered a yawn but she caught his smile anyway. "I don't need it, Jules. If you don't want it, let Mark have it."

"I never said I didn't want it." She lifted the laptop out. "You're sure you haven't used it? I'm not going to find pictures of all your girlfriends on here, am I?"

"Oh, shoot." He started to reach across the table, then sat back and laughed. "Don't give me that look, I'm joking."

"I'm not." She scrambled out of her chair and went for more coffee.

"Hey." He rubbed his jaw and gave a half shrug. "Sorry for being short with you last night. I was a little rattled."

"Really? I couldn't tell." Julia sat again and inhaled the aroma of the coffee that mingled with her mother's potpourri and last night's roast chicken. "Did you get much more sleep?"

"Some. You?"

"I haven't slept a full night in years."

"Jules …"

She held up a hand, sipped coffee and shook her head. "Let's not get into it." Snow still fell in light drifts and she watched a few flakes hit the kitchen window and slide off. "I suppose Cade told you he volunteered me to write an article for his friend. I don't know what he was thinking."

Reid's upper lip curled. "He was probably thinking you'd be good at it. You were a pretty talented writer once upon a time."

"Years ago. I'm not good at much anymore."

The rumble in his chest made her look at him again. His brows knit together in a frown. "When did you stop believing in yourself?"

She sat forward and splayed her palms on the table. "You want an exact date?" A smile slid away from her. "When somebody tells you you're stupid enough times, Reid, eventually you begin to believe it."

His hand came down over hers. She knew he wouldn't say what he probably wanted to, but his eyes did. He'd always been protective of her. It was just as well Frank was dead. She'd known it the moment he'd tried to get answers out of her that day up at the cabin.

But he didn't have the right to look after her anymore.

And she didn't have the right to want him to.

Julia pulled her hand away and stirred a spoonful of sugar into her coffee. "Maybe you can show me how this works some other time. I don't think I could concentrate right now." That was understating it.

Reid propped his elbows and rested his chin on his hands, piercing her with enquiring eyes. "What's going on inside that head of yours, Jules? What have I done now? I apologized for last night. What else do you want?"

Julia shook her head and left the table. Got out a bowl and the pancake mix, Mark's favorite breakfast meal. He'd be starving when he woke up. She blinked moisture and moved to get the milk and eggs, but Reid was in the way.

He invaded her space. Narrowed his eyes and tipped her chin upward with two fingers. "Talk to me."

She wanted to push him aside, pretend he wasn't even there. But he was. And that was the problem.

"I don't know how to do this." Exhaustion sagged her shoulders and pushed out tears. "I mean, how do we … how do I … accept the fact that you're going to be in Mark's life when every time I look at you, all I think is how you didn't want to be in mine?"

His shocked expression made her wish she'd kept quiet. Reid ran his tongue over his bottom lip, took a breath and folded his arms. "I thought we were past this. We talked about it. Can't you just let it go?"

"I'm sorry. But you did leave, Reid. You left and you never looked back. What guarantee do I have that you won't do the same to Mark? That one day he'll wake up and you'll be gone?"

"You have my word." His blue eyes searched hers, pleading, begging her to believe him. "I won't hurt him, Julia. Not like I hurt you. You're just going to have to trust me."

"I don't have much choice." She went to the fridge. "So how do we do this? Are you going to want him on weekends or what? Do we divide up holidays, school vacations? I don't know what this is supposed to look like."

Reid gave a muted groan. "Jules, it's not even 7 a.m. The world won't end if we don't have it all figured out by noon." He sat again and she stood at the counter, measuring, mixing, stirring. Trying to ignore him.

"Are you sure you know what you're doing over there?"

"I'm making pancakes."

"I remember the last time you made pancakes for me. Killer wouldn't even eat them."

Because her back was to him, she allowed a smile. "When I went down to Atlanta, I got a job in a diner as a waitress. The chef was an old guy, about a hundred years old. Oliver. When he found out I could barely boil water, he took on the task of teaching me how to cook like some mission from the Almighty. He had the patience of Job, but eventually I caught on. My good cooking was one of the reasons Frank married me."

Reid cracked his knuckles. "What were his other reasons? So he could have his own personal punching bag?"

Not so long ago, she would have fled the room in tears. Today, the acrid question made her laugh. She grabbed the coffee pot and walked to where he sat. "You always were a grump first thing in the morning." She gave him a refill, and debated with herself. It was too early to cook anything, so she had time. "How did you end up in New York?"

Reid ran a finger around the gold rim of the green UV mug, his old alma mater. She'd married him during his sophomore year. Cade had told her Reid left Vermont that summer. After he'd left her.

So many years separated them, yet so much history bound them, and so much she didn't know stood in the way of fully trusting him again.

"Do we have to talk about this?"

Julia gave him the stink eye. "I've just told my son that you're his father. I'd like to know what you've been up to for the last twelve years, so yes, we have to talk about this."

"Fine." The way he scrunched his nose said he was none too happy about it. He stretched his arms above his head with a groan. "It's not that interesting. After I left, I met up with a college buddy of mine who was transferring to NYU. He knew I had an interest in broadcasting, so he talked me into applying as well. I got in, and didn't come back up here much after that. The network hired me almost right after graduation. I'd worked summers there too. Started out running errands in the studio, doing a few stories here and there. After a couple of promotions, I landed a spot on the desk."

"And sky-rocketed to fame." She'd planned to start college herself that September. Instead, she ended up in Atlanta, pregnant, and then married to Frank. "I'm sorry. I don't mean to sound bitter."

"You do though." Reid leaned forward, his stare so intense she could barely meet it. "Do you think it doesn't bother me, knowing how different our lives have been? Knowing that you had dreams of your own? It bothers me more than you know, Julia. More than I can stand. But I don't know how to fix it. If you've got any ideas, I'd sure love to hear them."

"Nope." She pushed up the sleeves of her sweatshirt and tossed him a smile. "Fresh out of ideas I'm afraid."

"Then lets talk about something else."

"So why did you leave New York? Why not get another job with another network?"

"That's not how you change the subject." He tipped his chair back and pushed his fingers through his hair. "What happened to making pancakes?"

"I'll make them in a minute. I'd rather hear why you're back in Bridgewater pounding nails into two-by-fours instead of racing around the world racking up a seven-figure salary." She studied the polish on her nails, then shot him a tentative smile. "And Cade wouldn't tell me."

"I left because ... because it was the right thing to do." He gulped coffee and twisted his head from side to side, flinching at the crack the exercise produced. "I made a mistake."

"You made a mistake leaving?"

"No, I ..."

"Mama." Emily wandered into the room, trailing her pink bunny behind her. "I had a bad dream." Her eyes got a little bigger as she caught sight of Reid. "Mister Reid!" She scampered over to him and he scooped her into his arms.

"What'd you dream about, princess?"

"Monsters."

"Monsters?" Reid plopped her on his lap so she faced him, pushed her blond hair out of her sleepy eyes and tickled her under the chin. "Big fat ugly ones?"

"Uh huh." Emily nodded, a smile starting. "And gooey."

"Gooey and slimy?"

"Yesth."

"Ah. Those are the best kind of monsters ever." The morning sun lit his eyes as it streamed through the window. "They're the friendliest monsters in the world, and they love playing with little girls."

"Really?"

"Oh, sure. Especially ones with huge pink bunnies to keep them company all night."

His deep chuckle blended with Emily's happy giggles.

Julia let out her breath, hating the places her mind was going. Hating the strange pleasure found in watching him interact with her daughter. She'd always wondered what kind of father Reid would be. More and more as the years passed, and Frank's temper ruled their home. She'd lay awake nights and dream of things that would never happen. Prayed for the impossible. Prayed for the same scene that now played out in front of her.

Julia kicked off crazy thoughts and stood to start the pancakes.

This was not happening.

Reid Wallace would not become part of her family.

No matter what he said, he would be heading back to New York to resume his career at some point. He didn't have the slightest intention of settling down.

Not with her anyway.

Not again.

Chapter Twenty-Four

A blast of U2 jerked Reid out of sleep. He groped around on the bedside table until he found his cell. "Yeah."

"Um. Reid?"

"Jules." Reid struggled to sit, coughed and squeezed his eyes a few times. He hadn't talked to her since they'd told Mark the truth last weekend. Hadn't wanted to talk to anyone, really. "What's wrong?"

"Nothing. Are you ... I didn't wake you, did I?"

"Yeah." He tried to stifle a yawn and failed.

"It's almost lunchtime."

"Is it?" Reid yawned again and sank against the pillows. He'd been up half the night, tried to get rid the images that taunted his sleep, finally drifted off again, didn't even know when. He hadn't ventured out of the cabin for a couple of days. Today was ... Thursday, maybe? He lifted a hand and held it out straight. No shakes.

Progress.

"Reid? Are you okay?" There was a pause on the other end. "We were wondering how ... well ... if you needed anything. If you got snowed in yesterday."

"Yesterday?" Reid pushed himself out of bed and shuffled across the room. Snow lay in drifts up to the window. "Yeah. Looks that way."

"Are you sure you're okay?" He could tell she was working to keep the concern out of her voice. "Mark said you haven't called. He thought ..."

Crap.

Reid sighed deep and sank onto the bed. He'd gotten sucked under again. "Sorry, Jules. I … well, to be honest, I've had a bad couple days. It happens."

She stayed silent a minute. "You should have called us. Do you want me to … I could send Cade up. I'll call him."

"No, Jules. You don't need to. I'm fine." He glanced out the window again. He was going to need a snowplow to get out of here. "How's Mark doing?"

"He's all right. They had a snow day yesterday, which he was happy about. The roads are clear now. Actually, that's why I was calling. I have some time off this afternoon and …"

"Oh." A smile inched across his mouth. "Okay. Where do you want to go? Assuming I can get out the driveway, I can pick you up and—"

"No." Her voice got all squeaky like it did when she was embarrassed. Laughter floated into his ear. "I was going to ask if you could pick Mark up from school. I have some stuff I need to do. Research. For that piece I'm working on."

Reid lifted his eyes to the ceiling and shook his head. Way to be an idiot. Of course she wouldn't suggest they go out, hang out or spend any time alone together. Not unless he forced it on her.

"Right. Mark. Sure."

"Well, you didn't think … did you think I was asking you out?"

"Of course not." He shoved his cold feet under the covers again and grinned. "That would be completely out of character for you, Jules. You were always a pretty traditional kind of girl, as I recall."

"You recall correctly." Another low laugh tickled his ear.

"So what if I asked you out?"

"Like on a date?"

"Well. Another one. If you want to count your birthday."

"That wasn't a date. That was a kidnapping."

"Ouch. But okay, you didn't have much choice. So, I'm asking now. Will you go out with me again?"

Her laughter got a little louder, followed by a muted sigh. "Reid, I have to go. Can you pick Mark up? You need to be there about 3:15."

"Was that a no?"

"That was me ignoring your question. Can you pick him up or do I need to ask my mom?"

"I'll pick him up." As long as he could find the number for the snow-plow company.

"Thanks, Reid." She clicked off.

Okay. Reid groaned and stared at his cell. So much for that brilliant idea.

Julia might have allowed him into Mark's life, but she still seemed hell bound to keep him out of hers.

When Reid pulled up outside the school at the end of the day, he found his son surrounded by a group of girls, taking turns signing his cast.

Mark wasn't happy about having to get around on crutches, but Reid had to give the kid credit for using the injury to his full advantage. Crutches on snow and slippery sidewalks couldn't be easy, but Mark looked like he was managing just fine.

Reid smiled, waited a few moments, then honked.

Mark made his way over and Reid got out, grabbed his backpack and crutches.

"Where's my mom?"

"She had some stuff to do and asked me to come get you. You mind?"

"I guess not." Mark got into the front seat with some difficulty. Reid made sure he was comfortable, then backed out of the parking lot.

"You doing all right on those things?"

"Been a week. I figured it out."

"I saw." Reid waited until Mark stopped fiddling with the radio. "Hey. Sorry I kind of bailed the last couple of days. You can always call me if you want, okay?"

"Whatever. Were you sick or something?"

"A little. But I'm good now."

"Cool." Mark snapped his seatbelt in place as Reid pulled onto the main road.

"How was school?"

"All right. Got an 'A' on my English paper."

"Awesome." Reid held out his fist and Mark tapped it. His grin said more than Reid knew the kid would. Mark hid his feelings well, but they escaped anyway through angry outbursts or comments that could make Reid's heart skip a few beats. He was learning how to deal with it, deal with his son and the scars he bore. Now that Mark knew the truth, Reid hoped things would only continue to improve.

"My teacher wanted to know if you helped. And Janice Keeser asked me if it was true you were my real dad."

"Oh." Reid cleared his throat. He hadn't failed to notice a couple of adults staring and pointing his way. Rumors were probably already running rampant, but there wasn't anything he could do about that. He and Julia would have to work out the details of this new arrangement and do their best to ignore the looks and whispers. Eventually folks would find something else to talk about. News never lasted.

"What did you tell Janice Keeser?"

"What do you think I told her? None of your business, Cowface."

"Nice." Reid covered his mouth to hide a grin. "One of these days, kid, you're going to actually want to be nice to girls."

"Not Cowface. There's a reason she's called that."

Reid shook his head and concentrated on the road. He tried not to think about the mounting emails he was avoiding answering. Hilary had sent a couple more. Apparently the network bosses were still hoping he'd come back.

Part of him couldn't deny he might want to. There were some things he missed. Memories of his old life crept up on him in slumber and tried to convince him he'd made a mistake leaving them behind.

But his life wasn't in New York anymore.

It was here. In Bridgewater.

With ...

"Hey, that's Mama!" Mark tapped on the window as they drove along the winding road beside the river. Reid glanced across the white fields to where Mark pointed. He pulled the car over onto the shoulder and idled.

Julia stalked the old-covered bridge like a soldier ready to fire at a moment's notice. She snapped a few pictures as she went, crouched by the dilapidated wooden structure, and stayed there for a long moment, running her hand over a particular piece of wood.

They'd carved their initials into the old bridge a long, long time ago.

A lifetime ago.

Reid couldn't see her clearly, but he'd bet she was scowling.

"What's she doing?" Mark wanted to know.

Reid gave a short laugh and ran a hand down his face. "Hunting ghosts."

"Say what?"

Reid breathed deep and took off his shades. "That's Faith Bridge, Mark. It used to link two parcels of land together. One side was Wallace land, the other belonged to your Mom's family, the Connellys."

"So it's ours?"

"Used to be. Those fields off to the left belong to your great-uncle Walter. My family's farmland was sold a long time ago."

"How come it's all boarded up?"

"Well ..." Reid fiddled with the buttons on the dash, letting a little more heat warm his hands. "A long time ago, my great-grandfather, Zachariah Wallace, fell in love with a girl called Ruth Connelly."

"Uh, dude ..." Mark raised both eyebrows and Reid laughed. Smart as a whip this one.

"They were engaged to be married. Both families were thrilled at the prospect, and they planned to merge their two farms together into one big one. The two fathers forged an agreement stating both sides could have free rein of all the land the other owned. They built the bridge together, and looked forward to Ruth and Zach's wedding. The parents were friends you see, and ..."

Mark cracked a wad of gum and rolled his eyes. "Could you speed it up a bit? Did they get married or what?"

"No. They didn't. Zachariah went off to fight in the war and I guess he met a girl over there. Called off the wedding. Broke Ruth's heart. Old man Connelly was furious, wanted to break their agreement and take back the land they'd agreed to share, but the Wallace side wouldn't hear of it. They'd already built the cabin up the mountain where I live now. Of course it's been renovated over time, but I think the foundations are the originals. I'm pretty sure they never did any farming together, and as you can see, they didn't take care of the bridge."

The red paint was barely visible, most peeled off through years of winter storms and summer sun and rain. The floorboards were rotten, some missing. He and Cade had figured out the way to get across years ago, but if you missed a step, there was a good chance you'd be going for a swim in the river.

"That's dumb. If that bridge was fixed up we'd be home in no time."

Reid nodded. "I guess so, yeah."

"So why don't you fix it?"

"Well." Reid toyed with the ring on his finger. If he didn't tell Mark, he'd hear it someplace else anyway. "I don't know, really. I guess it never got fixed because ..."

"Because?"

"Because somebody died there, Mark."

"Cool!"

Reid scratched his head and sighed again. "No, not cool. Ruth was devastated by what happened. Never did get over Zachariah. He came home a few years later, without the girl. I forget what happened to her. But he begged Ruth to forgive him and take him back. She wouldn't."

"Well, I wouldn'a neither."

"Mark." Reid twisted his ring again.

"So, what then? The guy bumped himself off?"

"No. It was Ruth. She ..." Reid stared at the bridge, debating whether to say it. He'd probably already said too much. Mark didn't need any more gruesome images in his young mind.

"Go on. How'd she do it?" Mark's eyes got buggy. "You know I can find out even if you don't tell me."

Reid didn't doubt it. "She hung herself. From the highest beam inside the bridge. Zach found her, but he was too late."

"What he do? Off himself too?"

"No. He boarded the place up, went up the mountain and stayed there. He married eventually, had a few kids, but they said he never got over Ruth."

"I bet that bridge is haunted."

"That's what they say." Reid watched the way the sun lit Julia's blond hair. Bundled in her red coat and brown boots, she peered into the depths of the bridge, pulled her head out again and began to walk away across the fields.

"Whatever. I think we should fix it up."

Reid drummed his fingers to the country beat coming from the stereo. "Not all things are repairable, Mark. Some things are better left alone."

Two steps forward, two steps back.

They were like a couple on the dance floor, he and Julia, circling around and around, but when the music stopped, there was nowhere to go.

"You ever walk across it?"

"No." Reid leaned forward a little to hide the lie. "It's not safe. Don't you go near it, hear me?"

"You're just saying that because it's haunted."

"It's just a story, Mark. Who knows if there's any truth to it. All towns have ghost stories."

"I bet Aunt Hannah knows. She's good at remembering history."

Reid set his jaw and gunned the engine. "She sure is." Almost as good as her sister.

He pulled onto the road again and headed home.

Chapter Twenty-Five

"You wasted your time coming here." Reid didn't even let her get out of the car.

"Oh, stop being so dramatic." Hilary Fairchild slammed the door, pulled her fur coat tight around her and marched up the driveway. "You could have made it a lot easier if you'd just return my calls, but no, you wouldn't give me the courtesy, would you?"

"I have nothing more to say to you, Hilary. We're through. You need to get over it."

"I am over it. Completely." She clutched a leather briefcase and nodded toward the cabin. "Mind letting me in? This isn't a social call."

"It's not a good time." Reid folded his arms and met her hard look as she removed her shades. Whatever he'd once felt for her, if anything, stayed in New York. Packed away with the rest of the stuff he'd accumulated over the years.

Elaborate paintings he didn't really like. Vases he would never use, let alone look at, with price tags that could feed entire Tibetan villages. Furniture that wasn't even comfortable to sit on. And Hilary.

At first, sure, he'd been attracted to her. They seemed like a good match. Someone to have on his arm, to make him look good, boost his ratings and secure his spot at the network. They'd never really been friends. Just two sad and lonely people using one another in every way possible, caring only what was in it for them. Looking at her now, all he wanted was to see the red taillights of her car.

"Pardon me for interrupting your busy schedule." Her eyes traveled over his paint-stained coveralls and her nose scrunched like there was a skunk in the vicinity. "You look like a maintenance man, for heaven's sake. What on earth are you wearing?"

Reid pulled the brim of a ball cap at the back of his head and peeled a bit of white paint from his chest. "They're called coveralls. Very high couture up here in the sticks."

"No doubt." She tapped her gloved hand against her briefcase. "If you can find a little civility, perhaps you'd invite me in. It is rather cold out here."

He heard the front door slam and held his breath.

Mark hopped up beside him on his crutches, stopped and zipped up his parka. "I'm all done. Ran out of paint, but you said you had to get more anyways." Reid watched his son give Hilary the once-over. He didn't look impressed.

Hilary blinked a couple of times, her mouth pulling into a thin line. Her blond hair swooshed around her shoulders as she shifted her stance. "You didn't say you had company."

"You didn't give me a chance," Reid muttered. "Mark, I can run you home in a minute. Go wait inside."

"Nah, Mama called while you were out back. She's on her way up. She was out anyways, figured she'd save you the trouble."

"Oh." Great. Reid grabbed the back of his neck, his cheeks heating. He could hear Julia's old clunker chugging up the hill already.

"Who're you?" Mark rocked back and forth on his crutches, staring at Hilary with blatant curiosity. Reid might have smiled at the brief look of astonishment on her face if he didn't feel so much like hurling.

"Hilary Fairchild." She didn't miss a beat. Stared back at him through cool blue eyes that never revealed her true feelings. "And you are?"

"Mark Hansen."

Julia's car crested the hill and came to a shuddering stop just behind the shiny blue BMW Hilary had driven up in.

Reid wanted to shudder along with it. "Oh, look, your Mom's here. I'll see you tomorrow, Mark. Thanks for the help." He took Mark's elbow and tried to help him down the steps but Mark shrugged him off.

Julia got out of the car. Raised a hand in greeting, the corner of her mouth twitching as she caught sight of Hilary. The way she clutched her elbows said there was a storm brewing behind those brown eyes. Reid didn't have the slightest clue whether she knew who Hilary was, but he wasn't willing to find out. "Ready to go, Mark?" He nodded at Julia. "Thanks for coming to get him."

Julia shrugged. "Not a problem. Looks like you're busy anyway."

Hilary swiveled on the heels of her black leather boots and angled her head. Looked Julia up and down, then threw him a frosty smile over her shoulder. She took a step toward Mark. "Let me help you, you poor dear. How did you manage this injury?"

"It's kind of a long story." Mark hopped down the pathway toward the cars.

"He's fine. He doesn't need any help." Reid chucked Mark's backpack into Julia's car and prayed for God to grant him favor. Not that he deserved it. But it sure would be nice.

Julia tossed her keys from one hand to the other, her eyes darkening as she watched Hilary. "Haven't I seen you somewhere before?"

Hilary shrugged pulled on a pair of dark glasses. "I doubt it."

"You look familiar." Julia shifted, seeming suddenly uncomfortable. "I'm terrible with names, but I'm sure we've met before."

"I can't imagine where."

Reid couldn't either.

"You haven't met." He pinched the bridge of his nose as a short laugh escaped. Julia stayed put, unsmiling. Probably waiting for him to make introductions and ask them all in for coffee. So not gonna happen. "Well, look at the time. Um, didn't your Mom have that thing tonight ... you should ... you know ... get back and help."

Julia gave him the death stare. He hadn't seen that particular look in a long time, but it jolted his memory at once. Maybe he was still that young jerk she'd hurled angry words at in the middle of the night.

"Yeah. That thing. Right." She put one leg back in the car. "Well, it was nice meeting you ... again. I think."

"Okay. Take care." Hilary gave a little wave and a stifled sigh.

"Her name's Hilary. Fairis-something-or-other." Mark shot a few flaming arrows in his direction. "See ya later, Dad."

Reid raised a brow. Yeah. *Nice one, son.*

He sucked in his breath and willed himself to stand still. If he moved, he'd most likely crumble to the ground in the quivering sorry excuse for a man he'd just become.

Julia reversed into the lay by and the car disappeared down the hill.

"*Dad?*" Hilary turned toward him, mouth open. "Did I hear that correctly?"

Reid released air from his lungs and walked toward the door. "Since you're here, you'd better come in."

An hour later, Reid was wishing he'd kept at least one bottle of something stronger than soda on hand. For medicinal purposes. Because the heartburn Hilary was giving him would surely morph into a heart attack any minute now.

"Two days before Thanksgiving, Hilary? I know you don't look up from your laptop long enough to celebrate holidays, but seriously?"

"Oh, keep your shirt on." She'd taken over his couch, spread papers and files all over it. Now she tapped out a few more sentences on her laptop, gave him a cursory glance and shook her head. "Why is your Internet so slow? Never mind. All right. I'm done. Assuming you can stop playing house for a few minutes and sign these papers, I'll get back to my life, and you can get back to yours. I'm sure it's a wonderful one."

If he could get to the edge of the mountain fast enough, he'd jump. Or drag her with him and give her a push. "Look, I know you're angry. I didn't tell you about Mark because I didn't know. I just ..."

"You don't need to replay it." Her face said she couldn't care but her eyes told the truth. "I heard. You just found out. You explained it all quite well. I'm not deaf, darling. But you could have told me when you came back to New York to break up with me. You knew then. Things might have made a little more sense."

"I know."

"Five years. We were together five years, Reid. You didn't think it worth mentioning that you'd been married?"

"I'm sorry."

She shook her head, her eyes turning to thin slits of contempt. "So you've said. Can you please just sign those papers so I can get out of here?"

Reid studied the legal documents again, the rock hard lump in his throat refusing to budge. "I can't."

"Excuse me?"

He almost laughed. "I thought you just said you weren't deaf, *'darling'*. I can't sign these papers." He handed them back to her.

Hilary sat back, shut her laptop and tapped long red fingernails on the lid. She settled her I'm-all-out-of-patience-and-ready-to-pummel-you look on him. "Reid. Baby. What is it about, 'we're being sued', that you don't understand?"

He raked a fist full of fingers through his hair and cursed. She always brought out the worst in him.

Scott Gilmore's family had every right to sue the network. Reid didn't blame them. Their attorneys had apparently already had several meetings and they might be willing to settle. But he wasn't about to lie to save his own skin. Or the network's. "This says we were assured the area was safe. That we went into Saraqueb believing we were going to be okay, having been told that the rebels were well out of the area. That's not true, Hilary."

She huffed out her annoyance. "Oh, please. Did you have any way of knowing that bomb was going to go off? Of course not. For all we knew, it was perfectly safe."

"No." Reid shook his head, memories surfacing, shaking him, making him wish for the thousandth time he'd made a different decision that day. "Adar told me it wasn't safe. I told you it wasn't safe. You told me to—"

"Oh, no you don't!" Her eyes flashed in the dimly lit living room. "I'm not taking any responsibility for this fiasco. I told you to file something else. You went in there on your own, Reid."

So that's how she would play it. He shouldn't have been surprised, but her cool demeanor disappointed him. If he'd ever meant anything to her, like she said, she was over it.

"I went in there because I was pretty sure you would have me fired if I didn't."

The truth, simmering under the surface so many months, now dredged up, still stunk.

"That was your assumption. You made the final call. Not me."

"You think I don't know that?" He shot to his feet, nowhere to go, just needed to put some space, a lot of space, between them. "I haven't slept a full night since that day. You know I was having trouble before that. I should never have gone on that assignment. I should have quit a long time ago. But I went, and it happened. I can't pretend it didn't. And I can't lie about what I did, Hilary."

She rose, took the few steps needed to reach him and placed her hands on his arms. "Listen to me. We're willing to back you. Willing to go to court, if that's what it takes, or settle, if they will. It was just a terrible accident and nobody is to blame. But if you can't do this our way, if you insist on taking responsibility, then you're on your own."

"Then I guess I'm on my own." He breathed deep. Saw the confusion on her face. Understood it, but couldn't pander to it.

She shook her head. "You'll still drag the network down with you. Once the press gets wind of this, it'll be everywhere. The bosses won't stand for it. Our ratings have dropped since you left. If you want your job back, this won't work in your favor."

"I don't want my job back." The words sounded hollow. False.

"What's happened to you?" Hilary whispered. "I'm offering you a way out. Don't you get that?"

"I get it. You've been quite clear. And I hope I have as well. I won't perjure myself."

"Explain this to me." She sat down again and waited.

He pushed his shoulders back and wrestled with his thoughts. "What you're asking me to do is wrong. Maybe a few months ago I would have gone along, because I was willing to do whatever it took to keep my job. Nothing was more important than that. I was Reid Wallace, the people's reporter. And damn proud of it. And look where that got me. No. This time I'm making the right decision."

"You're a little young for a mid-life crisis, babe."

"I'm not having a mid-life crisis. I just want to do the right thing."

"Taking the moral high ground doesn't always pay off." She shrugged and began to pack away her things. "So be it. You'll have to come into the city. Lou wants a meeting. Maybe by then you'll have come to your senses. Next week Thursday good for you?"

"I'll check my schedule." The reality of what was happening suddenly barreled through his resolve, splintered it and sent him to the nearest chair.

"You do that. But be there, Reid." Hilary pulled on her coat. Cleared her throat a few times, then perched on the arm of the couch. "You know he looks just like you."

"Yes."

"Funny how you always told me you never wanted children."

"Funny."

"I suppose we were just kidding ourselves, you and I. As much as I wanted things to work between us, I see now that we're just too different. You've changed, Reid." She fiddled with a diamond earring, twisting the large stone around, staring at him like she was trying to figure out where the real Reid Wallace had gone. He kind of wondered the same thing. And he had half a mind to ask for those earrings, the chunky David Yurman bracelet on her wrist, and all the other expensive jewelry he'd given her over the years, back.

"No, Hilary. I changed when I went to New York. And now ... I've found myself again." The truth simmered, lit a long-extinguished fire of hope, and he let it burn.

Eventually her mouth moved into a thin smile. "I don't know what's going on with you, Reid, but let me tell you something. These people are serious. They want their son back. Of course they can't get that, so they'll take the next best thing. Money. A lot of it. If you go public with what really happened, they'll go after you. For everything you've got. Which, I'm betting, given the fact that you're now looking at college tuition, you're not going to be so willing to give them. But if you really want to take this all the way—confess to knowingly walking their son to his death, like a lamb to the slaughter—then I don't think any amount of money is going to placate them." She pushed her hands through her blond hair. Either the lighting was really bad in here or he might have seen a shimmer of tears in her eyes.

"You're risking damaging, maybe even destroying whatever future career you have in television. Think about that before you make your final decision. And you might want to get your own attorney."

"Fine. I hear you." He stood and went to the door. Waited until she composed herself, then managed to find the celebrity smile he hadn't used in a while. "Thanks for coming."

"You have nothing to thank me for." Hilary pulled on her gloves and fixed him with that scintillating gaze he could never get around. She should have gone into law instead of television. "All the time we were together, I always wondered, always sensed you were never quite there. With me. It was her, wasn't it? The boy's mother. Julia?"

Reid pushed the door open and stepped onto the porch. "I'll see you next week, Hilary. Safe trip. And Happy Thanksgiving."

"Uh huh." She sent him a half smile and hurried down the pathway toward her car. Snow fell around them and he glanced at the gray sky. Wherever she was going, she better get there quick. Because she wasn't spending the night here. Wasn't ever coming up here again, if he had anything to say about it.

Reid went back inside, steadied his breathing, finally found his heart beating at an acceptable rate, and then realized he'd never told Hilary Julia's name.

Chapter Twenty-Six

Julia checked on Emily but she slept soundly. She got ready for bed and went down the hall to Mark's room and stuck her head around the door. He sat up in bed reading.

"Good book?"

He looked up as she came in. "Moby Dick."

"They're making you read that in sixth grade?" She bent to pick up the pile of socks, underwear and discarded jeans that lay about a foot from the laundry hamper. Her son was definitely using being in a cast to full advantage.

"No." Mark rolled his eyes. "Reid let me borrow it. He's got ... has ... a ton of books up at the cabin, you know. We're building shelves for a library. You should see it, it's cool."

"I'm sure." Her stomach clenched and she focused on tidying Mark's dresser so she wouldn't have to look at him.

"Mama?"

"Yep."

"Reid has to go to New York next week, after my birthday. He said I could go with him, if you let me. Can I?"

"New York?" Julia closed her eyes, gripped the edge of the dresser and clamped her mouth closed.

Seriously?

"I don't think so, Mark." She crossed the room and sat on the edge of his bed. The scowl he wore, so much like the man's she wanted to smack upside the head right now, warned she was in for a fight.

"Why not?"

"You have school."

"It'd only be two days. You could get them to give me work."

"No. And you're in a cast. It's winter. What if the sidewalks are icy and you fall? You can barely get around here. Trying to get through all those people ..."

"I can get around fine." He shook his head, folded his arms and his look told her he wasn't fooled. "You just don't want me to go with him. You're still mad at him for leaving you! I'm the one who should be mad, Mom. He left me too. When you told him you were pregnant, he should have stayed. But he didn't."

"When I what?" Cold tendrils slithered around her neck and pulled tight.

"You know. How you were pregnant, but he left anyway." Mark shrugged and bit his bottom lip. "He told me the whole story. But I don't care. He's here now, right? He wants to be my Dad. So what's wrong with that? So what if he was a loser a long time ago. You should just get over it."

"Wait. Reid told you ..." Julia scrambled to pick up her scattered thoughts and fold them into neat little piles right along with Mark's clothes. "Reid told you he knew I was pregnant? Before he left?" She could barely speak the question.

"I just said that." Mark gave her his I-can't-believe-you're-so-dumb look.

Julia studied her hands and let the truth sink in.

Reid had covered for her.

Taken the blame when all the while, she was the one who'd kept her son away from his father. Intentionally.

Perfect snowflakes hit the window, illuminated by the full moon. She watched them swirl around each other, each one different than the next. When they touched ground they would mold together as one, in a thick blanket of white.

Was there anything that would cover her pain like that? Cover the mistakes of the past? What could she do to release the anger she held onto like a life preserver? It wasn't keeping her afloat. It was dragging her down. And if she didn't let go soon, she'd drown under it.

"You should get some sleep now, Mark. It's ten-thirty."

He squished up his nose. "Half an hour more? Tomorrow's Thanksgiving. I don't have to get up early. Please?"

"All right. Half an hour." She leaned over and kissed his forehead. "Love you."

His arms came around her neck in an unexpected hug. "Love you too, Mama. Will you talk to my … to Reid about New York?"

Julia sat back and allowed a smile. "I'll talk to him." The very next chance she got. She brushed a thick lock of hair away from his eyes. "You know, Mark, if you want to call him Dad, it's okay. I'm sure he'd be fine with it. But …" She leaned forward and pulled a few stray threads off his quilt, letting her hair cover her grin. "That was a potshot yesterday, throwing it out there like that in front of that woman." She'd silently applauded that particular potshot, but wouldn't be admitting it.

"Whatever." Mark rolled his eyes. "I didn't like her. Who was she anyway?"

"Somebody Reid used to work with." And a lot more, but Mark didn't need to know details. Julia pulled the quilt up around him. "See you in the morning."

"She's not staying for Thanksgiving, is she?"

Julia let out her breath. "I don't know." What did it matter? If Reid showed up with Hilary Fairchild in tow, there was little she could do about it. "If she is, you need to be polite."

"Okay. But Mama?"

She waited at the door, watched him shift positions, a half-smile curling his lips.

"Don't be mad at him anymore. Please?"

Julia sighed and shoved her hands in the pockets of her robe. "I'll try, Mark. But don't be getting any ideas about anything, all right?"

"Ideas about what?" He grinned and picked up his book again. "G'night, Mama."

Silverware and fine white china shone under candlelight. Mom always used her best china and crystal for holidays, set a magnificent table, and she'd outdone herself this year. Dad ordered flowers because her mother liked the house to be filled with them. Debby worked hard to make them perfect, and Julia envied the end result. Orange and red chrysanthemums and yellow roses added warmth to the display of dried summer squash and corn laid out in a display even Martha Stewart would be proud of.

Julia studied the happy faces around the dining room table and tried to smile. She'd looked forward to this holiday so much. Until Tuesday night, when she'd encountered Reid's girlfriend. She'd known immediately who Hilary was, and a few hours surfing the Internet with Hannah confirmed it. The fact Reid didn't bother making introductions told the rest of the story.

Fortunately, Reid showed up for lunch alone. But the combination of Mark's bombshell last night and the uncertainty of Reid's current dating status had her crawling the walls. She was still trying to process it, trying to figure out the best way to handle it.

She'd never been more furious with anyone than she was with Reid Wallace right now.

"You okay, Jules?" Blast the man. He could still read her mind.

"Perfectly fine, thank you." She lowered her gaze, poked tiny holes in her mashed potatoes with her fork and wished Reid would stop staring at her. Wished he wasn't even here. Maybe even wished he'd never come back to Bridgewater.

Cade and Debby had been trying to get her to talk all morning, tell them what was going on, but she wouldn't.

"If you say so." Reid didn't look too happy either. Whatever mission had brought Miss Fairchild to Bridgewater, she doubted it was a pleasant one.

"That was a great meal, Mom. Thanks." Cade cleared his throat, a crooked smile taking over his features. Debby squirmed in the seat beside him, her eyes shining a little too brightly. Reid sat back with a grin, arms folded across his chest.

Julia didn't have to guess what was coming. Her throat clogged almost at once and she twisted the napkin in her lap. Gathered her thoughts and forced a smile before looking across the table at her brother and best friend.

"Deb and I have an announcement."

"Well, get on with it, boy." Dad was impatient, but a smile settled on his lips just the same. Mom gave a little squeak. Even Hannah was smiling.

Cade nodded, put his arm around Debby and pulled her close. "I have no idea why, but this wonderful woman has agreed to marry me."

Cries of congratulations exploded around them. Dad stood, pumped her brother's hand up and down and kissed Debby on the cheek. Debby showed off her ring. Mom wiped tears and hugged them both while Emily jumped up and down and immediately asked if she could be a flower girl. Mark looked amused. It wouldn't be cool to go overboard, but Julia knew he was grinning on the inside. He adored his uncle.

"Congratulations." Reid raised his glass, his smile sincere. "To the two best friends a guy could ask for. May God grant you many years of future happiness."

"Hear, hear." They all toasted and drank and her father got to his feet. "I have a bottle of champagne I've been saving." He exited the room whistling 'Here Comes The Bride.'

"When's the date?" Mom asked, her face aglow with excitement. "Not too soon I hope. You have a lot to plan."

"Well, we were kind of hoping sooner than later," Debby told her. "No reason to have a long engagement really … maybe late spring."

"Oh, goodness!" Mom clapped her hands together. "Not impossible of course. And the weather will be lovely. I'll call your mother right after dinner."

Julia reached for the pitcher of water, refilled her glass and nodded toward her brother and Debby. "You should have the wedding of your dreams, Deb. You deserve it after waiting this long. Hopefully you'll have better luck than I did."

"Julia!" Mom pushed her chair back, her cheeks pinking.

She'd shocked them all, apparently. Cade stared like he couldn't believe she'd said it. Reid studied his empty plate, clenching and unclenching his fingers around the blue water glass in front of him.

"Seriously? You can't just be happy for us?" Storm clouds rolled across her brother's face.

"She was just making a joke, Cade." Debby pressed her lips into a tight smile. Julia didn't look at the kids. Or Hannah, who probably agreed wholeheartedly.

"I am happy for you." Julia shrugged, her throat tight. "I'm just being honest. I got burned a couple of times, but hey, that's life, right? I'm sure you'll have a wonderful marriage. Maybe I should find myself a new husband. What's that they say, third time's a charm?"

Reid caught her eye. "Jules, don't do this."

Mark shifted in his seat. "Mama, stop."

Mark's whispered request shook her to her senses. But the look of disapproval on Reid's face lit her temper.

"Don't do what, Reid? Dredge up the past? Drag your name through the mud again? I wouldn't waste my breath. Seems like you've got your own personal fan club sitting around you anyway. Shame Miss Fairchild couldn't join us. Mom's always got room for one more."

"Here we are. A little bubbly to celebrate the occasion!" Dad returned in time to end the conversation as he popped the champagne. Julia stayed silent and couldn't wait for the rest of the meal to be over.

At last it was.

She found Cade and Debby at the back door getting ready to go to Deb's parents place. Julia cleared her throat, walked to where they stood and offered a meager smile. "Please forgive me. I didn't handle that well. Actually, I was awful. I'm so sorry. And I'm very happy for both of you."

"We know." Debby's shining eyes said there was nothing to forgive. "Don't give it a second thought."

"No, really. That wasn't fair of me." She blew out a breath and blinked tears at the concern on their faces.

Cade pulled her under his arm and kissed the top of her head. "Give yourself a break for once, huh? It's done."

Debby nodded and took Julia's hand. "I want you standing up there beside me, Jules. Will you be my Maid of Honor?"

"Of course." Julia glanced at her brother and rolled her eyes at his grin. "I don't suppose I have to ask who your best man is?"

"If he agrees." Her brother laughed and raised a blond brow. "And as long as the two of you promise to put your guns away for the ceremony."

Julia saw them off and ventured back into the warm kitchen where she helped her mother and Hannah clear up. The guys retreated to the living room to watch the game.

"Sweetheart." Mom grabbed her arm as Julia fumbled with a plate, catching it just before it hit the floor. "Put that down before you break it. That's your grandmother's china and I intend to pass it on to my grandchildren."

"Sorry." Julia put down the dish and braced herself against the kitchen counter. She was already dreading it. How would she get through a wedding with Reid standing up there with her, watching her, they'd probably even have to dance again.

The more distance she tried to put between them, the more they were pushed together.

"I'm going to let the dogs out." Hannah called for them and went to the back door, unusually tactful.

Julia straightened and sent her mother a look of apology. "I behaved badly in there. I'm sorry."

Mom put her hands around Julia's face and smiled. "Darling, you've been through so much. But you're home now. You have the chance to start over." Her deep brown eyes studied her. "But let me say this. You will never start over if you don't forgive that man. Really forgive him. Get rid of all those old feelings you're holding onto. Give him a real chance. Do you understand what I'm saying?"

Julia's chest tightened at her mother's words. She was absolutely right, but somehow it didn't make it any easier to admit. "I'm trying."

"Are you?"

No. She wasn't really trying. For all she'd said, even promised before God, about trying to forgive Reid and move on, she knew she hadn't managed it.

"Fine." Julia went to the sink and picked up the last plate. "I'll try harder."

"That's my girl." Mom patted her back. "Now. I think I'll go put my feet up and let Emily watch a movie in my room. Do you need a rest?"

"I'm okay. I want to get some writing done." She'd brought her laptop downstairs before lunch, hoping to find a quiet moment at some point.

Mom left the kitchen and Hannah came back in with the dogs, grabbed a bag of chips and went to join the others. Julia sat at the table and opened her computer. She spent the next hour working on the article that was due on Monday.

"Got anything to drink?" Reid startled her as he walked by the table toward the fridge.

"No, we don't. My dad doesn't drink beer." The words shot out of her mouth, sharper than she'd intended.

He stopped walking, made a half turn and stared. "Soda, Jules. Mark asked me to get him something."

"Oh. Middle shelf. He likes root beer."

"Sounds good to me." Reid's smile didn't light his eyes like it usually did. "You, uh … look nice in that color."

"What?" Rational thought played tag with confusion and muddled her thoughts.

"Your sweater. I like it. Is it new?" He was already halfway across the room.

She glanced down at the Kelly green wool sweater she'd bought on impulse yesterday, let out her breath and put her head in her hands. Willed away visions of Frank sprawled across the couch, drinking beer after beer and yelling obscenities at the television. And her. She'd come to loathe Thanksgiving. And all other holidays.

The fridge closed. Julia looked up and met his questioning gaze.

He placed two cans on the table, leaned across it and put his hands around her wrists. "Do we need to talk?"

"No." She pulled her hands free and studied the words she'd written over the last hour.

"I think we do." Reid pushed down the lid of her laptop.

She gaped. "I was working on that."

"And it'll be there later." He held her eyes prisoner for longer than she was comfortable with. "Don't move. I'll be right back, and then you and I are going for a drive."

Julia pushed her chair back and fled the room the minute he left the kitchen.

She stalled in the hallway and wondered where to go. The living room was closest so she went that way, pulled the pocket doors together and sank onto the couch, her head pounding.

It took less than five minutes for him to barge into the room and pull the doors shut again. "I thought I said don't move."

She huddled at the end of the couch, hugged her knees and stared at the painting of the old red covered bridge above the mantel. "I don't like to be told what to do. I lived with that for twelve years. I don't need it from you."

"Fair enough." He sighed and pushed his fingers through his hair. "Okay. Let me try this again. Can you please get your coat and come for a drive with me? I need to talk to you about something, and I don't want to do it here."

There was no use in arguing. Might as well get it over with.

"Fine." She pushed to her feet and marched past him. "Because I need to talk to you too. You might want to take me somewhere I can yell real loud."

Chapter Twenty-Seven

They drove around the deserted streets of Bridgewater awhile, listening to music and not talking.

"You used to hate country music." Julia broke the silence, stealing a look at him. The corners of his eyes crinkled in an unexpected grin.

"Mark keeps changing the channel every time he gets in here, so I figure it's easier to keep it on. It's growing on me."

Julia bit her fingernails and tried to figure out how to put her feelings into words. Anger, confusion and sorrow were so closely linked it seemed impossible to separate them.

Eventually Reid pulled over onto a side street, turned up the heat and shrugged out of his leather jacket.

Julia fiddled with her scarf as she stared at the house across the road. "Oh." Memories danced across her mind and made her smile, but what she saw chased joy away.

The old Victorian was her favorite house in town. She'd taken piano lessons from a lady who'd lived next door, and every time she passed the large house, she'd dream of living there. She loved its pale blue color, with white gingerbread trim and neat shutters. The house had boasted a perfectly manicured lawn that rolled down to the sidewalk.

Patches of snow sat here and there, but didn't hide the weeds that had taken over. The red brick walkway used to be lined with beautifully kept rose bushes. Bushes that now sat abandoned and unkempt. Two maple trees stood guard at the bottom of the garden and showed off their splendor every fall. It'd been easy to imagine living here, and as she grew older, Reid was there too, sitting on the wraparound porch in summer, drinking lemonade and watching kids play in the yard.

The house was no longer how she remembered it.

And her dreams hadn't come true.

"My house. It's all rundown."

Just like every aspect of her life.

Run down, bedraggled and sorely neglected.

Maybe she'd reached this state through no fault of her own, but what was she really doing to make repairs? What real effort was she making to move on? Most days it was easier to enjoy the pity party. It didn't require nearly as much effort.

Reid peered through the car window, gave a shrug. "Doesn't look like anybody lives there. The windows are boarded up."

"It was so beautiful. How could they let it go like that?" She wanted to run across the deserted street and tear down those boards. Wash all the windows until they shone. Scrub away the dirt, dust and grime she envisioned within, until a new layer of shiny wood covered every room in the house. Pull up the weeds and tend to the roses before real winter came.

But none of it was hers to fix.

"Hey, it's just a house." His soft words made her turn his way.

Julia shook her head, gripping her elbows. "No. It's not just a house. It's special."

Reid smiled, reached out a hand and tucked a strand of hair behind her ear. "Still love that old place, huh?"

It sounded even sillier when he said it. "I know, it's stupid, right? I've never even been inside. It was just a dream anyway. I knew I'd never really live there." She shifted, much too aware of his presence beside her.

"There's nothing wrong with having dreams, Jules."

"Yeah." She ran her finger down the cold glass of the car window. "Just as long as you don't expect them to come true." Julia sighed and unzipped her coat. "Look, I'm sorry about this afternoon. I was out of line. Holidays are hard for me." There. She'd apologized. That had to count for something, right?

"I figured." He studied her through clear eyes. "But it also occurred to me that normally, you'd be thrilled to hear Cade and Debby are getting married. Which brings me to the conclusion that something is bothering you. And since I'm usually the one responsible for that scowl on your face, I'm guessing it's got to do with me."

"You'd be right."

Reid clenched his hands around the steering wheel. "Please, enlighten me. What terrible crime have I committed now?"

"Did you tell Mark he could go to New York with you?"

His cheeks got a little darker. "I mentioned it."

"Without talking to me first?"

Understanding blanched his face, followed by a smile that only served to stoke her anger. "Okay, I—"

"No, not okay. You can't tell him you're taking him to New York without discussing it with me, Reid. That's not fair."

"I merely suggested it. It's his birthday. I thought it would be a fun trip. I didn't tell him it was a done deal."

"He's a kid, Reid. In his mind, it is a done deal! And I'd already made plans for his birthday. Plans I've been trying to tell you about for days, but you've been impossible to reach this week."

"I'm not impossible to reach," he argued. "You called me several times. You could have just mentioned it over the phone."

"I wanted to tell you in person, so you'd feel a part. Not just give you some offhanded invitation over the phone. I intended to talk to you the other day, when I came to pick Mark up. But you were busy."

"Julia." He sighed, pushed his seat all the way back and leaned forward for a while. "I'm sorry." He looked up, his eyes shadowed by dark circles she hadn't noticed earlier. "You're right. I should have talked to you first."

"Well. I'm sure a trip to New York sounds like much more fun than a pizza party with a few of his buddies." Not that she'd agree to let Mark go, but it was easy to see why he wanted to. "Why are you going back to the city anyway?"

His jaw clenched and she watched him take a measured breath. "I have some meetings with the network next week. I thought it might be a good opportunity for him and I to spend some time together."

"With you in meetings?"

"One meeting. Maybe two. I wouldn't just leave him to wander the streets, Jules. Give me a little credit."

"What would you do then, leave him with your girlfriend?"

"What?"

"That woman who was here. Hilary whatever her name is."

"She's not my girlfriend."

"Oh, please. I've seen pictures." She sounded like a sixteen year-old who'd just caught her boyfriend making out with someone else. Julia folded her arms and studied the lines on her brown cords.

"Pictures? Where?"

She made herself look at him again. "Um, Google for starters. Facebook. You're not that hard to find online, you know."

Amusement jumped in his eyes. "Ah. I see you've discovered the joys of the Internet. Creeping my page, though, really, Jules?"

"How else am I supposed to find out anything? You won't talk to me."

His smile came and went. "Are you mad because I asked Mark to go to New York or because Hilary was here?"

"This is not about her at all." Julia slapped her gloves together and pulled them on. "I don't care what you do. Your love life is none of my business. But if my son is going to be spending time with that woman, I'd like to know about it. You didn't even introduce us the other day."

"I didn't think I needed to." He fiddled with the volume of the radio, consternation pulling lines across his forehead. "She came up here for the network, to discuss business."

Julia had stared at pictures of the two of them until she couldn't take it anymore. Couldn't stop comparing her frumpy wardrobe to the glamorous outfits the woman wore in every photograph. Couldn't stop obsessing over the fact that if there was any reason at all for Reid to be heading back to New York anytime soon, Hilary Fairchild was it.

And she couldn't help feeling like the biggest fool in the world to give over even the tiniest bit of her heart to Reid Wallace again.

"Are you going to marry her?"

"Am I what? Where did you hear that?" His jaw tightened as he matched her pointed gaze. "Have you been talking to Hannah?"

"She might have said something." Shown her every website she could find that had the dirt on Reid Wallace. Of course there was always a chance that some things weren't true.

Julia floundered for a way to come out of this unscathed. "When I saw her at the cabin, I knew she was your girlfriend. I assumed she'd arrived for Thanksgiving."

"You assumed wrong. On all counts." He blew air through his lips. "Julia, don't you think that if I were engaged to Hilary Fairchild, which I am not and never have been and God help me, don't ever intend to be, that I would have had the decency to let you know?"

"Considering the fact that you kissed me, yes, that would have been nice."

"I wouldn't have kissed you if I was involved with someone else! Would I?"

"I don't know. Like you keep telling me, I don't really know you anymore."

"God, help me, do you know how frustrating you can be?" He slammed his head against the leather seat and closed his eyes.

"Did you live with her?"

"Julia."

"Just answer the question."

"You want to know if I slept with her."

"I kind of assumed if you lived together the two would go hand in hand. But you can answer that question too."

"Sort of."

"You sort of slept with her? I'm confused."

A strangled sound of aggravation stuck in his throat. "She had her own place, but … okay. Hilary and I were together for a few years, that's true. But it's over, Julia. Completely. You have no reason to be jealous."

He was totally serious.

"Oh, you've got to be kidding me." Julia opened the door, jumped out and slammed it on him. Reid Wallace was the most infuriating man she'd ever known. Ever. She zipped up her coat and walked down the block.

As far away from him as she could get.

He caught her up as she turned into the playground. Didn't say anything. Just fell into step beside her.

"I don't know what you think, Reid," she spat the words as she walked. "But you and I . . . it's not going to happen. Not again. So if you think I still hold onto old feelings and some false hope that one day you and I might be together again, you'd be wrong. On all counts. Is that clear enough for you?" She headed for the swings, grabbed one, hopped on and swung until she was high in the air.

"That's pretty clear." Reid took the swing next to her and soon matched her height and speed. "But let me be clear on something too, Julia. I am not romantically involved with Hilary Fairchild any longer, and quite frankly I have no idea what I ever saw in her. And if you really don't have any feelings for me, then that makes me the world's biggest putz right about now. Because I'm pretty much done for every time you look at me. I don't know, maybe a good kick in the gut is as much as I deserve from you. But it won't change how I feel. How I've always felt. So put that in your pipe and smoke it, sweetheart."

Julia kicked hard and stared at the disappearing ground, her lips inching toward a smile. Esmé's favorite saying sang to her, reminded her where they'd come from. Who they used to be. And his words, thick with promise, both terrified and thrilled her.

They swung in unison for what seemed like forever. Gray clouds lowered into the afternoon sky and a few flakes of snow fell around them.

Reid reached for her hand.

"Don't." She clung tight to the iron loops, cold metal penetrating her gloves. Stared straight ahead and ignored the resonating laughter that floated around her.

"Come on." His teasing tone held just a hint of challenge.

"No. You'll make me crash into you."

"I will not. We've done it a million times."

"A million years ago."

"Trust me."

The winter wind trailed through her hair and burned her cheeks with cold, but his words lit something in her heart. Something new. Something that derailed her, took her completely by surprise, stole her breath away and stamped out all trace of anger.

Julia smiled and pushed higher, grabbed his hand and held on as they swung together. Minutes passed. Talking wasn't necessary now. All she needed was the thrill of going as high as she could go, knowing he was right there beside her, feeling the same way.

Just like always.

"Ready?" His grin took her back a few years, but the lines around his eyes reminded her where they were. And the way he looked at her said maybe, just maybe, they were right where they were supposed to be.

"On your count."

"One. Two. Go!"

They jumped together, landing on their feet into a run that ended in both of them collapsing onto the cold ground in laughter.

Julia sat up first, brushing dirt and leaves off her coat. "We're idiots."

"No doubt." He wiped his hands and gave his head a shake.

She took a few moments to catch her breath and order her thoughts. "Reid?"

"Yeah?" He sprawled beside her, still grinning.

She sat cross-legged, ignored the cold and concentrated on the light in his blue eyes. "Why did you tell Mark you knew I was pregnant?"

"Ah." He moved to a sitting position, pulled his knees to his chest and let his arms dangle over them. The sun escaped the clouds and light bounced off the ring on his hand, drawing her gaze to it. He hated wearing gloves, even in the coldest temperatures, but it was warm enough this afternoon. "You heard about that, huh?"

"I didn't know what to say." Still didn't. She swallowed raw emotion, pulled her own gloves off and shoved them in the pocket of her coat, suddenly warm from exertion and the current of feelings traveling through her body at warp speed. "Why didn't you just tell him the real story?"

"Because we don't know what the real story is, do we?" He hesitated a moment. "Say you *had* told me, we don't know how that would have ended. I might have come back, I might not have, I don't know. So I told him what seemed like a better version of the truth. I didn't want him being angry with you for something we can't do anything about now, Jules. Let's just leave it this way."

There was little choice.

And Mark loved him anyway.

She scrambled to her feet and walked the perimeter of the playground. Reid sat for a while, then showed up in front of her, took her by the arms and simply stood there.

A half-smile fixed on his lips, but a frown narrowed his eyes. "I'm sorry for talking to Mark about New York before I talked to you. But I have to tell you, Jules, I'm sick of saying I'm sorry. I'm sick of worrying that anything I say might dredge up a bad memory or remind you, yet again, what a jerk I was. I want to move on. I want us back. You, me, the way we were before all the crap." He drew a breath and let it out slowly.

"I know I screwed up. But I want a second chance. I want my best friend back. I want to explore these crazy feelings that make me want to sweep you up in my arms and take us back to when things were good, back to when we really loved each other. But that can't happen unless you can find some way to get past everything. If you can't, I need to know that. If all we're meant to be is friends, okay. I'll accept it. It's not what I want, but if that's really how you feel, I'll respect that."

Julia allowed his words to permeate her soul. Ignored the tears that trickled over her cheeks. A family moved across her line of vision, walking together toward the swings she and Reid had just vacated.

The man, a tall, rugged-looking guy, reminded her of Reid. They had a young boy and a small girl, with blond curls much like Em's. The kids ran off to play and the man stood behind the woman, put his arms around her and she leaned back against him. He kissed her hair and they watched the children together.

Julia looked at Reid again. Hidden in the depths of his eyes she saw her past, her present, and perhaps her future. She reached for his right hand and ran her finger over the ring he wore. "Why do you still wear this?"

He lowered his eyes in a silent moment that almost made her dread the answer he would give.

"Two reasons." Reid exhaled a shaky sigh. "It reminds me of the kind of guy I was back then. Selfish. Self-centered. Narrow-minded, and cocky as all get out. When I look at it, I remember who I was, and I remind myself who I am now. And those are two completely different people."

That was true. Back then he had been all the things he said, but she'd loved him anyway. She'd given him every bit of herself, almost from the moment they met. Yet somehow she had always known she'd never be enough for the Reid Wallace she'd married. "And the second reason?"

He smiled. "Hope."

One word, with so much meaning within it. So much she still didn't understand.

"Care to elaborate?"

The grey flecks in his eyes shimmered in the afternoon light, moisture tingeing his lashes. "It reminds me that things won't always be this way. Some days I don't know what hope feels like. But this says maybe one day I'll be better than the guy you married. Maybe one day my life will be filled with love again, and I won't take it for granted. I have to hope that maybe, one day, somebody out there—somebody I loved more than I knew and should never have walked away from—might find it in her heart to forgive me. And maybe give me a second chance."

His shy grin, so different from the usual stellar smile that put the world at ease, caused her to backpedal. Everything he said was everything she'd secretly dreamed. All she'd ever wanted. But something still held her back.

Who was this man?

The moment she thought she had him figured out, he changed course and sent her sailing into the wind, unsure of the direction she headed.

"I guess those are good reasons," she whispered.

Julia lowered her eyes, praying for the courage to go on. She was tired of turning from the truth. Tired of denying her feelings. Denying him what he needed. What she knew now she needed to give him.

When she was about seven or eight, she and Hannah used to collect butterflies. They would spend hours in the fields. Nets raised, they'd stalk the fragile creatures, wait for the perfect moment, then pounce with glee. Capture the delicate, fluttering wings and put them in jars. Julia wanted to let them out almost at once, release them back to the life they were born to, but Hannah refused. And soon enough, the butterflies died.

Julia slipped her fingers through his and held tight. "I forgive you."

Reid angled his head. "For?"

"All of it."

"You're serious?" He shifted a little closer, eyes glued to hers.

"Yes." She gave his hands a squeeze before letting go, wiped the moisture from her cheeks. "I know I said I was going to work on forgiving you. I asked God to help me with my anger, and I guess I kind of figured it would just disappear. But it didn't. It sort of got worse, because the closer you and I get, the more afraid I feel. I don't know if I can trust you or anyone again. I want to try but there's this huge cavernous gap that I need to jump across and …" She sighed in frustration. "This isn't making sense, is it?"

His smile told her it didn't matter.

Reid slid cold hands around her face and drew her close. "You make perfect sense, Julia Connelly. You always did."

"Not always." She placed her hands on his shoulders. "I want things to be different between us, Reid. Better."

"I want that too. More than you know." He ran a finger across her bottom lip.

Julia shivered under his touch as exiled feelings returned, swelled, surged to life and almost knocked her off her feet. She sent up a silent prayer of thanks as she remembered what happiness felt like. What it meant to be free. Truly free. In mind, body and spirit.

She smiled wide and slipped her arms around his waist. "I kind of lied back there."

He raised a brow. "About?"

Laughter escaped as she watched new light dance in his eyes. "About not having feelings for you … that's not exactly true."

"Really?" Mock surprise pulled up his lips in a wicked grin that made her knees wobble. "I'm shocked. I mean, not that you do … but that you would lie about it. Jules, that's, well, that's just sinful."

"Stop." She held onto his smile for a moment. "Would you be patient with me? I'm still healing, and I want to do this right. I don't want to rush into things too soon." Her breath tangled with emotion and took away words.

"Jules." He leaned in, rested his forehead against hers. He looked at her again through wet eyes. "If I knew there was a chance for us to start over, I'd wait forever."

"I don't think it will take as long as that." She pressed her hand against his cheek and enjoyed the pleasure his smile brought.

Reid threaded her hair through his fingers, drew her closer into his embrace. "Would it be okay if we didn't talk anymore?"

"You said you had something to tell me. Was it just the New York thing?"

"It doesn't matter." He folded her in his arms and held her tight. "Nothing else matters right now. Just this."

"Reid?"

"Yeah?"

"Remember that day at The Lookout? When you said you wouldn't kiss me again until I was good and ready?"

He leaned back a little, a grin starting. "I remember."

"Well." Julia smiled and slid her hands upward to cradle his face. "I'm good and ready."

Reid's answer came in a sweet and gentle kiss that melted through her, washed away the past and filled her heart with fresh hope.

Chapter Twenty-Eight

"What do you mean you didn't tell her?" Cade paced Reid's New York apartment, throwing a baseball between his hands. He'd been called in to attend the meetings as well, and give his account of how things went down. Julia agreed to Mark coming along a little quicker once she knew Cade would be there.

Reid stretched on the couch, stared at the Manhattan skyline and wished he were anywhere else. "I didn't see the point in worrying her. They're suing the network, not me."

"Not you, yet. Dude, if things don't play out well tomorrow, this could get ugly."

"Keep your voice down." Reid glanced down the hall to the bedroom. Mark had passed out an hour ago, but still, he didn't want him overhearing this. "I'm not going to lie about what happened over there, and neither are you. I told you what my attorney said. The network won't want to look bad, so they'll settle."

"You better hope they settle." Cade shoved the last piece of pizza in his mouth. "Because I don't have the kind of money you do, and I'm getting married."

"Chill out. It'll be fine."

"I still think you should tell her, man. If she sees this on the news, dude, she'll be blindsided."

"I'll tell Julia when there's something to tell, Cade. And not before." Reid closed his eyes. Sleep wouldn't come tonight, he knew that much. He only hoped his instincts were right this time.

Reid stared down the long conference table and fiddled with the tie he'd pushed up a little too tightly that morning. They'd been talking for three hours. Going round in circles, like being on a Ferris wheel, no way to jump off or stop it. He wished somebody would pull the plug on the thing soon.

"Do you want to retract your statement, Mr. Wallace?"

Reid glanced at his attorney. The man shrugged, raised a brow. Reid's call. Warm air from the vent above them blew down, stifling him and making him sweat.

"No. What I said stands. I walked into that area under my own admonition, knowing it was unsafe. I hold myself entirely responsible for the deaths of Paul Ellis and Scott Gilmore."

"All right, Mr. Wallace." The older looking of the three attorneys in the conference room stood, slapped down the top of his laptop and shot a scathing glance at Lou Fairchild. "Since we're clearly not going to get anywhere, I say we call it a day. We're going to offer the family a generous settlement. We're not going to mention any of this to them, unless they refuse. I trust they'll accept, and we can avoid going to court. What you've told us in this room goes no further. Is that understood?"

Reid reached for his water glass, his hand shaking. "Understood." He sipped and caught Hilary's stepfather staring him down across the table.

Lou Fairchild had married her mother when Hilary was in grade school. She never saw her real dad, and Lou had adopted her. He doted on her, gave her everything she wanted and then some. But for some reason, Hilary always held him at arm's length.

Lou hadn't been happy with Reid's decision to leave New York. He'd been furious. But Reid left anyway. He hadn't seen Lou since breaking things off with Hilary, and wasn't looking forward to the moment the room emptied.

But it did, and before Reid could move, it was just the two of them.

"All right." Lou let go a heaving cough that shook his large frame. "Now that those chumps are gone. How are you?"

Lou was a decent guy, but you didn't want to get on his wrong side. Reid had seen glimpses of the man's temper over the years and prepared to tread carefully.

"Doing better every day, Lou. Thanks for asking." Reid shrugged out of his suit jacket and checked his watch. Cade and Mark would be on their way to meet him outside.

"And you're coming back to work, when?"

"Uh ..." Reid messed with his hair and twisted the ring on his finger. "Lou, I don't think I'm coming back."

Bafflement didn't come close to the expression that crossed the big man's face. "Okay. You do understand what just happened in here?"

"You're willing to cover my butt. Yes, I understand. But if this goes any further, I'll take the fall. I won't lie in court."

"I don't think it's going to go further. But I want you back here, Wallace. You want to play hardball? I'll double your salary and you can have your own show. How's that?"

"C'mon, Lou." Reid laughed, pushed to his feet and began to gather his things.

"I'm completely serious. You and I talked about this before you left for Syria. I'm still interested. I think we both know the idea is solid. The public will eat it up, especially after your absence. We can't lose."

One of the large clocks on the wall ticked a little too loudly. Reid glanced at all the other clocks, checked the time in London, Frankfurt, Brazil ...

"I don't think so, Lou. Thanks."

"Sit down, Reid. We need to talk."

Reid sat. Stared at his hands and finally looked back at Lou. "There really isn't anything for us to talk about."

"See, now that's where you're wrong, son." Lou poured more water from the silver carafe. "When I let you leave, it was under the assumption you were coming back. I didn't fire you. You said you quit, but we know you were just calling my bluff. You still have a year left on your contract, Reid. A legal, binding document."

"I quit, Lou. Tear up the contract." Sweat slid down the back of his neck and Reid shifted in his seat.

"I'm not going to do that. I'm going to hold you to that contract. You're going to move back here where you belong, start work again, and make us all happy. Capiche?"

"Hilary." Reid breathed out her name, no doubt in his mind that she was behind this.

Lou lifted his hands and grinned. "What can I say? She's been a mess since you left. Unfocussed. Beyond miserable, and her mother and I have put up with it long enough. We tried to get her to see reason. As you know, she can be very persuasive."

"This is ridiculous. Hilary and I are done, Lou, find yourself another lackey." Reid pushed his chair back.

"What you and Hilary do is your business." Lou gave a low chuckle. "But I want you back on the air." He clasped his hands together. "I didn't want it to come to this, but so be it. Do you know what really happened down in Atlanta?"

"Atlanta?"

"Yes. Atlanta. The night Frank Hansen was killed. Ringing any bells?"

Reid met Lou's cold eyes and suddenly saw the man for what he really was.

A snake. A slithering, conniving snake, willing to stop at nothing to get what he wanted.

"I don't know what you're talking about."

"No? Perhaps you should go back to Vermont and ask your son's mother then. Julia, isn't it? The girl you married when you were barely twenty years old?"

"This is none of your business." Reid clenched his fists to keep from pounding them on the table.

Lou's chuckle rolled across the room like an impending storm. "Well, that may be. But I think your adoring public would find it extremely interesting to know the events surrounding the death of your ex-wife's husband. Did you know she confessed to pulling the trigger herself?"

"There was nothing to confess. It was an accident." His breath left him, the two bagels and coffee he'd consumed in a hurry that morning churning in his stomach.

Lou pushed a dossier across the table toward him. "Of course it was. It's all there in the police report. I'm sure you looked it up yourself, knowing you. Self defense. Never went to trial. Everyone knew what a sick puppy Hansen was. Nobody would have blamed her I suppose, if she had been the one to kill him. But that's not what really happened."

Reid's hands shook as he flipped through the papers, scanned the words. Read the statements. "That is what happened. It says so right here."

"Mmm. It does. And you really don't know, do you?"

"Know what?"

"The truth, Reid. Julia Hansen didn't kill her husband. Her son did. Well, I guess that would be *your* son."

A sharp knife slid into his stomach. Reid shook his head, stared Lou down and took slow measured breaths. "That's not true."

"Just because she didn't tell you, doesn't mean it's not true. She covered for him. Lied to the police. I've talked to my sources. The kid was hysterical when they arrived. Said he did it. Fortunately for her, the first two cops on the scene were more inclined to believe her story than his. I suppose it became a question of who was protecting whom. But a neighbor saw the whole thing."

"What?" He was suddenly on a dirt road in the backwoods, the tires spinning out beneath him. Not a thing he could do except brace for impact and take the fall.

"Yeah. Sad, really. Sweet old lady, according to my source. She heard noises and came over, looked in the window and saw the kid with the gun. She backed the mother's story for the kid's sake I suppose. But it's amazing what people will say for the right amount of money. And then of course, Julia's sister knows everything. She and Hilary had quite the conversation before Thanksgiving."

"I don't believe you." Reid closed his eyes, pretended he was back at the cabin. Back in the safety of his own bed, sleeping. Just having another nightmare that he could wake up from and pretend like it never happened.

Lou took the dossier back and put it into his briefcase. "It would be a shame for something like this to get out, wouldn't it? Splashed all over the news. The press would have a field day. A touching reunion story, you and your son together at last, but when the rest of it leaked … yeah, not so pretty. I wonder what the charges are for lying to the police, do you know?"

"What do you want from me, Lou?"

"Oh." The man actually smiled. Put his hands behind his neck and rocked back in his chair. "I think you know the answer to that question."

Their meeting was over.

Reid waited outside the building for a glimpse of Mark and Cade. He spotted them walking down the block toward him, smiled, raised a hand. The day's tension lessened as he watched Mark maneuver through the crowd on crutches. Every now and again the boy got impatient and made like he wanted to swipe someone's ankle with the end of one crutch. Cade carried several heavy-looking shopping bags in each hand. Reid didn't even want to ask what his son had conned him into buying. With the cash Reid had handed over that morning.

"Hey, Dad." Mark was out of breath but smiling.

"Hey." Reid grabbed Mark in a headlock and pulled him close. "Did you have fun?"

"Sure." Mark ducked away with a grin and that you-might-be-my-dad-but-let's-not-get-crazy look. Reid grabbed a couple bags from Cade. "What'd you get?"

"Don't even ask." Cade put down the other bags he held, shook his hands out and grimaced as he picked them up again. "How'd it go in there?"

"It went fine. They're going to settle." No point in saying anymore yet.

"Good. Let's go eat. I'm starving."

"Hard Rock Café," Mark interjected, pointing in that direction. "Ya'll promised."

"Yeah, yeah." Reid pulled the gray wool cap on Mark's head a little lower. "Maybe having a kid on crutches will get us seated quicker."

"Or maybe you could just do that 'I'm Reid Wallace, you *do* know who I am, don't you?' thing." Mark hopped off ahead of them.

Cade rolled his eyes as they walked faster to catch Mark up. "I thought your mother told you to behave," he yelled.

"Dude, I am behaving!" Mark yelled back.

"Well, it's not a bad idea." Cade laughed. "Glad he was the one to suggest it. Now I don't have to."

Reid grinned, but they were right. Sometimes the name-dropping thing worked. Cade had eaten with him enough times to know not to complain about the perks of being in the public eye.

"All right. Want me to get a cab, Mark, or can you manage a couple more blocks?" He didn't want to wear the kid out. His heart thudded against his chest as he tried not to replay the conversation he'd just had with Lou Fairchild. Tried not to think about what Mark had gone through that night. What he and Julia both knew, and had kept from him.

"Mr. Wallace?"

Reid turned to see a small band of reporters trailing them.

"Oh, crap." Cade took Mark by the arm, but they were already surrounded.

"Mr. Wallace, are you back for good?"

"Is it true you're getting your own show?"

"Are you being sued?"

"Is it true you were married and had a son you never knew about?"

"Is this your son?"

"What's your name, kid?"

"Are you being held responsible for the deaths of those members of your news team over in Syria?"

The questions railed like gunfire and Reid held up a hand. He looked over his shoulder at Cade. "Grab a cab. Get him out of here."

He moved away from Mark and Cade and the small group followed him.

This was how it would be.

There would be no more running. No more hiding from the man he was, denying the mistakes he'd made, the lives he'd destroyed.

"All right, all right. I know you have a lot of questions. I'll take them one at a time." Reid watched Cade and Mark get into a cab, faced the press and smiled. And then he came up with the answers he thought they wanted to hear.

It was time to play the game again.

Chapter Thirty

Reid dropped Cade off at Deb's the next afternoon and pulled up to the house with Mark around dinnertime. His head ached and his throat was scratchy. He hoped it was just stress. He couldn't afford to get sick right now. He'd wrestled with what Lou had told him the whole drive back to Vermont. There was a chance it wasn't the truth. That he was just making it up. But Lou wasn't stupid. Reid would find out easily enough if it weren't true. And everything in him said it was.

Much as he wanted to corner Cade and demand answers, he couldn't very well do it with Mark around. And he wasn't about to ask his son.

No, Julia was the one he needed to talk to.

He'd never been so angry with her. So hurt.

She hadn't trusted him enough to tell him the truth. And somehow, he doubted she ever would.

He helped Mark inside and pushed his duffel bag across the kitchen floor with one foot. He'd apologized a million times for the press attack yesterday, but still didn't like the wary look in Mark's eyes. And he didn't want to think about what Julia would do when she found out. If she hadn't already. It would be one more thing for them to argue about.

"There you are. You made good time!" Madge bustled into the kitchen, sleeves of a red polo pushed up over jeans. "Mark, honey, how was your trip? I've got a couple of pizzas in the oven, Reid, you're welcome to stay." She cast a worried glance in his direction. "You've had chicken-pox, right?"

"Uh ... I don't know." Reid scratched his head. A wail from upstairs interrupted the silence.

"What's going on?" Mark slipped out of his coat and let it fall to the ground. "Was that Em?"

Madge nodded, giving Mark a kiss on the cheek. "Your sister has chicken-pox. Your mother says you've had it."

"Aw, man. When I was six. It sucked." Mark grinned. "Poor Em."

Reid picked up Mark's coat as concern ran rampant over other thoughts. "How is she?"

"She's pretty sick right now, but she'll be over the worst soon."

"Well, look who's back." Jonas strode through the kitchen door, a smile on his face, but worry in his eyes. "Looks like you bought out New York, son." He grabbed the shopping bags Reid had put down a minute ago, and took Mark by the elbow. "Come on into the den and show me what you got. I want to hear all about your trip." Mark hopped ahead of his grandfather and Jonas turned back to Reid. "Don't leave. I just saw something on the news that I think we should discuss."

He was gone before Reid could reply.

Emily's cries floated downstairs again. Reid shook off his coat, hung it along with Mark's on the coat rack by the back door and took the stairs two at a time.

He found Julia sitting with Emily in the steaming hot bathroom.

"Hey." His throat constricted as he caught her eyes, took in Emily's flushed face and heard her coughing. Angry red splotches covered her face and upper body.

"Hey yourself," Julia whispered, her voice shaky and sounding on the verge of tears. "You missed all the fun."

Emily stopped crying long enough to lift her head off Julia's shoulder and look at him through those big brown eyes that had captured his heart from the minute they met. "Hi, Mister Reid." She held out her pox-covered arms and succumbed to another round of coughing.

"Oh, baby. C'mere." Reid scooped her up and held her sweaty little body against his chest, brushing her damp curls off her forehead. "Looks like you went a bit crazy with the markers, huh, doll?"

A giggle tried to escape but her cough chased it away. Reid walked the bathroom with her, watched Julia lean over the sink and catch her breath. Emily began to cry again, her chest heaving against his.

"It hurts."

"I know, princess. It's okay. We'll make it all better." Reid rubbed her back and tried to sound confident of that, but when Julia lifted her head, exhaustion shadowing her eyes, he wasn't. Fear jumped him, took hold and whispered awful thoughts. "How long has she been like this?"

"All day." Julia splashed her flushed face with water. Her t-shirt was soaked through. "It's chicken-pox, but it's a nasty case. High fever. Cough that won't quit. And she's—"

Emily stared at him through mournful eyes as the color fled her cheeks, opened her mouth and vomited. All over his shoulder.

"—throwing up." Julia sighed and reached for a cloth. "There goes that dose of Tylenol."

"There goes my shirt." Reid grinned despite the stench flooding his nostrils. He took the cloth from Julia and wiped Em's little mouth. "Feel better now?"

"Uh huh." Emily rested her head on his other, vomit-free shoulder. "I missthed you."

"I missed you too, princess." Reid kissed her hot head and reluctantly allowed Julia to lift her daughter off him.

"Let's get you cleaned up again and into some fresh pj's, Em." Julia made short work of washing her, wrapped her in a big towel and headed for the door. "I'll try to get her to sleep," she whispered, and disappeared down the hall.

Reid peeled off his shirt, tossed it into the tub, leaned over the sink and breathed deep. Ran the water cold and soaked his head in it. Took another deep calming breath as he ran a towel over his head and chest. Rearranged the swirling thoughts in his brain and put them into prioritized boxes.

Chicken pox. Did kids die from chicken pox? He delved into the vaults of his memory where he kept all the facts and figures amassed over the years.

Not usually. But once in a while, maybe. Yes, there was that study that showed—

"Jules!"

"What? Stop yelling, I'm right here." She stood in the doorway, changed into a dry shirt and yoga pants.

"Has she seen a doctor?"

"I told you, it's chicken-pox." Julia held a fresh towel toward him. "Her fever will break. She'll be fine in the morning."

"Fever can kill a child, Julia. We should take her to the hospital. Didn't she get vaccinated?"

"Frank didn't believe in vaccinations." Sudden, unexpected laughter rang around the bathroom. "She's already asleep, Reid. Her temperature is coming down. You're overreacting." She bent to pick a few wet towels off the floor. "Did you ever stop to think that all the research you do might actually cloud your judgment one day?"

"Forgive me for being concerned."

"You're forgiven." She inched closer, grabbed the washcloth from the sink and gently brushed his shoulder. "You missed a spot."

Apparently he'd missed more than one.

"Wow, she got you good." Julia rubbed the damp cloth up his neck in a soothing motion, oblivious to what she was doing to him. "How was New York?"

Reid sucked in air as her fingers brushed over his skin, all thoughts of hospitals, statistics and useless facts abandoning his brain quicker than they'd entered it. "Uh. It was interesting."

"Interesting how?"

"We'll talk about it later." Her touch blindsided him with a boatload of memories and trampled over any thoughts of getting answers from her tonight.

His anger still simmered, but the way she continued to wipe the cloth across his chest held it at bay. Put other thoughts into his head instead. Thoughts he had no business even contemplating.

"Where'd you get this?" Her finger traced a thin white scar that ran from the top of his shoulder to halfway down his torso.

"Windsurfing accident in Tahiti." He wondered how much sleep she'd had in the last twenty-four hours. Because the fact that he stood there half-naked seemed to be totally lost on her.

"And this one? This is new." She trailed her hand across his shoulder and down his arm.

"Um. Bike accident." Reid shivered and sank his teeth into his bottom lip. "Jules." It took a lot of effort to grab her wandering hands in his and remove them from his body. "Can I borrow a shirt?"

"Oh." Her eyes traveled over him again, finally met his gaze and she stepped back, exhaling in a reticent smile. "A shirt. Sure." But she didn't move.

"You want to get me one?"

"No. Not especially." Her lopsided smile got a little bigger and made her look really, really cute.

Whoa …

He needed a good slap but couldn't stop a grin. "Have you been tippling in the Tylenol?"

Her eyes flared and she backed up against the sink. "No. But you … um …" She reached out and pressed her forefinger to his chest. "You didn't look like this. Before."

His relentless hours at the gym were for his own self-preservation. He'd never imagined this particular scenario. Not in a million years.

Reid shoved off a smile and tried not to enjoy the smoldering look that captured her eyes. The one he remembered her using on nights when he'd been burning the midnight oil and she deemed his studying over. It was almost impossible to ignore the growing desire that threatened to trample over his innate decency.

She was gorgeous. Even in a baggy t-shirt that had seen better days, wet hair that clung to the sides of her face and shadows beneath her eyes. Those lips were just begging to be kissed. And, despite everything he now knew, all he wanted to do was take her in his arms and comply.

Julia Connelly captured him completely. Without even trying.

He wasn't angry with her now. He was beyond angry.

He was insane.

"Julia." His feet moved without permission, his arms going along for the ride, his hands running up her arms and across her shoulders until his fingers spread through her hair, tipped her face to his and she allowed his lips access to her soft mouth.

She wound her arms around his neck, pressed against him like she'd always been there, and returned each kiss he gave with a fervor that did absolutely nothing to encourage him to come to his senses and hightail it out of there.

He'd kiss her all night if he could. He wanted more than just her mouth. He wanted to explore every inch of her. And the way she was responding said she'd probably let him.

"Okay. Okay ... Jules." Sanity kicked down the door and jumpstarted his brain. Reid disengaged, drew her arms downward and clasped her wrists in his hands. He let out a deep breath and shook his head. "We can't do this."

Not like he would have taken the moment further anyway, with everybody downstairs and Emily in bed down the hall, but that the thought actually crossed his mind scared him witless.

Her too, judging by the frightened look on her face.

"You're right. I'm sorry." She thrust the towel against his chest, her cheeks an even darker shade of red than Emily's had been. "I don't know what I was thinking."

Reid gave a muted chuckle as she stalked out of the bathroom.

He knew exactly what she was thinking. He'd been thinking the same thing. But that didn't give either of them license to act on those feelings, no matter how strong they were.

Julia returned a minute later and tossed a T-shirt his way. "This should fit. Emily is still asleep. I'm going down to see Mark. You should say goodnight and go home."

He'd been dismissed. Just like that.

Chapter Thirty-One

*J*ulia stared at the phone on her desk at work. Glared at it. Willed it to ring. But it stayed silent. She checked her cell phone again. No messages.

"All locked up. What a day. Did you get those order slips sorted out, Jules?" Debby came in carrying a bucket of dark green holly which she placed in the long fridge at the back of the room. "Christmas will be here before we know it."

Julia pushed a stack of papers across the desk. "Sorted and entered into the computer as well, even though you won't go near the thing."

Debby laughed and picked up the pile of paper. "Why should I when you can do it for me?" She flicked through the forms and shook her head. "I have so many new orders, I don't know what to do. We'll have to go into Burlington for more flowers. Maybe tomorrow. Let's make a list."

"Has Cade talked to Reid?" Julia blurted the question before she lost her nerve. Debby rounded the desk, pulled up a white plastic chair and sat.

"You mean in general or about anything in particular?"

Julia picked at the polish on her nails and waited for her cheeks to cool. "I mean since they got home from New York. It's been four days and I haven't heard from him."

"You haven't heard from Cade? He lives above the garage on your property, sweetie."

"Not Cade. Reid."

"Oh, Reid. Of course. The man you insist you have no feelings for." Debby played with the diamond on her finger and tossed Julia a wicked grin. "Maybe he's staying out of sight until Emily gets better. Did he ever have chicken pox as a kid?"

"I don't know. What's that got to do with it?"

"Maybe he's got it too." Debby's giggle did nothing to soothe Julia's nerves.

"He just saw Em a few days ago. He wouldn't have it yet."

"Unless he got it at the same time as her. You know, church or whatever. Come to think of it, one of Marla's kids had it a couple of weeks ago. You guys were helping out with Em's class, weren't you?"

"I should go check on him." And inflict all kinds of embarrassment on herself. Just what she didn't want to do. But the thought of him lying alone in that cabin, sick, couldn't be ignored. Julia groaned and put her head in her hands. "Deb? I did something really, really dumb."

Once the confession was over, once Debby stopped laughing, Julia began to breathe easier. "It's not funny! I just … I had this awful feeling all weekend that he wasn't coming back, and then there he was. And he was being all fatherly to Em, then looking like some hot dude out of a movie, and …"

"Jules, I get it." Debby snorted and held up a hand. "Oh, hon. Don't bash your brains out over it. You're only human. And I bet he didn't know what hit him."

"It wasn't right, Deb! I practically attacked the man."

"And he probably enjoyed every minute of it." Her friend reached across the desk and placed her hand over Julia's. "But maybe this time, don't show him how you feel. Tell him."

"I don't know how." Julia inhaled and allowed the admission to settle in her soul. "With Frank, it was all physical. I had to do exactly what he wanted, when he wanted it, whether I wanted to or not. I learned to hate everything about being with him. I hated myself for the things he made me do. I hated him." She stared down at her bare fingers and accepted the truth.

"I haven't felt any real attraction to a man in years. And that night I was so tired, and Reid was just standing there … I don't know what came over me. He must think I'm …"

"Stop." Debby shook her head. "You don't know what he thinks and you won't know until you go talk to him. So go. Get out of here and go on up that mountain. Face those giants."

"You really think this is funny."

Debby sobered. "No. I really don't. I just think it's high time you found happiness. I think you need to learn how to feel again, Jules. How to love."

"And you think Reid Wallace is the man who's going to show me how to do that?"

Debby gave a knowing smile. "I think he already has."

Julia waited outside the school in the car until she saw Mark, then jumped out to help him. Just before she got him to the sidewalk, three or four adults surrounded them, some with cameras, one with a microphone.

"Mrs. Hansen? Are you Julia Hansen?"

"Were you married to Reid Wallace?"

"Is this your son?"

"Mrs. Hansen, could you answer a few questions for us? Julia?"

Julia's heart ping-ponged out of time with her brain as the questions kept coming. She kept her head down, one arm securely around Mark's waist, the other shielding their faces. She saw a couple of teachers coming to the rescue, making a path so they could get to the car. She managed to get Mark into the front seat just as the last question hit her.

"Mrs. Hansen, can you tell us how your husband died?"

Julia hopped in, slammed the door, hit the lock and started the engine. She glanced at Mark.

He stared straight ahead, pulled the brim of his ball cap down a bit and slunk in his seat. "Go, Mama."

Julia hit the gas and prayed the engine wouldn't cut out on her. It didn't. But her hands didn't stop shaking until they were on the highway.

"What in the world?" She didn't know whether to be furious or petrified. At the moment she was both.

"They know, don't they?" Mark's whisper sizzled with fear.

She squeezed his arm and shook her head. "Don't worry, Mark. Everything's going to be fine."

Reid had better make sure of it.

Julia banged on the door of the cabin for the fifth time. She knew he was home because his stupid gas guzzling truck or SUV or whatever he called it, sat in the driveway. She scanned the porch and her eyes landed on the two urns Esmé always filled with flowers every summer. And kept a spare key under. Right or left? Left.

Bingo.

Julia fiddled with the lock and let herself in. "Reid? Are you here?" Her breath floated around the cold cabin. "You better be, because I need to talk to you. Reid?"

A groan floated down the hall. She threw her coat on the couch and hurried to the room he'd claimed for a bedroom.

"I'm dying," he croaked, pain-filled eyes staring up at her as she edged a little closer. Anger melted into concern.

He sprawled on the bed, dressed in sweats and a white vest that clung to his sweaty chest. The virulent red blotches over his skin confirmed her suspicions.

"You never had chicken-pox?"

"I don't know. Can't remember." He gave a pathetic moan. "Jules, my head hurts."

She put a hand to his forehead and shook her head. "You, my friend, are one sick puppy. Looked in the mirror lately?"

"No." He flipped onto his stomach and groaned like a cow in labor. "I've puked like five times this morning. Make it stop."

"Reid. You have chicken pox. And a really high fever." Julia stifled a laugh and moved around the messy room. "Do you have any pain reliever in the bathroom?" He didn't answer, so she went on a search herself. She found them and forced a couple pills down his throat, found him a clean shirt and some tomato soup in the cupboard, which she'd probably have to force down him as well.

247

Eventually he ate, drank enough water to satisfy her, then fell asleep. Cade showed up with supplies. They took turns sitting with Reid through the night, helping him to the bathroom when he woke, Cade showering him off the times he couldn't get there.

Cade and Debby had an appointment at one of the hotels they were looking at for the reception venue the next morning. Julia didn't want him to miss it, so made sure her brother left early. He promised to make sure the kids were fine, and come back around lunch so Julia could head home and rest.

Reid slept. Julia cleaned. Wiped down every surface she could find. Admired the new bookcase and her son's handiwork. The place hardly resembled the run down cabin she'd turned her nose up at only months ago. It felt like home again.

She stoked the fire and looked through old photo albums. As she sat on the new leather couch and scanned the pristine room, she found the pictures on the mantel.

Julia walked across the room to pick up the silver-framed photograph and stared at it for a long time.

Were second chances possible?

Would it really be possible for them to be together, after everything? Or was she still holding onto a dream that might never come true?

She put the picture back in place and went back to the bedroom.

Reid's fever was up again. She woke him and plied more pain reliever into him. Held his hand and listened to his delirious complaining, praying all the while he wouldn't get any sicker. She'd read somewhere that chicken pox was so much worse in adults. That if your immune system was down, you could …

"You're still here," he croaked, opening his eyes a moment.

"Reid?" His skin was burning up.

"I feel like I'm going to die. I want to die." His eyes fluttered closed with another moan.

"You're not going to die. Go back to sleep." Julia pulled her chair closer and gripped his hot hand in hers. She sat in silence for a few minutes until she was sure he was sleeping. "You listen to me, Reid Wallace. You're not going anywhere. You and I have unfinished business. And if you must know, I'm pretty sure I've fallen in love with you again. I liked the guy you were, but the guy you are now is even better. So don't you dare leave me again, you hear me? Don't even think about it."

The tiniest of grins slid across his mouth. "Couldn't resist my charm and good looks, huh?"

Tears of relief pricked her eyes. "Something like that."

"You still love me, Jules?"

Her smile chased off fear. "I do. So put that in your pipe and smoke it, sweetheart."

He opened one eye. "I might need you to kiss me like you did the other night so I know you're serious."

He was never going to let that one go. "Go back to sleep. You're delirious."

"Yeah. Probably. But I'll take it." He rolled to one side and tucked her hand under his. "I love you too, Jules."

Chapter thirty-two

Reid made a slow recovery, but by the end of the week, when Julia stopped by with another casserole and an apple pie from her mother, she found him showered and dressed.

"You're up. Are you feeling okay? How's your fever?" The red marks on his face were fading, most already crusted over.

"Seems to be gone. But I'm still itchy. I'm almost out of chamomile."

She walked through to the kitchen and put away the things she'd brought. "I'll go get you some. After I pick up the kids, I can to the pharmacy."

"You don't need to. I'll go in tomorrow." Reid followed her back into the living room. "Listen, Jules, we need to talk."

His expression was too serious.

"I need to go. I don't want to be late picking Em up." She had a good hour and a half to kill before that, but the look on Reid's face sent her flight instinct into high gear. "I should go."

"Jules. Just stop." He pushed his fingers through his wet hair, leaned over and exhaled. Stared up at her through hooded eyes. "You've got time. Sit. Please."

Julia took off her coat, sat, and tried to ignore the hundred horrible thoughts running across her mind. "Did Cade tell you we got mobbed at school the other day?" She shook her head, angry again. "A bunch of reporters were waiting for Mark when I came to pick him up. Where do these people come from? What gives them the right—"

"Julia."

The tension in his tone made her stiffen and shut her mouth. He stared down at his bare feet and then met her eyes.

"Yes, Cade told me. The same thing happened to us in New York."

"It did? Mark didn't say anything."

"I told him not to worry about it."

"Did you answer their questions?"

Reid shrugged, but she saw the concern in his eyes. "I told them I was married a long time ago, and that I had a son. And asked that they respect my privacy."

"But they know who we are!" Julia wound her hands together. "They were outside Mark's school, Reid. Hounding us."

"I know. Which is why we need to talk." He exhaled. "Julia. You lied to me."

"I lied to you?" She rubbed her eyes.

"What happened the night Frank died?"

Her knees wanted to buckle and it took all her strength to stand.

She had to get out of here.

"Stop looking at the door. You're not going anywhere until you tell me the truth."

She shook her head, unable to speak it, even after months of reliving it all in her mind. Somehow she just couldn't face it. What Mark had done. What she'd pretended he hadn't. "I told you what happened."

"No, I'm not sure you did." Reid took a step forward. "You weren't holding the gun when it went off, were you?"

The room became suffocating. "I ... told ... you what happened," she whispered, sounding like a computerized recording. "It was an accident." Julia turned from him, reached for her coat and purse.

Reid took hold of her arm. "You didn't tell me the whole story. You didn't tell me the truth. Did you?"

She forced her gaze upward. His jaw worked as he tried to keep his anger in check. This was it. The moment that would end whatever they were starting before it really began.

"Answer me, Julia!" His shout ricocheted off the walls.

She shook him off and went for cover, looked for a table to hide under, a dresser to crawl behind, anywhere he wouldn't get to her.

Reid flew across the room and caught her in his arms. "Sorry. I'm sorry. Don't run." He pulled her against him and enfolded her in his warm embrace. "You don't need to run from me, sweetheart. You know that, right? I'm sorry I yelled. I just need to know the truth. I need you to talk to me."

Julia relaxed against him and forced herself to breathe. "How did you find out?" Visions of the story flashing across the six o'clock news sent a wave of nausea rushing through her.

"Somebody told me. In New York. I didn't want to believe it."

A ten thousand-pound boulder crushed against her chest. Rational thought wouldn't come. She took a step backward and shrugged.

"It's true, isn't it?" Disappointment, disillusionment and a myriad of other emotions took a walk across his face. "Oh, my God. Oh, Jules." Reid took her in his arms again.

"I'm sorry." She sank into his chest, giving up the fight. "I couldn't tell you. I thought if you knew what really happened ... I didn't know how you'd handle it."

"You didn't trust me." He pulled back, holding her at arm's length, studying her. "Why?"

She'd hurt him.

"I couldn't." Tears slipped down her cheeks and pooled in the corners of her mouth.

"I'm Mark's father."

"I know. I told you it was an accident, and it was. What difference does it make how it happened?"

"Jules." He let her go and sank onto the couch. Put his head in his hands for a long moment that worried her. "So Mark killed Frank?"

She nodded, her throat too tight for speech. Waited a minute until she could get the words out. "But it *was* an accident. Mark came into the room when Frank was threatening me. He tried to get the gun away from him. It fired while they were struggling."

"You lied to the police."

"Do they know? Is that why those reporters were after us the other day?"

Reid lifted his shoulders. "I'm not sure. But did you think about what you were doing? Why didn't you just tell the truth?"

Julia shook her head. "I didn't think. I was semi-conscious. Frank had … he'd beaten me pretty badly. And he pushed me halfway across the room when I tried to pull Mark away from him. The next thing I knew, my husband was dead and my son was holding the gun that killed him. All I could think of was protecting Mark." Somehow she'd stumbled to him, taken the gun from her son's shaking hands …

"There was a neighbor. She corroborated your story?"

"Yes. Nancy. We went to church together, when I went. She saw the whole thing. Got to me before she called the police, I was lucid enough to ask her to … help."

"How far did the investigation go? Were you taken into custody? Did the cops just take your word for it?"

"They believed me. Afterward, in the hospital, I told them Mark tried to get the gun from Frank, which was true, and I tried to intervene. I suppose, since Frank wasn't around to tell them otherwise, they had to let it go. I told Mark it was better that way, that we would be safe."

"But Mark still has to live with it." Reid pushed up, grabbed a few logs from a copper tub by the fire and soon had a few flames going. Julia watched the wood crackle and burn, her life going up in smoke right along with it.

"Yes, he does, but he's free. What should I have done, Reid? Watch my son get hauled off to juvie? Wait for some gung-ho junior prosecutor to get hold of him and throw him to the wolves? Put him through a trial?"

"It was still an accident. You don't know what would have happened."

"No, I don't. But I wasn't willing to find out."

"You're lucky you weren't charged."

Julia sniffed and pushed her hair off her face. "I had four broken ribs, a broken arm, a split lip, nine stitches above my eye and a shattered jaw. Self-defense wasn't exactly a stretch."

Reid stalked the room and muttered words she couldn't decipher.

"Reid, who told you?" A woman with platinum blond hair and a million dollar smile came to mind.

"It's not important." He stopped his agitated march at the window, staring at the white world outside. She didn't want to know what he was thinking. Couldn't bear thinking about what would come next.

She watched a shudder rip through him. Grabbed the quilt she'd discarded and wrapped it around his shoulders. "You shouldn't be up yet. You're still weak."

"I'll live."

Julia stood beside him, folded her arms and breathed out her next thought. "I remembered where I'd met her. Hilary."

"What?" He turned to her, fresh panic inching into his eyes.

"Yes. Hilary. Your ex. She was in Atlanta after it happened. Asking questions. Once the police ruled Frank's death accidental, she came to see me. Told me she'd pay a lot of money for my story. That it would make a good documentary. Or a primetime movie. I didn't have a clue who she was, so I didn't take her seriously. I asked her to leave and never heard from her again. I wonder if she had any idea at that time who I really was."

"I wouldn't put it past her." Reid uttered a low curse. "They're going to keep a lid on this if I agree to go back to work. I have a year left on my contract. They'll deal with the lawsuit and—"

"What lawsuit?" Everything was happening too fast, like a light show out of control, threatening to set fire to innocent bystanders. "You're not making any sense."

"I suppose I'm not. I've been keeping secrets too." He glanced at his watch, took her hand and led her to the couch. And then he told her everything.

The way things were in Syria. The bloodshed he'd witnessed. The war he'd tried to cover to the best of his ability. The children he'd watched fall from sniper fire on the street below his feet. The condition he'd done his best to manage, but could never quite control.

"I shouldn't have gone into that area that day. But I did. I put my job first, over the safety of my team. It was a stupid, selfish thing to do and I'll regret it as long as I live."

Choices.

Life was a menu of them. Good ones. Bad ones.

Life altering ones.

Julia sat on her hands to keep them from shaking. "You can't change the decision you made. Neither can I." This was so surreal it was almost like a dream. If only. "You have to live with what happened over there, just as I live with what happened that day in Atlanta."

"I know."

Silence settled over the cabin. Julia filtered through the questions in her mind, too many of them to wonder which to ask first. "What if they decide not to settle, what if it goes to court?"

Reid shook his head. "I won't lie on the stand. I knowingly walked my crew into an area that wasn't safe. I'll tell the truth and pay the consequences. Your father agrees it's the only thing I can do."

"You've talked to my father?"

"The night we got back from New York. He saw something about the lawsuit on television"

"I didn't know."

"I asked him not to say anything until you and I talked. I'd planned to tell you when I got back, Jules, when I knew what was going on, but then Em was sick and then I got sick. And since then, between sleeping and puking my guts out, I've been figuring out what to do about all this crap."

"Does Mark know about Syria?"

"No."

"Does he know you know what happened with Frank?"

"Not yet."

"I suppose you think he should."

Reid's steady gaze didn't make her feel better.

"Yes. I want him to know it doesn't matter. Whatever happened, it wasn't his fault. He needs to know I love him unconditionally." He shook his head and released a heavy sigh. "Just when I think things are improving, everything goes south again."

"Well, I guess there's nothing left to say, is there?" Her world had shifted the minute he'd entered the room and she met his eyes. And now it spiraled out of control.

"What?"

Julia went for her coat. "We were just kidding ourselves anyway. It's better this way."

"Wait, what are you talking about?" He followed her across the room and turned her to face him. "You think this is it? The minute things get tough, I take a hike?"

She registered the disbelief in his eyes, set her jaw and pushed back her shoulders. "Why wouldn't you?"

A shadow of a smile danced across his lips. "Because I love you. And I'm through running."

"But you have to go back to New York, Reid. That's what all this means, right?"

The look on his face told the truth. "I don't see another way right now. I have to protect Mark."

"How?"

"I'll do what they want. I'll go back to work. Lou keeps a lid on the truth. And Mark stays safe. But that doesn't mean I'm bailing on you, Jules. I'm not. I'm not bailing on us."

"There can't be an us." Her whisper slipped through the air and she let go of the new hope she'd found over the last few weeks. Let go of him. "Not anymore."

Their future had been decided long before it began.

Chapter thirty-three

Reid placed the last photograph into his suitcase, yanked the zipper around it and lugged it off the bed. He slammed an empty dresser door shut as he passed it. The last few days had been worse than the nightmares that still stole sleep. He and Julia talked the whole thing to death. Did a lot of praying. Some arguing. And a fair bit of crying. But in the end, all their questions came around to the same answer.

They had to do everything in their power to protect Mark.

Reid only had to recall that deer-in-the-headlights look on his son's face that day in New York as those reporters barreled down the street toward them. He understood it now.

Wished a thousand times over that he didn't.

But there it was. The truth, in Lou Fairchild's hands, was a lethal weapon.

And Reid would go through hell and back to keep his son from harm. Even if that meant leaving the woman he loved.

Again.

Reid locked up the cabin, dragged his bags to the car and loaded up.

For the short time he'd lived here, he'd felt like himself. Felt like he'd connected with Esmé again. Began to believe that maybe, even after everything he'd done, she'd forgiven him.

And lately he'd started to believe in second chances.

Believed he'd been given one.

A second chance with Julia and the kids, and with the God he'd turned his back on.

The Lord gives and the Lord takes away.

Blessed be the Name of the Lord.

Reid didn't know what to do with that today. Today, he didn't feel like blessing anybody. Still, his conscience nudged him. With the cabin in the rearview mirror, he could still hear Esmé's voice. He'd called her for advice more than once after his decision to leave Julia, questioning himself, wondering how to make things right. And then, when he'd heard Julia had married Frank, it was too late.

"I've lost her, Essie. Made the biggest mistake of my life."

His grandmother's chuckle filtered through the phone. "Don't you give up, Reid Wallace. God's got a plan. And His plan is good."

Right now, he wasn't all that convinced.

He pulled up outside the Connelly house and trudged through the snow to the back door.

Hannah opened it before he could knock. "Reid, I just want to say …"

Reid inhaled, bit back his first response and held up a hand. "Save it." He pushed past her and entered the warm kitchen.

"Well, I am sorry." She scurried ahead and wisely made a hasty exit. He couldn't care where she went, so long as he didn't have to look at her.

He'd come close to telling Julia that her sister was the cause of all this mess, but somehow stopped himself. Seeing Hannah today, he could reverse that decision without a second thought.

Madge bent over the oven, lifted out a steaming loaf and turned his way. "You always did have a nose for my pumpkin bread."

Reid nodded, but doubted he had the stomach for it today. "I can't stay."

"I know. I'm wrapping this up for you. And there are more goodies in that basket over there."

"Madge …" Reid pushed down the traitorous lump in his throat and tried to smile. "Thanks."

She shook her head and came toward him, her eyes bright. Took his cold hands in her warm ones and fixed him with a smile that pulled moisture toward the rim of his lids. "Surely there's another way?"

"There isn't." He allowed her to hug him. Let her cry a bit, then drew back and shrugged out of his coat. "Where are they?"

"In the living room."

Decorating the tree.

Madge rejected the whole decorating for Christmas right after Thanksgiving regime. She preferred to do things at a leisurely pace. Put up all her crèches first. Then hung garland on the stairs, a wreath on the front door. The outside lights next. And then, finally, the tree.

"Mister Reid!" Emily saw him first, jumped up and pulled a pile of tinsel along with her as she hurtled toward him like a rocket. He picked her up, held tight and breathed in Mr. Bubble, kiddie sweat and excitement, and the faintest scent of her mother's perfume clinging to the pajamas she hadn't yet changed out of.

"What's this? Pajama day and nobody tells me?"

Emily giggled and pinched his nose. "No. We just had breakfast. Didja wants some pancakes too?"

"No, princess. I don't want any pancakes today." He glanced across the room. Mark sprawled on the couch, his face darker than a Caribbean thunderstorm. His cast had been removed yesterday and they'd gone out for pizza last night, to celebrate, but the only one who'd really had any fun was Emily.

Julia sat on the floor, cross-legged, sorting through a box of ornaments, her hair falling forward in a way that probably made her think he couldn't see her tears.

"You want to help us do the tree, Mister Reid?" Emily's big eyes implored him as she tightened her hold around his neck. Silently begged him to run back to his car, hightail it up to the cabin, unpack every last bag and tell them he was staying.

Forever.

But forever only happened in books and movies and fairy tales.

And his life was none of the above.

His life had become a well-scripted play, written months ago, directed by people who didn't care one whit about his feelings. Didn't care that he was about to do the hardest thing he'd ever done.

Walk away again. When he'd promised not to.

After an hour of helping Jonas string the lights, Reid glanced at his watch. He had a long drive ahead. Five hours if he was lucky, with no traffic. Cade questioned the validity of Reid taking a vehicle back to the city, but somehow he couldn't leave it here. He needed it as a reminder of what he'd left behind. And what he hoped, one day, to be able to come back to.

Miracles still happened. He'd reported on enough of them.

Maybe he needed to start believing in them again.

Jonas and Madge corralled Emily into the kitchen with the promise of fresh baked cookies. Mark poked at the ornaments on the tree. He'd been sullen and silent since Reid showed up.

Julia cleared her throat, gave Reid a shrug. "*You should talk,*" she mouthed.

Reid nodded, picked up a few stray threads of tinsel and balled them in his hand. "You want to rest that foot, bud. You've been on it a while."

"As if you care."

"I'll be in the kitchen." Julia followed her parents and Emily out of the room.

Mark shuffled to the couch and stretched out. Grabbed the remote and turned on the television. Loud.

Reid adjusted a few ornaments on the tree. Tried to figure what to say, gave up and headed for the couch. "You wanna scooch up a bit?"

Mark grunted but made room.

Reid squashed in between Mark's feet and the end of the couch. "I need to tell you something, Mark."

"I'm not stupid. I already know. You're leaving today. My mom told me."

"Okay. Well, yeah, I am leaving. But that's not what I wanted to tell you." Reid looked at his son, his heart ripped to shreds by the bitterness of Mark's words. "Actually, I wanted to tell you a story. A true story. About what happened to me in Syria. Before we met."

Somehow he was rewarded with Mark's astute gaze and the time to tell his tale.

"So that's it." Reid swallowed air and clenched his fingers. "It was the biggest mistake of my life, well, one of them, but I can't fix it. I can't bring that family's son back. If they take me to court, I don't know what will happen. But sometimes we just have to trust God. Because there are too many things in life we can't control. No matter how much we want to."

"I know." Mark's cheeks pinked and his eyes got a little bigger. He rubbed his nose with the back of his hand, didn't say anything for a few minutes. Then he fixed on Reid. "I did something. Something bad."

Reid could only nod, his throat tight. He lifted the boy's legs and put them over his. Moved down the couch until he could put an arm around Mark's shaking shoulders and wiped his tears away with a trembling hand. "Your Mom told me what happened with Frank. It was an accident, Mark."

"I know. I didn't mean to kill him," Mark whispered, the words muffled as he shoved his chin to his chest. "I didn't even know how to use the stupid thing. But he was like, kicking her and punching her ... so bad ... he said he was gonna kill her this time." His breath came in spurts as he tried to recount the story. "I just wanted to get it away from him. And then after the gun went off, I was glad. 'Cause he was the one on the floor and he wouldn't be able to hurt her no more. Then Mama said we could never tell, that it was better this way. But I wanted to tell you. I just couldn't. I'm sorry. I'm so sorry."

"Mark. It's okay." Reid pulled Mark against him. Let him cry it all out. Listened to his son's aching sobs and wished for a way out of this deep, murky pool they'd waded into.

But there was no way out, and the sharks were circling.

"Hey." He tried to smile as Mark raised his head. "You don't have to be afraid. Nobody's coming after you, Mark. It's done."

Relief raced across Mark's face. "I thought, that day in New York, when I saw all those reporters, and then at school—"

"No." Reid hoped he sounded convincing. "Don't worry about that. If anyone asks you any questions, just walk away. Walk away and don't look back."

"Yessir." Mark rubbed his face, his eyes brightening. "So you'll stay now? You don't care what I did?"

"What?" Confusion threw a surprise party, invited Reid at the last minute. "Mark, that's not why I'm leaving, bud." But it was. And there was no way to explain that to Mark.

"Mama said you were leaving because you had to get back to work. But I thought it was because of me. Because you found out what I did and you didn't want to be around me no more." Mark shuddered, trying to keep his tears in check. "Anymore."

Reid pulled his son against him again. "No. I have to fulfill my contract, Mark. It's not my choice, but it's what I have to do." That was as close to reality as he was willing to get.

"Well, that sucks." Mark wiggled out of reach and folded his arms. "What about Christmas?"

Good question, kid.

"I'll try, Mark." No promises. Reid leaned over his knees. He couldn't say for sure where he'd be in three weeks. Lou Fairchild was calling the shots now. "Your mom and I will talk about it. Maybe you can come visit over your break."

"I might be busy."

"Yeah. Well." Reid forced himself to stand. "I left a box of books in the kitchen for you. And some photo albums that my grandmother kept and some other things. Stupid stuff, from when I was a kid. Pictures and medals and stuff like that. But you can have them if you want."

"Lame."

"Yeah. I figured." Reid pinched the bridge of his nose and prayed for strength. This was sucking life from him.

And he hadn't faced Julia yet.

"I need to get going, Mark."

"So go already."

"You have my email. And all my numbers, right?"

"Long distance. Grandpa doesn't like spending money, in case you didn't know. And my mom don't got none."

Reid nodded toward the tree. "I put some presents under there. You can open the blue striped one with your name on it any time. My number is already programmed in. And your mom said it was cool. So call me, okay?"

"Whatever." Mark stared at his feet, his cheeks blistering.

His dark hair was getting long again. Reid had meant to take him into town for a cut this week, along with getting those new pants they'd bought in New York hemmed so they didn't pool around his ankles. And he'd wanted to take him to the new thriller that was just released, as long as he could arrange it without Jules finding out until after the fact.

He'd meant to do a lot of things.

Saying goodbye hadn't been on the list.

"All right. Well. I'll call you tonight when I get in. I'll see you soon, Mark. I love you, dude."

Silence. The room throbbed with it. Screamed at him to get out and never come back.

Reid stood and headed for the door.

Made it halfway down the hall.

"Dad! Wait!" Mark hopped toward him, holding something in his hand. His face contorted in pain. "Dangit! Came down hard on that stupid ankle."

Reid slid his arm under his and let Mark lean against him. "What's this?" He stared at the silver-framed image of him and Mark, taken in Central Park. Before their world catapulted out of control without permission.

"Uncle Cade took it. I was gonna give it to you for Christmas. But maybe you want to take it now. Just in case."

"Thanks, bud." Words became difficult. And then, as Mark put his arms around his waist and held tight, impossible.

"Please come back." It was a whispered request, maybe even a prayer, one he probably wasn't meant to hear, but his son's words shattered Reid's soul.

Reid shoved the picture under his arm and placed his hands around Mark's tear-stained face. "Remember who you are, Mark. Your name might be Hansen on paper right now, but you're a Wallace. You're mine. Don't forget that. I am not leaving you. I'll be there for you whenever you need me, any time, no matter what."

"What if you're halfway around the world?"

"Then I'll fly back halfway around the world."

"What if you can't? What if you get hurt someplace? What if you marry that stupid Hilary chick and have more kids and she doesn't want you to see me? What if you—"

"Mark." Reid's laughter was bittersweet. He hugged him tight and shook his head. "Dude. I will not be marrying that stupid Hilary chick, I promise. You've got your mother's imagination, that's for sure." He smiled at Mark's anxious expression. "Listen. I know this is hard. But it's not forever.

Like I said, sometimes we just have to trust God. I'm learning that. It's not easy, but God's got this. We need to believe that."

"That's what Uncle Cade and Aunt Deb and everyone keeps telling me. God has a plan, yadda yadda, big freakin' deal. I don't like this plan. What if He messes up? What if you never get to come back?"

A strange peace settled over him as Reid kissed his son's sweaty forehead. "God doesn't mess up, Mark. If there's one thing I've finally learned through this, after all the years I've traveled the world, seen the things I've seen—destruction, death, tragedies you just can't explain no matter how much you want to—it's that. God's plan is good. And he doesn't let us go. Ever."

"If you say so." Mark straightened. Rubbed his face with both hands. Smiled and shrugged his scrawny shoulders. "I'll keep your bike running."

"I'm counting on it."

"I know how to change the oil and everything."

"Good. Make sure you run her at least once a week over the winter. Don't let the engine seize up."

"No, sir." A grin teetered on the edge of Mark's lips. "It'd be much easier if you just let me ride her."

"Nope." Reid laughed and nudged his shoulder. "Nice try though. Admirable effort."

"I learned from the best." He held up a fist and Reid tapped it with his own.

"Don't fight with Em. And look after your mother."

"Dude." As if he hadn't been doing that his whole life.

"I know." Another ragged sigh escaped. The longer he stood there, coming up with meaningless instructions, the harder it would be to walk out that door. And he had to. "All right. I'll see you, dude."

Mark rubbed his nose again and gave a practiced upward tip of the chin. "Not if I see you first."

Reid nodded and turned back down the hall.

"Hey."

Mark's voice stopped him again and he pivoted.

His son leaned up against the wall, arms crossed, his dimple flashing. "Love you, Dad."

Reid took four steps back and folded Mark in his arms one last time. This was home.

The only place he wanted to be.

The one place he couldn't be.

Defeat dragged him back to the kitchen.

Julia sat with her parents and Emily around the table. No sign of Hannah, which was just as well. Jonas and Madge rose as he came into the room. Jonas gave him a silent farewell and a handshake. They'd already said enough. The judge assured him he was doing the right thing, and he approved. Madge had no words. He knew if she opened her mouth, she'd burst into tears. Instead, she hovered at the door, waiting to take Emily into the other room.

Julia took the dirty plates to the sink, dishes clattering, water running.

Reid forced his feet forward until he stood over Emily, watched her color in her Dora book for a few minutes. He'd been stockpiling everything Dora the last few weeks. He could probably recite most of the DVD's and books by heart. He'd even spent an evening with Jules recording their voices on one of those storybooks that Em could play back again and again.

How was it possible for one little girl to step into his jumbled world and set it straight? All she had to do was look his way, and he was spellbound.

She wasn't his. He knew that. But she might as well be.

He already loved her that much.

Her cute button nose, the way her eyes squished together as she concentrated on the task at hand, the way she let out a little sigh of frustration whenever she made a mistake.

Just like her mother.

"Hi, Mister Reid. You want to color too?" She stopped her endeavors and set that mesmerizing gaze on him.

Reid crouched beside her and pushed an errant curl out of her eyes. "I wish I could, princess, but I have to go. I came to say goodbye."

Emily put down her blue crayon. Fixed him with the look and crossed her little arms. "Where're you goin'?"

"Back to New York. I have a job there." Reid remembered all the reports he'd done on the military. He'd been with them in their final moments before deployment, watched the way they said goodbye to their kids and their wives. Holding on until the last minute, like they'd never see each other again.

Today he got it.

Boy, did he get it.

"Oh." She scratched her nose, her eyes widening. "I thoughts your job was here. Fixin' up the cabin."

"Yeah. Well, the cabin is all fixed up now. So I need to get back."

"You gots things to fix up back there? In New York?"

"Sort of."

"But you're comin' back for Christmas, right? We already gots you presents."

A stifled noise came from Julia's direction, but he didn't dare look her way. "I'm not sure, Em. New York is pretty far away."

"Are ya taking Mark with you? Like last time?"

"No, baby, Mark is staying here. With you and your mom."

"Oh." She let out a shuddering sigh and her bottom lip began to quiver. "Are you sure you hafta go?" Emily stretched out a hand and ran a chubby finger down the side of his face, chasing away the tear that was trying to escape unnoticed.

"Yeah. I have to go."

Her mouth turned downward, almost touching her chin. "Oh. Well. 'Cause I ask-ed Santa and Jesus and God if you could stay here. And be my new Daddy."

Reid's smile faltered. Might as well rip his heart out right there, slap it on the table and let them all dissect it.

Something that sounded like a glass crashed against the sink. Or what used to be a glass.

Reid sat on the chair next to Em's, scooped her up and placed her on his lap. Held her close as she wrapped her little arms around him. "Em, can you do me a favor?"

"Okay." She nodded, full of importance, ready to do whatever he asked.

He leaned in close and whispered in her ear. "Keep praying for that, okay? Keep asking God if I can be your Daddy. Because I really, really want to be."

"Can I ask Santa too?"

He laughed and kissed the top of that precious nose, wishing he could stop time at that exact moment. "You can ask him, princess, but just between us, God's got more clout."

"What's clout?"

"It doesn't matter." Reid hugged tight and breathed deep. "I love you, Em."

"I love you too, Mister Daddy Reid." Her grin said they shared a special secret. She smacked a kiss on his cheek, scrambled off his lap and skipped over to her grandmother. Reid watched them go, helpless to do anything but sit there.

Eventually Julia joined him at the table.

Placed her hand over his and shrugged. "I guess I get to take the blame this time."

"Jules." Reid brought her hand to his lips and kissed the soft skin. "I don't know what else to do. If I didn't think Lou Fairchild was serious, I wouldn't be going." Lou had already played his first hand, having those reporters sniffing around outside Mark's school. "We can't risk this being blasted all over the news. Mark's in enough turmoil as is."

"I know." She extricated her hand and got to her feet. Walked around the table to the chair he'd flung his coat around earlier. Picked it up and held it toward him.

He needed to go.

Needed to walk out that door and not look back.

His entire being revolted against the idea.

She stood there, trembling, almost swallowed up in a thick red sweater, eyes filled with tears. "I should have run you over when I had the chance."

Reid walked to her, took his coat and placed it onto the table. Threaded his fingers through her hair and pulled her toward him. "I'm glad you didn't." His heart thundered as her arms came around him and she placed her head against his chest. "You've given me my life back, Jules. I know who I am now. And I know who I want to be."

"Is that right?" She raised her head to look at him. Her smile didn't go far. "And who is that? Mr. Wallace, Superstar of The Evening News?"

"No." Reid shook his head. "It's Mr. Wallace, Mark's dad—the guy who coaches basketball and baseball and whatever else they need me to do. Mr. Wallace, Emily's dad—the guy who shows up every Tuesday at 2, for dance lessons, and ends up tying big pink bows and fixing broken elastics on ballet slippers. Mr. Wallace, the guy married to the most beautiful woman in the world. The guy all the other dudes are jealous of, because I get to wrap you in my arms every night."

"There is that little issue of us not being married anymore." Her mouth curled upward. "But it sure sounds like one amazing dream."

Reid smiled as the truth fell over him like sunshine. "I never believed dreams came true, Jules, but this time … this time I'm holding onto the hope that they do."

Doubt flickered in her eyes. "What if they send you back overseas? What if you can't handle it? What if you get hurt?"

"I'll be fine."

"What did your doctor say?"

"Take your meds and keep your head down."

"I can't lose you." Julia's face crumpled. "Not again. I couldn't stand it."

"You're not going to." Reid pressed a finger to her wet lips. "We'll make this work. I love you, Jules. I've always loved you, and I always will. No matter what."

He watched her try to rein in her emotions. She'd tried to be strong up until today. Every shuddering breath she took tore away another piece of his heart.

"Why is it that Frank Hansen still possesses the power to ruin my life from beyond the grave?"

"He doesn't." Reid rested his forehead against hers and breathed in. "We'll get through this, Jules. I promise you. I'm not letting you go this time."

"You've made promises before, Mr. Wallace."

"This is different. This time I know what I'm letting go. And I know who I'm coming back for." He smiled. Didn't want to, but somehow her look of chagrin forced it from him.

"Here." Reid pulled back, fiddled with the ring on his right hand, and, after twelve years, twisted it off his finger.

He took Julia's trembling hand in his, slipped his ring on the third finger of her left hand and pressed her fingers under it. "Keep this for me until you can put it back where it belongs. Remember what it meant the day you gave it to me. It means even more now. I'll love you forever, Julia Connelly. Until I take my last breath."

Tears streaked her face as she nodded. "I'll love you forever, Reid Wallace. Until I take my last breath."

"No buts?"

"Fresh out."

"Good. Me too." Reid took her in his arms, pressed his lips to hers and lingered there. If wishes came true, they'd all be magically transported to a foreign land, given new names, a new life, never look back. But he was all out of wishes.

Prayers would take precedence.

Chapter Thirty-Four

$\mathcal{J}$ulia exited the building that housed the offices of *The Bridgewater Bugle*, shivered in the January wind, but couldn't stop a smile. She'd just gotten a job.

Her cell phone sat in her purse. Reid was somewhere in the Middle East again. They hadn't wasted any time getting him back on the air, putting him in the path of danger. She could hardly stand to watch the news these days.

Once again, her life had come full circle.

Except this time, he knew how much she loved him.

If only it was enough.

Julia went home and wandered through the empty house. Dad was in court and Mom had volunteered to get the kids that afternoon. She didn't know where Hannah was. Her sister seemed to be avoiding her lately, more than usual.

Up in her bedroom, she put away clean laundry and fiddled with the photographs on her dresser. Stared at Reid's smiling face as he sat with the kids, an arm around each of them.

Wished for the thousandth time since he'd left that things could be different.

"Julia?"

She sighed, put the picture down and turned. "Hannah. Thought you were still at work."

"No. I …" Her sister stood in the doorway, hesitating. "Can I talk to you?"

"Sure." Julia headed for the old rocker in one corner of the room. Hannah sat on the edge of one of the twin beds. "Hey, I got that job at *The*

Bugle." She had to tell someone. "The editor was super nice. Said I could start on Monday. I won't be doing much on my own at first, but he likes my writing. One of these days you might even see my name in print."

"That's great, Jules. Really." Hannah smiled, looked around the room, her eyes misting over. "Oh, gosh. I don't know how to say this."

Julia's pulse jacked. "Hannah, what?"

"I'm assuming Reid didn't tell you, because you're still talking to me, but I can't stand it any longer. I told someone, Julia. About what really happened in Atlanta. I know I'm not supposed to know, but Mom was so upset when she came back from seeing you after it happened. She told me you guys were coming back here, and she told me what you said to her. That it was really Mark who had the gun that day, not you."

"Hannah." Julia inched forward in her chair, her stomach clenching. "Who did you tell?"

"Reid's ex-girlfriend," Hannah whispered, staring at her knees. "She was here just before Thanksgiving. She seemed nice enough, took me out for coffee, and … I don't know why I did it. I …" She pushed off the bed, pulled at her ponytail and shook her head. "No. I do know why I did it." Hannah squared her shoulders, her mouth tight. "I wanted Reid to leave. I wanted the two of you to be apart. I wanted … I wanted to hurt you."

Julia sucked in a breath and drew her knees to her chest. "Why?"

"Because you hurt me!" Hannah cried. She sank onto the bed again, her face almost as white as the snow on the ground outside. "All those years, being your kid sister … you have no idea how hard it was! You were the smart one, beautiful, popular. And I was fat and ugly and I didn't have a lot of friends. I wanted to be like you, but I knew I never could be. You, Reid and Cade pretty much ignored me most of the time. When we did hang out, I always felt like I was in the way. Like I wasn't really wanted."

"Hannah, that's not—"

"You can say it's not true, Julia, but it is. You know it is."

She did know. Julia fiddled with the chain around her neck. Held Reid's ring between her thumb and forefinger, heard the truth, accepted it and hated it.

"I guess I could have tried harder. I just … I had my own life, Hannah. I didn't know you felt that way."

"You never asked. And you never asked if it was okay with me if you left in the middle of the night without saying goodbye. Never asked if I cared that you were suddenly gone, no longer a part of our lives. I missed you, Julia. I might have pretended to hate you, but deep down, I idolized you. You were my big sister. I wanted to be like you because I loved you. But you left, and never came back."

"Hannah." Julia wiped her eyes and sat next to her sister. Reached for her hand and held it tight. "I'm sorry."

"I know." Hannah rested her head against Julia's shoulder. "So am I. I've been so stupid, holding onto this all these years. If I hadn't opened my big mouth, Reid would still be here. Mark would—"

"It doesn't matter." Julia shook her head. Giving in to anger and denying her sister forgiveness would just add to the mess. "It'll be okay, Hannah."

"Are you sure about that?" Hannah narrowed her eyes. "Because if anything happens with you guys, I'm going to hold myself responsible."

"No." Julia stared at the picture on the dresser again. "If we're making another mistake, Hannah, it'll be our fault. Nobody else's."

Reid walked down the hall toward the kitchen, bleary-eyed and desperate for coffee. So desperate he could smell it.

"I thought you were going to sleep all day. Welcome home." Hilary's voice purred.

Reid blinked. Maybe he was still on the plane. Still dreaming.

Or having a nightmare.

"What are you doing in my apartment, Hilary?" He spied a sweatshirt on the back of the couch and pulled it on over his bare chest.

She came toward him, still smiling. Holding a big mug of coffee. "Stop being grouchy. Sit. I'm making breakfast."

Reid took a swig of the strong stuff for sustenance. Put the mug down and put his hand out. "Can I have my key back, please?"

"What?" Her eyes rounded, bottom lip beginning to quiver.

"Hilary. Let me be very clear. You and your father can pull every trick in the book, but that's not going to change how I feel. I've been back in

New York three months. Nothing has changed. You and I are over. I appreciate your friendship, but that's all I'm interested in. Got it?"

She rolled her eyes and shot him a grin. "Oh, fine. It was worth a shot."

Reid exhaled and allowed a mega-second of relief. "Key."

Hilary foraged through her massive Marc Jacobs bag and handed him his keys. "Are you still researching that story? The child porn ring?"

"Yup." Reid put the keys on the table and picked up his mug. "It'll probably take me a couple months to put it together. And I'll be gone a week in June. Cade's wedding."

"Thought that was April."

"It was, but Deb's dad broke his hip last week. They figured it'd be better to move it forward."

"Okay. Just make sure you get this one filed before that. It's hot." The glint in her eyes worried him. "You got those leads I gave you?"

"Yeah. Haven't had a chance to follow them up yet. Maybe if I can stay on US soil longer than a couple days at a time, I'll get this story done."

"I'll talk to Lou." Hilary left the kitchen and pulled on her leather coat.

He walked her to the door. "You doing okay, Hil? You need to talk about anything?"

"Who me?" She tossed her head and gave a smile. "No. We'll talk, but not today. You'll know when. Meantime, eat your breakfast. There's a message on your machine from the love of your life. She wants to know if you're still expecting the kid to come see you this weekend."

"Are you sure it looks okay?" Debby turned again, checking out her reflection in the mirror.

"If you ask me that one more time, I'm going to leave." Julia adjusted Debby's veil, straightened her train and shared a smile with Deb's younger sister. Debby's other sister stood in front of her, doing last minute touch-ups to the bride's make-up. The room was thick with the heady scent of flowers, perfume and anticipation of a day they'd all waited too long for.

"You look amazing," Julia breathed out as Lucy stood back. "Cade's not going to know what hit him."

"Well, I'm going to hit him if he's not standing at the front of that church." Deb's laughter petered out as Julia took her hands.

"He'll be there. After everything you two have been through, how could he not be?" Debby blinked back tears. "Thanks, Jules. You look beautiful by the way."

Julia did feel beautiful today. But a sadness she couldn't explain shadowed her. "No tears." She pulled Debby into a light hug, careful not to touch her face. "Last I heard, Cade was handcuffed to Reid. He's not going anywhere. And I gave Mark permission to let the air out of the tires of every car in the church parking lot if he saw either of them heading for the back door."

Debby smiled and sucked in a deep breath. Music from the string quartet they'd chosen floated down the hall. Mr. Jamison appeared in the doorway, smiled and held out an arm for his daughter. "Let's get her done, sugar."

"You didn't cry at our wedding." Reid snuck up behind her as Julia picked through the buffet. She put a few shrimp on her plate and stabbed a piece of pineapple.

"It was a two minute ceremony in front of a JP. I didn't have time to cry."

"Marry me again and you can cry all you want."

"Very funny." Julia ducked away, heading through the crowded lawns of Debby's parents' home. An informal outdoor reception had been decided on rather than a hotel venue, and they'd all been praying for a cloudless sky for weeks.

There were storms in the area, but so far, they'd stayed away.

Reid followed her to a table. There was no head table so the bridal party could sit anywhere. Speeches had been given and the bride and groom mingled with friends and family. Julia had somehow made it through the ceremony without staring at Reid the whole time, but now she allowed her eyes to linger just a little.

The man sure knew how to look good in a suit.

He'd shown up late last night, gone straight to Cade's to make sure he was still there, and only been able to visit a few minutes this morning before the chaos started.

And now it was over.

Julia looked at her watch. "Wow, look at that. You've been in town for almost twenty-four hours."

His handsome face darkened. "Did you tell Mark I couldn't stay?"

"I had to. He had the whole week planned. Fishing, biking, who knows what else."

Reid pulled on his tie. "I tried, Jules."

"Oh, I know. Having your own show must be so difficult." She sipped punch and scanned the crowd. Cade and Debby were mingling. Hannah was talking to the new high school teacher, Colin something or other. Emily was with Mom, and Mark was. Come to think of it, she hadn't seen Mark since they'd taken pictures several hours ago.

"I said I'd been offered my own show. I didn't say I was going to do it."

"Why wouldn't you?" It sure sounded like a done deal to her. "It's not like you have a choice, Reid."

Things had been better at the beginning, just after he'd left.

He'd shown up for Christmas, only for a couple of days, but it meant the world to the kids. He'd flown Mark out to the city on several occasions. But over the last few months, he'd been traveling more, out of touch, his visits more infrequent.

Julia did her best to stuff down that feeling of foreboding, but something in his eyes put her heart on full alert. But she couldn't worry about that now. Debby and Cade were about to leave.

She stood and went to join the crowd to see them off.

It was late afternoon by the time she was ready to go home. Emily was with her parents, but Mark was nowhere in sight. She walked across the lawn to where Reid chatted with a few of her relatives, took his arm and pulled him aside.

"Did you and Mark talk today? I haven't seen him in a while, have you?" She shielded her eyes from the setting sun. "Where is he?"

Reid shifted is jacket from one arm to the other. "Probably off sulking somewhere. He's pretty mad at me."

"You think?" She could relate.

"Relax. Let's go sit. We don't have to leave yet."

He led her to a table and grabbed a couple drinks for them. Sighed and pulled at his tie. "We'll get through this, Jules."

"You keep saying that, but it's getting old. And you can't expect me to adjust my schedule whenever you have some free time. I just can't up and go to drive Mark to the airport at the drop of a hat. I have a real job now."

"I know." He leaned back in his chair and set that smile on her. "Miss Editor in Chief. I'm proud of you, Jules."

"Whatever." She smiled anyway. The job was more than she'd hoped for. A few stories here and there at the beginning, but soon she had her own column. Last week her boss had announced his intentions to retire, and put her name forward to take his place.

It was preposterous really, to think she could slide behind that desk with little to no experience, learn the ropes in a few short months, but by the time he'd emptied his last drawer and handed the keys over, Julia felt like she'd always been there.

Where she belonged.

"It's the *Bridgewater Bugle*, Reid, not *The New York Times*."

He grinned. "I think it's great. I have an online subscription you know."

"Congratulations." When she thought about the past year of her life, she realized just how far she'd come. It had taken some time, but she was starting over. Starting a new life. Becoming a woman who knew who she was and what she wanted.

Healing.

The only part of her life she hadn't yet figured out sat across the table from her.

"Jules. I need to tell you something."

"And here it comes." She'd known for a while now that one day he'd come to his senses.

Anybody with a brain could see where Reid Wallace belonged.

And it wasn't in Bridgewater running car-pool and coaching basketball games.

"Julia, you don't even know what I'm going to say."

"I do." She pulled on her shades even though the sun was sinking behind dark clouds.

"Ms. Hansen?" Mark's friend Jeremy appeared beside their table, looking like he'd just run the entire state from top to bottom.

Julia's nerves jumped. "Hi, sweetie. What's up?"

"'Kay, please don't be mad ..."

Reid pushed out of his chair. "Dude, what's going on? Is everything okay?"

Jeremy shook his head, his face getting redder by the second. "Nuh uh. Mark's stuck on the bridge. We need you to come now. Before he falls in the river."

"What!" Julia shot to her feet, not missing the look Reid sent her. He was more panicked than she was. "What bridge?"

"I know what bridge." Reid grabbed her hand and they ran for the car.

Chapter thirty-Five

The sun slowly inched down beyond the trees and cast Faith Bridge under an orange glow. They only had an hour or so of daylight left. Reid pulled into the lay-by and saw a few bicycles thrown against the embankment. Three other boys hovered at the mouth of the bridge, still in their Sunday best. He ripped off his tie and muttered under his breath at their guilty expressions.

Julia ran across the road, a flurry of light pink and bouncing brown curls. She ignored the boys and peered into the bridge. "Mark?"

"Ma!" A thin wail floated toward them. "My foot got stuck. I can't move it or the board might break."

Reid moved Julia aside, crouched at the entrance and allowed his eyes to adjust to the dim light. The musty smell of the old boards accosted his nostrils and the raging river below blared in his ears. His chest tightened as he surveyed the condition of the old bridge. They'd broken a couple of boards that blocked the entrance to get in. "Mark, can you hear me?"

"Yessir."

"Good. Do not move. Got that?"

"I just told you, I can't."

"Yeah." Reid straightened, took a few deep breaths and glared at the group of boys. "Whose brilliant idea was this?"

"Mark's." They all spoke together.

"I dared him." PJ Taylor stared at the ground.

"Great." He sighed. "I'll deal with the four of you later. Meantime, start praying."

Julia paced the area in front of the bridge, on her cell. He had no idea who she was calling, didn't really care. All he cared about was getting his son back onto solid ground.

Reid talked himself off the ledge his mind dragged him onto. His pulse raced and familiar tendrils of fear crept closer. He made up his mind and headed for the dark cavern.

Breathe. Do. Not. Panic.

"What are you doing?" Julia squeaked.

"Going to get my son."

"Are you crazy? You can't go in there. You'll send the whole thing crashing down!"

Reid gripped her arms, met her frantic eyes and waited until she was silent. "Julia. Right now, I need you to be quiet. And pray. Have a little faith. Can you do that for me?"

She nodded, color draining from her cheeks.

He let her go and pulled off another board to make the entrance wider.

Left, right, five steps forward.

He and Cade had written down the route they'd discovered could get them safely across and back again, but that was so many years ago. And Cade wasn't here to talk him through it.

Tonight it was just Reid and God.

"Dad?" Mark's voice filled with fear. "No offense, but I don't think those boards are going to hold you."

Reid crawled forward on his hands and knees as the wood shifted beneath him. Cracking. Creaking. The wind whistled through the bridge in mournful melody that did nothing to calm his nerves. He wouldn't think about the cold water surging below.

Thunder rolled in the distance and he felt the first few drops of rain hit his face as it splattered through the holes in the roof.

Inch to the right, move forward five paces. Or six.

He couldn't remember.

Mark was straight ahead, prone on the planks, one foot stuck between them.

Reid sucked in his breath as another board cracked. "Dude, when I get you out of here, I'm going to employ my paternal rights and ground you forever."

"I figured." Mark scratched his nose and dared to grin. "But I woulda made it over if my foot hadn't got stuck. Maybe. There's like a ton of boards missing at the other end. We can't get out that way."

"Good to know." Reid belly-crawled to where Mark lay, somehow managed to reach for his foot. "Stay still. I'm going to pull your foot out."

Thunder came closer and rain fell harder. Reid prayed and pulled. Mark's foot slipped from the boards and he yelped in pain. Figured it would be the ankle he'd already broken. "Sorry. You okay?"

"I'm okay."

"Good." Reid breathed deep and stared into Mark's frightened eyes. "Want to tell me how we're getting out of here?"

"Carefully?"

"Reid?" Jonas' voice boomed through the darkened bridge. "I'm throwing in a rope, son. Can you see it?"

Reid squinted, fumbled in his pocket for his phone and turned on the light. "See it." Mark jumped each time the thunder rolled. "Okay. Mark, I'm going to turn around, and you follow me. When I say stop, stop."

"Okay. Dang, I hate storms."

"That makes two of us." Reid felt around the slimy boards, testing each one as best he could. His nose itched from the musty smell but he didn't dare sneeze. He swiveled and moved forward. Felt Mark's hand on his ankle, but kept moving. "You hold on, Mark. Tell me if you feel anything moving." He wiped dirt, sweat and rain off his face and reached for the rope. A few planks had disintegrated after he'd crawled over them the first time.

Reid pressed on the boards to his right, figured they were solid enough, and went that way. If he could get Mark to the edge, the part of the bridge that was on land, they just might make it out.

"You all right in there, sir? We can push a ladder in."

Reid eyed a couple of firemen. Shook his head. "Boards wouldn't take it." He glanced down at the angry river. Big mistake.

"Dad, this board feels real shaky."

"Don't come any closer then. Stay where you are."

Oh, Lord, please get us out of here.

Reid crawled backward until he reached Mark again. "We have to get over to the side. It'll be the safest area." Lightening split through the bridge. Mark leaned against him, his breath shaky and shallow. Reid made a calculated decision, tipped Mark's chin upward and met his eyes. "You need to go in front of me."

Mark obeyed without question.

Somehow his son had figured out the formula. Reid could tell by which boards he tested, which ones he avoided. When one broke, he shifted his weight to the next. It probably took ten minutes for Mark to reach the side of the bridge.

It felt like ten hours.

Mark scrambled to his feet and held onto the planks. "It's good over here."

"All right. You go on. Keep going, Mark."

"Mark?" Julia appeared through the small crowd. "I see you, honey. Come on, walk this way."

"Dad?"

"Go, Mark." Reid felt the nail dig a little deeper into his thigh. Searing pain shot through his leg.

He'd known he was stuck a few minutes ago. And the two boards he sprawled on felt spongy. Any minute now he would plunge into the drink and hit the rocks that hid all through that part of the river. And he didn't want Mark around for that.

"Mark, come out!" Julia pleaded. "Reid, what's the problem? Are you hurt?"

"Stuck." More sirens reached his ears. He inched forward, grabbed the second rope they'd thrown in and saw Mark crawling toward him. "Mark. Go back! You're in enough trouble as is."

"I'm not leaving you."

If he hadn't been about to go bungee jumping in the river, Reid would have smiled at the familiar stubborn look on his son's face and the irony in his words.

"Mr. Wallace?" The fire chief crouched at the entrance of the bridge. "We've got a chopper on the way. We can break through the roof and pick you up that way."

"Great idea. If I survive the concussion from boards falling on my head, I'll be forever in your debt."

"Oh. We'll just … cancel the chopper then."

"Yeah." Reid rolled his eyes and grinned at Mark. "What's it like on the other side of me?"

Mark moved forward slowly, testing each board as he went. Reid sent up another prayer, pushed up and felt his flesh rip. White pain almost made him pass out. But he was free.

"Dad, we're almost out, just … hey!" Mark yelled in protest as one of the firefighters reached in and yanked him off the bridge. "Let me go! My dad's still in there!"

Five feet separated Reid from safety and his son's screams. His vision blurred, his heart beat faster and he knew he wasn't going to make it.

"Nice going in there, Mr. Wallace."

Reid opened his eyes to a couple of paramedics hovering over him. He was safe, on land. In an ambulance.

Alone.

He took one look at the ugly gash showing under his ripped pant leg and passed out again.

Julia, Mark and Jonas met him in the emergency room. After a dozen stitches and a hefty dose of morphine, they drove him home. He stayed the night at Cade's, woke up groggy and disoriented, spent an hour on the phone changing his flights and spent another hour trying to explain to Hilary why he wasn't going to make it for tonight's scheduled taping.

He was just picking up his duffel when someone rapped on the door.

Reid limped across the room and let Julia in.

"Good, you're still here. How'd you sleep?" She wore jeans and a T-shirt, wet hair hanging limp against flushed cheeks. Her eyes were red-rimmed.

"Off and on. Leg's pretty sore. How's Mark?"

"He's fine. His ankle is a little swollen, but he's got an adventure to brag about."

"He's lucky." Reid rubbed his eyes and scanned the room. He hadn't been here long enough to make a mess; the thorough check was force of habit. "Thought you guys would be at church." He'd wanted to go himself, but then got tied up on the phone.

Julia shook her head. "I sent the kids with Mom and Dad." She let out her breath on a shaky sigh. "I wanted us to have a chance to talk before you left."

"Okay, well, I need to get going in about fifteen minutes."

"This won't take that long."

Reid backed up and sat down.

"I've been doing a lot of thinking the past few weeks." Julia paced the room, arms crossed. "I can't do this." She walked back to where he sat. "It's not going to work, Reid."

"What's not going to work?" His throat tightened as he tried to focus on her.

"You and me. You're never here anymore. I'm tired of waiting around for you to show up when you can. Tired of waiting for the phone to ring, wondering where you are, if you're all right." She pushed fingers through her hair, didn't look at him. "I think we both knew it wasn't going to work from the beginning. We just didn't want to admit it."

"What are you saying?" Reid stood on shaky legs. Reached for her hands, but she pulled away.

"I'm sick of this thing hanging over us. I don't like being afraid every time I turn on the news or see an article about you somewhere. I don't want the truth to come out, but I can't live like this anymore, Reid."

"Julia. I don't think you understand."

"I do understand." She waved him off, her eyes dull. "Go back to New York. Live the life you were meant to live. We'll figure things out with Mark, he can spend vacations with you there or something, but he can't keep hopping on planes whenever you call. He's missed enough school since you left."

"You've met somebody else." It was the only logical conclusion. But the fire in her eyes his words ignited told him it was the wrong one.

"Don't insult me." She shook her head and stared him down. "Don't you see? If I'm not in the picture, maybe the press will leave you alone. Go out with a few other women. Give them something else to talk about, Reid. As long as you're in the position you are, I'm always going to be in the spotlight, and so is Mark. If Lou Fairchild could find out the truth, what's to say somebody else can't? I don't want to wake up one day with a hundred reporters at my door while the police show up to question me." She pulled at the chain around her neck. He saw his ring at the bottom of it. Watched her fiddle with the latch, slip it off the chain and hand to him.

"No." Reid swallowed down the lump in his throat. "No. You're not doing this."

"It's for the best." She lowered wet lashes, unmoving. Finally she took his hand in his and pressed his ring into it. "For what it's worth, I'm glad we tried."

"Julia." Her name sounded hoarse on his tongue. His world crashed and tumbled down around him as she turned and headed for the door. "Julia! Don't leave. Wait. We can talk about this. We'll work it out!"

"There's nothing left to work out, Reid. It's the right thing. You'll see."

Déjà vu.

"But I ... I love you, Jules."

"I know." She smiled through her tears. "And I love you. But we'll get over it."

Chapter Thirty-Six

Julia drove past the house every day on her way to work. The trucks started showing up in early May. Contractors, roofers, landscapers, all went to work restoring the beautiful Victorian to its original splendor. By the time Cade and Debby's June wedding had rolled around, she began to see the place the way it used to be.

At the end of August, as the leaves started to turn and the kids went back to school, the moving trucks pulled up.

Whoever the new owners of her dream home were, Julia envied them.

Because the place held such history, she played with the idea of writing a story on it. Wondered if she could get an interview with the lucky people who had bought the house she'd once dreamed of living in. Over lunch last Sunday, her father informed her he knew the family.

They'd been reluctant at first, but he'd managed to set something up for the first weekend in September. They were from out of town, but would be all settled in by then. Yes, she could take pictures if she wanted.

She stood in front of the old home now and marveled at the transformation.

New shingles sparkled under the Sunday afternoon sun. The siding was painted in the original robin's egg blue she loved so much. The gardens had grown in, bloomed all summer long, and the brick walkway was lined with rose bushes right down to the sidewalk.

White wicker furniture sat on the wrap around porch, arranged in comfortable groups where one could sit, enjoy the shade and watch the world go by. She'd never been around back, but imagined it was spectacular. The lawns would reach the river at the end of the property—the same river that rushed through town and ran right under Faith Bridge.

After that fateful night, the night she'd wondered if she might lose Mark and Reid, her father and Reid agreed to fix the bridge. It was repaired and fully functioning now, but she still couldn't bring herself to drive across it. Because on that night, waiting, crying and praying for them to come out unscathed, something inside her had shifted.

Julia made a conscience decision not to be held captive by fear any longer.

Having spent the last twelve years of her life that way, it was time to let go.

Even if that meant letting go of Reid.

He hadn't understood. He might never understand.

But Julia believed she'd made the right decision.

Mark adjusted to seeing Reid on an infrequent basis, and they kept in touch through Skype and emails and texts. Over time and intensive therapy, Mark's anger began to fade, his scars a little less apparent. Their son was growing into a handsome young man, finished out the school year at the top of his class. She couldn't be more proud, but as always, he was a bittersweet gift.

Every smile he gave her reminded her of what she'd lost.

But slowly, as the days passed, she made peace with her decision.

God did have a plan. And He had been faithful thus far, providing her with a job, a roof over her head and a safe place to raise her children. One day soon, she hoped to start looking at homes in the area. They wouldn't need anything big. Her parents had already broached the subject of providing her a loan.

Life was good. Lonely at times, but all in all, she couldn't complain.

And Mark was safe.

Julia walked up the path, stopped to smell a few roses, admired the lavender, lilacs and purple hostas in the flowerbeds that snaked around the front porch. Two golden retrievers, puppies still, raced around the house toward her, yapping, tails going like mad. She let them sniff her hands and they allowed her to move forward.

Julia slipped off her sunglasses and knocked on the front door.

After a minute or so, she knocked again. Checked her watch. She was right on time.

Surely they hadn't forgotten? She knocked again, then walked across the porch to peer through one of the long windows.

Her cell phone buzzed in her purse. She frowned as she reached for it. Hopefully they weren't calling to cancel on her. "Julia Connelly." The pups jumped around her feet. She walked to the other window and looked through, but the house was dark and she couldn't see much. "Hello?"

"Don't you know it's rude to peek through windows, Jules?"

She stepped back from the house and almost dropped her phone.

"Reid?" They hadn't talked in a few weeks. Maybe a month. Not that she was counting.

"The door is probably unlocked. You could walk right in if you want."

Julia blinked, stared across the lawn, her heart hammering against her chest as she pressed the phone to her ear. "Where are you?"

"Hmm. Interesting question. I guess you'll have to find out."

"Reid?"

Dead air.

Julia looked down at the dogs. "Want to tell me what's going on here?" They circled her legs, playing with each other. She pushed hair out of her eyes and walked to the front door. "Okay, if I get arrested for trespassing, it's on your heads. You don't make very good guard dogs. Just saying."

Beyond the front door was the most beautiful foyer she'd ever seen. Highly polished walnut floors shone under a small chandelier. A curving wooden staircase stood at the end of the entryway. Large potted plants and Persian rugs were placed in perfect positions. A hall table sat to her right, a few stacks of books, a purple orchid, and an expensive looking glass bowl arranged on it. It all looked like something out of a decorating magazine.

To her left, double doors complete with beveled glass blocked the next room from sight. Feeling every inch the intruder she was, she picked up her phone again. Scanned her contacts until she hit on Reid. Punched him in the face.

"Wallace."

"You know it's me, so stop being silly and tell me what this is all about."

"That's a nice greeting, considering you haven't said two words to me in the last six weeks."

"It hasn't been that long. And there were those times you didn't return my calls."

"You dumped me. I wasn't exactly thrilled about it."

"I didn't dump you. I let you go."

"Semantics. Did you meet the dogs?"

"Ferocious beasts that they are, yes." Julia inched toward the double doors, the puppies at her heels.

"The one with the pink collar is Ruth. Her partner in crime is Zach."

"Ruth and Zach?" Why were those names familiar? Julia shrugged off the thought, forgot good manners and pushed open the doors. "Holy crap."

Reid tut-tutted. "Language, Jules. What if Em were to hear you?"

She clicked off his chuckle and stood in the center of the room.

A room she'd dreamed up in her mind a million times.

The deep blue walls, rich bold colored rugs, leather couches with thick cushions that beckoned her to come sit and stay a while. White California blinds on the windows, opened to let the sun in. Palms in bronze pots waved under the breeze of a gently moving fan. Even a baby grand sat in one corner of the room.

Everything was just how she'd imagined it.

Planned it.

A huge fireplace with an ornate wooden mantel drew her gaze.

And then she saw the pictures.

She quickstepped it across the room, stopped and stared, afraid to touch them.

Afraid if she closed her eyes, none of this would be real.

The photographs were Reid's.

There was an old one of her, Cade and Reid when they were kids. The picture Cade had taken of Reid and Mark in New York. A picture of Emily at her dance recital. And the picture of the two of them on their wedding day.

"Oh, God, please tell me what's happening."

"You might find out sooner if you ask me."

Julia held her breath, shut her eyes, opened them again, and made a slow turn.

Reid stood in the center of the room.

Smiling like a kid on Christmas morning, taking great pleasure in her confusion.

"You're here."

"I am." His dark hair was longer, a faint shadow of scruff covered his jaw, and he stood barefoot, in khaki shorts and a faded navy blue polo, looking like he owned the place.

She opened her mouth to speak again, but couldn't. He was beside her in two strides, his arms around her waist as her knees buckled.

"Figured you would do that." He swept her off her feet and grinned down at her. "Hi, Jules."

"Put me down." Julia steadied her breathing as he lowered her onto the couch. "You bought my house."

"Actually, no." Reid crouched beside her, moving her hair out of her eyes. "You need water?"

Julia pushed his hand away and sat up. "No, I need answers."

"So do I, but you go first. What do you want to know, Jules?"

"I want to know what you're doing here. Whose house is this?"

"Well, mine." His grin sent that dimple jumping.

"You did buy it."

"Nope." Reid got to his feet, the dogs following him around the room. "The house belonged to my grandparents. Esmé was a city girl, so Grandpa figured she'd be happier living in town. But she loved the cabin on the mountain, so I guess they just stayed up there and rented this place out. I never knew they owned it until she died."

"I think I'll take that water now." Julia followed Reid through the house. Passed an exquisite dining room, a study and another room until they came to the kitchen. "Oh. Wow."

"Nice, huh?" He tapped the green granite counters and opened a dark wood cupboard door for a glass. Everything sparkled. The butter-yellow walls, stainless-steel top of the line appliances, even a copper hood above the range.

It was all just a little too perfect.

Julia picked up an apple from the basket of fruit on the oak table. Put it down again. "Reid? Do you ... remember how I used to talk about ..."

"This house?" Her handed her a glass of cold water. "How you would decorate it if you lived here? What rooms you would use for what, the kind of furniture you'd have, the colors you wanted? Yeah, vaguely." His teasing grin cut the safety net she'd erected around her heart again in an instant.

She took a few gulps of water and put the glass down. "Tell me why you're here. Why you did this."

He shuffled closer, smiled and gave a shrug. "You mean you haven't figured that out yet?" He laced his fingers through hers. "I'm done with New York."

"You can't be. You ..."

Reid raised a brow. "Let me finish?"

Julia grinned and bit her lip.

"I was doing some research, doing a piece on child pornography. And ..." A shadow fell across his face and he shrugged again. "Unfortunately a few of my leads kept taking me down the same path. Right to Lou Fairchild's desk."

"No." Julia's stomach churned.

"I'm afraid so. He was arrested last week. Hilary had a few stories of her own to share with the police. He'll be going away for awhile."

"Oh, no, Reid. That's terrible." She'd never liked Hilary Fairchild, but Julia's heart went out to her.

"For them. Yes." He ran a finger down the side of her face. "I shot my last segment a few days ago. Handed in my resignation. And then I came home."

"Just because he's in jail doesn't mean he won't talk, Reid. And what about Hilary? She knows too."

"Hilary has had a change of heart. She'll be okay." He shrugged. "Jules, I can't promise you this will go away. But if the truth gets out, we'll handle it. Together. As a family." His eyes crinkled with his smile. "So there you have it. You have your answers. Now I want mine."

"Reid." She took a deep, shaky breath as he dropped to one knee. Shook her head in disbelief.

But he held her left hand in his, and a ring in the other.

The biggest diamond ring she'd ever seen.

"Julia Connelly, I love you. I know you love me too, even though you've spent the last little while convincing yourself you don't. So, I'm going to ask you, one more time, if you will do me the great honor of agreeing to be my wife. Again."

"Can you get up, please?" she whispered, gripping his shoulders. "I don't feel so good."

Reid scrambled to his feet and curled his hands around her arms. "You're not fainting before you answer my question."

Julia smiled, pressed her hands to his chest and her lips to his mouth. "I will. I'll marry you again. But this is the last time."

Reid's laughter echoed around the sunny kitchen. "I should hope so." He slipped the ring on her finger, drew her to him and kissed her.

An achingly slow kiss, that sent waves of pleasure rushing through her and blood rushing to her cheeks. "Let's get married tonight," he growled against her neck. "Your dad can make it legal in five minutes. Then I can show you the bedroom."

Julia laughed and stood back to see his face, trailed her fingers through his thick hair and shook her head. "Tempting, but no. We're doing it right this time. And my dad will be walking me down the aisle."

Reid smiled and kissed her again. "We should go tell him that then." He tipped his head toward the glass doors.

Her parents sat at a picnic bench down by the river, while Mark pushed Emily on a swing-set nearby. "You thought of everything."

"Yes, I did." He ran the top of his finger down her nose. "Like you said, we're doing it right this time." Reid took her hand, opened the door, led her outside and let go a shrill whistle.

Julia walked across the lush grass as Emily jumped off the swing, raced toward them at full tilt. Reid crouched and held out his arms, waiting for her to hurl herself against him. He swept her high into the air, his laughter mingling with her shrieks of delight.

"You're back, you're back, you're back!"

Mark reached them next and Reid pulled him in for a hug.

"What'd she say?" Mark asked.

"What do you think I said?" Julia winked at her son, realizing he'd probably been in on this too. Mark high-fived Reid and let out a whoop.

"Can you be my daddy now, Mister Reid?" Emily bounced in his arms.

"Absolutely, princess. Now and forever." Reid rubbed noses with Em, held out his free arm and Julia squeezed in under it.

Mark put his arms around both of them, his sigh filled with contentment. "Finally."

Julia looked up at Reid, met his eyes and smiled. "Welcome home, Reid."

He returned her smile, his eyes wet as he leaned in to kiss her again. "Welcome home, Jules. Welcome home."

Thank You!

It's never easy to fully express my heartfelt thanks and gratitude after each book I write. So many people along the way have done their part, encouraging, pushing me forward and praying me through as I write the words I pray will touch hearts.

Thank you, God, for loving me, for giving me the stories, the ability to write them, and the desire to never stop telling them. To be able to do what I love is a rare gift, and one I hope I'll never take for granted.

My husband, Stephen, who bravely lives alongside this crazy writer and encourages my dreams, no matter how far-fetched they may be. I wouldn't be able to do this without you, my love. You are a true hero.

My kids, who always cheer me on and tell me it's all going to work out. Your love and support means more than you know, and I'm so excited to share our journeys together.

My Dad, stepmom and all my family – you keep me going and give me fun and laughter, memories to cherish and moments to look forward to.

Family and friends near and far, who never stop believing and encouraging.

As always, my agent, Rachelle Gardner, I couldn't take any of these steps without your guidance, you are truly a blessing in my life.

And to all my amazing friends who write fabulous words and inspire me to be a better writer every day – you are my lifeline in more ways than you could possibly know, and I am so grateful for the communities who've embraced me and given me a place to call home. I'm beyond thankful for each one of you, and for all you do to bring joy to my life.

Until next time …

Also by Catherine West

"...the writing is witty and fast-paced and the love story is perfection."
-Amazon reviewer on
Yesterday's Tomorrow

"...a beautifully written story that will simply stir your soul."
-Amazon reviewer on
Hidden in the Heart

Available now from Amazon

Yesterday's Tomorrow
Vietnam, 1967.

Independent, career-driven journalist Kristin Taylor wants two things: to honor her father's memory by becoming an award-winning overseas correspondent and to keep tabs on her only brother, Teddy, who signed up for the war against their mother's wishes. Brilliant photographer Luke Maddox, silent and brooding, exudes mystery. Kristin is convinced he's hiding something.

Willing to risk it all for what they believe in, Kristin and Luke engage in their own tumultuous battle until, in an unexpected twist, they're forced to work together. Ambushed by love, they must decide whether or not to set aside their own private agendas for the hope of tomorrow that has captured their hearts.

Brace yourself for a heart-thudding love story amid the raw and real backdrop of Vietnam during one of the most turbulent times in American history. Without question, this is a novel that will woo and win you heart and soul, written by a gifted storyteller who will do the same. —JULIE LESSMAN, award-winning author of *The Daughters of Boston* and *Heart of San Francisco* series

This compelling love story, set against the backdrop of the Vietnam War, transported me through recent history. Cathy West's debut novel is beautifully crafted and thoroughly engaging! —DEBORAH RANEY, bestselling author of the *Clayburn Novels* and *Almost Forever*

A beautifully told story, crisp and accurate in its detail, filled with emotion and deftly handled by a writer who understands the hope of prayers asked and the beauty of prayers answered, Yesterday's Tomorrow is a story to savor. —LISA WINGATE, national bestselling author of Larkspur Cove and Dandelion Summer.

I do not exaggerate when I say Cathy West writes an unforgettable and powerful novel with *Yesterday's Tomorrow*. I read the book several years ago and some scenes remain vividly etched in my mind. West is one of my favorite authors because she writes real, she writes raw, and she does it with a mastery of prose that woos readers. —BETH K. VOGT, author of *Somebody Like You* (PW starred review)

Hidden in the Heart
For the first time in her life, Claire wants to know where she came from ...

After losing her mother to cancer, and suffering yet another miscarriage soon after, Claire Ferguson numbs the pain with alcohol and pills, and wonders if her own life is worth living. Adopted at birth, Claire is convinced she has some unknown genetic flaw that may be causing her miscarriages. She must find a way to deal with the guilt she harbors. But exoneration will come with a price.

With her marriage in dire straits and her father refusing to discuss her adoption, Claire leaves everything she's ever known, determined to find the answers she needs.

But what if the woman who gave her life doesn't want to be found?

Through her novels, Catherine West reaches out to her readers, asking them to examine the deeper issues of the heart: how our failures shape our futures, what real faith looks like, and how much heartache can a marriage survive. In *Hidden in the Heart*, West explores the many facets of adoption, writing with gut-wrenching honesty and yet a tenderness that kept me turning pages late into the night. — Beth K. Vogt, author of *Somebody Like You, Wish You Were Here*, & *Catch a Falling Star*

Catherine West intricately weaves a story about one family's journey toward truth, healing, and wholeness. *Hidden in the Heart* is a touching tale that will leave readers with a sense that even in the midst of great hurt, God can redeem what's been lost." — Katie Ganshert, author of *A Broken Kind of Beautiful, Wishing on Willows* & *Wildflowers from Winter*

Catherine West's adept prose unfurls moments with the power to change lives, giving us both the dismay of heartbreak and a call to redemption in the story of two women who did not know how much they needed each other. — Olivia Newport, author of *The Pursuit of Lucy Banning*

Hidden in the Heart is a compelling love song of a novel about finding a true home in a lonely world. Gifted author Catherine West writes with lump-in-the-throat power to transport you through a family's journey from brokenness to grace. A page-turner full of honest spiritual insight and poignant characters, this is a luminous story of forgiveness that will take hold of your heart and lift its hidden burdens. — Rosslyn Elliott, award-winning author of *Fairer than Morning* and *Sweeter than Birdsong*

Hidden in the Heart is a thought-provoking and powerful story that explores the depths of human despair– and Christ's redemptive and soul-changing power. As I read Claire's story, I realized how each of my experiences, faults, mistakes and triumphs are woven together to make me who I am. And that person– flaws and all– is exactly the person that God created for His purposes and His designs. Full of witty dialogue and poignant examples of faith, Catherine West has captured one woman's journey to find her true self in a way that will touch each mother, daughter, sister or friend. — Erin MacPherson, author of "The Christian Mama's Guide" series.

Hidden In The Heart takes you on an emotional journey through the life of Claire Ferguson. A journey of loss, hope, and a promise for the future. Claire struggles through darkness, until a sleepy Maine town and its inhabitants show a glimpse of light and rest. Catherine's gift for writing the family saga has made her one of my favorite authors. She has the talent of being able to weave together stories with such emotional power, that you feel truly blessed when you reach the end. A Catherine West novel is a must-read novel. — Lindi Peterson, award-winning author of *Her Best Catch*

Hidden in the Heart goes beyond the quick fix of discovery and delves into struggles with faith, commitment, complicated circumstances, and difficult decisions. If your family has been touched by adoption, you will want to read this well-told story. — Lori Wildenberg, co-author of *EMPOWERED PARENTS: Putting Faith First.*

From the first page, Catherine West pulled me into the broken life of her main character Claire Ferguson. A love story on many levels, *Hidden in the Heart* spoke to my heart about the value of forgiveness and the ultimate beauty of love. — Sue Harrison – International Bestselling Author of *Mother Earth, Father Sky.*

Catherine West has penned a well-told story complete with flawed characters who must deal with their mistakes, heartbreak, and pain. *"I'm not so sure God deals in guilt. If anything, I think He deals in forgiveness."* A lesson for us all. — Eileen Key – Author of Cedar Creek Seasons & Sundays in Fredericksburg.

Hidden in the Heart is a beautifully told story of a young woman's search for her birth mother. Loosely based on her own journey of discovery,

Catherine West infuses a transparency and depth of emotion that is both heartrending and immensely satisfying. I couldn't put it down. *Novel Rocket* and I give it a very high recommendation. — Ane Mulligan, Sr. editor, *Novel Rocket*, author of *Chapel Springs Revival*.

About the Author

Catherine West is an award-winning author who writes stories of hope and healing from her island home in Bermuda. *Yesterday's Tomorrow* won the INSPY for Romance in 2011, a Silver Medal in the Reader's Favorite Awards, and was a finalist in the Grace Awards. Catherine's second novel, *Hidden in the Heart*, was long listed in the 2012 INSPY's and was a finalist in the 2013 Grace Awards.

When she's not at the computer working on her next story, you can find her taking her Border Collie for long walks or tending to her roses and orchids. She and her husband have two grown children. Catherine is a member of American Christian Fiction Writers and Romance Writers of America, and is represented by Rachelle Gardner of Books & Such Literary Management. Catherine loves to connect with her readers and can be reached at Catherine@catherinejwest.com

Catherine's Website – http://www.catherinejwest.com

DISCARD

Made in the USA
Lexington, KY
13 August 2015